The Keeper of Fates

The Jewel
of the
Sorcerer

By

Nicholas T. Daniele

Layout and design by Ryan Twomey-Allaire
Cover images provided by Shutterstock

ISBN: 978-1-936476-09-1

For Mom, Dad, and Kevin

Contents

The Keeper of Fates

THE JEWEL OF THE SORCERER

"It is a high council that I once heard given to a young man, 'Always do what you are afraid to do.'"

– Ralph Waldo Emerson

Prologue

Night of the Golden Star

It was unusually chilly for an August evening, and Martrum Tuckle, enjoying the end of his eightieth summer, found himself a bit more bundled than he was used to as he perched upon the hillock overlooking his flock. Standing his staff against a nearby tree, he stooped to sit, and when he found a suitable position glared out across the field, observing.

Much of Martrum's herd was of the same mind, having taken to cradling their lanky, awkward legs beneath their wooly coats to enjoy a quiet night's rest. Their worries–shepherd and flock alike–were always few. Maxxie and Rufus, descendants of an ancient line of Tuckle sheepdogs, were adequate security. Ever alert, the shaggy beasts could detect intruders from a mile off, whether squirrel or wolf, and with that particularly comforting knowledge, Martrum Tuckle closed his weary eyes.

Upon opening them, the old shepherd noted that night had fully fallen, and that it was a particularly starry night indeed. *Magnificent!* he thought, gaping slightly.

Taking hold of his staff, he struggled to his feet. His flock below was quiet. Maxxie, lying beyond the outer ring of the herd, was bathing his bear-like paws with his coarse tongue; Rufus, who had fallen asleep along the inner wall of sheep, was shuffling noisily in the grass, apparently rapt in an adventurous sort of dream.

Good thing I'm not paying you, he said to himself, a smile beginning to tug at the edge of his lips. *Big oaf—*

But suddenly, with a wild jerk, Rufus woke, springing to attention as though detecting something menacing in close proximity. The look he had in his deep, black eyes Martrum knew him only to bear when trouble was near. Rufus's reaction was such that Martrum himself became startled and nearly lost his footing. But nearly as abruptly as Rufus sprung awake, he lay back down, closed his eyes, and went to sleep again.

Poor old fellow, thought Martrum. *I think age is starting to catch up with—*

Just then, out of the corner of his tired eyes, Martrum Tuckle thought to see a gold light shimmering through the boughs of the tree above. Trying to dismiss it for starlight, he turned his attention away, only to find that the light became brighter the more he tried to ignore it. *What the—*

Martrum did not remember taking shelter behind the tree, but peering in fright from the safety of its cover he saw a beam of golden light descend from the stars, touching down softly only thirty yards or so from his station. It was a light so strong and fervent that Martrum was blind to all of the surrounding area, but he could not look away. Transfixed, he stared blankly until the golden beam subsided to a dull, flickering glow before dying out completely.

When it was all but extinguished, Martrum's sight was blotchy, and even when he closed his eyes it remained as if he was staring at that horribly radiant orb. But now he heard voices, and struggling through his foggy vision, he distinguished three shapes standing where the light had been.

The first voice was very gruff, and unmistakably male. "It would be in our best interest to seek another mode of transportation next time." The figure of the speaker seemed larger than the others, and he was stretching, craning his neck as if to crack out the stiffness. He stood looking out to the field beyond. "A peasant village, honestly?" he continued. "Could Father have been more cliché?"

"As far east as can be managed was his command." The voice that responded was female, and so melodic that any ominous thoughts Martrum was concealing began to subside, though he now clung to the tree as tightly as he had ever clung to anything. "And 'next time?'" she continued. "It was my understanding that this would be our only visitation."

"At least for a long while," said the third voice, also male, yet his bore elegance that was absent in the other's. "If we are to respect Father's wishes, of course."

"Remove any thoughts of disobeying Father's orders from your mind, Nepsus," said the female sternly, and though the other was in shadow, Martrum thought to see him cower. "We are to fulfill his final wish before retiring to the realm to attempt to restore him."

Martrum heard the hoarse voice of the first male give a slight chuckle.

"I would have you tell me what amuses you, Charon," said the female sharply, anger rising in the chimes of her voice.

But the one called Charon was not fazed. "You need look no further than yourself, dear sister," he answered.

"Children, children," interjected the second male— Nepsus, Martrum thought he heard the woman call him. "Surely we are all recovering from a lengthy and uncomfortable trek, but must we bicker here in the open? We cannot know who may be listening."

"Then go seek out eavesdroppers, little brother," answered Charon bluntly, and when he stood up to Nepsus, Martrum could see that he was larger than him in every way a man could be larger than another.

This remark caused the woman to guffaw. "Now *you* give the orders?"

"Be silent, Nephromera," said Charon sharply, turning from his brother and advancing on her. "I have endured enough nagging from you for one apparition."

"Yet the stubborn little boy," she answered under her breath, and her voice sounded as if she had spoken from behind clenched teeth.

Turning from the towering Charon, Nephromera began to walk away down the hill where Martrum's flock was resting, seemingly ignorant to the open quarrel waging just above them. She thrust her hand to the heavens, and, in a flash of purplish light, a staff manifested out of nothing, and she continued to walk on.

It was then that Charon followed her, and called from the ledge, "Yet the foolhardy, sniveling girl."

This insult made Nephromera stop cold for a fraction of a second, and in that time she made as if to turn and retort, but clearly thought better of it. Continuing away, she swept past Rufus, whose tongue was now dangling from his slightly ajar mouth, and out in the direction of the nearby village of Amar.

"Now you have done it," said Nepsus accusingly.

"What have I done now?" replied Charon defensively.

But presently Nepsus was following in the woman's wake, springing along as briskly as a young buck.

"She started it," muttered Charon to himself before he too cantered off to join his siblings.

Under the starlit cover of night the three figures of Nephromera, Charon, and Nepsus traversed west, where, faintly across the bleak and rolling expanse of field, what lights were left burning in Amar could be distinguished. Seizing his own staff, Martrum Tuckle labored down the hill after them as stealthily as his eighty year-old, creaking limbs would allow.

Before he endured the field ahead, he roused Rufus who woke excitedly as though startled out of dream.

"Will you relax?!" Martrum squealed in the loudest whisper he could muster. He clasped one bony hand around Rufus's mouth to prevent the enormous dog from making an audible-enough sound.

"Listen, you mutt," he continued, "Daddy's got to go for an important walk." The elderly shepherd averted his gaze to see that his quarry was still within range. "Look after this lot, will you? And tell Maxxie when he wakes."

He had to hurry; otherwise, the ground his weary legs would have to cover to gain on the three strangers would be a difficult errand. Martrum sighed as he watched the black shapes grow smaller in the distance. "Daddy will be back soon enough. Don't you go fretting now. That's a good boy."

Rufus whimpered almost inaudibly, as though lamenting his master's decision to temporarily leave, but the old shepherd's heart would not be swayed. As briskly as he could manage, he set off on the trail of the odd company.

To his advantage, their pace was leisurely, as though the business they were seeing to was not an urgent matter. But their manners were certainly edgy. Even the foreboding figure of Charon seemed to flinch at the slightest sound of movement.

Quiet, you old fool! Martrum scolded himself whenever he kicked a stray rock or broke a branch. It was difficult to manage stealth and speed in the darkness of the field, and he found himself dodging behind outlying trees more often than suited his purpose.

The voices of Nephromera, Charon, and Nepsus were only audible enough to determine that they were speaking. Their words, however, were indistinguishable, though Martrum believed them to be bickering again.

In nearly half an hour's time, the outskirts of the village was upon them. By now, there were sufficiently fewer lights than Martrum had seen from his perch, as most of the residents were almost certainly asleep by now. On a bridge beneath which ran a slow-trudging stream, the three stopped.

Martrum took to hiding perhaps fifty yards behind them, where the girth of one of the remaining scattered trees afforded him shelter. Here, in the open beneath the unveiled moon, the features of the three strangers were finally perceivable. The woman was without question the most beautiful Martrum had ever seen. Her flowing locks of gold ranged beyond the slopes of her slender shoulders to the small of her back in a decorated braid. The surface of her face seemed smooth even from the distance that separated Martrum from the three, with high set cheekbones and crystal eyes that seemed to pierce through him even when her gaze was elsewhere. Yet there was a twinge of something strong in the features of her face as well—something masculine and stern—such as inclined

Martrum to believe that she was the leader among them. A brightly colored shawl was draped upon her shoulders atop a dark blue satin robe that dragged behind her as she walked.

Her brothers were equally breathtaking to the eyes of Martrum Tuckle. Never before had he seen young men who looked like them. Charon was indeed a paragon of his kind—boasting a magnificently brutish figure and standing well over six feet in height. Upon his chest, he wore a shimmering breastplate that was presently reflecting the starlight. Behind his back, his dark blue cape flirted with the dusty earth and was beginning to take on stray pieces of loose straw. The outlines of his face were sharp at the edges with a very distinguishable jawline and a deep delve in his cleft chin. His hair resembled more of a lion's mane than anything—a brilliant, white-gold, lion's mane. His eyes were very much alike to his sister's, though they seemed to be embedded deeper into his face than hers. At his side swayed a glittering scabbard out of which a marvelous sword glimmered from guard to pommel.

Nepsus, whom Martrum determined was the youngest of the three, dressed as peculiarly as his older brother. He was a fair size smaller than Charon (perhaps by nearly half a foot), and his hair, though the same, mesmerizing hue, was much shorter and more kempt. He had an arrogant gaze upon his face, though his mannerisms did not suggest that he was arrogant, and at his side, like a staff of his own, he carried a spear whose point was fashioned to resemble what Martrum could only guess was the head of a golden swordfish.

Nephromera stood peering out beyond the edge of the bridge, looking into Amar before they entered it completely. For a long while, they remained quiet and unmoving. Nepsus had taken to sitting on a nearby ledge of the bridge, but Charon paced impatiently. Finally, he broke the silence with an air of frustration. "Well, now is as good a time as any to do it, if you have to."

"I daresay she is seeing to that, brother," said Nepsus lazily, playing with the fingers of his non spear-hand, which seemed to be piquing his interest.

Even from the distance that separated Martrum from the three siblings, he could hear Nephromera muttering something. It seemed unrelated to what Charon and Nepsus were discussing, which now concerned how to properly respect your elders. Leaning on her staff, her chant grew louder and more animated. After several moments, it seemed her staff was supporting the entirety of her weight, until finally she fell to her knees in exasperation and Nepsus raced to aid her to her feet.

Martrum was not prepared for what happened next. The staff to which Nephromera had clung a moment ago was standing balanced in its lonesome, wreathed in an eerie, blue-purple glow. Now the staff seemed to be shrinking, and as it shrunk, changed form until it was nothing more than an odd little heap upon the ground.

"It is done then?" asked Charon, wonder at the edge of his rasping voice.

Nephromera struggled in Nepsus's arms, and, short of breath, answered. "It is done."

Charon stooped low beside the bundle and raised it in his arms. For a moment, his back was to Martrum, but when he turned his broad shoulders to show his sister what he had lifted from the ground, the old shepherd saw that it was fleshy-colored and wriggling.

A child? he asked himself in wonder.

Martrum's thoughts were confirmed. After a moment or so, he heard the very distinct cries of an infant, muffled by the cloths surrounding it. Nephromera's face came alight as she took the child from Charon's arms and held it like her own. Silence fell over the three for what seemed like a long while.

"Hello, little brother," Martrum thought he heard her say. The child had been in Nephromera's arms for the breath of a moment before it stopped crying and fidgeting entirely. Martrum thought to see its little eyes, alert and wide, peering from within its heap of rags.

"I still do not understand," said Charon, striding away from his crumpled sister. "Why was this Father's final wish? Why subject the youngest of his children to walk among the damned?"

"Because it will be his responsibility one day to rid them of their plight," she said resolutely. "You know he will be the only one over whom Parthaleon will have no power."

"Honestly," said Nepsus, "do you ever pay attention?"

Charon shot Nepsus a furious stare, but remained quiet. When the silence was broken at last, it was he who spoke. "This world, it has grown fond of war. Its affair with bloodshed will never cease. Our brother will live amongst them—amongst these . . . these *ants*—never knowing his true potential—"

"We have played our part, dear brother," said Nephromera, and her voice was weak and tired. "Now we must allow the Fates to play theirs."

Charon turned aside, and a hint of sadness crept into his voice. "*He* controls the Fates now."

But whom Charon was alluding to, Martrum did not know.

"Not those most hallowed," replied Nephromera. "Not the Mountain's most sacred. And I daresay Lucian's is the most sacred of all."

"There is no time," said Charon. "Sorcerian feeds on every perished soul, and every death makes him stronger. By time Lucian comes of age and acquires his gifts it may be too late."

"Brother," said Nephromera, "your heart is steadfast. Father will need your strength now. You must believe in his cause, and that of our brother. It is our faith that we must place in him—in both of them."

Just then Nepsus spoke. "The sun will rise before long," he said with worry.

"Then let us do this," said Nephromera wearily. "Nepsus . . . I do not think I can make the tread on foot."

"Fret not," answered her younger brother, and before Martrum could even comprehend the words that Nepsus had spoken, a large, black horse stood where the youngest of the three had been.

"No, Charon," said Nephromera, grasping her brother's

shoulder. "Not yet. First, I must ask you to help me."

Charon stooped low, and lifted his sister—child and all—effortlessly on to the back of the horse that was Nepsus. Now, every glimmering feature of Nephromera became dull and dreary—from her sparkling robes to her white-gold hair. In an eyeblink, she bore filthy, weatherworn rags and seemed to have aged fifty years.

When she spoke again, her voice was that of an elderly woman on the brink of death. "Now you, Charon."

At once, the massive form of Charon shrunk, and in his place stood a boy of about eight years of age. His garb, too, was dirty and poor, and his face, though perhaps fair, was smudged with dirt.

"Let us go on, then," said Nephromera wearily, "and leave our brother to his new home."

Nepsus bowed his horse-head as if in agreement, and Charon, taking up a reign, led the pack on into the streets of Amar. The village was ever quiet. Not a soul passed along the dirt roads to question them (and this truly would have been a questionable sight this late at night).

After a short while, the company stopped before an old inn. Martrum knew of this place scarcely, as he had enjoyed breakfast here a time or two in his younger days. He once favored the company of Mary, the old innkeeper, in an earlier stage of his life, and felt quite embarrassed to have wandered all the way here from his hillock beyond, provoked or not. But it was too late now to be bashful. Hiding in the shrubbery of a nearby establishment, he watched as the young form of Charon received the child from Nephromera's arms.

"Farewell, little brother," he heard the boyish voice of the formerly mighty Charon say. Then, reluctantly, he placed the child gently upon the steps of what he saw Mary had finally named the Mary Ol' Inn. Stooping his bushy little head sadly, Charon stepped away.

Nephromera spoke from atop Nepsus's back. "We may yet see him again, Charon," she said optimistically, but the air in her tone suggested that even she was not entirely sure of the truth behind her statement.

As if in agreement, the head of Nepsus bowed.

"Shall we risk taking our true form?" asked Charon. "It will make for easier passage to Zynys, I deem."

"I am afraid we must," answered Nephromera. "I fear I am weaker still in this form. Help me, please."

Charon was the first to materialize into his true form, and stood again in the glory of his brutish figure. Now he was able to help his sister down from horseback, and she was barely on the ground before she too was in her real likeness, along with Nepsus.

"I feel somewhat better now," she said, as if to herself. Stooping low to survey the child, sleeping peacefully on the doorstep of the inn, she kissed him on the forehead.

"Lucian," she said, as if tasting the name. She stood for a moment staring at her little brother, then turned to walk away when abruptly she hurried. "I almost forgot." Pulling a rolled up bit of parchment from her robes, she stuck a message within the child's rags. "That ought to explain enough," she determined.

Resolved, the three siblings stood, preparing for their return trip to wherever it was that they were going, when Nepsus spoke. "And what of the shepherd?" he asked.

Martrum's heart jumped.

"He has followed us since the field," he added.

"Ah, yes," said Nephromera, "we mustn't forget. Charon—"

Before Charon's name was finished being spoken, a vice-like grip yanked Martrum from hiding, and he was lifted above the head of the hulking man. In a fraction of a second, all went blank.

A moment later, Martrum Tuckle woke alone, his staff severed and his hair unkempt, wondering how on earth he ended up in front of the Mary Ol' Inn, and why indeed a child was sleeping on its doorstep.

Part 1

" . . . let us step into the night and pursue that flighty temptress, adventure."

– J.K. Rowling

1

Lucian Rolfe

Seventeen years later . . .

Lucian Rolfe stepped onto the balcony outside his room at the Mary Ol' Inn. A diffusing sleep had somewhat refreshed his seventeen-year-old limbs, a slumber credited to the potent rum he had consumed the night prior around the bend at MaDungal's Pub. It was midday, or so he guessed, for the sun was now high and unveiled upon his modest village of Amar, as whatever clouds may have resided with the new day had almost dispersed entirely.

Of all the towns abroad, perhaps his was quaintest. Here, each bend twisted off into an equally peaceful section. There were shops whose windows were always polished to allow passersby a very thorough look-in at various sorts of little goods or crafts. Here and there were scattered small market stands where farmers often sold their farm-fresh produce. Amid the multitude of little cottages were various pubs and inns. Surely, there was just about everything one would need to go about his or her daily life.

County Road perhaps endured the most traffic. There was Edwin Jacobs, the burly blacksmith, who was the marshal's source for arming his officers. Pike Pennylabel kept his pottery shop close by as well and made a fine profit (there were a plethora of well-tended gardens). Gawain the goldsmith, who always busied himself by building new pieces of jewelry and other gold-crested items particular to the fancier houses, conducted business just beyond that. And then, at the end of County Road, was Mary's Inn, voted finest in the village, from whose balcony Lucian now stood peering. His face was fair still, though much of the boyish look he once possessed was threatening to leave him entirely. He wished he had a copper coin for every time he heard that from his adopted mother Mary Rolfe, the innkeeper, or his half-dozen female admirers from school. Finally, he was beginning to notice the hint of a beard's stubble upon the contours of his sallow cheekbones—a glimmer of his advancing adulthood. Normally his brown locks were tidy and well kept atop his head; but today they drooped like willows over his brow. Some would describe Lucian as shy, which is a rather accurate way of putting it. He seldom spoke unless spoken to, with the exception of moments when he was with his neighborhood friends going on with their usual schemes about town. But those closest to him, namely Mary, regarded him as a common seventeen year-old boy, who loathed his studies, loved his friends, and who mischief had a natural way of finding.

Speaking of Mary Rolfe, she had been calling for Lucian for the better part of ten minutes. But, as was normally true of her requests, she might as well have been engaging the wall. Lucian did not pay any heed, though he heard her voice plainly. The beauty of that fine Saturday morning (or afternoon, whichever it might have been), was too beautiful to be spent indoors doing chores. Stretching, he gave a refreshed exhale, long and extended. "All I need is a—"

Suddenly his bedroom door slammed open with authority. "All you need is a new set of ears, Lucian Rolfe!" said Mary, thundering through his bedroom and onto the balcony. What Lucian *had* been thinking was that the only missing component of his balcony was a comfortable, cushioned chair—preferably a rocker—but it was hard to continue thinking of comfort with the elderly innkeeper aggressively prodding him. It was not Mary Lucian feared, it was the involuntary smirk he felt fighting to be made at the edge of his lips. It was certainly difficult to retain a grin, for Mary had blundered onto the balcony in her chocolate-stained apron, smelling of cakes from an entire morning of baking, and her gray hair began to sprout from the protective bonnet atop her head. But all his effort, alas, was in vain.

"You wipe that smile off your face, young man, or it's the kitchen for you today. And I'm not kidding, either."

It was rumored around the village that Mary's eyesight was quickly fading, but she still detected grins on Lucian's face before he made them.

There was no point arguing with her, Lucian decided. Instead, he answered, "I'm sorry, I couldn't hear you calling."

Mary snorted. "The Bennetts probably heard me calling, and they're down by the creek. You ought to think hard about changing some of your ways, young sir. You can't just lounge around here all day without a care in the world. It's a shame you never knew your parents. Perhaps they may have taught you the things I've been trying to teach you since you came a-thumping on my doorstep!"

In fact, though it could never be certain, it was Lucian's biological mother who had come "a-thumping" on Mary's doorstep some seventeen years before, when she found Lucian nestled there in a bundle of rags. She looked everywhere for the woman who had left him, but her search was empty. Thus, she took him in and raised him as her own. Initially, Mary believed Lucian's arrival to be a bad omen. In that year, she was close to losing the inn to the bank. Her business was failing miserably. She was unable to keep up with her bills and taxes. Now, atop all her already-existing financial issues, she had a child to support. But she could not just simply leave the boy to die.

In time, however, circumstances changed quite dramatically. The marshal's young nephew had spent a night at the inn after a long return from business elsewhere, and in the morning stayed for breakfast. He took a firm liking to Mary's hot apple pie, and apparently raved about it in his uncle's hall, and from that day forward Mary never encountered a poor day of business. Needless to say, her financial turnaround could not have come at a time more apt.

As to the whereabouts (or other information) with regard

to Lucian's mother or father, she did not care to broach the subject. She was a firm believer in the philosophy that there was no need great enough to drive a mother to forsake her child, especially on a doorstep in the rain. Though, when she inquired among her close acquaintances, no one could offer the slightest hint as to whom Lucian's mother might have been. "Mary," they would say, "you are the boy's mother now. You are all he's got."

"You're right," said Lucian, hoping to evade one of Mary's rants. "I'm not sure I was thinking clearly."

Mary gave an annoyed chuckle. "No, last *night* you weren't thinking clearly, when you practically fell through the front door upon the witching hour. Nearly took all night for me to haul you up to bed. And the vomit! Next time I'll make you sleep in it."

It now became apparent that he had more rum the previous night than he originally thought—or remembered. But now that the subject was broached, he noticed his shirt *was* stained something awful, with crusty, brown smudges here and there, and when he brought it up to his nose for further inspection, he was greeted by a putrid stench.

The rant, which he so carefully tried to avoid, was inevitable. Mary continued on by nagging about how he never studies and hardly attends lectures; how he sits around like a log and never helps around the inn; and, because a rant of Mary's would not be complete without it: how he never tidies his room.

She might have carried on all afternoon had it not been for the rising smell of burning bread coming from the kitchen. "Oh dear! The bread! I'll see you downstairs for brunch, Dear." Then, before slamming the door in disgust, she warned, "Ten minutes!"

Stretching one last time before starting for his bedroom, Lucian acknowledged once more the lovely day that had fallen over his quiet town. Walking into his room now, he sat upon his bed, noticing that he *did* feel somewhat dehydrated. *I think I'll stick with ale from now on,* he determined confidently. As though it would make his newly discovered headache subside, he rubbed his temples.

Upon doing so, he wondered how indeed the headache had been inflicted. Was it Mary and her rant? A hangover? A combination of the two? It *had* been a long while since his last consumption of rum, or any hard liquor at that. Usually he preferred MaDungal's fine ales, of which there was a plethora; but last night he supposed he would add a dash of spice to his evening—a debt he was paying presently.

Lying down, just for a moment, he thought about his childhood, as he was accustomed to in quiet times. The unclear waves of his past touched down foggily and rippled away into various distorted visions. Ever since Mary told him how she took him in, he pondered the features of his mother, wondering what she looked like before he was born and now. He envisioned a tall woman, with olive skin and silky, flowing hair—like his own, but longer—with thin arms and slender legs. Then his mind automatically strayed toward his father, and what his name might have been, and what size shoe he wore, and how big his arms were, and how deep his laugh was. Perhaps he was a warrior, who met a glorious end in battle in the name of his country. Or perhaps a lesser fate claimed him, something much less admirable than those of old stories.

But, whatever the terms by which his father passed, if in fact he passed at all, Lucian figured he would never come to know. That did not bother him. What truly bothered him was the fact that he was not sure if he cared.

Mary was now at the point of spontaneous combustion. She called Lucian with a tone that suggested it was the last time she would do so before action was taken, and thus he heeded her. That afternoon, several paying customers were enjoying brunch in the dining room—a large sitting area with six long tables, decorated with floral designs and flowerpots. Large square windows were set within the stained-wood walls here and there, their curtains drawn to let sunlight frisk freely through.

Meanwhile Mary labored, running back and forth from the kitchen to the dining room where her guests patiently anticipated the arrival of their orders. Lucian came down and joined them, and the ten or so guests greeted him as he assumed a seat. He knew everyone present, if only by name; the town was far too small to know at least that much. Mr. and Mrs. Blackwell sat closest to the stairwell, accompanied by their children Samuel, Rebecca, and Susan, all under the age of seven. The Godfreys and their daughter claimed the table beside him, and the Cromwells sat closest to the kitchen.

Though the customers greeted Lucian kindly, he could only manage nods and feigned smiles. The pounding in his head had become nauseating. Eventually Mary glided over to Lucian's side attempting to mask the contempt in which she held him. "And what can I get for *you,* dear?" It is indeed an art form to speak through clench teeth, yet Mary had mastered it.

Lucian moaned. "Got any tea?"

Mary feigned an exaggerated smile. "Of course! On its way."

When she was gone, Lucian cupped his weary, heavy head inside his hands, trying to discern why he felt worse now than before. He surmised that it must have been the trip down the stairs that compounded his hangover; the fluctuation of colors and lighting could very well have played a significant role. Just then, Mr. Blackwell, whose youth had never fully fled from him, leaned in to tap Lucian on the shoulder. "Rough night last night, friend?" he asked knowingly.

Lucian's dreary eyes peered at him. "Complete with MaDungal's finest rum," he replied quietly, so that Mary's selective hearing would not detect him.

To Mr. Blackwell's countenance came a look as though he had been poisoned. "That stuff can wash paint off the walls! How much did you have?"

From the cover of Lucian's skinny arms, Mr. Blackwell heard, "I don't remember much past a bottle." Then the boy looked up again, remembering to be respectful. "And I'm not sure I want to."

"You're probably better off—"

Just then, Mary entered from the kitchen, her feigned

cheer now all but blatantly false. "And one cup of tea for the young sir!" Moving then to the Blackwells' table, she checked if all was well. Mrs. Blackwell confirmed that their brunch had been delightful, and in time, Mr. Blackwell paid their bill and bid everyone a fine Saturday.

Then it dawned on Lucian: Saturday, the sixth of April— the eighteenth birthday of his best friend Jemstine Fryer. *That explains it,* he thought, referring to the feeling he had since he had woken up. For hours now, the foreboding sense that he was forgetting something had been hanging over him like a dark cloud. Now he wished it was something much less important. Of all the things he had forgotten of the night before, the one thing he remembered was seeing Jemstine off before he left for the pub, promising to meet him at the miller's creek that morning to spend the day fishing. With a hard *THUD,* he set his cup of tea down and raced quickly out the door, thinking, *You've done it this time, Lucian Rolfe,* all the way up the road.

2

The Miller's Creek

Lucian's heart sped as he raced the half mile to the creek. He could only be thankful that it was not yet summer; otherwise, the sun would have overpowered him in his current condition.

I deserve to faint, he thought. *Trampled by comers and goers without them even noticing.* If only he had not been so selfish. It was unforgivable to forget his one true friend's birthday—a day during which he promised to join him. Lucian could only hope that the Fryer boy would still be there.

He did not spare a look to admire the glorious Saturday that had fallen over the village. Though early April, it was exceptionally warm, and the sun was allowed to work without hinder in a cloudless sky. He saw the glittering creek, quiet and serene, running east to west like a sparkling silver thread, and soon passed atop the small, wooden bridge arching over it. Exasperated from his overlong sprint, he looked desperately about, but Jem was not in sight. Now the rum on his breath seemed fouler than it originally had, and began to sicken him. It was the only thing that deterred his thoughts away from potentially having ruined his lifelong friendship.

Once again, it seemed a night at the pub thwarted Lucian's dedication to his only legitimate companion, who did not care much at all for the pub or its atmosphere. Jemstine Fryer seldom drank, and even when he did, it was among family. He could enjoy himself without alcohol, which is why he hardly ever accompanied Lucian to MaDungal's. Perhaps their social preference was the only difference between the two boys—that and the fact that had the tables been turned and it was Lucian's birthday, Jem would have been with him at dawn.

Like we were supposed to, Lucian reminded himself.

Now, like the ringing of a monotonous trumpet, he recalled the words he told Jem the night before. *I'm excited for tomorrow! It's been too long since we've been fishing.*

And Jemstine replied, *It will certainly be a fine Saturday! Just you and me, like when we were younger.* And then they laughed and embraced before going their separate ways.

Neither could have guessed those two ways would have led to this. Jemstine had probably sat and waited the entire morning, from sunrise to high noon even—hoping that Lucian was only being kept by Mary for some last minute chores, or that the old inn-keeper needed an extra hand in the kitchen for an hour or so, or whatever other scenarios Jem might have played through his mind to save himself from the possibility that his best friend had simply forgotten. Jem's faithful mind could never have imagined the truth of the matter—that on the eve of his birthday, Lucian Rolfe stumbled through his door in the wee hours of the morning, drunk enough to end all drunkenness, slipping in puddles of his own vomit, and condemning himself to bed until noon, practically unconscious.

It was a hopeless matter, Lucian thought. The reality was probably that Jem had returned home by now, heartbroken and cursing Lucian for forsaking him—again. Lucian stood up from the bridge, gave one last look around as though Jem might have been there, and began to walk away when a splash sounded from the creek below.

The Fryer boy's voice called up. "Lucian!"

Lucian gave a sigh of relief. "You're still here!"

Jem, dripping wet, pulled himself up on to the low hanging bridge. Lucian latched on to one of his forearms and helped pull.

"Well, what do you know?" Jem said. "I thought you had changed our plans again."

Lucian gave an embarrassed chuckle, unsure if Jem was kidding. "Not exactly."

The adrenaline that had coursed through his body while racing to the creek took his mind off his very present headache somewhat. But now that his feet were under him, he rubbed the back of his head and winced. "I overslept," he said, grimacing. The thought of alcohol made him want to throw himself over the bridge.

Jem snorted. "Late night?"

"I suppose you could say that. Happy birthday, by the way."

"Well, it is now." Once he finished drying himself, he threw on his shirt. "Five more minutes and it would have been disappointing. I was about to leave, but I decided to take a dip in the creek. Current isn't that fast today, and it's exceptionally hot for April, no?"

Lucian wiped the remaining rails of sweat from his brow. "You can say that again."

"It's exceptionally hot for—"

Lucian rolled his eyes. "You know what I meant." He gave a weary look to the idle creek slipping away beneath them. "Anything biting today?"

"Not yet. I've gotten bored a couple times today and wound up jumping in, so I didn't fish as much as I would have liked to."

"Want to have another go?"

Jem smiled. "Sure thing. My rods are sitting up against the end of the bridge."

It was evident now that had Lucian been attentive at all to his surroundings, he could have spared himself a load of worry—for there, in plain sight, were Jem's fishing poles perched up against the helm of the bridge; though he did feel he was deserving of his few moments of despair. The two then took to fishing. Several fishless hours passed as they sat talking about past memories they shared, like the time Jem—who currently worked as a stable boy on his father's farm—went to stand up beside a beast of a steed, tripped, and in the act of trying to stop his fall smacked the horse on the hide and sent the entire barn into an uproar.

Lucian claimed to have been able to hear the ruckus from the inn, which, in Jem's defense, is not unlikely, for only two streets separated both properties.

At last, to spare further embarrassment, Jem suggested retiring while a hint of daylight remained, when their line caught abruptly. Both boys froze and looked with incredulous delight to each other, then to the pole, then back to each other, as if it were the first fish they had caught in their lives.

"Reel it in!" Jem exclaimed. "Go on!"

Lucian worked at the pole for quite some time, using every bit of his strength to twirl the spindle and haul in the line. Now he switched hands as his right arm became spent.

"We've got a fat one!" Lucian proclaimed in his struggle. Weariness hardened his voice, and sweat now fused his shirt to his skin. Jem came to his aid, and together they steadied the line. At an upward angle, they were able to prop the rod as to make the process a bit more manageable, and with both their strengths at hand the line began to slug its way to the surface.

"It's coming now!" cried Jem, his voice wrought with excitement. "She'll be up any second!"

Suddenly, with a great jerk, the two boys fell back. The weight that had burdened their line subsided entirely, and they lay bewildered and tired upon the bridge panting. Lucian was first to peer at the rod they had labored so tirelessly over. Upon the hook, the worm they employed as bait remained alive and squirming. Beneath it, tangled in an odd way, was a key—and a defiantly odd one at that. No fish of any size was in sight, neither upon the bridge nor scurrying away in the ever-moving creek below.

Observing the key, they saw that it was uncommon in every way but its shape. The shifting light of the high sun seemed to conduct a strange phenomenon: for one moment it seemed ordinary and, in another, sacred. Upon close inspection, they found that it was indeed unlike any other key they were accustomed to. It had an elongated shaft, bathed in pure gold, from which sprouted jagged, silver teeth that appeared as though they had once been flat. Now they almost resembled fangs. The feature most enthralling to the boys was its crown-shaped base, which rose up into three separate points like little mountains. And, such as mountains bore white caps of snow, these were helmed by their own individual jewel: an emerald, ruby, and sapphire, respectively from left to right. What was more, the emerald and sapphire appeared to be alight, even in the brightness of that afternoon, like trapped little beacons. The ruby, however, flanked by the two glowing jewels, was noticeably dim.

For what seemed like hours, the boys were without ability to speak. Since their eyes fell upon the trinket, the surroundings seemed to fade away, and all was silent save the slow, precise beating of their hearts.

At last, Lucian muttered slowly, "That's odd."

His voice came to him with the sluggishness of a dream, echoing as though he had spoken in the deepest of mines. Time was now an idea they overlooked. Their gaze was held by the oddity in Lucian's hands, this entity beckoning them in the form of a key—a key laced with gold and jewels and magnificent splendor—and they felt alone in the outskirts of the small village, as though they were all who dwelt within.

Suddenly, a horse's braying woke them from their trance as a kindly gentleman passed them in his carriage. Now it was as though their bodies slowly began retrieving a sense of proper function as they became wary of their surroundings once more.

"I can't say I like this thing," Jem whispered, looking both ways as though in earshot of others. "It's strange, I think. Who would craft a thing so common with such glamour? And why is it in the creek of all places?"

"It's probably a reject of Gawaine's," suggested Lucian, as if to himself. "He's quick to temper. Always throwing things out if he can't get them right. He probably just got rid of it."

"I don't know," said Jem, grimacing. "Gawaine's talented and all, but he's never made anything quite like *this* before.

And besides, he normally signs his pieces with that fancy 'G' of his. No sign of that anywhere on here." Glaring hard upon the key, his eyes became studious and unwavering. "What do you think we should do with it?"

For a short while, Lucian did not respond to Jem, for he remained caught in the remaining stages of whatever possessed his focus. At length he began stammering. "I—I don't know, Jem." His gaze, if possible, fixed harder upon the key. "But we found it. So by right it's ours for the keeping."

Jem said nothing, returning only a bewildered glance. "You mean to—to keep it?" he muttered. "But it's only a key—a golden key . . . with . . . shining stones." He paced back and forth as if in thought, then added in earnest, "This isn't meant for us to pester with. What if it belongs to someone? Someone *else?* Someone dangerous."

"Like who? Everything belongs to someone, Jem; and now it belongs to us. I wonder what its worth would be. Maybe we can find some profit for its exchange."

Nervously, Jem continued to pace forwards and back, considering Lucian's words, then he said finally, "No, no, no—I don't want any part of that. Folks go to bed at night and wake up in the river for that sort of thing. Suppose it belongs to a lunatic? It would mean our heads if he found out we sold it!"

As the boy presented his thoughts aloud, he became nearly frantic, much to the amusement of a pair of young ladies who were now passing by. Lucian, embarrassed, waved to them with a makeshift smile, as though oblivious to Jem's apparent dilemma.

When the girls passed out of range, Lucian caught at Jem. "Alright," he said, "first—look at me—" he grabbed hold of Jem's plump face, damp from sweat accumulating on his rosy cheeks. "No one knows this thing is here. It's ours by chance, and for the time being we're going to keep it."

"But . . . but, no . . . I mean how . . . I mean—" he stammered wildly. Lucian could find no other alternative to suppress Jem's mounting fit than to smack him, and though he momentarily regretted striking his best friend on his birthday, it managed to calm him down.

Lucian proceeded to speak patiently. "If it brings you this much worry, you don't have to be part of this. I'll take it."

Lucian, for all he was worth, could not determine why Jem was so frightened. In time, he sat down again, panting as though having endured some sort of physical strain. Jem had never been the overly nervous sort, but for some reason he was experiencing enough paranoia to shake a village from its very frame. Lucian wondered confusedly why he was reacting so dramatically. It was only a key after all. Astonishment was natural, due to its very splendor. But paranoia? Lunacy? He sat down beside Jem, who was shivering for the dampness of his attire.

"Is everything alright, Jem?" Lucian dared to ask. For some strange reason, he was not sure if he wanted to know the answer.

His friend *did* seem rather distant, as though he harbored some secret he wanted to share but simply could not. "It's just—" Jem started at last, and his gaze shifted headlong, "—lately I've noticed a strange man around town—someone I've never seen before. My father has seen him too. Normally, I see him when—" then his gaze passed over a nearby part of the outlying forest and froze there, too horrified to look away. Soundlessly, his lips moved as though he meant to speak but simply forgot how, and he could only direct Lucian's attention to where he was looking with a clattering hand. When Lucian followed his troubled gaze, he too saw the man, cloaked and barely visible, comprised almost entirely of shadow, standing casually in the eaves of the wood peering toward them, seemingly without much intent. From far off, their eyes fell upon him, and from there, he seemed more like a ghost than a man; one who had manifested in that place rather than ventured there from wherever he had come.

Lucian now fumbled for words himself, though he was more discrete about it than Jem. "Surely I've never seen *him* before," he said, his nerves unraveling slightly as he spoke. "We shouldn't make it obvious that we're—" but before he could direct Jem to casually proceed away from the creek, the Fryer boy had already leapt up and began walking at an incredible pace back toward town. Alone, and feeling much more vulnerable on the bridge, Lucian followed, slipping the key into his pocket. Out of curiosity, however, he turned and gave one final look to the wood before traversing homeward. To his surprise, whoever had been standing there was gone.

3

Mascorea's Council

The great hall of Mascorea, King of Medric, was located in the center of Medric's capital city of Adoram, and was widely referred to as Magnis Abitaz. Without denial, as Medric architects had boasted since its construction, it was the most beautiful structure in the west. Certainly, a most elegant edifice, it had a tendency to sparkle even on rainy days. Some argued that it was even more dazzling within its confines, in which the white, blue-veined marble floor seemed to stretch for nearly a mile. High white pillars flanked the main corridor, and above, the decorated ceiling boasted grand designs in a slew of various hues. Sapphire tapestries draped down between every other pillar, with Medric's sigil of the prancing bear embroidered on their midsections in white. Every other fifteen feet or so, man-sized window slits afforded the pale sunlight entrance, thus all was often bathed in its splendor.

It was indeed a busy corridor. The traffic passing to and fro never seemed to subside until the sun died away. From dawn until dusk, attendants, advisers, lords, ladies, generals, soldiers, recruits, artists, singers, musicians, merchants, traders, and school children (there were hundreds more), rushed in and out to visit Mascorea and bring him gifts or tidings. Seeing as how he was not the type of king who demanded this of his people, they were more inclined to do so of their own accord.

But no visitations would be had this day—no choir of children or blacksmiths displaying the latest models of weaponry. This day was to be spent entirely in Mascorea's council chamber, a small anteroom located at the end of various hidden passageways beyond Magnis Abitaz. For the king had summoned his Secret Council earnestly, and, scurrying about from their previous stations, his small band of councilmen rallied to his hidden chamber.

Among these councilmen were the lords Patrid and Haldus, who had begun their royal service under Mascorea's father and predecessor Varon. In their velvety-blue, gold-flecked robes, they scurried among the fray within the main corridor anxiously. When they were finally out of earshot, Lord Patrid spoke.

"What do you suppose caused His Grace to rally us so suddenly?" he asked. He was small for a Morok, though in his younger years his body may have hosted more brawn.

"I cannot say, councilman," answered Lord Haldus, who matched the other's eager pace. "But I do not know His Grace to succumb to petty worry. Whatever his need, I trust it is most dire."

Haldus was larger than Patrid. Whereas the years had withered Patrid's face to a sallow, sunken shell of its former self, Haldus yet bore much of the form he boasted during his years of military service long ago.

The din of the busy corridors was behind them now, and they passed into darker confines of Magnis Abitaz until the marble floors gave way to stone, and a large, sealed door to which only the Secret Council bore keys opened to a dark, damp, and very small tunnel. They trudged on slowly, crouching, as there was not enough room to stand completely.

"I daresay a better spot could have been chosen," said Lord Patrid, struggling in his pursuit behind Lord Haldus, who chuckled in response.

"Almost there," assured Haldus, his voice also strained. "I see the light ahead of me."

And in nearly a minute's time, they stepped out of the dusty tunnel and into another brightly lit room that seemed to be a shrunken, square replica of the main corridor itself. Here, the same marble floor was beneath them and four white pillars—one in each corner—rose up and joined the colorful ceiling to the floor. And before them, in front of which waited yet another member of the council, was the entrance to the chamber. It was a room known only to exist by those summoned to it. With the doors closed and latched, it served as more of a vault than anything; not even a whimper would be heard from outside had an explosion occurred within.

The councilmen recognized the other Morok to be Navys, Master Chief of the Medric fleet. Decked in his handsome armor, he stood with his helmet cradled under his arm. As they staggered toward him, batting away the dust from the lining of their robes, Navys turned a hard and impatient stare toward Patrid and Haldus.

"Sagestone," he said, seemingly annoyed. "An impressive display to boast, yet a hindrance when trying to get any sort of important business underway."

Navys was alluding to the enchanted door of the council chamber. It was comprised of an element called sagestone, found only in the sacred realm of Mount Zynys. Legend told of its impenetrability against any earthly craft, and thus the earliest Morok king employed it to enclose his council chamber. Yet indeed its only flaw was the time it took to open completely. Comprised of three layers, it opened in such a manner that one layer slid sluggishly away at a time, and only then after a secret knock was performed.

"I knocked perhaps fifteen minutes ago," said Navys grudgingly, watching intently as the third layer of the door was just getting itself moving.

When the door slid away at last, the three councilmen were afforded a look within. It had been long since either of them had been summoned here, and they had forgotten the eerie splendor the chamber possessed. It was a circular room, with torches fastened around its circumference. Their firelight reflected off the sapphire jewels wrought throughout, and worked to splay a ghostly, pale-bluish gleam across the room. On the far wall, the tall, distorted shadow of a man danced like a black lick of flame—a shadow that belonged to none other than Mascorea himself, sitting behind a mounted desk of stone, rubbing his temples with his long and slender hands, seemingly at his wit's end.

There was another who was present, sitting below the desk in a chair of stone. His name was Stór, Chief General of the Morok legions. A hard and difficult Morok, he seemed to have no function outside of a disciplinarian. Upon seeing him, Navys, Patrid, and Haldus had little trouble understanding why Mascorea seemed so vexed. Yet when the king saw them enter, his old, pale-blue eyes fell upon them warmly, and he rose with a weary smile and his arms outstretched.

"Ah, good councilmen," he said, his voice aged and hoarse. "Do sit down, do sit down."

Stór followed suit and stood as well. He too cradled his helm beneath the crook of his arm, the massive, dark blue plume of which was wisping around his broad shoulder. The general was a grisly, bear of a Morok. It was a wonder, especially to Patrid, who loathed him, how the armory ever managed to find a suit that fit his massive contour. He always thought it was difficult before he gained his belly, when he was comprised of nothing but solid muscle. But now, nearly two centuries and a hundred pounds later, he was surprised the bearded brute was not bursting at the seams.

"About time," barked Stór, in his best attempt to say something under his breath. "Perhaps we may be able to feast at a reasonable hour."

Haldus ignored Stór's remark and merely bowed to Mascorea in greeting. Patrid gave a mock smile, pretending not to be annoyed. But Navys, ever the combative type, stepped into Stór's proximity, his pointed chin nearly flush with the bristles of the general's.

"I daresay you can afford to miss a meal or two," he said, patting Stór's armored stomach for good measure.

"I would be wary of where I point that pincer of a chin if I were you," growled Stór.

"Gentlemen." The voice was Mascorea's, and though he spoke collectedly, Stór and Navys ceased their mild bickering and stood to attention as if he had shouted.

Then Mascorea, in his robes of white and blue, swept up to his altar, and bid his council members sit with a gesture of his hands. "Now that we are all gathered," he began, clearing his throat. "It is in earnest you have been summoned here. Long has it been since our last meeting, yet I believe no meeting of such importance has ever been held within these walls. It has been brought to my attention that the Key has resurfaced—"

At these words, the four members of the council erupted into errant chatter.

"The Key?"

"It cannot be!"

"Gentlemen—" Mascorea urged.

" . . . regarded as myth . . . "

" . . . destroyed . . . "

"GENTLEMEN!"

Mascorea was supporting himself against his podium with much effort now, as though he had expelled the remainder of his energy. His councilmen, like cowering children, sat down quiet and alert. Even the mighty Stór seemed startled as he took his seat and placed his helmet at his feet.

The king continued as collectively as he was able. "Yes, indeed this is of some shock to you. I yet find myself believing I received these tidings in a dream. But as it happens, the Key has resurfaced—Kal Glamarig, as the legend names it—the Jewel of the Sorcerer of Nundric, and the only instrument that has the power to unlock his Chamber of Fates."

The council was aghast. Lord Patrid was the first to find his tongue. "Where, my lord?" he asked, embarrassed at the way his voice wavered. And his question quieted the others for a moment as they turned their gaze attentively to their king.

Mascorea regarded Patrid with his crystalline eyes, which, though aging fast, still bore much of their potency. "Off the shores of the east," he answered plainly. "In a village scantily domiciled. It is there we must focus our doings, before the same tidings reach the land of Dridion,

21

and Melinta assembles his own reconnaissance team."

Stór stood, and his voice bellowed firmly throughout the small chamber. "Are we so far from a truce that we cannot join forces with Dridion?" he asked, a subtle twinge of desperation lingering at the edge of his gruff voice. "Is Melinta so far gone that he cannot be swayed?"

The calm voice of Mascorea answered. "In another time, perhaps my first action would have been to call for the aid of Dridion, when Melinta's father Viridus reigned and all was well between our lands." Then he turned his gaze away from Stór and bent his head as if lamenting. "But Melinta's mind is overthrown, as you know, by his need for vengeance. Word has reached my ear, even, of his allegiance with Nundric."

At this news the councilmen became distressed, and muttered to each other words of fear.

"We cannot reach out to Dridion," continued Mascorea resolutely. "Had a truce between us been forged, the issue of trust would be ever present. There are indeed enough foes to fight; let us not compound that matter by trying to convert some of them into friendship." Then his gaze became utterly sullen. "I fear we are alone in this."

Lord Haldus stood, his hard stare filled with intent. "If this is indeed the way it must be," he began, "I move to send our own reconnaissance fleet to the shores of the east, and retrieve Kal Glamarig before the enemy."

Lord Patrid nodded slowly, considering. Navys rolled his eyes and folded his mailed arms. Stór grunted.

But Mascorea seemed interested. "And how many ships do you suggest, good Haldus?" he inquired.

Lord Haldus contemplated. "Three or four," he said finally. "I cannot rationalize sending any more than that. If seen from shore, a fleet so small in quantity would not raise suspicion. We do not know how the mortals have progressed in the years since they fled east. That was generations past, mind you—their great grandsons and granddaughters could be somewhat established by now. Our troops could be met with hostility."

It was then that Navys stood, apparently unable to

conceal his take on the matter any longer.

"That is why we must travel with full force," he suggested eagerly. "Such a mission must be completed on a grand scale. I offer you, your grace, a hundred ships, and my finest crews."

Now it was Stór's turn to rise, a wide, chipped smile flashing from beneath the dark thicket of his beard. "Ah, the cub bears his teeth!" he roared. "To think I ever took you for a woman." He gave Navys a swift pat on the shoulder. "This lad's plan holds promise, my lord. I will offer a thousand of my best on top of his crews. And as you well know, I have many fine soldiers at my disposal—every one of them raring to defend his country."

All eyes turned to Mascorea, who stood contemplating, yet his long and weathered face seemed unsatisfied.

"Keep in mind," said Mascorea after a long while, "that we are not waging war. These are peasant villages to which we strive; not cities like Adoram, around which loom daunting walls. Your offers are generous, and I am grateful for your willingness to aid in whatever way you can, but I refuse to subject a hundred of my ships, or legions of my soldiers, to the fury of the ocean, though I well know it must be crossed somehow."

All were seated again, and the anxious air that for a moment was present in the room was vanquished.

At last, Lord Patrid stood to voice his opinion. "My good king," he began, "I too share your stance in this. Master Chief Navys and Chief General Stór are decorated figures, and have served our country well. But to risk them, along with thousands of others, is too steep a price to wager. War is certain to reach Medric, regardless of our part in obtaining Kal Glamarig. The Lord of Nundric will stop at nothing to destroy the remaining free lands that oppose him. We cannot risk our strength in arms to be depleted so."

"Your stance is heard," replied Mascorea, "and well received. I share in Lord Patrid's views, gentlemen. I will not subject that many souls to an uncertain cause."

Just then Navys stood. "Respectfully, my lord, but once

you have risked one life, you have risked a thousand. Is one so different than a multitude?"

"I respect your honesty, Master Chief, but you must understand that we are on the cusp of a war not even your forefathers endured, and in such times sacrifices must be made. The finding of Kal Glamarig means that Sorcerian's forces are prepared to move. That Key is the only mechanism by which the Chamber can be unlocked and thus undo him. They will stop at nothing to retrieve it, and thus we must stop at nothing. There is no denying that a great risk lies in our decision to send a team, however large, across the Mid Sea. But in this also lies great reward."

Lord Patrid turned to Navys. "You know well the fury of the Mid Sea, Master Chief, perhaps better than the rest of us," he said. "Can you not attest to its rage? Its malice? It is April, no less, and the rising temperatures play strange workings upon the sea."

Now, a twinge of anger flooded through Navys's voice. "I need no lesson in crossing oceans, councilman. I have crossed my share and am here to speak in this chamber today."

Navys then stood up to Lord Patrid, whose small figure backed away slowly. Haldus and Stór stood quickly to prevent any sort of grapple. But in time, all began shouting at one another, expressing their own thoughts and ideas as to what should be done. Mascorea, meanwhile, agitated and weary, leaned back in his great seat and took to rubbing both temples again with his slender fingers.

Allowing them to argue amongst themselves, Mascorea tried to fend off his gathering enervation, and, when he felt he had enough strength to stop them, he shouted, "ATTENTION!"

The raging council was cast into abashed silence.

"It is clear to me," began Mascorea, plainly agitated, "that a verdict will not be reached tonight." The four members of the council, realizing how childishly they had behaved, gathered their wits and sat back down.

Mascorea continued. "Bear in mind, however, that this is a task entirely dependent upon speed. Sleep, and let your blood settle. In two moons' time a decision will be reached and set in motion." He took to looking each one of his councilmen sternly in the eye before muttering, "Dismissed."

Sluggish and embarrassed, the four members of the council stood to leave like scolded children. Mascorea, as though he had physically had to tear them apart, plopped down in his chair consumed by exhaustion.

What Mascorea remembered most about that defiantly strange evening was how unusually cold it was. Having lived through many Aprils, he could not recall a colder April night, and no matter the mechanisms by which he sought warmth, he simply could not attain a comfortable temperature. His bedchamber was secluded in the uppermost chamber of Magnis Abitaz, with a comfortable four-poster bed, upon which soft blue fabrics were draped. The enormous brown pelt of a bear was strewn across the dark stone floor, and he sat staring contemplatively into its blank eyes.

A servant was feeding the fire blazing in his hearth, but Mascorea dismissed him after his many failing efforts to warm the room. He was not planning on getting much sleep as it was. Occasionally stealing through the cracks in the wall were invisible tendrils of a northerly wind, causing the furs on the floor to billow, and the ornaments on the walls to chime.

Since he left the council chamber, the riddle of Kal Glamarig played constantly through his mind. How could they obtain it before Sorcerian's forces? Surely, they were already in motion. *Speed and secrecy,* he told himself. *That is what this task depends on, as I have said before.* Then he recalled the behavior of his councilmen and became dismayed. *It was unlike them to react that way . . .*

Melancholy, he walked to the corner of the room adjacent from the hearth, where his shrine to the Sages of Mount Zynys was glinting in the firelight. Here he bent upon his weary knees in prayer, imploring them desperately for a sign or message. Yet it was hopeless, as he had feared,

25

knowing full well that his inquiries were futile, and that the Mountain, as it had for centuries, would remain dormant.

Nevertheless, he rallied his faith and prayed aloud. "By the grace of Zynys, sway my hand toward a proper plan. See that I do not lead my people astray . . . "

As if in answer, the slow, soft whistle of a strand of wind howled momentarily and was gone.

I might have known, he thought disappointedly, when abruptly the red gleam of the fire ignited into a rich, blue-white flame, and in a flash, the roomed was filled with its blinding glow as though the fire itself had escaped. There was a sound like thunder, accompanied by a wildly flickering light as though the very world itself was malfunctioning. Mascorea, bent and afraid, found himself cowering on the ground and backing away in fright, when, as suddenly as it occurred, the terrifying experience ceased, leaving only chiming ornaments as remnants.

The horror subsided so suddenly, in fact, that it was some time before Mascorea realized he was no longer alone in his bedroom. A man whom he did not recognize was standing by the foot of his bed, wrapped in a thick, dark cloak, through which Mascorea thought to see some form of light yearning to escape.

The stranger was stretching his arms over his head, as though his body had been worn by a long journey, and he seemed to be muttering to himself. The king could only distinguish part of what he was saying. " . . . blasted means of transport, truly . . . "

Had he entered through the window? Impossible—the chamber was nearly half a league from the ground. Fear gripped the old king. "Who are you?" he implored nervously. He was not sure how much more his weary heart could endure.

It was as though Mascorea's voice startled the stranger to attention, and he stood upright to reveal his true height. As if in answer he unveiled himself, and the room was ablaze with a lustrous radiance. Mascorea felt throttled, as though all the furies of the world and beyond united into a spear-point and stabbed him. He understood now that this was a being not of this world. The old scriptures bore tales of people who experienced visitations—or so they claimed—from the eternal realm of Mount Zynys, Land of the Sages, but never had he believed them to be true until this moment.

The being glided forward, but the light that was radiating off his body was too violent for Mascorea to behold any of his features. "I am Nepsus, Sage of the Sea," answered the stranger at long last.

Sages were said to appear in some sort of guise—old men or women, birds or beasts—but Mascorea was certain that he was seeing Nepsus in his true form; that by which he left Zynys and by which he would return.

The old king, his voice wavering, answered. "Good Sage! I beg of you—extinguish your light; make it so I can look upon the target of my prayers!"

At his request, Nepsus strode forward, and it was as though his form blotted out the incredible light that had been blazing. Now Mascorea could look upon him plainly. His glittering, silver armor was wrought with the ancient runes of Zynys, and they glowed fluorescently from amidst his breastplate. Behind him was draped a cape, blue like the ocean, and in his hand he carried a mighty spear, whose golden point was crafted to resemble the head of a swordfish.

An errant tear coursed slowly down Mascorea's cheek. "Forgive me, good Sage, if I have done wrong. Forgive me, if ever I have despaired."

Nepsus extended a lean, muscle-roped arm to the groveling king's shoulder, and spoke gently. "Good Mascorea, such a king this world has not boasted in a long while, but you must listen closely. You are right to plot the retrieval of Kal Glamarig, but know that this will be the only instance a son or daughter of Zynys will speak with you plainly. It is imperative for your forces to cross the Mid Sea, and thus I shall take it upon myself to tame her. You must, however, abide by my orders. It is in one ship only you shall send your force, and entrust one Morok to the task. Give this Morok an able crew and no more. This ship must bear all the trappings of a common merchant vessel. The sails you wave will be neutral, and bear no resemblance to those of your own fleet. By now, Sorcerian has certainly planted agents in every crevice of the world. His spies patrol the air, land, and even the sea by now. Yet I believe such commonality will not draw even his attention."

"And . . . and this will work?" asked Mascorea sheepishly.

"I cannot promise the vessel will go unnoticed, but it will at least stand as cause for debate, sparing enough time to arrive safely and begin the quest."

Mascorea contemplated for a moment. "It will be difficult to select a mercenary," he said thoughtfully. "My generals are proud—especially Stór. He will surely have his own selection in mind."

Mascorea was dismayed to see a glimmer of frustration flash across Nepsus's face. "This is not a time for heroes of the likely sort," said Nepsus shortly. "Yours are honored warriors, but you must send someone who will surely go overlooked. I know of one who, if given the chance, could best any soldier your generals hold dear."

The old king drew a look of doubt. "I would know of this soldier, who could best any in my ranks."

"It is a name that has surely been discussed among your council. Gamaréa, son of Gladris. He is prepared for his chance, and it is you who will appoint him."

Mascorea considered for a moment. "I have heard of this Morok," he said at last, though he was not definitely sure. "If my memory serves me correctly, however, I recall only foul reports of him."

Nepsus's voice became stern, and he spoke as though disgusted. "It is a sad fate that he has suffered at the hands of your generals, who have chastised him under the premise that he is half man. But I bid you hear me now. I can attest otherwise. You have the promise of a Sage to call forth! Your predecessors believed that a bloodline could be judged based on outward appearance. To uphold those beliefs upon inheriting the crown was your right as king, but it is a flawed way of thinking. Gamaréa is one of many to have suffered the prejudice of your nation. It is time to give him the opportunity Medric has so long denied him."

It was such an absurd and obscure order that Mascorea was not sure how to react. "You are sure of this?" he asked, puzzled.

But in response, the room erupted again in a thunderous cacophony. Rage and horror overtook the chamber once more, and all was, yet again, violently ablaze. Mascorea's heart gave a shuddering jolt, and outside he could hear his servants scratching and clawing desperately to flood the chamber, but their way was locked.

Now all within range could hear Nepsus wailing. "I am the Sage of the Sea, son of Ation, King of Kings, creator of this world and its populous! This is the final decree of Zynys before retiring to dormancy to revive the greatest of all lords. And you, Mascorea, son of Varon, will see it done, and question me no more."

The light extinguished in its abrupt manner and all fell silent again. The doors, which had apparently unlatched themselves, allowed the servants passage, and a whole host of them rushed into the chamber, crying and muttering frantically to each other. At the foot of his bed, splayed upon his bear-pelt rug in his night-robes, they found Mascorea shivering, his eyes wide, his body trembling, and the slightest hint of a smile tugging at the edge of his lips.

"That is an absurd order," argued Chief General Stór two dawns later. "I refuse to adhere to this."

Lord Patrid nearly burst. "My lord," he said sheepishly, "your servants described how they came upon you in your bedchamber. Though I won't get into detail before the council, I will say that we must understand the discrepancies between reality and fever dreams—"

"And lunacy," added Master Chief Navys. "He is a savage, this Gamaréa—a murderer. He should have been banished long ago along with all the other mortals who fled east."

Mascorea sprung from his seat, his voice raised and frenzied. "Four hundred years of life and yet you still think him mortal, Master—Chief—Navys?" Mascorea annunciated every word of Navys's title as if to suggest a man of his rank should bear better sense.

"Several solid arguments were raised in my chambers last night, gentlemen," continued Mascorea succinctly. "And you are fools to believe that I will deviate from the orders of a Sage."

Stór spoke. "And so you elect to send this murderer across the sea to do the will of our people? This traitor whom none of us can trust?"

"He murdered one Morok," replied Mascorea frankly. "And he was a child no older than a school-aged mortal. And, for your information, given Jax's reputation I daresay it would not surprise me if the general's fate was deserved."

"You can say this plainly?" said Stór, not menacingly, but disbelievingly. "He was a good soldier, Jax—and he was my friend. How can you stand there and insult him in defense of such filth—"

"It is no insult to say the dead have claimed their graves, general. And your words are rash this morning—seek to hold them in check. I know I said that we would continue our little debate this morning, but as you well know, the matter has been settled. An errand runner has been set in motion and Gamaréa is perhaps already in the city. I merely sought to inform the council of the decision. One ship, one crew, no flags. This country will not fall into the nets of conformity like the Fairies of Dridion. I know you harness your separate doubts, but I ask you now to trust your king, and believe that I will not lead you astray."

Lord Haldus spoke. "I have never had dealings with this Gamaréa, son of Gladris."

"I have," said Stór shortly. "Long ago, when he came to my camp as a recruit. No respect, no honor—wrought from nothing but bone and pale flesh . . . "

"He was seven," answered Mascorea bluntly. "Show me a child of that age who is not assembled so."

The general inhaled deeply. It was clear to the council that he was summoning all his power to control his rising fury.

"I respectfully move to be excused, your grace," muttered Stór.

Mascorea nodded his white-capped head. "You may leave," he said. "The doors are beginning to open as we speak, unless my ears deceive me. When they part you may take your leave, Chief General."

And in moments, the last layer of sagestone doors was heard jawing open behind them, and before long the silhouette of Gamaréa, son of Gladris, appeared in the shadows of the doorway.

4

The Summoning

Podrick Worthwent had been a stable boy this time last year, but by a fortunate series of promotions, mismatches, rights, wrongs, and opportunities, he somehow found himself a thirteen-year-old errand-runner of King Mascorea. His mother and he took up residence in the poor, seaside village of Dwén Alíl after his father perished on an ill-fated fishing vessel in the northern seas. Since age seven, he was employed in several little occupations to help with the finances of the Worthwent household, and now it was his duty to report every Thursday to the forum outside Magnis Abitaz to await instruction from one of the king's advisers. Adoram was only six leagues or so from Dwén Alíl, and it was a journey that Podrick did not mind in the least. Not with the incentive of a hot meal to spur him on.

But for Podrick, this Thursday was a Thursday unlike any other that he had been alive for. Not only did he actually receive an errand, but received it from King Mascorea himself. Surely, this was an encounter none of the other errand-runners could boast. Those who knew Podrick, his scrawny frame and his ever curious stare, quipped that it was simply due to the fact that he was first to arrive on that particular Thursday, but it was no matter to the young Worthwent boy. Let the envious envy.

His errand was strange, however. Normally, the errands consisted of running into the marketplace in the center of the city to procure goods and deliver them to the king's stronghold; but never before had he heard of delivering an actual person.

"My dear Podrick Worthwent," Mascorea had said, "it is with great care that you must fulfill this task. Venture to the coastal town of Titingale, fetch one Gamaréa, son of Gladris, and escort him here to Magnis Abitaz."

It took most of the afternoon to venture down the southerly roads into the small farmsteads of Titingale just as nightfall was encompassing the area. Leading his bay at a leisurely pace down the gravel roads, Podrick went on until he found an affordable stable. There he met an aging Morok named Tamm, sitting in a small booth in front of the stables with his hands folded.

Tamm stood quickly in the presence of the approaching rider, initially having only seen Podrick's silhouette. He settled himself, however, when he saw that the rider approaching was a child.

"Not 'customed to gettin' children ridin' in at dusk," said Tamm, in the casual twang of the southern Morok provinces. "'Can I do for yeh there . . . ?"

Tamm seemed to be inquiring Podrick's name.

"I am Podrick Worthwent," Podrick introduced himself formally, "and I am here on official business from Adoram, by order of the king."

"You don' say!" Tamm's voice sounded thoroughly surprised.

"I do," replied Podrick matter-of-factly. "Or, well, I did. I need a temporary respite for my horse."

Tamm seemed amused by the businesslike conduct of the young rider. "You've come to the right place there, Pod!" he exclaimed. "You don' mind if I call yeh Pod, do yeh? Well, anyway, we'll tie her right up for yeh. Won't have to worry 'bout a thing."

Podrick dismounted, and saw now that he was only as tall as Tamm's waist. "What do I owe you?" he asked.

"Well now, let's see—what've yeh got?"

Tamm felt somewhat guilty for charging a young boy the full price for a stable, which, in terms of copper, stood at about ten pieces. But to Tamm's surprise, Podrick reached into his traveling cloak and pulled out a glittering silver coin.

"I trust this will suffice?" he said plainly.

Tamm did not answer right away, but eventually took to nodding his head.

"The king himself has funded this trip," stated Podrick, incase Tamm had been wondering. It was the first time either had been in possession of an actual silver coin.

In no time at all, Tamm found a suitable stable for Podrick's bay, and the Worthwent boy took to carrying off on foot, which, luckily, was a manageable means of transportation in the small, shabby town of Titingale. The streets were divided into small blocks between which ran narrow avenues of dirt passageways. Folk littered some sections more so than others. Every so often, a small, run-down-looking establishment played host to a fair-sized crowd of drunkards.

But there was one building—The Adder's Nest—that proved livelier than the others, out of which a boisterous and laughing crowd spilled outside and into the street. Podrick made his way through the various strangers, up the rickety stairs, across the dirtying, mildewed floor, and up to a chipping bar counter, over which a disgruntled-looking Morok the customers referred to as Prig was peering.

"Sorry, young lad," he heard Prig's voice carry over the din. "Fresh out of orange juice and milk, we are. Can't do yeh fer anythin' but beer or liquor."

From where Prig stood, Podrick was a dirty-blonde clump of hair, but it answered: "I am not looking for a drink; I am looking for a person."

Prig laughed, displaying a black-toothed smile. "Got plenty o' them, we do!"

"A specific person," Podrick said bluntly.

Prig's demeanor tensed up somewhat. "Well then, you'll need teh be more specific."

"Gamaréa, son of Gladris. By order of the King, I am to escort him this night to Magnis Abitaz."

Prig's eyes flickered. "Well I'll be," he answered in astonishment.

"You know him, then?"

"Not personally, see, but he comes in erry now an' then. But *every*one in Titingale knows *who* he is."

Prig gesticulated toward two swinging doors in the far corner behind the bar, then shifted a knowing look back to Podrick. "Just take the stairs."

Podrick Worthwent, who felt that his errand was getting stranger by the second, hesitated a moment before making his way through another labyrinth of tall, conversing Moroks. His descent into the lower level of the pub proved more difficult than expected. Moroks cluttered every step, inattentive to where they were holding their overflowing pints. An anxious air was about them. Every set of eyes was peeled in one direction, on something that was apparently worth bodily injury to see.

"On with you, then!" voiced young Podrick as he fought down the stairwell. "I am on important business here!"

The stairwell spilled into a myriad of eager faces, their eyes all fixed on the same spectacle. Podrick could not see anything of the basement until he was nearly halfway down the stairs, but when he looked out across the crowded floor, he saw the audience's attention was focused on a boxing ring of sorts, in which a Morok of a good, strong build was dodging quick blows from a burly, short-haired opponent. As he danced and punched and dodged, his shaggy, unkempt locks flew wildly, adding an animalistic look to his already-grisly appearance. Finally, after the stout Morok missed with an errant jab, his shaggy-haired combatant rammed a shoulder into his midsection, hoisted him up, and slammed him directly into the wall of the ring."

"That's it, Gammy!" he heard a spectator shout.

"Finish him off!" another called out from the stairwell.

The shaggy-headed fighter, whom Podrick determined from the cheers was the Morok he was looking for, finished his opponent with three swift punches—two to the ribs, and one flattening blow to the face. This toppled his rival, and, after a moment's frustration, the fallen brawler decided it was in his best interest to charge Gamaréa, who with relative ease threw him from the ring and into the crowd.

Alone and unscathed, Gamaréa proceeded to urge on the crowd, which cheered their approval wildly.

Seizing the opportunity to speak with him alone, Podrick darted forward and made as if to get into the ring himself. He was bumped aside, however, by whom he presumed to be the match's dictator. Leaping eagerly into the ring, this well-dressed Morok, bearing a smug grin upon his plump face, raised Gamaréa's muscled arm enthusiastically.

"The victor, and undisputed champion!" he called loudly, and the crowd roared in excitement. "That's all this evening, folks. Get home safely! Ah, yes! That's the spirit! Be sure to tip the staff!"

As the room cleared, Podrick saw the Morok that had been flung from the ring stagger to his feet and join a groaning group of others who must have been mangled by Gamaréa that evening. There was a momentary hesitation for Podrick as he thought to approach the fighter—who was leaning against the flimsy ropes, his back taut and strung with cords of muscle and strands of scars—but time was pressing, and the night would not wait.

Edging forward, his little steps cautious, Podrick stuck a finger out and poked Gamaréa gently.

"A word, sir," he said, sheepishly.

Gamaréa turned as if expecting someone larger before looking down at Podrick with a momentary hint of surprise on his bearded face. "Bit late for you to be out and about, is it not, kid?" Raising the sack of water again, he enjoyed another long drink. "And in the Underground, no less," he added, as if an afterthought.

Podrick cleared his throat. "I am on specific business for—"

"Must be close to midnight, come to think of it," Gamaréa interjected, speaking as if to himself before pouring a bit more water over his already-damp and matted locks.

"Yes, well," started Podrick, somewhat annoyed at having been interrupted, "if you would kindly let me finish, sir. Right, then. As I was saying—I am on specific business for Magnis Abitaz."

Gamaréa's main concern, however, seemed to be

stretching out what must have been a stiff leg. Finishing off his water, he tossed the empty sack aside and released a lengthy yawn. "For who?" he asked, quite passively.

"It is not a *who,* sir; it is a *where.*"

Gamaréa guffawed, as though coming to a sudden realization, and Podrick's heart was filled with promise. His frustration returned, however, when Gamaréa answered: "Weres are only myth, boy," and his tone suggested that he did not have time for such rubbish.

Stooping between the two flimsy ropes, he stepped out of the ring and leapt down, making as if to leave, brushing ever-so-slightly past Podrick as he went. Though he was barefoot, he was without question the tallest Morok Podrick had ever seen. But the young errand-runner would most certainly have none of that nonsense, however, regardless of the imposing figure Gamaréa struck. *Speaking to me as if I am a commoner or one of his ogling admirers.* Spinning around, his fury rising to a boil, Podrick stamped after him.

"For your information—" he called out, but his voice was muffled as he found himself constantly hindered by passerby. To his encouragement, however, Gamaréa seemed to have reacted to his words. *He is not out of reach yet.*

"For your information—" he shouted toward Gamaréa again.

"Run on home, boy," interrupted Gamaréa, glancing slightly over his shoulder as he strode away. "Your mother is probably worried sick."

But Podrick had broken into a run now, and before long grabbed hold of Gamaréa's worn breeches.

"For—your—in—for—mation," said Podrick, his breath finally catching and his knuckles turning white as they clung to Gamaréa's breeches. "I am not speaking of *weres,* sir."

Gamaréa now at least seemed moderately interested in the persistent boy threatening to unpants him. When Podrick felt certain that Gamaréa would at least stay still for a moment or so, he relinquished his grip, and clasped his hands over his knees to catch the remainder of his breath.

"I am speaking—about—a—place," Podrick panted, bending over, hands returning to his knees. After a moment, he straightened up and grimaced as air filled his lungs anew. "A place we must be off to at once," he finished.

A moment of silence fell between them. Podrick's eyes were brimming with anticipation, and Gamaréa's, to the boy's surprise, seemed encouragingly contemplative. Yet his only response was a bellowing roar of laughter. Stroking his frizzled, brown beard, he looked down at the boy with playful eyes. Smiling, he smacked one of his thick hands onto Podrick's shoulder. It was all the boy could do to keep from whimpering. *I wonder what those other fighters must feel like right now,* he thought quickly as Gamaréa began walking away again.

Podrick pursued him to a small bench upon which various articles of clothing lay scattered, and Gamaréa, selecting a filthy, brownish rag of a shirt, slung it over his bare chest. "You are here alone?" he asked, a hint of suspicion audible in his voice.

"I am, sir," answered Podrick. "But we must not tarry. Important business awaits us in Adoram."

Gamaréa gave a wary look beyond Podrick, as if searching for someone or something obvious enough to complement this random, businesslike child and his urgent message. When nothing out of the ordinary presented itself, however, a disappointed look crossed over his face. "I see Prig has been serving minors again," he said with a sigh.

A sneer came to Podrick's face as though he had just taken a swig of sour milk. " . . . I beg your pardon, sir—"

"What was it, boy? A shot of bourbon? Whiskey? I'd think by now Prig would at least have the common sense to—"

"Now wait just a minute!" and even Podrick was surprised to hear himself shouting, waving a stumpy little finger at the towering Morok in front of him. It took a moment for Podrick to collect himself, especially since Gamaréa had once again begun to walk away. "If you think I am some drunken loon—excuse me, miss—" he bumped into an inattentive Morok woman, "—I assure you, you are quite mistaken. For the last time, I am on an important—"

"Wait right here."

Podrick rolled his eyes. They had reached a wooden door in the far corner of the Underground. Inside were two plump Moroks, lounging comfortably in decorative attire. One sat behind a desk, the other on a tall stool before him. Pipe smoke poured out in thin gray clouds when the door opened, accompanied by the sounds of their laughter. When Gamaréa entered, the two reacted as if they knew him well, leaping to their feet to congratulate him on "another splendid show." The Morok behind the desk then handed him a jingling velvet sack, and that was the extent of their meeting. Gamaréa walked back into the open, tossing his reward into the air with a smug grin on his dirtied face.

"Can't forget the winnings!" he said cheerily when he saw Podrick waiting. "Now then, Patrick, as you were saying . . . "

Seeing his chance, Gamaréa darted toward the stairwell, which had emptied sufficiently compared to earlier, when it had been overrun by spectators. Podrick resumed as they climbed. "I am here on an important matter from Mascorea's hall of Magnis Abitaz. He commands your presence."

Gamaréa chuckled. "My presence, you say?"

Confusion struck Podrick. Why was Gamaréa laughing as though he had told him the cleverest of jokes? "Why do you laugh?" he asked demandingly.

But now they reached the distraction of the top of the stairwell to find that the bar area had inherited many of the spectators who had taken in Gamaréa's fights. It was only a matter of seconds before a drunkard nearly toppled into both of them, spilling the contents of his pitcher as he staggered to and fro. That was when—to both Podrick's horror and relief—Gamaréa clasped on to his brittle arm and began escorting him forcefully through the boisterous throng. In no time at all, the cramped, dust-riddled lodgings of The Adder's Nest were behind them, and Podrick enjoyed a fresh intake of the crisp, night air.

"Never been in a pub before, I'd guess?" said Gamaréa,

smiling as he noted Podrick's apparent discomfort.

Podrick took extreme care in dusting off his clothes. For some reason he felt itchy. "I suppose I can scratch *that* off the bucket list," he sneered, brushing off the left sleeve of his coat.

Gamaréa was silent for a moment, the smile having yet faded from his face. It was not long before he spoke again. "Magnis Abitaz." It was a near whisper, as if he was speaking to himself as he gazed aimlessly down the quiet streets beyond.

"It's been a long while since I've seen Mascorea's hall," he continued contemplatively. When his eyes fell upon Podrick finally, there was a distinct sternness present within them. "You are sure of this, boy?" And now it was Gamaréa's whose voice was purposeful. "You are not some jester or storyteller?"

Normally this question would have offended young Podrick, but, believing that Gamaréa was indeed beginning to buy into his errand, he merely gave a relieved smile. "I would not have gone through all this trouble if I were, sir," he assured.

Gamaréa turned his gaze away again, and looked beyond Podrick contemplatively. "So the lord Mascorea requests my presence in the Sacred Hall," he mused softly. "Magnis Abitaz, the White Forum. How is Adoram these days, boy?"

Podrick hesitated. "Um—well, it's—"

"—Come now, ten minutes ago I couldn't get you to keep your mouth shut! I'm sure it is as bustling as ever." A fondness then clouded his eyes, as though of one remembering a past love. "It was a grand sight, indeed."

"It is perhaps better than when you last saw it," assured Podrick. "It is the most beautiful city that *I* have ever seen; but, then again, I have not seen many."

Gamaréa was silent for a moment, his eyes filled with the blankness of reminiscing. "I have," he said at length. "Your judgment is accurate enough."

Together they wandered silently into the night, leaving the din of The Adder's Nest behind them, until even the sporadic eruptions of laughter sounded only as faint whispers.

"I have heard Mascorea has been utilizing errand-runners of late," said Gamaréa as they wound up a narrow side street. "The rumors must be true then, of the Great War that is soon to come?"

Podrick looked at him incredulously in the darkness. Gamaréa returned his gaze questioningly. "You are accustomed to the way news travels, boy," continued Gamaréa. "You are employed because the king will not risk his soldiers or advisers to capture or assassination on the road. It is a discrete method indeed—"

"I only aim to aid my house," snapped Podrick. "Coin is hard to come by in Dwén Alíl and other villages by the sea. The fishing seasons have proved unfruitful, and men have to venture further out than they have ever dared to catch anything of value. Yet there they find only storms and death, or worse."

Gamaréa's tone brimmed with interest. "Worse, you say?"

Podrick nodded. "Word has reached the coast that sightings of beasts have been seen as close as Stormbeard Bay—the very port where our ships are moored. And what the Mid Sea harbors one can only dare to guess. The fish are gone, wrecks are frequent; the storms of the open seas are said to work in violent ways, but I have never heard of them destroying ships with such consistency." Podrick's voice then dropped and became sullen. "My father was killed this past season, along with nearly a hundred others. Dwén Alíl still mourns their losses."

Gamaréa frowned. "That is truly a sad tale. My heart weeps for—"

"Words will not return him," said Podrick, not unkindly. "But action can avenge him."

Gamaréa smiled, as though obtaining a new understanding of what Podrick was about. "So it was vengeance that drove you to Titingale, then? Your hope to avenge the dead?"

"As I said before, sir, I am merely an errand-runner for the king. I would welcome vengeance for my father, mind you, but I believe King Mascorea has other plans for you—and I daresay more urgent."

They halted at length at the stables, nearly lost now in shadows. It would have been easy to miss had it not been for the noise issuing from within. Tamm, they found, had fallen asleep, slouching in his chair and snoring.

"Alright there, lad," said Gamaréa, gently nudging the leg of Tamm's seat with his boot.

The stableman shook himself awake and peered closely at Gamaréa and Podrick until his vision cleared.

"Indeed, indeed! I remember you," said Tamm, with the obvious pretense that he was fully awake. "Come back fer yer bay, I s'pose?"

"I have," answered Podrick.

"Say there, stableman," said Gamaréa, "we are on an important errand—Adoram bound, if you take my meaning. Magnis Abitaz is our destination. It comes to it that I am in the market for a good beast; one that can travel the night to the Capital without the need for pause."

Tamm frowned. "I'm afraid this is merely a temporary lot, sir. Comers and goers drop off their horses, see—come back an' get 'em later on. None o' these buggers is actually fer sale."

Gamaréa fumbled around his belt, and Tamm must have thought he was going to draw a weapon of sorts, for he backed away nervously. A surprised grin came upon Tamm's face when Gamaréa handed him the sack of coins he was given in The Adder's Nest.

"Take this in exchange," said Gamaréa casually. The sack jingled when he placed it in Tamm's bony hand. "Forty in silver."

Tamm had perhaps never seen that amount of coin before, for he stammered at his words like a drunk before exclaiming that Gamaréa could have any horse he desired, and that he would reimburse the owner in due time. Thus it was he proudly saddled a black thoroughbred, which seemed to welcome its rider fervently, and along with Podrick Worthwent wasted no time riding off into the night. They had much ground to cover before sunrise.

5

Son of Medric

Adoram was built around and atop bluffs in the open terrain of the Medric plains. When seen from above, the blue roofs of the city buildings afforded the capital a divine glow that made the city seem alight even in darkness. Architects of every generation sought to amass its beauty, constantly presenting new designs and plans to further boost the city's already-blazing splendor. And as Gamaréa rode in before the coming sun, he reflected that it now stood worthy of Zynys itself.

Like a blue-and-white garden sprouting from the plain, Adoram stretched for four leagues, encircled by Détremon—the thick wall that had earned the reputation of impregnability. There, like small, darting shadows, Gamaréa glimpsed several guards scurrying about, whom, Podrick was quick to mention, were expecting them. And, as the riders thundered across the fields, Détremon jawed opened and all of Adoram was revealed.

It was long ago that Gamaréa had last visited the capital city of Medric. Then the roads had been comprised of dirt and dust, when now they were laid with fine stonework. The pattering pursuit of their aggressive horses diminished whatever secrecy Podrick hoped to achieve, their clapping hooves racking the silence of the still-sleeping streets. Yet it was not long before smoke rose up from surrounding chimneys, and the lone riders were joined by merchants arriving with loaded carts to begin setting up for what were usually promising days of profit.

But Podrick and Gamaréa did not stop until climbing the high, hilly, building-cluttered roads, and as they progressed toward Magnis Abitaz, the roads grew steeper still, until the White Forum was upon them and the ground flattened into Mascorea's white-and-green courtyard. Crisp and broad, the pillared walls along the perimeter of the rotund forum rose high. Marble monuments decorated the circular layout, and the trickling of fountains spluttering down into wide, granite pools cast a calming ambience upon the stillness of the morning that was yet to fully rise. Lining the walkways were finely kempt lawns and evergreen trees that had grown tall and strong, but even they were overshadowed by Mascorea's tower, encompassing all in shade despite the dawn.

Lord Patrid, who had been standing eagerly outside the great doors of Magnis Abitaz, issued forward hurriedly to greet them. "Adoram welcomes you, Gamaréa, son of Gladris!" he exclaimed, his white-and-blue robes flowing from his outstretched arms. He introduced himself to Gamaréa formally, and then turned his attention to Podrick. "As for you, young sir, I must commend you on a job well done. It is not often one discovers a responsible lad such as yourself. Do help yourself to a warm breakfast!" He gestured toward the inner reaches of Mascorea's hall. "It will be prepared within the hour. And expect your Thursdays to be much livelier from this day forth."

Then Lord Patrid turned on Gamaréa and Podrick, and began to patter up the stairwell to the doors. "Now, if you would kindly follow me, there is much to be done!"

He led them onward. Once within the massive hall, Gamaréa and Podrick said their farewells, parting each other's company for the first and final time.

"Breakfast will be served just that way," said Lord Patrid, and Podrick with a swift bow scurried off to fill his belly.

Lord Patrid then escorted Gamaréa along several glistening corridors. Being as it was merely sunrise, Magnis Abitaz was quiet, and thus their passage went unhindered. But an uncomfortable silence fell between them now, such that Gamaréa felt the need to speak.

Clearing his throat, he said, "This is a lovely establishment indeed. Have you been employed here long?"

But Lord Patrid did not seem to be the sort for small talk. "Right this way, my friend, right this way," he answered cordially. "We haven't any time to waste."

After passing down two more corridors, and reaching an odd little door no larger than a wall-mounted portrait, a strange feeling began to disquiet Gamaréa. "I don't suppose you can tell me why I am here?"

Lord Patrid looked nervously to and fro, as if to make sure they were quite alone, and jarred the little door open. "Best left unsaid until within safe quarters," he said in a cautious whisper, gesticulating toward the innards of the tunnel he just revealed.

"After you," said Gamaréa.

And Lord Patrid crept through, to Gamaréa's surprise.

What was this odd little place? Where was he being led? Gamaréa found it unsettling that Lord Patrid would not risk any of his own people overhearing him. The tunnel ran narrowly deep into the bowels of Magnis Abitaz, and before long the cramped, slit of a passageway grew cold and dank.

Lord Patrid remained silent, until at length they reached the exit door at their destination, coughing and batting dust from their clothes. They were met by two guards armed with spears and outfitted in the decorated steel plates of the Medric legion. Together, they aided Lord Patrid out of the tunnel, but stood aside as Gamaréa finagled his own way out.

Some things never change, he thought as he struggled out.

Behind them, directly across from the exit door, was an enormous doorway comprised entirely of fine, bluish stone. *Sagestone?* Gamaréa wondered with fascination. The guards turned upon the door, and, using their spearheads, tapped a sort of code onto the stone. Gamaréa was amazed to see that the doorway almost instantly began to part by its own will, layer by layer.

"Zynys appears to have been fruitful," he said, extracting a small grin from Lord Patrid. The guards' faces, however, remained stern.

The first two layers had slid away completely when Gamaréa began to walk through in earnest, and as the third and final layer parted for him, he locked eyes, almost instantly, with a familiar face. Chief General Stór was on his way out—uproariously, it seemed—wearing a scowl that could have frightened a wild boar. It had been many years since Gamaréa found himself in the general's presence, but he saw not much about him had changed. *Bit of a belly, though.* Stór had always been the burly sort, and bearlike in his manner and actions. In Stór's youth, when Gamaréa first fell under his whip, Stór was at the pinnacle of Morok form. Before him now, however, was a grizzled and bitter version of a once illustrious soldier.

A blatant hatred filled the general's eyes when they fell upon Gamaréa, answering his unasked question of whether or not Stór would recognize him. Grunting, the general blundered past; sure to brush Gamaréa with his armored shoulder before leaving. A chill air encompassed the chamber Gamaréa now entered. It was a room cast entirely in shadow but for the blue torchlight emitting from the braziers along the rotund wall, and, bathed in their pale-bluish gleam, were three eager faces.

Lord Haldus stood immediately to introduce himself when Gamaréa appeared, sandwiching one of his hands in the cold embrace of both of his. Nearest him, his armor tinkling in the ghostly gleam in the chamber, was Master Chief Navys, who remained seated, and whom Lord Haldus took it upon himself to introduce. But Gamaréa could only stare past them to where the unmistakable figure of King Mascorea stood behind his mounted seat, the centerpiece of the dark chamber. It seemed as though he attracted what little light was present in that room, like a white magnet, and Gamaréa was quietly infatuated. Almost involuntarily, he bent to one knee and laid a hand atop his breast. It was the first time Gamaréa ever saw Mascorea in the flesh.

Mascorea, sweeping down from the mount on which he stood, bid the others leave before the doors latched again. They did so hesitantly, but only Navys openly retorted.

"It was not a request, Master Chief," said Mascorea, calmly.

And with that, Navys stammered off, muttering to himself as he went. " . . . rotten . . . half-breed . . . " Behind them, the doors latched at last with much verve, echoing momentarily in the crevices of the chamber.

As Gamaréa had his head bowed, he was startled when Mascorea spoke from directly in front of him. "Do you know why you are here, Gamaréa, son of Gladris?" he asked, as though a teacher asking a simple question of a pupil. "Do you know why I have summoned you to Magnis Abitaz?"

Gamaréa's face flushed, feeling both embarrassed and unworthy to be in the presence of his king, and spoke with his eyes cast to the floor. "Am I at some fault, your grace? Is the price for an ill deed due?"

As if in answer, Mascorea placed his long hand gently on Gamaréa's shoulder. "You may look at me, you know, son of Medric," he said amiably.

Gamaréa hesitated for a moment, but having been encouraged, risked a look at the figure of Mascorea. He was taller than Gamaréa imagined him, and much thinner than is characteristic of the Morok race. His face was bare and gaunt, with dark blue eyes sunken beneath his furrowed brow, and his graying mane of hair flowed down past his shoulders.

Gamaréa remained quiet, and Mascorea's voice intercepted the silence once more. "I know what they have spoken of you," he said softly. A silent moment fell between them in which Gamaréa braced for what was to follow. "I regard those accusations merely as words. I see before me not a crossbreed of Morok and man, but a pureblood, and an able body."

Mascorea's words invigorated Gamaréa, who spoke openly for the first time. "How do you know this . . . my lord?" He nearly forgot the proper way to address his king. "I have been made to believe otherwise ever since I was a child."

"Apparently so was this nation and my generals," said Mascorea curtly, with a twinge of frustration in his voice.

"But dark days are upon us, Gamaréa, and there are more pressing concerns than the composition of one's blood."

The king brushed away then, and made for his altar.

"Rise," he said, and Gamaréa did so. Taking up a pitcher, Mascorea poured himself a glass of mulled wine, then gestured as though asking Gamaréa if he preferred one.

"No thank you, my lord."

Mascorea smiled. "You will find that it is most polite to accept a king's offering, even if you do not desire it."

"In that case, I'll have one, your grace."

The king laughed. "You are going to need it, I am afraid."

Gamaréa accepted the glass from the other side of Mascorea's stone desk. Bringing it to his lips, he smelt the sweet fragrance of the draught within his cup, and soon savored the palatable wine with much satisfaction. It had been a long while since he enjoyed a drink as delectable.

"I trust you fancy the wine?" asked Mascorea hopefully.

Gamaréa's answer came out distortedly from within his cup, but Mascorea interpreted it to mean he did.

"Now then," continued the king, "to matters most important. In your travels, which I gather have been various, have you at any time come upon the tale of Kal Glamarig?"

Gamaréa returned a perplexed stare. "No, my lord," he answered embarrassedly, "I can't say that I have."

"It bears several labels, I am sure. Ation's Key, being one; The Jewel of the Sorcerer being perhaps the most prevalent."

Recognition shined abruptly on Gamaréa's face. "I have certainly heard that one," he answered resolutely. "Is Kal Glamarig its true name?"

"Indeed it is—the original title given to it upon its forging. In the ancient tongue of Zynys, it translates to *King Gem,* or, *Jewel,* if you will. My study of ancient dialects is not very extensive. Anyway—"

"I have certainly heard of The Jewel of the Sorcerer," contemplated Gamaréa, speaking this time with much certainty.

"And what do you know of it?"

"It is a legend—the Key that once belonged to Ation and now resides deep within the pit of the earth in the land of Nundric, and—"

"Resides in Nundric no more, I am afraid," interjected Mascorea. "Whispers have reached our shores that Kal Glamarig has surfaced in the scarcely populated villages of the Eastern Seaboard. We must take care to retrieve it, before the gathering forces of darkness reach full strength and launch their own assault."

Mascorea's voice remained in the chamber even after he finished speaking, falling away into fading echoes.

Gamaréa contemplated before speaking. "Why retrieve it at all if it would cause so much woe? What purpose would it serve in the keep of Medric?"

"It would indeed serve no purpose for us, but we do not seek it for want of gain. As you may or may not know it is the only device that can unlock Sorcerian's Chamber of Fates, in which he has molested the fates of the world and turned them toward evil courses. When once it was the fate of all to live eternally in the realm of Zynys, our souls are now doomed to be ingested by him. He has become a creature that feeds on the very essence of death, an elixir of damned souls that works to revive him back to his full strength. Every death makes him stronger, and with a war on the verge of beginning I fear he will rise again before long."

Gamaréa's brow furrowed. *"That* I didn't know," he said frigidly. "Feeds on death, you say? On the very souls of the dead . . . And this chamber of his—this Chamber of Fates— if it is opened—"

"The original Fates will be restored, and all his progress lost," answered Mascorea plainly. "He will revert back to the helpless state of dormancy in which Ation's spell originally sent him, if not worse. To open the Chamber, in essence, is to destroy him."

Gamaréa considered for a moment. So obscure were the tidings Mascorea was sharing with him that he felt as though he merely commented on some fabled tale. "And if he isn't destroyed?" he asked at length. "If he tallies enough souls to return to power . . . "

"At that point all we could do is pray, I fear," Mascorea answered quietly. "For unless the Sages themselves have worked to rejuvenate Ation, there will be no one strong enough to combat him. The defenses against him will have to be set by Medric alone, and though strong I fear they cannot hold against the Lord of Nundric at full strength with all his host behind him."

"And Dridion?—"

"We cannot reach out to Dridion, I am afraid," said Mascorea with a hint of disdain. "The alliance between Melinta and Sorcerian is all but complete. The Fairy King fails to see the strength we would boast had our forces been joined. He has reasoned, inexplicably, that there will be no hope for those who oppose the will of Nundric."

A silence fell between them again. Within his chest, Gamaréa's heart began to race uncontrollably. Rising to the forefront of a whirlwind of emotions, he began to understand the reason he was standing before Mascorea today.

"What is it you would have me do, my lord?" he asked, somehow feeling that he already knew the answer. He heard himself speak before he realized what he said, and he wished more than anything that he could recall his words.

Encouragement flickered on the old king's face, and Mascorea answered, "A vision came to me, or maybe something more. I was in my bedchamber two evenings ago when the Sage Nepsus revealed himself to me, speaking of Medric's duty to retrieve Kal Glamarig and launch a campaign to seek to open the Chamber of Fates—"

"The Sages are more than myth, then?" Gamaréa had never counted himself among the spirit worshipers. No deity ever aided him, eased his pain, or thwarted his evils, and he knew of no other who could say otherwise.

"Before me, Nepsus was made flesh and bone," answered Mascorea, "and he expressed the Mountain's interest in aiding our cause *if we hurry.*" He annunciated the final three words as if to stress the need for haste. "He

52

specifically instructed me to seek you out, and lay on your shoulders this most harrowing of burdens."

Gamaréa did not answer for a moment or so. Looking into his cup, he noticed sadly that only one small swig of the sweet wine remained. He gulped it down, placed the empty cup on the arm of his chair, and stood to pace before the king's desk. There was a tingling in his toes.

How could it be? Of all the Moroks worthy for the task, why was it he whom Nepsus selected? But he would not dare accuse the king of lying, or call him mad as did his councilmen just hours before.

"But none know the whereabouts of the Chamber," said Gamaréa finally. "At least, I have never learned of it."

"Ah, yes," said Mascorea, as though Gamaréa had simply shared with him the day's weather forecast. "Nundric is a tricky location. Most of it is underground—that is to say, beneath the world itself. There, beneath the ashen fields, lies the black plain of Parthaleon. I am sure you have heard of it."

"The Land of the Dead."

"One of its many epithets, yes. There, Sorcerian has trapped the spirits of the deceased since he established his realm many ages past. It is within this hellish kingdom that the Sorcerer resides, slowly regaining the strength he expelled when he launched his assault on Zynys, claimed Kal Glamarig for his own, and weakened Ation indefinitely."

"No living soul can walk the plains of Parthaleon," said Gamaréa absentmindedly, "or so the tales say. He who tries would be dead before touching down upon the black soil. And even if he did, it is guarded by beasts of unmatched power. It can't be entered."

"This would be troublesome for Sorcerian, if in fact he were still a living entity. The spell he conjured to subdue Ation was beyond even his power to wield, but he went through with his plan nonetheless. It can be debated that he fully expected to sacrifice himself in order to bring down the Lord of the Sages."

"Yet you say he is alive."

"Regaining much of that which he lost, yes. As of yet, I

do not expect him to be more developed than those poor, mindless souls who infest his dwelling; and certainly not whole enough to risk leaving Parthaleon."

"That is why he needs Melinta."

"Very good, yes," said Mascorea, with a hint of relief that Gamaréa was catching on. "He needs not only eyes, but bodies upon the ground to do his bidding while his true malice gathers in Parthaleon. But he does not look to them merely as agents, mind you. Fairies are immortal, as you know—nearly as pureblooded as the Sages themselves. Their souls are worth three if not five times that of a mortal's."

"They are sacrifices . . . "

Mascorea nodded gravely. "By sending them to war he hopes to achieve victories of many kinds. Yes, I fear the filth with which he has begun to infest this world is nothing compared to what waits to be unleashed."

"And so I am to sail east and claim this Key?"

Mascorea's voice grew sullen, and he said, as though under his breath, "It is the will of the Mountain, yes, but the choice, I trust, is yours."

It was truly odd to think of the tumult of events that came to pass over the past several hours of his life. Part of him believed that he would wake up to find that it had all been a dream.

"If it is the will of the Mountain," said Gamaréa reluctantly and at length, "then I will not decline."

Not even he knew why he said this. The words seemed as though spoken by another. He could not prevent them or call them back to his tongue, but could only listen as his acceptance reverberated off the walls and back to him. It was as though he signed a contract with his voice, and now that his name was down in ink, his agreement was finite and irrevocable.

"There will be no leisure in your task," said Mascorea bluntly. "No step of yours that is not pursued. Forgive me, I have known you but moments and have managed to set upon you woe to outlast a thousand years."

Gamaréa gazed into Mascorea's old and troubles eyes.

"There is nothing to forgive, my king," he said. *You've only sent me to my doom.* "I will do what is in my power to return with Ation's forgery, and see the coming war shift in our favor."

Yet not even he believed it when he said it.

For a moment, Mascorea glared at Gamaréa so closely it was as though he sought to decipher the very coding of his soul. Whatever days Stór had been speaking of were obviously well behind Gamaréa now. Here the Morok's magnificent figure stood, nearly a head and shoulders taller than his king, and, though his cloth was frayed and poor, the muscled contours of his arms and legs were easily distinguishable, and, though his face was dirtied and bristled by a shaggy beard, he saw that it had indeed been fair once.

Such courage, Mascorea thought. *Such ignorance of fear. Or is it? Nepsus seems to have not misled me in his judgment. I am only thankful his years of strife here have not made him vengeful. Yet I must tell him . . .*

"I will not give you false hope," said Mascorea. "Your journey will be riddled with peril. Thus I must expel whatever demons still linger within you."

What end does he seek? wondered Gamaréa, becoming perplexed.

"I have had errand-runners and advisers scour the archives for the Medricacies," said the king contemplatively, reaching under his desk and revealing a weathered sheet of stained and dusty parchment. "It holds the family crests and histories of every Morok family to ever domicile this country. Yours is but a matter of paragraphs on this one page. Would you care to hear it?"

Gamaréa muttered his approval, curiously.

"I thought you might," Mascorea began. "Gladris, your father, was a soldier, it says, who fell upon the slopes of Shír Rezgard fending off Sorcerian's henchmen in the year 222 Anthium—being the first age of recorded history, of course. Did you know this?"

Gamaréa shook his head slowly. "I never knew my father."

"Your mother, it says, was the daughter of a merchant. Arysei, they called her, who married Gladris in a fort of Hrothgale in the year 217 Anthium. She conceived a child at the end of year 221, and gave birth to a son a month or so after the fall of her husband. The birth was premature, it says briefly, the child smaller than the midwives were accustomed to. And with the father absent, and none to vouch for the boy's true parentage, they regarded him as a bastard. A mortal, they surmised, must have laid seed to Arysei, leaving her with a child less than pure—"

"So Gladris is not my father?—"

"Let us not be hasty! It says here that the child of Arysei rose through the ranks of the Morok training camps, but with a poor record: Disrespect and misconduct under then general Stór, and high treason in the camp of Adoram, murdering the late Chief General Jax."

Gamaréa wondered when that would surface. "My lord, that—"

"Is pardoned, son of Medric."

Gamaréa looked upon Mascorea incredulously. "My lord?"

"You were not the first to be subjected to the malice of Chief General Jax. He himself went as far as to kill frail recruits. You, I fear, would have been no different had action not been taken."

Gamaréa could not think of anything to do but give a bow of thanks. "My lord."

"You fled, then, after the death of Jax—to where I know not—a hiatus of nearly a century, but returned to Hrothgale in the year 335 for brief employment as a blacksmith before taking up residence in Titingale doing the Sages know what—" and with his eyes he alluded to Gamaréa's scratched and dirtied face.

"When I fled," began Gamaréa heavily, "I didn't know where to turn. I remember the beginnings of an accident at sea, and I woke on the estate of Tartalion Ignómiel, who trained me as my generals could not, and afforded me shelter and friendship."

"Ignómiel," said Mascorea softly, as though speaking

the name of a friend. "So the wise Fairy lord still lives."

"And has separated from Melinta, to my knowledge."

A thought passed over the king then. "Where was his establishment, might I ask?"

Gamaréa hesitated for a moment, as if trying to recall details of a distant dream. "Guinard," he answered finally, "a small coastal province outside of Deavorás, the Fairy capital. He has moved since, I hear, and no longer considers himself of Dridion at all."

Mascorea shook his head in disappointment. "We are not afforded the time to seek him out, I am afraid. Ignómiel would have been an invaluable ally indeed. But come! We cannot tarry here."

Mascorea sped into a darkened corner of the room, returning with a long sword, sheathed in leather and wrapped in its straps, and a long bow of yew complemented by a full quiver of blue-feathered arrows. "Days this dark will need a dawn," he said proudly, "and thus I lend my former sword to you. Dawnbringer is its name; may he bring you good fortune when times grow dark. Unleash him! Fill the night with fire!"

With a deft swipe, Gamaréa unsheathed Dawnbringer and stared in wonder at the double-edged blade. Made of fine steel it worked to reflect the blue torchlight shining around them. The guard was fine and curved, with a small sapphire that seemed to burn upon its mid-section. The hilt was long enough for him to fit two hands with room to spare, running down to a circular pommel upon which a small wispy-rayed sun was etched.

"Go with all speed, Gamaréa, and smite what obstacles lay siege to you," continued Mascorea. Gamaréa sheathed Dawnbringer and took to fastening his newly gifted weapons to his person. "The day is new," Mascorea added, "and the hourglass is already overturned. The sands of time are funneling as we speak!"

Gamaréa hadn't even the time to thank him for the beautiful weaponry. It had been long since he fought with anything but his hands, and the sword and bow felt heavy, firm, and strong. He could not wait to feel the grip of a sword in his grasp once more, or the light pinching of the bow between his fingertips.

Mascorea began leading him urgently through the great doors. "Now," he said, "arrangements have already been made." The sagestone dragged aside and the two Moroks assumed a quick pace throughout the breadth of Magnis Abitaz.

"You must fly, dear boy, and with all speed," continued the king as they sped on. "Your horse is worthy, and replenished enough. See that he is foreign to fatigue, and knows of nothing but haste."

The great doors to the King's Tower were open to the brightening morning spilling openly across Adoram. There in the square, now littered with onlookers, Lord Patrid held firm to the reigns of Gamaréa's black steed, which was beginning to grow restless in the adviser's grasp as it laid eyes on its approaching master.

As Gamaréa mounted the braying beast, Mascorea grabbed hold of him once more. "Go with the will of Medric and the strength of your forefathers," he said urgently, the gleam of tears welling in the crevices of his pale eyes.

The horse swirled eagerly around when Gamaréa took to the saddle and pranced back to whinny fervently. This was his moment, Gamaréa told himself. Whatever falsity he thought Mascorea had been about, he knew now to be inaccurate. The actuality of his errand was beginning to sink in. It was all so real that he almost wanted to be sick.

"Onward!" cried Gamaréa, and as commanded his horse brayed enthusiastically and sped away.

In the light of the low-rising sun, Mascorea saw only the silhouette of the horse and its rider, sitting upright and brandishing his sword skyward. He watched as they blundered out of the square and across the great bridge beyond the forum, where they could be seen by the keen eyes of Magnis Abitaz no more.

On then, son of Medric, thought Mascorea as he watched. *Now you pass from my sight, but I pray that Zynys has eyes on you still. Go with all strength, and let courage drive you, for you cannot know the dangers toward which you strive.*

This is it, then, rider. Now you embark on the path wrought only for your steps. I would have liked to meet you when the world was good and darkness but a subject of the night. Yet we meet instead in your most trying hour, for the first and perhaps final time; and I pray with all the hope that is left in my sad heart that your steps pass through my hall anew, and bear on them a legend.

When there was nothing left to watch beyond the tower, those present turned their anxious eyes as if in question to the lone figure at the bottom of its steps. Mascorea met none of their gazes, turning away from the brightening world and vanishing into his hall where he imagined he would contemplate the events of that morning until the end of his days.

6

The Port of Dwén Alíl

The cluttered little red-roofed town of Dwén Alíl crested Stormbeard Bay like an old, worn cap. In the slight glimmer of the birthing morn, activity began to manifest within its weathered, cobblestone alleys. The Hardy Harpist Inn opened unusually early today—not for want of profit, but response to duty, for it was well known, though he was retired almost a decade, that Captain Gawaire could not declare his morning begun without a tall cup of steaming tea.

In the darkness that preceded dawn, he sat alone, letting the rejuvenating minty steam flutter over his face like a warm bath, recalling his meeting with Master Chief Navys only hours prior.

The last of the torchlight in his modest apartment on top of Morton Street had been extinguished, and Gawaire, yearning for the touch of his wife already abed, nearly had his hand on the bedroom door when he heard the knock out front.

At such a late hour? he wondered, warily opening the door to see the familiar face of his former superior.

Gawaire welcomed Navys cordially, and setting his torches aglow once more led Navys to the dining room.

"I welcome your hospitality," Navys commented, "and at such a late hour indeed."

"Not often one comes rapping past the high moon, Master Chief," replied Gawaire. "Is all well in Adoram?"

It was the only proper question Gawaire thought existed.

Why else would Master Chief Navys ride throughout the night to seek *him* out when he had dozens of able Captains still at his call?

Navys, however, was uncertain how to respond to Gawaire's inquiry. "Yes and no," he said at length. "There is much ado now about the Great War, which we thought until recently to be but rumor."

"The bastard is moving, then?"

Suddenly the few torches that were alight flickered. Gawaire sensed Navys was slightly on edge.

"We mustn't speak of him so," said Navys. "We should not even allude to him. But yes, it would seem he is—or will be, at least. Kal Glamarig has surfaced; his ever precious jewel."

"Kal Glamarig." Gawaire's words were soft and strung out, as he peered into the nervous eyes of his former commander. "That is why you have come?"

Navys nodded. "I am here on behalf of King Mascorea."

Then Navys lowered his slender face as if in sorrow, and spoke again without averting his eyes. "My friend, I know I cannot ask more of you than the fine years of service you have already tallied, but these darkened days have cast all ways into shadow but one, and the only path that is alight has led me to your door. In the wild East the Jewel of the Sorcerer has emerged, and the king believes it his charge to claim it before the Dark One's forces become keen to its whereabouts."

"He means to sail eastward, across the Mid Sea?" Gawaire's tone was ever incredulous.

"With one ship," added Navys. "And I cannot think of a Captain more able for this task than you."

Gawaire, who had been slouching moderately, straightened his poster and stroked his gray-flecked beard. A look of wonder came into his dark and weary eyes, and he tapped a wear-worn finger on the wooden table.

"Let me ask you," he said at last, "Mascorea—does he pay much attention to occurrences outside Adoram?"

Navys's countenance suggested he didn't quite understand what Gawaire was implying.

Gawaire continued. "I can't speak for any other regions of this country, but Dwén Alíl has been in mourning for months since the dismantling of the last fishing crew that risked those waters."

A look of recognition crossed Navys's face. "I have heard of their misfortunes."

"Every day there's a funeral, it seems. I haven't seen a woman wear a bright gown around here for the Sages know how long. And now Mascorea wants to pose a ship of his own fleet against the fury of the Mid Sea? It's folly. There are strange things at work beneath those waters—malice beyond reckoning awake in the chasms of the deep. Not only will he fail to obtain Kal Glamarig, but he'll lose a worthy crew in the attempt."

Navys drew a grave expression. "My friend, I understand your concern. Your reluctance stems from years of uncontested experience, but this is not a common errand. Of all my Captains yet at my call, need drove me to your doorstep alone. It is a mission, I think, that can only be engineered by a waterman of your skill."

Gawaire considered. Navys had never been complementary of any of his officers. Not even during Gawaire's service did the Master Chief express his adoration for his talents.

The Master Chief continued. "I too can attest to the sea's malice. But I also know, with you at the helm, we stand a fighting chance at reaching those forsaken shores. It is a venture to which I would entrust no other."

Silence fell between them that consisted of hard stares and contemplation—Navys praying Gawaire would accept, Gawaire wondering what would become of him if he accepted or refused. He looked to the darkened hallway down which he had previously sought his wife. That moment seemed as though it were weeks past. Solemnly, Gawaire mused on the possibility that, if he accepted, tonight may be his final chance to do so. Something diffcrent lurked in the still air of the crammed apartment, quiet now save their breathing. It was the calmness one clung to before the horn of duty bellowed, the sullen angst preceding a final farewell.

But Gawaire felt something coursing through him also; something that he did not express openly yet found difficult to compress. The thought of clashing iron, the salt-filled scent of ocean waves, the rocking of his galley, and the call of the gulls all came rushing to the brim of his memory, tugging at his mind as if imploring to be remembered.

Things in Dwén Alíl were rather dreary these days, he mused. Since his final voyage on *The Sojourn*—the war galley that had retired with its Captain—Gawaire found unusual difficulty adapting to civilian life. Every night he would stare at his wall-mounted sword before going off to sleep, remembering all the adversaries he had bested, down to the expression on their faces, before sending them to the afterlife. There now, in the ringing silence of his kitchen, the Captain's skin began to crawl with life.

"I have two conditions," said Gawaire at long length. "I will helm no ship but *The Sojourn,* and employ no mariners but my own."

So it was the still night was breached by the clattering of doorknockers as Master Chief Navys and Captain Gawaire ran about the small portside town. When their work was completed, eighty mariners stood at Gawaire's call, all more than qualified to man forty oars along the ribs of the galley. Gawaire's former First Mate, Larstus, was one of the last to be summoned, and did not need the slightest bit of convincing.

Master Chief Navys suggested bringing boatswains aboard as well, Moroks who would surely boost the morale of the rowing crews in the rough and sludgy sea. Gawaire could think of no better choices than Lot and Irie, who once walked the decks of *The Sojourn* perhaps even more than he. He also knew where to find them, though they were none too pleased for their premature departure from Lady Luck.

Now they were all of them coursing through the nearby alleys in service to *The Sojourn* once again, under the coral-colored blanket of sky over the bay, and for the first time that morning, Gawaire took a sip of his tea. It was not long before Larstus found him, sweat already on his brow from having hauled heavy crates into the galley's hatches.

"I'll say," he said, "you're quick to summon the lot of us from bed, but once it's time to lift a finger you're nowhere to be found."

Gawaire laughed. "Why don't you pipe down and allow an old Morok some peace and quiet. The Sages know I won't be getting any for a while."

"You might end up with eternal quiet eventually, from what I've heard—if the beasts out there are more than myth." Larstus pulled a chair from under Gawaire's table and took a seat himself. "Might all have our own lockers down there before this thing is through."

Gawaire's stern eyes peered at his First Mate from over the brim of his mug. He set it down with a clank. "Now that's no way to be talking."

"Maybe not, but I'm sure you've heard the tales?"

"Blast the tales. That's a lot of ocean out there; we could easily go unnoticed."

"It's eighty-five leagues to the eastern shores, mate. That's a vast expanse to be tip-toeing, but I'm with you nonetheless."

There was silence broken into every now and then by Gawaire's sipping. Then Larstus said, "Say now, what do you know of this passenger we're taking along? This rider from Magnis Abitaz. I overheard Navys talking about him outside."

"I suppose he's the one to do the king's bidding," answered Gawaire. "Didn't ask any more than I cared to. All I know is that his business is none of mine. My charge is to get him there and back again, and that's what I'm fixing to do. You'd do well to keep your nose out of it."

Silence fell again. Eventually Larstus whispered, "Navys was saying that he was . . . chosen by a *Sage,* or some codswallop along those lines."

Gawaire grunted. "Might as well have been. Hopefully, whoever selected him sticks around and comes aboard."

Larstus knew that tone. "You think this mission folly, don't you?"

"For the first time, mate, I don't know what to think,"

said Gawaire, sliding his mug away. "My dreams have been troubled of late, and now this. I saw the fear in Navys's eyes, and heard the doubt in his voice. But we can do nothing but see to our charge and hope for the best."

Just then one of the boatswains—Irie—bounded through the door, his face red from toil and his black beard matted and furled.

"Captain Gawaire," he said, his voice deep and stern, *"The Sojourn* is almost fully prepared."

"Is the crew accounted for?"

"The entire sum, Captain. Eighty mariners. Sergius somehow made them all breakfast; Lot is rounding them on board; Gellun is assuring his compass is working properly. Waiting on the rider now."

"Have a seat then, Irie," said Gawaire, alluding to an empty chair with one of his burly arms. "You look as though you've been working hard. Might be your last chance to rest for a good while."

Irie was much obliged, and found his seat almost before Gawaire was through telling him to do so.

"You know," began Irie, picking something from his leather jerkin, "they say this rider is quite the sight."

"You don't say?"

"I just did. Say he's the pick of the litter, they do. Or was it the runt?—it could have been the runt."

"Well if it's the truth," said Larstus, "then he's nothing to write home about. But I'm assuming he's worth all this trouble, at least."

"He'd better be," added Gawaire.

Full morning now encompassed the sky over Stormbeard Bay, a pale blue, cloudless morning beneath which the chopping water glistened. Gawaire, Larstus, and Irie made their way out to the pier, beside which *The Sojourn* was bobbing like a restless steed imploring for a chance to run. By now the mariners had all but boarded, the first wave of forty rowers prepared to grind their galley across the sea. Gawaire was ascertaining the galley's readiness when Gellun—the quartermaster Irie had spoken of briefly—gave a shout from the stalk of the crow's nest halfway up the mast.

"Rider!" he called. "I see the rider!"

Gawaire was surprised at how anxious he became. He quickly climbed aboard and shouted orders. Those who weren't already there took to their stations, and soon it grew quiet enough that they could hear the pursuit of the rider's horse as it raced up the cobblestone streets. Having stopped before the pier, they watched as the rider dismounted, a dark brown jerkin of leather laced across his wide chest, a loose shirt of evergreen pinned beneath. Under these, a shirt of scaled mail jingled somewhat loosely off his arms for what they could see through his fur-lined, travel-worn cloak of brown that was draped around him. Strapped around his shoulder and running diagonally across his body was a fully loaded quiver. A Medran bow of yew was slung around that. At his waist was sheathed a sword exceeding a yard in length.

There was nothing rich about his appearance, no article of clothing or jewel on his person that suggested he was the descendant of a prosperous house—except perhaps his sword. He rode without much swagger and walked the same, introducing himself without the slightest bit of arrogance to the Captain who came to greet him.

"Are you the one from Adoram?" asked Gawaire firmly from the galley's deck.

"I am," replied Gamaréa. "Forgive me if I have kept you, but I departed from Adoram at dawn."

Gamaréa dismounted and patted his horse as if to say farewell when a stable boy rushed up. "Allow me to offer your horse temporary lodging!" he said, excitedly. Gamaréa noted that he was perhaps only a year or two older than Podrick.

"How long do you expect you will be away?" asked the boy.

Gamaréa eyed the galley for a moment, and then cast a contemplative look beyond the bay. "Never mind that," he replied, not unkindly. "This horse belongs to the Worthwent household. See her delivered there as soon as possible—to Podrick, her master."

The boy rushed off to do so, and Gamaréa stood to meet Gawaire.

"An endearing mare, I'll say, to make the journey in a matter of hours," said the Captain, obviously impressed.

"Ready when you are, Captain!" called Larstus from the prow.

"Right then," said Gawaire to Gamaréa. "Shall we? This will certainly be a marvelous race indeed if we are to reach the eastern shores before the foe."

7

The Galley's Voyage

So it was Gamaréa took to the decks of Gawaire's galley, finding himself welcomed instantly. Gawaire himself seemed to be a noble-enough Morok, and one of the friendliest he had ever met. He told Gamaréa stories of wars at sea, and of pirates off the icy coasts of the north, and his part in the mighty fleets of old that sailed along the foul coasts of Zenak in the Black Sea, flanking the hordes of Nundric driven toward their nets by Medric cavalry. It was a grand tale, and one of valor—and several more followed.

His first mate Larstus, whom Gawaire took to referring to as Lars, also proved friendly, though his manner was less gentlemanly than that of the Captain. Where Gawaire shared stories of war and valor and noble pursuits, Lars implemented stories of wenches and maidens, and all the brothels he had visited in his many years at sea. By the time he was finished, Gamaréa thought he had heard every female name that had ever existed, but he found the lanky First Mate amusing nonetheless.

Lars and Gawaire would constantly get into arguments about details. Gawaire would claim an enemy force was smaller than Lars remembered it to be; Lars would claim a woman he swooned was more beautiful than Gawaire gave her credit for—and the list goes on. These moments of bickering did not bother Gamaréa in the least, however. In fact, when Gawaire and Larstus left him, he longed to have those moments of bickering back. Their voices seemed to compress the ocean somehow, making it seem much smaller than it actually was. When they dispersed, however, *The Sojourn* felt as though a child's play thing lost in the midst of the endless, murky sea.

The trek across the sea was silent but for the waves licking at the sides of the galley, the mechanical chopping of the forty oars against the sea, and the muffled shouts of Lot and Irie urging the rowers onward. Gamaréa found himself not speaking unless Gawaire or the others initiated conversation, and as the days went on their talk began to dwindle. Gamaréa was immersed in thoughts about the duty given to him. Tartalion Ignómiel, his mentor, always told him that it was the duty of a warrior to accept any and all tasks appointed to him without question—that the prosperity of his country was more dear than his own, and if it meant giving his life to achieve that prosperity, so be it. Such premises had coursed through his mind when Mascorea presented this task to him. Yet up until then, Tartalion's lessons had been only words; he could never have been certain how difficult it was to accept a task from a king, let alone the task of all tasks.

The Mid Sea stretched on, whether his thoughts were on it or not. Five days passed, or so he thought. At sea, the days and nights all seemed to weave together as one. He lost track of time constantly, being unable to judge the sun or the stars, or much of anything for that matter. The consistent bobbing of the galley left him queasy, and his little bed in his confined cabin afforded him little sleep. But when he slept, he remembered.

When Gamaréa was born, speculation rose immediately as to his true composition. His skin bore a complexion much paler than that of his kindred, and his eyes were much less alert than was the tendency of normal newborn Moroks. His parentage already cloudy at the time of his birth, Gamaréa became subject to the scrutiny of his people in the first moments of his first hour, before even knowing what scrutiny was or could possibly be.

Under the kingdom's tireless watch, Gamaréa grew and prospered until at last, eight years after his birth, certain speculations were fast becoming solidified. Gamaréa had difficulty with his studies, to the extent that his teachers found need to reprimand him daily. Much lankier than his peers, it became very apparent that his body lacked the means to grow into even an average Morok build.

Confusion evolved into suspicion as Gamaréa progressed into his teenage years. His studies still faltering, and his body still bony, he was ever the subject of the Morok council. He lost count of the amount of times he was verbally analyzed by councilmen and physicians, and every time it was determined that he was simply not ripe enough with age to distinguish anything definitive.

Nevertheless, when it was time for the children of Medric to leave their homes and attend the military academies, Gamaréa was allowed to join the recruits—a decision not made by him or his guardians but wholly by the council. It was determined that if the boy's composition was truly of Morok blood, he would outlast the historic camp; but should he bear a lesser make—a mortal make—his return would be unlikely.

The time he spent in training camp was a blurry, cruel nightmare, where one hour's sleep was considered quite replenishing indeed. Bearing the brunt of Medric's scalding afternoons, recruits were ordered to tend the fields, where they plowed and farmed the largest agricultural acres of the nation. The older adolescents fell into the chore of carrying large stones to the center of Adoram. This of course was meant to add bulk to their physiques, and, more importantly, teach valuable lessons in endurance and perseverance.

But throughout his first three years, Gamaréa achieved nothing but sore backs and numerous spells of heat exhaustion, to the extent that the commanders began to suspect the ever swarming rumors to be true. Was there truly a half-breed amongst them?

Gamaréa was eleven years of age when he was first brought into Stór's tent, then an acclaimed general of the Morok legions. Stór's stature overshadowed even his numerous honors in war, and at his huge feet, Gamaréa was placed without any form of introduction.

"This is the one," was all that was said. And Stór stood and lifted the child effortlessly with one arm, balancing him like a toy that could stand.

"Recite the code," Stór's gruff voice mumbled sternly.

Gamaréa, terrified to the bone, stammered, but eventually remained silent.

The general grew impatient, his lips quivering beneath his thick beard. "The code!" he roared.

Wordless still, Gamaréa returned but a blank stare. Then Stór reached down, took the boy, and brought him to a pavilion of punishment where he wrung his frail wrists around a pedestal and bound them tightly. In one swift yank, Stór angrily ripped the shirt from Gamaréa's back, exposing the soft skin of the child he still was. Stór, then, with finality in his voice, said, "You will recite the Code of Medric, or suffer lashes for words unspoken."

But Gamaréa did not respond. He could not respond. And Stór's whip fell hard and fast without conscience of the chaste soul at his lash's end. Now the general flogged the boy without fatigue, and it became as though a separate entity possessed him. Soon even his own guards became dismayed, and took it upon themselves to still the hand of Stór before the boy was truly undone.

When the whipping ceased, one amongst them fell back, his breath catching at the sight of the lifeless child having slid to the ground bludgeoned like a rack of meat in a butchery. Blood covered the entirety of Gamaréa's back, and his hands were perched awkwardly over his head, stuck in their coils. But that was not the thing that baffled them. Instead they noted, every one of them, that the boy had said nothing, cried out, or even begged for mercy. He did not even wince. One guard thought to see a single tear traverse down the slope of his soft face before his eyes went dark and his consciousness fell, but that was all.

Though none said it, all knew that only a Morok could endure such a beating and awaken to his veins still pulsing. But that was no matter, for even when the boy recovered he was yet considered the half-breed who luckily defied the whip of Stór. And thus the notion followed him, looming tirelessly above him like a scavenger anticipating the moment he would drop. They studied his mannerisms ceaselessly, even things as subtle as the way he wiped sweat from his brow, as if seeking the slightest inkling that his movements deviated from their own. And the scrutiny cast a shadow over him too thick to penetrate, too dense to see him clearly, and though his peers came to know him well, they stared with renewed confusion every time he came their way, as if some quality about him changed since they saw him last—as though he were a foreigner.

A flash of lightning. A clap of thunder. Gamaréa focused his vision as if returning from a daydream and went above deck again. With all it could muster, the vessel endured the Mid Sea over waves like mountains, weaving around towers of sharp rock, all the while the helm spinning nearly from its hinge. Gawaire's voice, made small by the maelstrom, was heard shouting. "Press on! Now is our test; no hour ours but this!"

The senses the Captain had mastered guided him, for no star was present in the storm-riddled sky. Gamaréa peered out from beneath the mount of the helm. *Nothing but mist and shadow out there!* he fretted. *No smells but salt and rain.*

"You there!" he called up to Gawaire, his voice barely distinguishable over nature's roar. "How is everything at the helm?"

Rain raged down upon the deck, splattering off the wood thousands of times over like miniature explosions at their feet. Gawaire gave no answer, his focus only on the storm at hand. Clinging to the rail, Gamaréa walked starboard to get a better look. Waves were overlapping each other, as if the entire sea had declared war on itself before them. Lightning illuminated the surroundings, veining through the pitch-black sky above and fizzing out in the vast fury of the white-capped sea beyond.

Cowering, Gamaréa took for the lower deck where he sought solitude in his cabin, determining he would be of better service if he simply stayed out of the way. His garments were now soaking wet and leaking vigorously as he slipped and slid to his cabin. Once inside, he was quick to shut the door—and leapt in fright to find a shrouded woman standing behind it.

The room was too cramped for him to draw his sword, but even if he wanted to the woman had fallen upon him so quickly that he could barely move despite his strength.

Getting a better look at her now, she having flung back the hood of her shroud to reveal her flowing, white-gold locks, he realized that this was the first time he had seen her aboard *The Sojourn*. But she was beautiful, no matter the reaches of her viciousness. The grasp she had upon his wrists threatened to crumple them into dust, and perhaps would have if his were a smidgen smaller. Yet he was smitten by her gaze, peering into her gorgeous eyes like crystal lamps, aglow with a fire either venomous or passionate. Something inside of him did not want her to relinquish her grip. Her voluptuous lips furled as if to speak, and her eyes met Gamaréa's, then grazed slowly to his lips and back, as if she for a moment thought to kiss him.

His heart was pounding so relentlessly that he was surprised the skin of his chest was not pulsating. Was it the fleeting sensation of his sudden fright, or the essence of beauty clutching him, that made him react so? It had been long since he felt a woman's touch. Despite the fact that this fairest of beauties was a squeeze away from dismantling his wrists, it felt nice to feel the softness of her uncalloused hands, the length of her slender fingers curling around his wrists and holding him still—completely immobile, entirely at her mercy.

"Who are you?" he dared to ask, salty water dripping from his beard. He shivered, whether from the chill of the sea and the storm or otherwise.

"Not yours to question," she answered sternly, yet with a voice that chimed like music. She released him then, and his wrists fell to his side. Gamaréa looked upon them as if surprised there were no furrows where her fingers had pressed. The woman peered outside his cabin's door before shutting it firmly. Turning to him she said, "This storm will pass soon—my brother is on the deck seeing to its riddance. It is only a matter of time before the sea clears."

Gamaréa was confused by her words and looking carefully upon the fairest of all faces saw now that silver runes were etched on the rise of her cheeks, almost too faint to see unless you knew they were there. All words fled from him.

"You are . . . " he began, "is it—?"

"It is," she answered hastily. "I am a Sagess, Gamaréa son of Gladris; Nephromera is my name, love and tranquility my charge. But I fear in times as dark as these, such things are left to memory. Above deck, my brother Nepsus tames the waves, and when his toil concludes this galley's passage will go unhindered. But once your vessel reaches the Eastern Shore, I fear her crew shall leave our sight, along with all my father's creations."

A heavy sadness fell over Gamaréa at that moment, as though bidding farewell to someone he had known his entire life. "It is done then, Sagess?" he asked dishearteningly. "I lived my entire life dismissing your people for legend, yet the moment you prove your existence is when you forsake us?"

The galley leapt as though climbing a wave, and Nephromera fell forward into his arms. "The eyes of Zynys have been ever attentive—" she protested, slightly offended and slipping out of his hesitant grip as though it would turn her to stone, "—gazing even on those who neglected us."

An awkward silence fell about them, and Gamaréa found the need to speak—to say anything—to remedy the lifelong absence of the Mountain in his life. But Nephromera spoke first, "Now it is time to shift our focus onto more dire things. This war cannot be won without us, Gamaréa, son of Gladris. Mascorea seeks Kal Glamarig, and he is right to do so; but delivering it to Medric alone will do nothing but bring quicker destruction to his lands."

"Then I am to dismiss the charge I am sworn to?"

"Never!" exclaimed the Sagess, grabbing on to his arms as if preparing to scold a child. "See its retrieval done before Sorcerian's forces obtain it, along with the one who has found it . . . he is very dear to us . . . "

"I am to deliver a mortal to Medric as well?"

Nephromera was silent for a moment, as though carefully plotting what she was going to say. "In essence, yes," she said at last.

In essence? he thought. *A yes or no would have sufficed.* "To what end?" asked Gamaréa coldly. "The mortal race is all but desolated but for the scattered few to which we sail. Peasants, the lot of them. What role is this man to play in the trials to come?"

"There are questions to whose answers even your king is blind, son of Medric. Have you reckoned a hundred leagues much? Have you considered all the contours of the west—with its boundaries and expanses, vastness and breadth?" The look upon Gamaréa's face was of an ignorant child proven wrong by a superior. "Mascorea believes he is alone in this fight," continued Nephromera, "and he may well be if Lu—if this mortal does not join you."

"But you instruct me to seek one man, and leave me without answer as to how this man will change the course of the war."

The growing fury on Nephromera's face was all but palpable. "All in time, son of Medric; the days beyond not even I have answers for. But this is the will of the Mountain—the will of my father—and you must see it done."

The hurry in her voice was disquieting to Gamaréa.

"And what of him?" asked Gamaréa skeptically. "Why is your father not here when we need him most?"

Nephromera's expression became as hard and sharp as mountain stone. "The Lord Ation has been under Sorcerian's spell since the First Age, unable to stir or waken since. But with the skill of all the Sages in Zynys, we may be able to revive him. This is why our focus must turn from all below, and leave you to your own doings. But the path must be set right. Instructions must be given before the start, and that is why we are here now. But I must warn you, Gamaréa, we will not return again. Not for a long while, at least. And you must see to the completion of your task alone."

Then, as if the world itself stopped, *The Sojourn* calmed, and the sea became placid. Nephromera's attention was to the small corridor outside the cabin, where two sets of shod footsteps banged against the floor.

Gamaréa could hear their voices. It sounded as though they were bickering.

" . . . could have made a neater job of it . . . ," he heard one say.

" . . . could have stayed home . . . ," he heard the other respond.

The Sagess opened the sliver of a door to reveal the unmistakable figure of Nepsus, his armor glinting even in the dark, standing outside, and an even larger figure behind him, a green tinge in his otherwise fair, bearded face.

"Have you shared words?" Nepsus asked Nephromera, seemingly neglecting Gamaréa's presence.

"You mean to say you were unable to hear her from above deck?" asked the Sage behind Ncpsus.

"If you had not noticed, Charon," replied Nepsus, "my hands were quite tied—"

Nephromera jerked forward and the others quieted. "I have told him all there is to tell," she said resolutely, sliding out of the way as Nepsus swaggered in and stood before Gamaréa. The Morok was not used to looking up to anyone, not even slightly, yet even he found the Sea Sage's presence daunting.

His eyes of blue, like globed remnants of the sea itself, peered into Gamaréa's own sternly. "You have been selected by none other than my father, the Lord of Lords—Ation of Zynys, Forger of Souls—before you or any of your ancestors drew breath upon this earth. It is his will you see to now. Mind you, son of Medric: this is all a cruel game and you are but a small piece upon the board. We no longer obtain the luxury to move you as we please, for the matter of our father's revival concerns all our strength and fortitude if we are to have further hand in this. For now, and for what I fear may be a long while, your people will be alone against the gathering darkness. But fear not! Yours is a fantastic tribe, and fate certainly works in cunning ways. May this only be our first meeting, son of Medric, but until we meet again, this is farewell. Go forth with all the gall you can muster. It is to you all the free lands of earth must pray now."

Suddenly a blinding light filled the cramped cabin, as though a little sun had burst before him, and it radiated heat that for a split second was unbearable. When it was gone, Gamaréa was temporarily blind to all before him, yet he could make out the slender outline of the beautiful Nephromera, and she said softly, "Now, as the world hangs at the end of a thread, it is in his creations that the maker rests his hope."

Then, to Gamaréa's sweet surprise, Nephromera kissed him lightly. The touch of her lips lingered upon his own for so long it was a great while before he realized she had vanished. Upon opening his eyes, Gamaréa determined he would have been content if that were the last sensation he ever felt.

8

The Eastern Shore

So it was in nine days' time *The Sojourn* moored on the Eastern Shore, sliding along a grated wharf upon a rocky cove at the bottom of sheer cliffs. Gamaréa watched eagerly from the galley's rocking prow all through the final evening, for Gellun had informed them all that land would be upon them soon. All that day the crew was merry, singing boisterously as *The Sojourn* swallowed up the waves. Even Gawaire was piecing together songs of valor and courage, and of the forgiving sea the galley had weathered.

For a long while, there was no conversation that deviated from the subsided storm a few nights past.

"I've never seen anything like it," Gawaire had said, "and I've seen my share of sea storms, mark. Came out of nowhere and left the same! It was as if the Sages themselves—no, no, that's enough of that silly jabber; but you take my meaning."

Weathering the Mid Sea raised the spirits of the crew to a level none thought reachable, but a new dismay began to fill the Captain, for their food supply was running low and he and his eighty mariners would be needing a place to stay. Not as suited for travel as Gamaréa, it was decided with much hesitation that *The Sojourn* would take to exploring the east coast for coastal towns with ports and inns, villages not lost beyond cliffs and forests.

"Follow the coast," Gawaire instructed. "You have my word that we will not stray. Surely you'll find us."

Though Gamaréa implored them to stay, he knew it had

to be done. It was not fair to ask a group so large to plod through leagues of unknown territory with nothing but the ragged clothes on their backs. So it was Gamaréa bid farewell to *The Sojourn* and her hardy crew, and stood on the rocky wharf waving until the rowers' songs faded and the high masts bent away under the blue-red crest of the coming dawn.

He turned away then. The soft tides of the eastern sea rolled up under his boots, and looking up he saw a great forest sprouting high above, running east and west for a good distance. Far away under the rising sun were mountains shrouded in morning mist, the wondrous silhouettes of their peaks black as night against the gradients of purple and red, rising up and away to where it was dark still. But he would not go by that way—not yet. For he suspected that, in those places, nature was not the only foe.

The mortal lands ran far, deep, and uncharted from there, and Gamaréa knew there would be much traveling ahead for him. Luckily, his cargo was light and essential for venturing off on foot, clad in much the same manner as when he set out from Stormbeard Bay nine days ago. Dawnbringer swung idly at his waist, latched over his shoulder was his quiver full of arrows, and his fine bow was snug securely in its leather sling.

Looking around, he admired the landscape, which was practically untouched, and breathed in the cool, salty air of the morning breeze off the tide as it reached up and ebbed away. Throughout his life, he made a point to keep a union with the land, and he trusted his senses would serve him well here, though the east was foreign to him.

Ahead the path was steep as he climbed upon the cliffs, and reaching the ledge, he saw the cove was now but a flickering string many meters below. Having reached the high eastern ridge, he sat and peered out, his body aching and weary. He set his gear beside him, laying each piece of equipment down gently as if it was a small child.

Presently the morning spilled across the waves, and like diamonds beneath the valiant sun the coast glistened as it streamed in from further out. Above and from some meters outward he heard the songs of gulls that had perhaps just woken, and saw them now collecting over the sea. Here and perhaps for many miles, there was no village, nothing but a far country of forest said to proceed for tiresome leagues. When he felt refreshed enough, he looked out to the mouth of the wood where he had hoped to find the foremost of scattered towns. Then he walked along the face of the forest and peered into its shadowy innards through which he would soon venture.

"Desolate," he said to himself, gazing into the darkness of the wood. "This venture reliant on speed may well go ill in here. Where are you, mortal? And how do I get there?"

Ready as he would ever be, he started along a path through the woods, realizing now that he was still tired and sore, for his gear pulled at his back awkwardly and it took some time for him to get adjusted to its hold. As he paced through the woods, he noticed the path ran on, consistent at times but dipping every so often. He hiked for hours, coming to sweat beneath the late-morning sun.

Nothing but cluttered wood met him for a great distance, a majority of which he could not see on account of the amassing trees. On multiple occasions, he passed by potential meals, but he left them alone. It was much too soon to tarry, and he felt he lacked the strength to carry or drag a buck along his path. And, what was more, he did not care to attract the presence of wolves.

He took his first rest at dusk, reaching a steep incline in the forest that had been difficult to mount, thus at its pinnacle he lingered a while. So it was that in a flat area, he sat against a stone, its rough, random edges oddly comfortable against his back, and he lit his pipe and looked ahead through the cluttered wood. As he smoked, he stretched his legs out in front of him, closing his eyes as if to rest. *Now I'm here,* he was thinking. *Now half my duty is done.* Soon the crickets began their twilight serenades; the boldest of them chirping first, promptly followed by the others.

When he was through with his pipe, he stood up and continued on. He would not sleep—not in the forest. The wood had grown dark, and a crisp chill was alive in the air. Trudging onward, untrusting of the foreign confines of the darkening woods, he went on until he could journey no more.

I could risk a bit of rest, he determined, lying down in a patch of soft grass. *I won't fall asleep. I'll just lie here.*

But it was not long before weariness shrouded him like a great cloak, and after several moments, he succumbed to dream.

There was not a lord of Medric unaware of tales regarding the half-breed, and their accounts suggest Gamaréa arrived in Adoram at the age of eighteen to begin his training with the country's recruits.

By this time, word had spread of his defiant reputation (if one can classify merely surviving a lashing from Stór as defiant), but this rumor was enough for his officers to at least regard him somewhat closely. His appearance was irksome to the guards, as he generally presented himself in poor rags too big for his lanky, boyish frame. To further their annoyance, he was unaccustomed to using his long and slender hands in any way that was beneficial. He held the weapons he was issued awkwardly, almost as if he was unaware how, and his form was awful—slouching when he should have stood upright as though a weight were on top of him.

His commanders soon became impatient. It was obvious to them that, in Gamaréa's case, the elementary skills all Morok boys normally developed by now had not been sharpened by a worthy father, or perhaps any father at all, and they could not spare extra effort instructing him in the fundamental ways of battle.

Though his presence was common around the camp, none of his peers quite knew who he was or where he came from. It was one of his first few days in Adoram that the training soldiers watched as Gamaréa awkwardly crept about with a cold look on his face, as though he could not quite place where he was or how he had arrived there. The recruit stood aside as the others labored about the fields, watching with something of a smug grin on his face, as if he knew the secret to a better method and chose not to tell.

Thus the others came to regard him with nervous angst, as though he were a lurking predator who prowled amongst them and at any moment would lunge. Finally—and to the relief of the others—he was fetched one day by a soldier who bid him follow, and was taken to where Stór sat and supervised.

General Stór, who knew well of him by now, paced around, musing. Now and then, he looked up at the boy, his face fair still, his brown hair long and disheveled in thick curls running past his ears. Through his years of instilling shrewd discipline, Stór had grown accustomed to young recruits cowering in his shadow, but Gamaréa stood before him seemingly without a care, as though he had never heard of the acclaimed warlord or desired to—as though his back had not once been subject to the relentless lash of his whip. Then without much conversation, Stór issued him to Inérceo, a province in the foothills of the mountain Shír Rezgard, where young soldiers trained to gain positions in Mascorea's legions.

When Gamaréa was brought away and out of sight, Stór said, "They call him Gamaréa."

An officer asked, "Is that his right name?"

"It is the name he has been given, I gather. By whom and for what reason I cannot say."

Then another officer spoke. "In all my years I have never heard of a Morok with such a name. It does not even seem reminiscent of our people; it sounds almost—"

"Mortal," Stór finished, musingly.

Perhaps this was the first time that Stór, whose eyes had perceived six hundred and ninety-seven winters, thought more of a simple name than any other spec of time in his long life. For the general, a name was and always had been simply the title of someone's story. But watching Gamaréa closely over the last ten years caused him to regard his name as much more—not simply as the title of his entire person but as the cause of his actions.

Once in Inérceo Gamaréa did not speak to anyone, and

none attempted to converse with him either—though this is not to say he was disregarded. Passively, he sat away from where his peers trained, but still within earshot of the officers who commanded them. The residents of the barracks to which he was assigned did not sleep easily, having heard of the rumors surrounding him. To make matters more uncomfortable, Gamaréa often spent the long nights standing longingly against the post of the barracks, looking out across the darkened plains. Now and then, when it was warm, he sat outside smoking a pipe in the grass.

One particular night a peer of Gamaréa's met him outside of the barracks where he was sitting and approached him hesitantly. Though he sensed the other's presence, he initially paid him no attention.

The recruit fumbled for words momentarily, then said at last, "You there—why is it you never retire?"

For a while Gamaréa did not regard the other. Then the soldier continued hesitantly, "You there—why do you never speak?"

Disappointedly, the recruit turned and walked off when Gamaréa said finally, "Do you know the way to the city?"

The other, baffled at the sound of Gamaréa's voice, stumbled with his speech again. It was not a sinister voice, but instead a voice that—had the soldier not been looking at him—he would have mistaken for that of an elder; cold and hoarse like a fleeting breath of wind.

"The—the city?" he replied.

"The city, soldier—do you know the way?"

Against his better judgment the recruit told him, though Gamaréa would not explain why he requested the information. The unsuspecting recruit assumed the stranger sought a road to freedom, and if it would ease the troops around Inérceo he saw no harm in aiding him. But two days later Gamaréa returned along the back-roads of the encampment, and the trainees watched as he was seized by guards and taken to the Chief General of Mascorea's armies—a Morok perhaps more feared than the infamous Stór of Adoram.

None knew his right name, but those who had been stationed there long enough referred to him as Jax. And he glared at Gamaréa, who was flanked by the guards carrying him by his arms, like a beast acknowledging helpless meat. Loudly, he commanded Gamaréa to explain himself for fleeing, but the young Morok would not say. At last, when Jax would say no more, he bound him by his wrists to a post nearby and tore the cloth from his back, revealing to all in the vicinity the protruding scars that Stór had once so ruthlessly inflicted.

Jax, taken aback at first, eventually laughed and said, "I see your arrogance has influenced the many."

Then he asked Gamaréa one final time to explain himself before belting him across the back with a thick rod.

SMACK.

Nearby, the guards who beheld his face noted that the only expression the young soldier wore was of anger. Against the post, Gamaréa felt nothing but the rough edges of the wood digging into his cheek as he rested upon it, almost at peace.

SMACK.

Nothing was audible except his own voice inside his head, saying constantly: *They do not know you; they cannot know you. Perhaps something will happen. Something* must *happen.*

SMACK.

Then all that was around him became clear again, and he heard the rod pound against his back once more, and the enraged Chief General panting wildly as he struck him.

SMACK.

Now the guards saw the whiteness of the young soldier's wrists as he labored in his effort to pull free.

SMACK.

Every individual muscle in his arms, shoulders, and chest bulged from his skin as he grimaced—not in pain but in determined struggle to rid himself of bondage.

SMACK.

Finally the coils around his wrists were undone. Gamaréa screamed triumphantly aloud, spinning quickly with enough time to seize the rod from Jax as it was bounding to where his back had been. Then, in outrageous fury, like a beast newly dispersed from a cage, Gamaréa broke the rod across his thigh and thrust a jagged fragment through Jax's heart.

Bewildered and astonished, Jax fell upon his knees, tugging confusedly at the wooden rod protruding from his burly chest. Gamaréa stood above him, moist with sweat and blood, and after a moment of peering almost into the kneeling man's soul, belted Jax across the face with the other half of the rod.

SMACK.

The blow sent Jax to the ground in an instant, where he drew his final breath.

In horror the others looked on, even the boldest left amongst them too frightened to move as Gamaréa's gaze now passed over them all. Then Gamaréa too sprang back as though acknowledging for the first time the grim reality of what just occurred. He could hear nothing but the racist names the onlookers screamed at him, remarks reminiscent of the rumors that haunted him for the last eighteen years.

Run.

It was as though that small word comprised the entirety of his vocabulary. Alone through his throbbing veins it coursed like blood, raging like a thick, black stream with currents impenetrable, through which no deviating thought could pass freely.

Run.

He stumbled. The guards broke after him.

They must not have me. They cannot take me yet.

Ahead he thought to see a clearing where he could escape their mounting pursuit. Now inside his chest his pounding heart thundered, like the boldest of all drums, so much that his inner voice fought to be heard over the din it created. But of all the words he wished would sound in his mind he heard only the one—that which told him to turn and flee and never return.

Gamaréa woke feeling dawn was pressing. Standing, he stretched his body in order to shake off his lingering weariness and unsheathed Dawnbringer. In the fading moonlight he practiced his form, closing his eyes and focusing intensely as though meditating, and at sunrise he set off again, moving quickly and without rest. When evening came again, he decided not to tarry as he had the previous night, for he determined he wanted to complete his mission sooner rather than later.

When the next morning came, Gamaréa found himself nearly sprinting through the final length of the wood. The path ahead was clear, and seemed to be tapering toward an open space that was far off still. Two hours after sunrise the mouth of the forest was in reach, and Gamaréa, in quick stride, stepped out into a vast field that perhaps was as green as those of Dridion, which in time gone by was famous for such things. Long and far the field stretched, running in soft folds for quite a distance.

Trekking across the plain, he eventually reached a small, cluttered village where mortal folk were busying about their simple lives. He did not wish to cause a disturbance—as seemed to be the case wherever he went—thus he lingered passively on the outskirts of whatever town he had come upon, concerning himself with no one and keeping his presence discrete.

The town was called Eveland, though Gamaréa would not have known this at the time. Some time around noon an honest man named Simon White, who had been walking in the far country through which Gamaréa had recently passed, was returning home whistling a lively tune to himself. Atop his shoulder he carried a pack that contained the contents of his unfinished lunch. Mr. White's clothes were more like rags, layered as though the dead of winter.

He saw the stranger in his peripherals and thought it wise to continue his tread, for he did seem truly odd, and most certainly not a resident of Eveland. But instead, Simon's morals forced him to stop and turn to get a better look. Though the stranger's face was bold enough, his lazy and complacent manner suggested to Simon that he was indeed weary. A number of questions crossed Mr. White's mind, all of which he meant to ask but refrained.

To both of their surprise, Gamaréa presented the first audible question. "What is the cost for a piece of meat in these parts?"

Then Simon was certain he *knew* what the stranger was about. It was definitely a strange phenomenon to Simon that, although the other had not moved, he could almost foretell *how* he would move—slow and weak as one with famine. Mr. White nearly even guessed the sound of his voice—dull and soft, concealing a subtle sharpness like the ringing of an old sword.

And Simon, who had disregarded the question for a long moment, answered finally, "More than I can afford. And, meaning no offense, I reckon more than you can as well, friend."

Gamaréa looked away, as if Simon had not been there, and released a breath of smoke.

Mr. White continued. "I've got a small house down the road a ways. The wife is there. We haven't much to eat but it would be of no charge. There's a fire in the hearth as well."

Gamaréa sat musing, as though he had not heard Simon. He was in fact, however, weighing the humble man's offer. The talk of meat sparked a flame of hunger within him that perhaps had been there for a good while. He truly realized, now that it was within reach, how much his body needed sustenance and good, clean water—not to mention a comfortable place to rest for a time. So it was after a long pause Gamaréa stood, his pipe drooping from the corner of his mouth, and agreed to follow Simon White to his quaint cottage, which turned out to be only half a mile down the small dirt road that led into Eveland from the far country.

Once there, the first thing Gamaréa noticed was a relatively attractive young woman busying herself with pottery. Across from the door was a small table flanked by thin, wooden benches. There was a small room in the left-hand corner big enough to fit their tidy bed and a rocking chair that was perhaps a perfect size for the frail Mrs. White. Her ball of yarn lay slightly unraveled on the floor in front of it. To the right was the hearth in which Mrs. White had built a healthy fire. Above that, a small cauldron hung perched on a makeshift overhang that Simon had installed some winters ago, or so he mentioned.

"Great for boiling water or stew," he explained excitedly. "I daresay it's the next big thing!"

Gamaréa quite honestly did not care, not with the fire crackling like it was.

It was some time before Simon's wife noticed that her husband was accompanied. When at last she looked up from her errands she seemed to almost freeze. The familiar comfort of her husband's image in the doorway no longer seemed familiar—not with his guest beside him. Now instead it was haunting, almost threatening, and she backed away somewhat as though the two men meant her harm.

Simon stepped toward her lightly. "Evelyn, my dear," he said softly, "it is quite alright—"

Her plain face paled more intensely, if possible, and her thin lips worked as if searching for a word. Finally she invoked her husband. "You've brought a guest, Simon?"

"I have!" Simon was openly excited by his deed. "Found this fellow sitting just outside town. Poor lad probably hasn't eaten in a couple days, I suspect, eh?" He looked to his guest, whose eyes were fixed on Mrs. White. Gamaréa could hear nothing but what seemed to him like senseless words working within the small confines of the home, swirling like a great wind, and distracting him from all possible thoughts except that Evelyn's face reminded him of a face he had touched once—soft and ageless and free of hate.

Emmanuelle.

Suddenly, as that name crossed his mind, Evelyn's ears perked up attentively. "Emmanuelle?" she said inquisitively. The woman's voice was wavering, almost like she was in tears, and her face, upon which she wore a frightened look until now, seemed filled with grief.

89

To Gamaréa's surprise, he realized he had spoken the name aloud.

"Is that your name?" inquired Mr. White cheerfully, breaking the uncomfortable silence. Upon the sound of his voice, the stifling air that Gamaréa had felt within the room abruptly subsided, as though it was a candle Simon himself had blown out. "I don't recall you telling me your name, in fact."

Gamaréa, slightly flustered, answered after a moment. "I didn't." Then he thought of an alias quickly to keep his identity safe. "Seafarer," he said at last. "Thomas Seafarer."

Mrs. White excused herself, as Mr. White mused over the stranger's name. "Seafarer—Seafarer—no Seafarers in these parts, I don't think. Where's your town?"

Gamaréa thought quickly. "By the sea," he said absently.

Simon laughed. "Naturally, of course!"

Mr. White was about to inquire about another matter when Evelyn called him into the bedroom. The door closed gently behind him and for a few minutes Gamaréa could hear the subtle sounds of a stable conversation occurring between the couple. In moments the Whites emerged, Simon very enthusiastically.

But it was Mrs. White who spoke, her small figure standing firm in front of her husband. "If you would like," she began, "we have some pillows and blankets to spare—if you should decide to spend the night, of course. It certainly is a long way to the—sea—from here."

Gamaréa nodded. "I know that well enough, my lady. But I wont burden you or your husband, though I appreciate your hospitality."

Simon stepped forward urgently. "Nonsense, Mr. Seafarer! Do stay. Stay as long as you'd like, my friend."

A look outside suggested that it would be dark soon, and thinking of his trials ahead, Gamaréa wondered if indeed there would be anymore suitable sleeping arrangements in the foreseeable future.

"I suppose I will stay for the night," he obliged at last.

9

Repairing Broken Promises

"We shouldn't jump to conclusion, Jem," said Lucian calmly. The two had made their way back to Mary's inn, and Lucian had taken to sitting Jem down in the dining room for some hot tea.

"Are you hungry?" Lucian asked. Jem, with a blank stare still across his pale, plump face, shook his head subtly. Then Lucian sat also, the fresh scent of the minty tea ascending past his nose and clearing out his senses. The Rolfe boy gave a refreshed exhale, then said at last, "When was the first time you saw that man?"

Jem was not looking at him. Instead he stared without much emotion into his cup of tea, watching it softly ripple toward the edges as the steam crept up past his eyes. "A couple days ago," he said at length. "By the blacksmith's."

"Arty's?" Lucian said surprised. "What was he doing there?"

"Getting a blade tended, I'm sure, but he had an odd look about him. He never revealed himself from under his cloak, and Arty himself seemed unnerved by him, though they wound up talking for a while."

"Then he must be somewhat sociable or well-mannered," Lucian surmised. "Have you seen him anywhere else?"

Jem thought. "Twice on Thursday; once at dusk, and again as he was heading south past the farm before I went to sleep. Saw him straight through my window, I did."

Lucian mused for a moment. "Were all your chickens accounted for in the morning?"

Jem snorted. "This is hardly the time to joke."

Lucian laughed. "I'm sorry, Jem. It just seems that the more we talk about this man, the less threatening he seems." He fetched the kettle. "More tea?"

Jem declined. "Think of him as you will, but he scares the life out of me."

Sitting back, Lucian rolled his eyes. He caught at his stomach. "I'm starving, but I think Mary's gone to bed."

Jem's stomach, as if in answer, rumbled loud enough to make Lucian sit upright. "Now that you mention it," he said, "I could use a bite too."

Lucian laughed. "Sounds like you could use multiple bites. Let me treat you to some food down at the pub. Come on! Just me and you—no one else. MaDungal's got the finest pork around!"

"Well, I do like pork . . . " Jem contemplated.

"That's that then. Let's go."

Even if Jem wanted a choice, Lucian would have forced him. But he *was* hungry—starving, in fact. And there was no denying that MaDungal's housed the finest pork in any villages within thirty miles of Amar. The chicken there was also very good. Just thinking about the possibilities had Jem's mouth watering the entire way.

Before they even turned down Pub Street, they could hear the lively festivities of a typical Saturday night at MaDungal's. The fiddler was sawing away on his prized fiddle, and his tunes were ecstatic with exhilarating life. There was also a flute playing along with him, whistling lively. Booming laughter had sprung up, subsided, and sprung up even louder every other moment it seemed. And when they finally made it to Pub Street, they could see the brightest building of them all—the cottage and makeshift tavern, MaDungal's Pub.

The lights were glimmering so brightly that everything else around it was blackened and nearly invisible. Many men stood outside with their pints and pipes, smoking fine smelling tobacco and laughing merrily, shoving one another as if to keep themselves from falling over in a joyous frenzy. There were those who at the drop of a hat (or pint glass) locked eyes and began fighting while everyone else around them seemed oblivious to their quarrel. Or perhaps they were so encompassed by the lively atmosphere that they genuinely did not notice.

Nevertheless, MaDungal's was a place that Lucian came to forget his worries—whatever the worries of a seventeen year old boy may be—and he was happiest above all else that Jem was now accompanying him.

They approached the bar and sat centered as Macintosh MaDungal busied himself behind the counter, shouting orders to bartenders and barmaids and barking into the kitchen at the cooks. His apron was dirtied and damp with alcohol, but there was no denying he was the finest bartender in these parts, even if he was also the clumsiest.

"Let's hurry this up, Macintosh!" Lucian shouted from his seat as MaDungal nearly fell over in a fury. He hated when people referred to him by his full first name. The stout, red-bearded bartender turned around with a ghastly scowl on his crimson face, but when he saw that it was Lucian who had called him, he gave an enormous smile, which Jem, for one, didn't think he was capable of.

"Well if it isn't my friend Mr. Rolfe!" MaDungal exclaimed. "Bit behind schedule this evenin', I see. I thought I'd finally get a Saturday to meself fer once."

"Sorry to disappoint you, Red Delicious—" this was also a nickname he loathed, "but I'm here now, and ready as I'll ever be. I believe you've already met my friend Jem Fryer?"

MaDungal looked hard at Jem, as though trying to place him. "The face looks familiar. You're old Fryer's boy, ain't yeh?"

"That I am, Mr. MaDungal—"

"Now hold on there, lad. *Mr.* MaDungal is me father, bless his soul. You call me Mac. Now be quick about it, ladies, the adults are waiting—"

"Well for starters," said Lucian, "we're starving." Then he slung an arm around Jem's shoulder. "And it's this 'lady's' birthday."

MaDungal gasped, genuinely excited. "Say now! Then he eats on me. Well, not in the true sense, 'cause that would

93

get awkward pretty quickly, but yeh take me meanin'! You, on the other hand," he turned his gaze to Lucian, "I hope yeh've got some coin. I assume yeh'll be havin' the pork?"

"How well you know me, Mac. You know, when you're nice and busy behind that bar, you really *do* look like a Red Delicious."

"Watch it boy." He took a dagger from underneath the bar—much to Jem's dismay—but then patted Lucian friendly on the head before shouting, "Two orders of pork!"

MaDungal took to straightening up his liquor bottles behind the bar. "Drinking tonight, boys?"

"Of course," said Lucian. "Jem?"

"I might have one," Jem answered hesitantly. He was then startled by the fiddler who had jumped in the empty seat next to him playing an incredibly upbeat tune on his glowing amber instrument. The flute player—a fine, young woman, hopped to the side of Lucian.

Lucian nudged Jem. "Isn't this great?" A broad smile came across his face. "Nothing like this place. Now, if I were you, I'd stick with ale. MaDungal has the finest ale around, and it doesn't make for headaches in the morning."

Jem chuckled. "He seems to have the finest *everything* around, eh?"

MaDungal, who had been perusing back and forth tending others, passed just at the right time. "Yeh don't agree, my friend?"

Jem was frightened by MaDungal's menacing, yet joking, tone. "Oh, of course I do, sir." MaDungal started laughing and patted Jem on the shoulder rather roughly with one of his enormous hands.

Lucian began schooling Jem on the different kinds of beer that MaDungal carried. For Jem, it may have been too much to take in at once. "Let's start with ale," he began. "These are probably the lightest of the beers here. They've all got fresh, almost fruity tastes to them in some cases, but you probably won't taste it on your first go. We've got the Huntington Street, the Smithhouse Blueberry, Cracklewhip, Whippersnapper, Bay Hound, and Eveland Cherry—brewed just down the road in Eveland, and my personal favorite. Then there are the stouts, which are by far the heaviest beers."

"What do you mean by 'light' and 'heavy'?" asked Jem concernedly.

"Several things! Taste, body, alcohol potency—heavy beers will fill you up quicker, whereas the lights won't. The stouts, for instance, are dark and creamy, but their taste is very bitter. If you look there—" he pointed to the tap handles, "Mac's got the Huntington Street Stout, Newbury Stout, Whitmore Alley Stout, Old Peddler's Brew, and Uncle Mason's Medicine. But I think we should avoid those entirely."

"Then why even get into them?"

"Because it's important to know, of course. You never know when you might need this information."

MaDungal walked by again. "So what'll it be, lads?"

"Pint of Eveland," ordered Lucian.

"Can I just have a water, sir?" asked Jem politely.

Lucian was appalled.

MaDungal laughed. "Oh come now, it's yer birthday! Have some ale! You won't regret it. It'll be on your friend, anyhow." He winked at Lucian.

Jem tried to retort, but before he could get a word out MaDungal slammed two overflowing pints of Eveland Cherry in front of the boys, and even took one himself.

"To the young master on his birthday!" toasted MaDungal. Then the three pounded their glasses together and drank. Lucian and MaDungal did not take breaths until they had consumed the entire glass, while Jem began sipping as though the fresh beer was scalding hot tea.

Suddenly the fiddler looked up from his instrument. "Did somebody say birthday?" he exclaimed merrily. In fact, Jem thought he seemed overly (and uncomfortably) excited. Upon his long, slender face came a grin that could only mean he was thinking something incredibly exposing and embarrassing. Doubling back to where Jem was sitting, he began playing a tune that caught the attention of everyone in the pub. Even those outside began filing in to witness what was about to happen.

The crowd began to clap to the melody of the lively tune. Suddenly, two enormous men flanked Jem and picked him up, stool and all, hoisting him over the crowd and bobbing him up and down as though he were out to sea. Lucian and MaDungal, with satisfied looks on each of their faces, sat back and watched with smiles, clinking their refilled pints together and taking it all in.

A random man lifted up his glass after a time and began slurring words to a song:

> *Today's your day, young master*
> *Today is yours alone*
> *The music's playing faster*
> *And hardy is our song*
> *You've come out for your birthday*
> *Don't let it fall apart*
> *You must enjoy the splendor or*
> *We'll knock you on your arse!*

The crowd laughed wildly, and cheered, because apparently the man got the final line wrong. "It's *"And we hope to never part!"*" shouted MaDungal from behind the bar.

Now another man stood on a table, covered in whatever he—or perhaps someone else—had been drinking, and sang:

> *Oh once there was a meadow,*
> *And in it lived a sheep.*
> *The art of life did he know:*
> *Always a few pints deep.*
> *When he came home from parties,*
> *His wife was sorely torn.*
> *Said he, "Mine drinks be hardy!"*
> *Said she, "Sleep in the barn."*

Again the crowd cheered, having been amused by the drunken man's outburst. Lucian looked to MaDungal, who was shaking his head as if to say "This is what I have to deal with." Regardless, Lucian and the bartender were thoroughly enjoying the cruel form of torture the crowd had devised at Jem's expense.

Jem's back was turned to him, but Lucian wished he could have seen the look on his face. It must have looked like he was about to cry and soil himself simultaneously.

As the tune played on, a plump, older woman began to sing:

> *He fainted in the meadow*
> *Before a sleeping ox*
> *Ahead were but the shadows*
> *Behind him was a fox*
> *And in his drunken stupor*
> *He let out not a squeal*
> *He had himself a party*
> *And made himself a meal!*

The ladies' voices were heard above all others cheering in the pub just then, as their companion completely insulted the man who had sung before, though he would never have known it. Jem realized it was a small game of sorts, to see if the next person could match the previous person's verse— or something of that sort. Finally the behemoth men put Jem down, but as they turned him around and lowered him to the ground, the boy became dismayed. For, sitting in a dark corner of the pub, beneath a dying lantern near the rear exit, was the cloaked man, smoking his pipe, his dark eyes intent and aware, focusing solely on the birthday boy. It seemed like an age before the large men finally set him down again.

Jem returned to the stool beside Lucian, blankly staring down at his empty glass.

"Oh, I'm sorry, Jem," said Lucian, "I finished it. Hey, Mac, can we have—"

"I saw him," said Jem.

Lucian stopped. "Saw who?"

"Him."

"Sorry, but there are a lot of 'hims' present at the

moment—"

"The man in the cloak." He was whispering furiously through clenched teeth.

Lucian's eyes became wide and attentive. "What? Is he outside?"

Jem directed Lucian's attention to the area where the man was sitting, though it was blocked by MaDungal's shelves of liquor in the center of the bar.

"What do we do?" asked Jem. "He looked right at me; nowhere else. I think he's on to us. I think he wants that . . . that *key.*"

"Listen to yourself. We stumble upon one beautiful little thing just in time for its psychotic owner to find us? I don't think so. Things don't happen that way. We found it by chance, and we're keeping it by right." MaDungal came over to converse again. "Say, Mac," inquired Lucian, "that man over there—who is he?" MaDungal turned his head round to look about the room. "The one in the cloak."

MaDungal did not need to investigate further to know who Lucian was talking about, apparently. "Haven't gotten a name," he said. "He says he's just here for an important matter, though what Amar has that's so important, well, damned if I know. Odd fellow—speaks in riddles. Harmless, though, if yeh ask me."

"Jem here thinks otherwise," replied Lucian. Jem hated when Lucian drew unnecessary attention toward him. If he really wanted the attention, he would have voiced his opinion himself.

"Is that so?" said MaDungal curiously, looking at Jem studiously. "I could see how one would find him a little strange. But he's been in here before—last couple nights, at least; hood and all. Always pays—tips well. Respectful fellow, from what I've seen. All the pleases and the thank yous. I wouldn't worry, especially not you two. What would an outsider want with a couple of school boys anyway?"

MaDungal gave a bellowing laugh. "I mean, ain't like yeh stole something from him or anything!" His laugh grew almost as heavy as the two boys' newfound discomfort. Lucian and Jem looked hard at each other. Could this man be there for the key they had found? Was it possible that at the very instant they found it, the man somehow appeared in the woods? It seemed like too much of a coincidence. But, then again, there had been sightings of the man dating back to the beginning of the week. Maybe he lost the key and was inquiring about it around the village? If that was the case, he knew it was in Lucian's possession, having watched him fish it out of the creek.

And he wanted it.

Lucian tried to subdue the tempest of his thoughts. "I'll have another," he muttered softly.

10

Crowley's Quarters

The night waned into the early morning hours, and in time the last of the pub-goers had finished dispersing. Lucian and Jem remained at the bar, despite having offered countless times to help MaDungal with his cleaning. Saturdays were always the busiest night at the pub, MaDungal often told Lucian, and the place looked nothing short of a war zone. Through the lingering haze, still clinging to the dusty air around the bar, they noticed the hooded man was gone, perhaps having left with most of the crowd. Nevertheless, strained and perplexed grins remained painted across the boys' faces, as MaDungal noted when he broke from his chores.

"You two still pestered by that hooded fellow?" he asked. His apron was damp, and stained with various hues of brown.

Jem, who fixed his gaze on nothing or no one in particular, replied, "I just know it's his." In response to this, Lucian kicked his shin beneath the stools.

"Ouch!" exclaimed Jem. "What was that for?"

But Lucian was not quick enough, for the interest of the bartender had officially been piqued. "*What's* his?" he asked, in a tone of uneasy curiosity.

With haste Lucian tried to begin another topic. "The pork was rather dry tonight, Mac."

Macintosh MaDungal looked furious. "Wha'd'yeh *mean* dry? I checked all the slabs meself, thank yeh very much. Yeh go eat in other pubs around here and then tell me

whose pork is *dry*. Dry! Don't know a thing about dry . . . "
His voice trailed off as he stole away from them, pretending
to keep busy with other things. The old bartender was
never one for constructive criticism, or any sort of criticism
at that. But nevertheless, Lucian's plan worked.

Meanwhile the two boys continued speaking under their
breath. Lucian, if he had not already made it apparent,
was uncomfortable raising the discussion of their new key
to anyone. But the notion was formulating within Jem's
mind that the presence of the key and the hooded stranger
were connected. Much too soon after he had parted from
them, MaDungal returned, incredulity wrought across his
plump face. "Was it really dry?" he asked.

Lucian laughed lightly at the sincerity of his lifelong
friend, worrying around with his big, burly body within
which was no harmful bone. "I was trying to get under your
skin, Mac," he said.

As though relieved, the bartender released a long exhale,
but then Lucian noticed his eyes fix on something suddenly
and MaDungal's gaze became transfixed on the odd lights
gleaming through his pocket.

"Say now," said MaDungal, as if entranced, "what have
you got *there?*" His words flushed out slowly, as though
he had not meant to say what he just uttered and did so
unwillingly.

The lights of green and blue glared pretentiously even
through the thick cloth of Lucian's coat, and MaDungal
explored how it was possible he hadn't noticed them earlier.

"Where?" played Lucian, though he knew well what
MaDungal was referring to.

"That shiny thing in your pocket."

Lucian's heart leapt. "Well—wh—ho—pockets?"

"Yes, pockets—the things you, you know, put stuff in."

"Well, Mac," said Lucian scholarly, "you can put stuff in
a lot of things: bins, boxes—"

"Alright, Lucian Rolfe, let's hear it." MaDungal was
growing impatient. There was no insult harsh enough to
draw his attention away now.

"I haven't a thing in my pockets, my friend," said Lucian

finally. "Perhaps the ale has taken hold of you."

As though waking from a dream, MaDungal shook his head somewhat. His eyes became clearer and more aware, and behind his voice was purpose as he repeated, "Let's hear it, Lucian Rolfe."

Without choice, Lucian did a double-take of both directions before slowly pulling the key out of his pocket and setting it on the counter. The blue and green lights lit up the dim bar as though it were day.

"I fished this out of the miller's creek this afternoon," Lucian began. "We don't know what it is."

MaDungal's eyes took in the glittering thing before him—the stones of emerald, ruby, and sapphire; the heavy gold molding of the plate upon which they rested; the way the emerald and sapphire beamed like small lamps. In all his long years, this was the closest he had ever been to something of this magnitude. Initially he thought of profit, as Lucian had earlier that day. Perhaps with his earnings he would finally be able to afford a pub as big as Mary's inn down the way, with three levels and as many full bars. But then his eyes looked away, and when they doubled back to the two boys they bore the look of shame. And then Macintosh MaDungal peered down again and saw the trinket for what it really was. This was no mere nugget from some distant mine, or some heirloom from a faraway kingdom. It was just a key—a truly *odd* key, but a key all the same.

"That sure is a decorative key, if I've ever seen one," MaDungal said at length.

Jem, who had seemed to be in a daze himself, replied, "We think it belongs to that odd man." He gestured toward the area where the stranger had been sitting.

"It must open his wardrobe," Lucian joked, "because apparently he's been wearing the same thing since he's been here."

MaDungal looked up sharply. "Alright now," he defended, "he's a nice man by my judgment."

"You've spoken with him?" asked Lucian attentively.

"I ain't *spoken* with him, exactly. Said my hellos and

goodbyes and that's about it. But he doesn't seem to be any trouble. A little odd, I'll give yeh that—but not a threat."

"He's eerie," commented Jem. "Much too eerie. And strange."

"Well," replied the old bartender, "everyone has one or two things that gives them the creeps. I, for one, am deathly afraid of—" and then MaDungal's eyes peered upward, when as if on cue a black widow perused down toward his nose by its string. "Spiders!" MaDungal exclaimed in utter horror. He fumbled wildly for anything to strike the eight-legged beast. At last he took hold of an overhanging pan and began wailing away at the counter. Somehow he ended up on the floor, and when he emerged his hair was ruffled, and needless to say, the pan was dented and the counter chipped.

"I think I got him," MaDungal observed. He inspected multiple sections of the counter where the spider had been. "I must have got him."

Lucian rolled his eyes after witnessing what he believed to be an unnecessary scene, and while MaDungal's attention was elsewhere he returned the key to his pocket.

"Anyway," said Lucian, *that's* what was in my pocket."

The bartender drew back and focused on the boys again. "So if I'm hearing this story right," he said, "yeh've fished out a key that looks to be from an ol' castle o' sorts, and now yeh think it belongs to a man in a hood who has followed it all the way here so he can have it back?"

Lucian and Jem nodded simultaneously. Then MaDungal, in his usual bellowing manner, bent in a fit of laughter.

The two boys disappointedly rose from their stools and walked solemnly to the door. "Thanks for the time, Mac," said Lucian, slightly under his breath. Then they left the old bartender in his lonesome, accompanied only by the echoes of his own laughter.

Gamaréa sat before the fire like a statue, his eyes transfixed on the hearth, knowing nothing more desirable than that which he currently looked upon. He did not take in any scent but the burning wood, crackling lightly beneath the flames. Since he sat in the chair, the White family had taken care not to pester him. The woman—Evelyn—busied herself with her remaining chores and dinner preparations, while her husband tended to errands that brought him in and out of the house.

It was one of these particular moments, when Simon was absent, that his wife approached the traveler seated at her fireplace. She did not enter the room entirely, but stood timidly in the doorway watching him. And he felt her eyes on him—felt her innocent gaze observing him studiously. It was a gaze that suggested the woman saw more in him than what he let on, that he perhaps was not Thomas Seafarer from "by the sea" but someone else entirely—someone whose purpose could not be spoken of in a sentence or perhaps even in a book.

He felt her eyes upon his neck like the small twinge of a nearby flame, though he determined nothing foul about them. Evelyn emitted only warmth, like her fire, and Gamaréa felt only the secure feeling that he was being watched over; that perhaps, although his story could not be believed, he himself could be believed in.

Evelyn for many moments searched for the proper thing to say, but even the words she felt most confident saying fell to ruin as they sought to pass from behind her lips, stifled in the dryness of her nervous mouth.

When she found courage enough she approached Gamaréa slowly with a pail from which the steam of warm water rose up in clear tendrils, dispersing just before the shallow ceiling. Though at first she could not imagine herself conducting such an act, she knelt before the stranger, whose gaze was calm as it shifted down to meet hers. The flames from the lively hearth she saw reflected in his eyes, and his lips parted slightly beneath the cover of his beard before he asked what she was doing.

Her hands were exploring his travel-worn boots—soft like velvet, fixed in some spots with leather straps and fastened here and there by rusted metal buckles. Evelyn slid her fingers along them for a time before she set about unfastening the laces. Soon his feet were exposed, and—to Mrs. White's surprise—appeared as something soft. Then she took the pail and the clean rag that was soaking within. After wringing out the cloth, she draped it over one of his feet and worked it earnestly with both hands. It was as though she knew his pain—how broken he had become, how far he had ventured. Now she took the damp rag to his other foot and cleansed it thoroughly.

Gamaréa had not felt comfort quite like this since Emmanuelle. Perhaps he looked at Evelyn so longingly because he replaced her face with that of his love, lost now to memory.

Mrs. White tended his feet gingerly for a good while before she stopped to grab hold of her wrists as though having worked them to their limit. Gamaréa wore a look that was a cross between blankness and embarrassment, as he searched for the proper thing to say in the awkward silence.

Then, without looking into his eyes, Evelyn muttered. "You don't have to say anything, sir. I can't say with any confidence who you are or where you're from, but the Thomas Seafarers of the world do not come clothed as such." She saw the shirt of mail now glinting mildly through his wrapped cloak, gleaming somewhat in the firelight. But her words did not sway him. It was as if he chose who and what to listen to and left all else unheard.

The woman stood then, and in her eyes was a look he believed was of sorrow. Whether sorrow for him or the poor trajectory of the passing days, he could not say. But when she dispersed with her pail to expel the water within, he took it upon himself to leave. Evelyn returned to find the living room empty, and the rocking chair swaying gently where the stranger had been.

Amar was certainly pleasant during the day. There was something about the way the sun hit everything perfectly. The quaint houses bunched together, intricately placed, following the twists and turns of the road systematically. Not one pair of houses bore the same color. Perhaps that was the most dazzling aspect of them. Certainly there were many different gradients of blues and reds and greens, but none bore the same exact hue. The inn, for example, was a very lovely shade of brown with red shutters—the balcony from Lucian's room the color of sand. The house to the left bore an off-white tinge with green shutters and doors, while the one to the right was purple. Maybe it had been an unwritten law of sorts that no two houses in Amar could bear the same color, some often wondered. Regardless, it certainly benefited the eye. This was a place that knew no strife—that seemed completely separated from the neighboring villages. Everything here was at peace.

But to Lucian Rolfe and Jemstine Fryer, this night was disquieting. They left the pub together and started the half-mile or so to their homes. The town had fallen quiet with sleep under the glaring moon. All streets, no matter which way they went, were barren. Even the crickets seemed to be on leave. But despite the utter silence, they were not certain if they were alone. Somehow the shadows felt heavier—the wind colder. From all directions it seemed eyes were piercing them—separate entities circling them mischievously.

The streetlights all but waned. Jem grew nervous. "Lucian," he whispered, "can you feel that?"

Lucian had been walking with quick strides. "Feel what?"

Jem shivered. "Strange air of sorts, I suppose."

Jem had not taken to notice, but Lucian had been walking with his hand over his pocket, as to cover the gleam emitting from the key he carried. "It *does* feel strange around here," he replied.

Lucian barely broke stride when they passed old man Fryer's farm, which came two streets before the inn. He waved a hasty goodbye to Jem, and bid him happy birthday one last time before speeding home. Everywhere his eyes lingered a heavy feeling was present, and it seemed to follow him at his own pace. If he went slowly, the feeling went slowly; if he raced, it raced as well. An immense density encircled him that he could not seem to shake—

an isolated, powerful energy that he could not control or evade.

As he strode he thought to hear footsteps. *You're scaring yourself, Lucian Rolfe. Pull yourself together.* But the footsteps seemed too authentic to have been imagined. He stopped short, as if to surprise the sound that he could have very well been imagining. Nothing. No footsteps or any other unnatural noise for that matter. He chuckled slightly. The inn was in sight now, and a sense of security and relief fell over him like a snug blanket. Ever so gently, he opened the door as to not wake Mary. Softly, he paced up the stairs and headed into his bedroom. His balcony doors were still opened—perhaps since he had woken up that afternoon—and his bed was untouched. *Then why do I feel so different?* He could think of no explanation except that the key was causing his newfound paranoia and anxiety. But he couldn't understand why.

It's just a key, he thought. *Isn't it?*

He got up to close the balcony doors and decided to stand outside for a moment. Even at night the town was graceful—quiet and motionless, like the stars that studded the heavens above. His wary eyes scanned the street before him, sizing it up from right to left: the potter's shop and living quarters, some of his most prized works decorating the front lawn; the painter's small workshop with his tiny apartment above; the hooded man standing perched against a tree; the glassmaker's—

Lucian's attention suddenly shifted as he went from progressively sleepy to attentively awake in a split second. He knew he saw him. The hooded man had been standing right there, clearly looking up at him within the shadows of the great oak that stood between the painter and glassmaker's buildings. But he was gone now.

Or was he?

Lucian, for one, was growing tired of this stranger that had entered his town uninvited. He was a stalker, and for some reason, since Lucian laid eyes on him at the pond, he had now seen him three times. Backing into his room, Lucian shut his balcony doors and was sure to lock them.

And just as extra precaution, he slid a chair over and placed it under the handles. Changing into his night clothes, he placed the key on his bed, and inspected it further when he got underneath the covers.

He failed to understand why, in fact, someone would bother to make a key as though it were a jewel—as if it were of great value. After all, things of great value usually have many uses. Diamonds, for example, could be used for decoration, numerous kinds of jewelry, and as a means for profit. But what would anyone do with a key? Keys unlock things. And the purpose of a key would be nullified if it could unlock *numerous* things, wouldn't it? Otherwise, why have any locks at all? He imagined, then, what it was the key was charged to open. But one thought crossed his mind before sleep crept over him, and like a nervous person it paced to and fro along the corners of his mind. *If the key is studded with jewels, whatever it unlocks must be of greater worth.*

Jewels were scarce to the point of non-existence in Amar. Perhaps the wealthiest residents owned a slightly studded necklace or ring that had been passed down as an heirloom, but this key was by far the most ornamented item in the village. Lucian was willing to bet his life on that.

So how did it end up here? Why in the miller's creek?

He sighed, wearing himself away with all the internal questions he was asking. Sliding the key under his pillow, he closed his eyes.

The bowels of night waned on soundlessly. Lucian tossed and turned, unable to find a position comfortable enough to fall asleep. Suddenly he began hearing what sounded like odd swishes of wind, but looking outside through the doors of his balcony he saw the leaves of the trees were motionless. The unidentified noises soon became hauntingly audible voices, whispering quickly from every direction—calling his name, demanding the key.

He quickly checked beneath his pillow. The key was gone. Looking this way and that, he frantically went searching for the shining lights of green, blue, and red, but they were nowhere to be found. Suddenly a searchlight glared brightly through his room, then came back after a moment or so. And it was upon one of its revolutions that he saw the silhouette of the hooded man standing in the doorway of his bedroom—and after another revolution he saw that he was standing directly over him. No features of his face could be distinguished—no human element about him perceivable. There was only shadow; only shadow as he reached with a long arm and grasped him tightly by the wrist.

"Let go!" shouted Lucian, shooting up from his bed. "Help! Help!" But no one heard.

There was a shattering sound, a woman's cry, and when he was fully coherent again he saw Mary near the doorway, drenched in sunlight, a pile full of broken plates at her feet.

"Ugh!" grunted the old innkeeper.

Lucian bit his tongue. "Mary!" he said. "I wasn't—I didn't mean—"

"Quit your yammering, boy, and help me pick up these dishes. Mr. Goldswell will be very displeased when you tell him he needs to make me a brand new set. He brought these over only last month."

When the pile of broken glass was tended and Mary was completely downstairs, Lucian sat on his bed filled with disbelief. Had he dreamt that entire scenario? It seemed so real. He shook his head wildly for a moment, as though his nightmare had evaporated in a cloud of dust and fell atop his matted hair. Then he hesitantly checked beneath his pillow, relieved before even removing it completely that the lamps of blue and green were still present.

I've got to get rid of this thing. But how?

So many thoughts paraded through his mind that he cupped his head within his hands and sighed. His anxiety would not subside even the slightest bit, and to conflate matters his right wrist was randomly in pain. Raising his sleeve he noticed a red ring around it, as though someone had grabbed him there and held him firmly. Dismissing it momentarily he rose to dress himself when he was abruptly reminded of his dream. Looking at his wrist a second time, he realized that it was wrapped in a ring of broad fingerprints.

Jemstine Fryer looked half asleep when he answered the knock at his door, and there was Lucian Rolfe with another one of his proposals.

"I'm going to throw it back in the creek," he said resolutely.

Jem rubbed the last of the sleepiness out of his eyes. "Are you sure that's a good idea? What if that just makes that hooded fellow even angrier? It finally surfaced after who knows how long, then it's right back at the bottom of the creek?"

"I had a nightmare. I think you're right, Jem—I think this man wants the key for some reason."

"Maybe it's a keepsake of his family or something?"

Lucian's tone grew short and nervous—a tone Jem, for one, was unaccustomed to. "His problems are no concern of mine. I'm taking it to the creek."

"But—"

"He knows where I *live,* Jemstine. He knows where I live." Jem's eyes grew wide with horror, partly because Lucian only called him by his full name when discussing important subjects.

"I saw him last night before I went to sleep," Lucian continued in a whisper, "from my balcony window. He was standing against the tree in front of the painter's house. That's as close as I ever want to see him again."

Jem's heart plummeted to the pit of his stomach. Not often was he able to think to himself that he had been right about something, but he believed an "I told you so" unnecessary.

"Do you want to come in?" asked Jem, turning and continuing on from the doorway.

Lucian walked in and looked around momentarily, as if he suspected the stranger was looming somewhere in the Fryer household. Jem's voice startled him suddenly. "Lucian?" Jem had not spoken loudly, but it was enough to wake Lucian from whatever trance he had found himself in.

The boys went into the kitchen where Jem took a kettle—that had apparently already been filled with water—and set it over a fire that had been started. "My father is out of town for a few hours," he said. "But he started this fire and fetched water from the well. Tea?"

Lucian obliged, nodding. His gaze, however, was spaceward, the look about him perplexed and oblong. A slew of compromising emotions channeled through him—of sadness, anger, fear, but nothing positive.

Jem startled him to attention a second time. "Lucian, are you alright? You're starting to scare me."

Lucian's face was of someone who wished to say something but could not find the words, and remained that way for a long while—shapeless, not defiant yet not oppressed, just simply musing, as though he had been placed there unknowingly and heeded the events of somewhere else entirely. But when at last he looked at Jem, the other acknowledged that something haunting was behind his dark green eyes. A shadow seemed to callus there, and everything about Lucian now seemed dark. For what Jem perceived as a long while, Lucian appeared this way, until at last his eyes assumed a state of normalcy and he spoke again. Then he told Jem of the dream he had and showed the marking on his wrist, which if anything had become clearer since when he first woke up.

Jem grew nervous. "You said he grabbed you by the wrist—in your dream?"

Lucian nodded absentmindedly.

Now Jem took a seat and stared blankly also. "You mentioned a nightmare," he continued. "You didn't mention that it had an actual affect on you."

"How would you expect me to feel, Jem?" Lucian's tone was not unkind. "One moment I was dreaming of getting grabbed by the wrist, and the next I wake up with markings that suggest I actually had. It is not something I expected—and certainly not something I prefer discussing much."

"What are we going to do?" Even Jem could hear the wavering of his voice. "I knew this was an awful idea. But no—what do we do?—we're careless as usual. Well, *you* were careless as usual. I said we should have let it be. I said back *there* we should have let it be."

"Now isn't a proper time to throw out accusations," Lucian retorted, apparently offended.

Jem laughed slightly, though no sign of amusement had crossed his face. "And when would it be a proper time, Lucian? When this lunatic actually kills someone? Kills you? Kills me? *Then* would it be proper to deal out accusations?"

Lucian was not looking at his friend now. Instead his gaze had fallen to the floor, off of which the small fire glinted somewhat. Jem eventually recoiled from his sudden rage, and poured two cups of tea, pitying his friend. He set a glass down before Lucian, then sat across from him at the table.

"Sorry," he said softly, and slightly embarrassed. "It was wrong of me to get so angry. It's just—I'm scared too, you know."

After a moment Lucian looked at him. "And you think I'm not? I've all but brought this man home with me. I want him out of my mind as much as you do. I don't know when I'll be able to sleep again."

Jem stood again and walked over to the window. The kitchen faced the back of the farm, and from there he saw the folds of the hills stretching far out until they reached Buckland nearly ten miles south. The sky over the fields was cloudless, shining with a splintering shade of blue that did not deviate from its hue. He looked as far as he could see, and remembered his younger days. Jem could hear his father telling him, *Now, Jemstine, you can only go as far as the old apple tree. I don't care what Lucian says or does, you are not to go past the apple tree.* And of course, Lucian would always go slightly further than that point, and poke fun at Jem when he was too nervous to do the same.

Lucian hadn't touched his tea. His face looked nearly ill at the table. Suddenly he shook his head. "I can't stay here, Jem," he said directly. "I have to bring this back to the creek."

A separate voice sounded through the room, boisterous and raspy. "Bring what back to the creek?" It was Samuel Fryer, Jem's father. He had entered through the side door of the house with five or six logs of wood, and he tossed one in the fire burning in the kitchen before throwing the others on the ground near the window.

The two boys looked sharply at each other, expecting the other to answer. Samuel scratched his head, already unconvinced at the answer the boys had not bothered to provide yet.

Jem opened his mouth to reply when Lucian said, "A fish."

Jem's father acquired an almost ill-looking expression. "A—fish?" he said. "What are you taking a fish from Edward's creek for? Rainbow trout perhaps make the most boring pets on earth."

Lucian smiled nervously. "That's exactly it! Not to mention it's begun to reek and Mary has threatened my living conditions if I decide to hold on to it any longer."

Samuel was fixing himself a cup of tea. He grunted something of a laugh. "She'd be wise to do that regardless." He sipped his piping hot drink and scratched his brown, burly beard, which was graying in some spots, oblivious to whatever offense his statement may have caused Lucian—not that it had, of course.

"Met an odd fellow today down in Eveland," he continued.

Jem looked up from his mug. "What were you doing in Eveland?"

Samuel squinted at his son. "Don't you ever listen when I talk to you, boy? I told you I needed to meet with a friend of mine about building a new stable. Damn beasts out there nearly tore the one I have to shreds. Sooner or later that thing is going to cave in on them." Then he mused. "Although they'd probably deserve it. Anyway, before I left I ran into someone I ain't never met before—nearly in the literal sense. Damn fellow almost knocked the logs right out of my hands. Like a brick wall, he was! I asked his name, and it was one I never heard in these parts, for sure.

114

Seafarer, he told me. Anyway, he seemed to be in quite some hurry, though he didn't seem to know exactly where he was going."

The look Lucian and Jem exchanged must have been one of sheer incredulity and terror concocted into one horrified glance.

"What in the heavens is the matter with you two?" asked Sam.

His words seemed to wake the two boys out of a dream, as they shuddered and sat upright again.

"Nothing," Jem replied. "It's—it's nothing."

Samuel looked at his son hard for a moment, as though he was analyzing the very essence of his thoughts. Then he turned the same gaze to Lucian, if not more intense. His eyes peered directly through him, similar to the way Mary caught Lucian in a lie. But as though he flicked a switch, his eyebrows raised and he became oddly cheerful. "Well, I suppose I'll leave you two be. Thanks for the tea, son. I'll be out in the barn if you need me."

He walked out whistling, shutting the door firmly behind him.

"A fish?" Jem cried immediately.

Lucian threw up his arms in contempt. "Well what else would someone bring back to a creek?"

Jem shook his head, mostly in disbelief of their current predicament. Then Lucian stood up from the table and glanced out toward the door where Jem's father had exited. "Are you coming or not?" he asked.

It may have been some time around noon when the two boys set out for the miller's creek. This Sunday afternoon was typical, it being slightly brighter than Saturdays usually were, though neither of them could quite comprehend why. Lucian's notion was that this was nature's way of teasing children before another week of school resumed. The townsfolk seemed joyful. There was the laughter of friends visiting friends, and of course the small children running about haphazardly, playing their mischievous games. Now and then Lucian and Jem would pass a glance to each other, silently reminiscing on the days when they had done the same.

Yet as much as Amar glistened today, neither of them stopped to admire the beauty. Instead they passed anxiously with ceaseless strides down the winding roads and even past some friends who tried to say hello. It might as well have been the most horrid of days, for that truly is what it felt like. It seemed that every corner gave cause for more tension, and in every shadowy portion of the road they thought to see their stalker, hunched over and watching them within the cover of darkness.

But the hooded man made no appearance on their way to the creek, and when at last they stood upon the bridge they gazed warily around them. The area was motionless save the barely rotating mill working in the light breeze. Then their eyes passed to the eaves of the wood and saw that it was uninhabited.

"Alright," said Jem, "he's not here. Throw it in."

Lucian took the key from his pocket and held it in his palm, looking at it studiously for a moment. He noticed upon close inspection that only the emerald and sapphire were alight. The ruby, like an extinguished lamp, was dim. *That's odd,* he thought. *Why the ruby and not the others?*

It *was* beautiful, there was no denying that—despite being something as common as a key. Lucian had seen many keys in his short life—Jem as well—but he could not remember a key more glamorous than this. In fact, when they thought hard upon the matter, they recalled few items of *jewelry* more glamorous. There was an unexplainable allure about the way the smooth, glittering gold complemented the shining gems.

Lucian, as though observing himself from above or elsewhere, found himself involuntarily tracing his finger along the key's shaft, then over the stones. He felt a sensation similar to when he first found it. The environment slowed down around him. Every subtle sound was intensified— the gentle rippling of the pond, the nearly inaudible sliding of his finger running softly upon the key, his heart beating methodically in his chest. Then he heard his name called softly on the air. *Lucian. Lucian. Lucian*—

"Lucian!" it was Jem. Lucian shook his head as though waking from a deep sleep. "Are you going to throw it in or not?"

It was then that an odd sensation overcame him—something he could not explain: a literally pressing feeling, as though someone was squeezing him. His surroundings seemed to condense, no longer wide and vast on all sides but enclosed like a closet. And he heard the words wiggle free from his tongue, though he had no conscious desire to say them.

"I—I'm not sure I want to now."

Jem looked at him bewilderedly, his jaw separated, and his eyes sunk beneath his brow. The Fryer boy stammered for a moment, then sat vexed.

"You can't be serious," he said incredulously. Jem's words were distant, as though he was speaking only to himself.

But even Lucian was unsure if he was entirely serious. The words had simply trickled out, seemingly unprovoked. All that was present in his mind was a sudden need to at least learn about the key before disposing of it completely. Somehow he felt it was right. After all, he did not fall upon the key unjustly, but by chance. He thought again of the possible fortune it could bring him. Perhaps if he sold it he would be able to travel the world or open a shop of his own in the town—though he was not sure what kind of shop exactly.

He sat down beside Jem and put an arm around his infuriated companion. Jem was quick to twist out of his grasp. Lucian's gaze became crossed. "Come on now, Jem," he said softly. "I just want to find out a little more about it, that's all. It's much too beautiful to get rid of so quickly. Perhaps it's worth something? Maybe there's a reward to be had?"

Jem snarled. "I don't know about all that, but I can tell you what it's *not* worth: worrying about from sunup to sundown. And it's certainly not worth having some stalking madman lurking about town. My reward is my sanity. With this thing outside the creek, I haven't any."

Jem looked suddenly at the key gleaming in Lucian's hand as if it had beckoned him. Then his gaze fixed again on his friend, who, he was sad to think, was becoming more and more like a stranger himself.

Lucian paid no heed to Jem's desperate words. "I think we can agree on something?"

The Fryer boy's look grew stern. "No! There is nothing we can negotiate that would ease matters. We can't keep this key a minute longer."

Lucian sulked back, as though disappointed, and remained that way for some time. Suddenly he straightened, and a light was in his eyes. "How about this:" he started, and stood up excitedly, "we'll take it to Crowley, and ask him about it. He must know something—wouldn't you say? After all, he must be far more knowledgeable of trinkets and foreign affairs than anyone else around these parts."

"The marshal?" Jem mused for a moment. "But his quarters is nearly half a day's walk from here—past the far country."

"And we're already on our way. We can't have more than another couple hours to go."

Jem thought hard for a moment. "Do you really think it's in our best interest to bring this to the authorities?"

"A minute ago we were going to just throw it away," replied Lucian. "I don't see the harm in asking about it. Who knows, I hear Crowley appreciates an honest man. If we bring him something of value that we've found, he might reward us on the spot."

"And if we go and he tells us what he knows—which is probably little to nothing—what then?"

Lucian looked away, as though he had not taken Jem's question into consideration. Then he answered: "On our way home, we'll return it to this creek and toss it in, I guess—no questions asked. Just a simple flick of the wrist, a tiny splash, then sleep."

Jem mused. "Then I'll go with you, on the condition that we take horses instead. It's become far too hot to walk."

They anxiously doubled back to Samuel Fryer's farm.

There they saddled two fairly sizeable mares—Lucian's brown and specked with white, Jem's gray and flecked with black. They were an honest pair, and in decent shape for long distance riding. In no time at all, it seemed, they were on their way.

The marshal's quarters was a straight enough journey, down the main road of Amar and through the far country until it crossed into Eveland. They traversed the backcountry of that town from there, traveling northeastward until the hill on which the marshal's quarters sat was upon them.

There it was perched, plainly built, like a shepherd looking out over his modest flock. Flags swayed gently in the breeze from atop the stone pillars standing before the large doors, and flanking the entranceway were two large statues of lions. Beside these stood two armed spearmen.

Lucian and Jem were taken aback. Neither had taken the possibility of security into account. Lucian, for one, hadn't a clue what to say. He did know, however, that whatever he did say would have to be a lie. Nevertheless, the two boys fastened their horses to the provided stone posts before the quarters and carried slowly up the stairs. The guards, who had been slouching nonchalantly and joking, straightened as the boys approached, and their faces grew stern.

The one on the right said. "You there—halt! What business do you have at the marshal's quarters?"

Lucian and Jem passed a quick look to each other. Lucian had all but opened his mouth to babble a makeshift story when long, skeletal fingers appeared from behind the guards, settling on each of their shoulders. Stepping aside, the spearmen revealed a weathered man, old and straggly, with hair of gray drooping in loose wisps. He wore robes as they imagined a king would, falling loosely atop his frail body and rustling behind him as he walked.

"I thought he'd be bigger," Lucian whispered to Jem.

"I thought he'd be younger," Jem replied.

At the base of his face a sharp chin protruded, and his nose was hooked like that of a scavenger's beak. There was no quality about him that was admirable, no movement or piece of garb suggesting that he was an honest man, as they had often heard. Standing in the shadows of his guards his beady eyes pierced the two boys, and he stepped forward only slightly as though frightened of the light.

Then he spoke, his voice shrill and raspy. "Children? What brings children to my steps?"

Lucian and Jem exchanged another look, as though deciding who would answer. Then Lucian said at last, "We've important matters at hand in Amar." The story seemed to flow naturally off his tongue.

Crowley's voice escalated nearly to an exclamation. "Amar? You have traveled far then, boys. And so young." He surveyed each of them for the better, head to foot and foot to head. And when Crowley's eyes passed over Lucian they seemed to pause a moment or two at his pant pocket where he kept the key. His pupils seemed to contract there, and Lucian worried that he caught the glint of the gems. But then the marshal looked away, and Lucian was unsure if Crowley had noticed anything at all.

The boys wanted to wriggle out from beneath his silent scrutiny, but they stood firm and confident waiting for the next word. Then as if from a dream the marshal's eyes became attentive again, and he looked up and smiled. "Right," he said kindly. "Come then! Let us not tarry here if we've much to discuss."

He beckoned them enthusiastically with a wave of his arm and led them into the main room of his modest quarters. They realized now that its inner portions were much more spacious than it had appeared from outside. The ceiling stretched upward triangularly, tapering to a high point. They passed along a creaky, stained wooden floor. Heavy wooden pillars lined the walkway down to where the marshal's chair was perched in the center. There they saw the desk at which they guessed he normally sat, littered with parchment and jars of ink from which quills poked out.

As they passed the main room Crowley spoke hurriedly. "I thought I had forgotten about an appointment of some sort," he said anxiously. "When you reach a certain age, boys, things seem to happen faster. And most of the time you find yourself unable to keep up."

"I don't understand," Jem replied.

"You tend to lose track of time, my boy. Time—such a precious thing! Before you know it years seem like months—" then he stopped, and almost solemnly looked over his shoulder, "and you see a crumpled version of yourself in the looking-glass; old and gray, so foreign you cannot recall how you could possibly have wore a youthful face."

Then an awkward silence was driven between them as no one spoke for a long moment, until Crowley abruptly propped up cheerfully and began walking on, and with a long hand gestured for them to follow. "But noting the spontaneity of our meeting, I do apologize if I seemed . . . confused or unwelcoming before. Not often do I receive visitors of the youthful variety, let alone Amarians, who indeed have far to go."

They had come upon another room now—a dining hall of sorts. "Ah! Here we are!" It was a rectangular space with a wide, old table placed in the center. Lining each of the two longer sides were four chairs. Pewter plates and utensils were placed at each of the chairs, and here and there along the shabby walls was a lovely painting or two of landscapes in chipped frames. A wide window, concealed by thin, stained drapes, stretched nearly the length of the room to the boys' backs, looking out into a far drop of green field, beyond which the eves of a dark forest loomed.

The marshal's voice remained cheerful. "Do sit! Do sit, my boys!" He no longer seemed to bear the intimidating aura they felt had radiated off him at the doors. Instead he was now rather grandfatherly.

Lucian and Jem sat abreast of each other across from Crowley, who was smiling widely. "You two have joined me at an exceptionally convenient time, for I was about to dine!" Just then, as though summoned, a relatively well-dressed man entered the dining room with a platter of fine-smelling food, and when he set them on the table they noticed the centerpiece of it all was a sparkling glazed ham. It was not until now that Lucian and Jem realized how hungry they truly were.

"Now," said Marshal Crowley, "do not be timid! I know you two must be famished from that dreadful ride, and I simply will not accept shyness at my table. Feast!"

For more than an hour they dined until Lucian and Jem were uncertain if they would be able to stand. When they each had their fill, Crowley set his cloth on the table. "Now," he began, "I trust my dining room is private enough for our meeting? For as it goes for privacy in this place, this perhaps is my most confidential room."

For a while Lucian had forgotten the true reason they had come there. Though the key sat thoroughly in his pocket, Crowley's hospitality caused their minds to stray from their immediate purpose. The feast was perhaps the grandest either boy had ever enjoyed, and the fine wine he shared was a pleasant change from the hardy ale and rum at MaDungal's Pub.

"It's just right," said the Rolfe boy at last.

"So what is it I can do for you?" said the marshal, clapping his hands together loudly. "Surely your cause is of high importance to bring you way out here? Is there trouble brewing? Shall I station officers around your village?"

Lucian and Jem looked to each other, hesitant to speak.

"No, no," said Lucian finally. "It's nothing like that—"

Then, without knowledge of a proper way to begin, Lucian took the key from his pocket and placed it on the table. Having grown used to looking at the key, the boys forgot the impact it must have had on others who were seeing it for the first time. The marshal's eyes presently brimmed wide with curiosity, and his lips parted somewhat.

His voice seeped out soft and hauntingly. "What . . . *is* this?" Yet, though he seemed to be seeking information, his manner was as of one who already knew.

Lucian answered quickly. "It's a key, sir, and that's all I can really say. I fished it out of a creek not long ago, and it's been in my keep ever since."

Crowley had picked the key up from the table and had taken to caressing it as though it were a small pet. His eyes passed over it in the strangest of ways, as though he had become unaware of his surroundings; as though Lucian and Jem had fallen into memory and it was he alone in the room—he alone with the key he now possessed.

The marshal's eyelids drew back to reveal each eye to the utmost extent. Tiny red veins ebbed within the whites, like little sunrays emitting from his irises, which themselves were such a dark shade of brown that they nearly gelled with his pupils to create the illusion that he was glaring through two black globes. Now he seemed to be speaking softly to himself in a low, rhythmic tone that almost sounded like he was humming.

Upon watching Crowley nearly salivating over the key, Jem leaned in toward Lucian's ear and said, "Bit of an odd fellow, wouldn't you say?"

But it was not Lucian who responded. "Everyone is odd in some way, my friend," said Crowley. Jem sat back, embarrassed to have been heard. Though the marshal kept it to himself, he had been experiencing the same phenomena that Lucian had on the bridge earlier that day. He had been thrown into an ever-wheeling trance in which he could hear only his name. Everything else in his surroundings had grown dark and dreary, and when the sensation went away Crowley felt nothing but sadness and despair.

An ominous silence fell over the table. The marshal was still examining the key under his long, pointy fingers as Lucian and Jem sat back and watched him, their suspicion of the old marshal steadily growing. So it was the longer the key was in his grasp, the more nervous Lucian and Jem became, and the more they regretted having sought him.

At last Crowley became attentive again, seemingly waking from the dream-like state in which he had been enveloped.

"It is a key," he said confidently. Lucian and Jem hosted the same blank stare.

Lucian answered. "We were sure as much," he said. "We *aren't* sure, however, what it's for or where it came from. Of all things, who would make a key like this—and why?"

Then Crowley rose, the key firm now within his grasp. His fist was clenched around it, as though protecting it from others who might try to seize it. To and fro he paced thinking hard upon something, his fist covered by the long sleeve of his scarlet robe. Then he began mumbling words to himself for a moment, only this time Lucian and Jem did not recognize the language. All that kept them from fleeing the hall entirely was that they believed Crowley knew something, for he paced before them as one on the verge of solving an equation. Perhaps he had the pieces but could not figure out how they fit together. As he paced, Crowley's gaze would constantly shift back to the key in his hand—as though he did not trust that it would still be there—then he would continue mumbling.

Lucian was growing impatient. "Sir?" he said nervously. The marshal either had not heard him or was ignoring Lucian completely. His eyes now were squinting intently, as though he tried to weld the pieces of the mystery together in his mind. Suddenly he stopped, and as he stopped it seemed the stifling atmosphere that had encompassed the room stopped as well, and they could think and breathe for the better.

"It cannot be true," he muttered, as if to himself. But Lucian and Jem were paying such close heed that they heard him clearly.

Lucian shifted anxiously in his seat. "What can't be true?"

The marshal spun round, as though he had forgotten he was in the boys' company. His eyes were different than Lucian and Jem remembered them being moments ago, and were no longer the elderly eyes of an old gentleman. They were not even deep and black with no deviation between pupil and iris. Now instead there was a flicker in them—a wild, sinister flicker, and it frightened Lucian and Jem to the bone.

Again he fiddled with the key, as a predator looked upon its pray before eating. "It is mine," he whispered, quick and shrill like the hiss of an asp. "Mine to deliver. The path to my glory! He did not mention how easy it would be."

Lucian sprang up. "Glory?" His voice was a wavering shout, shaken nearly to the brink of tears. Jem became welded to his seat in horror.

Lucian shouted in protest. "That's not your key!"

Then Crowley guffawed, and it seemed unlike a human laugh. This instead was a deep and bellowing howl, as though multiple voices had possessed his own to cry out in one vile proclamation.

"It is mine to do with what I will," he shouted harshly. "And it shall be me who receives the utmost glory. It will be me who achieves that life most prosperous from his Highness far below!"

Now he craned his vile head and his mouth grew wide as he laughed the louder, bearing his oddly-shaped teeth, sharpened nearly to the point of fangs.

Lucian—out of either desperation or simple reaction—leapt upon the table and forced himself on the demented marshal with a shout. In an infuriated tangle, the two bodies wrestled upon the floor. Crowley shouted something in another language repetitively, cocking his head away from the scrum and beckoning toward the door for his guards. All the while Lucian struggled to stay with him (Crowley proved much stronger than he anticipated). Suddenly, with a cry, Lucian grabbed the marshal's wrist and bit into it hard until his mouth leaked with Crowley's hot blood, which to his utter dismay was black as the pit of night.

Loud and shrill the old marshal wailed as the key fell free upon the floor. Jemstine Fryer darted from the table and grabbed it as Lucian released his grasp on the old man. Then, as fast as their feet could carry them, the boys stole away through the hall, passing the large guards who patrolled the front door, seemingly unaware of the condition of their master. Mounting their steeds, their hearts pounding uncontrollably, they fled into the coming night—the key secured in Lucian's pocket.

And even as they fled they heard Crowley howl from afar—screaming not for his wound but through rage that the key, once firmly in his grasp, had slipped away.

11

Darkness Gathers

The night wheeled past them as they bounded ceaselessly toward the reaches of Amar. Behind them the marshal's hall had vanished, but they were still a considerable distance from home. Neither could recall a time they rode so hastily, but whether by terror or other means they managed exceptionally, though Jem felt very queasy after.

Soon the path became familiar again, and far away they saw the streetlights on the bridge above the miller's creek. But suddenly the horses slowed to a stop simultaneously, as though they had coordinated it, and stood blankly in the middle of the road despite the constant nudges from the boys.

Lucian grew furious and dismounted. A sudden apprehension came over him, for he realized then—when everything slowed down—that he had not checked his pocket for the key, which apparently *was* as important as they had once guessed. To his relief, it was still there.

Jem dismounted also, a green tinge present on his plump face. "Perhaps they're tired," he suggested wearily. "We *have* been speeding for nearly an hour, I'd guess. Even if someone was pursuing us from Crowley's hall, they've given up by now. And I'm sure whatever horses he's got are better than these old beasts." As if in retort his horse grunted and nudged Jem slightly with her head.

Jem did raise a valid point, however—at no interval had Crowley's men pursued them. But the disquieting realization remained that the marshal knew now that they were from Amar . . .

Lucian rested his tired head upon the hide of his horse, sweat pouring from his face and his hair now sticking to his forehead. He could not get Crowley's haunting laughter or screams out of his head.

"What could Crowley have wanted the key for?" he asked softly, as if to himself.

Jem shrugged his shoulders. "Off his marbles, that one," he said worriedly. "Few candles short of a birthday cake, if you know what I mean."

"Yeah, but did you see the look in his eyes? He knew what this key is, and maybe what it's meant to unlock. Didn't you see them, Jem? Didn't you see his eyes? It was like he changed—or was beginning to change—right in front of us. He seemed . . . *evil.*"

"I did notice," replied Jem nervously. "I was sitting right beside you. The way he looked at us, as though we had startled him—as though he had forgotten we were even there. I can't imagine what was going through his mind."

Lucian sighed, oppressed by perplexity. "I can," he answered. "I've also felt strange things while handling the key. It's as if it has a separate life-force all its own—like it has a heartbeat, feelings, a sense of its surroundings. That's why I failed to throw it back in the creek. That's why I attacked Marshal Crowley. Even now I feel it pulsating in my pocket, as though it's living—as though the slightest movement I make could harm or suffocate it."

Jem looked blankly at his best friend who he had known for seventeen years—whom he learned his first skills with, played his first games—as though he had never known him. Though Lucian was not menacing or eerie, as the marshal had been, Jem sensed a very foreign air about him—an air of sadness and fear and shame. What troubled Jemstine Fryer mostly was the tormenting realization that he could not help.

"Lucian," said Jem softly, the worry seeping through his whisper, "I don't know what you mean, but I do know—"

Jem was suddenly interrupted by the alarming wails of the steeds beside them, as they each reared upon their hind legs and whinnied loudly into the night. Something had frightened them to the point of panic, and they bounced their hooves wildly upon the ground before speeding away. Jem yelled after them as Lucian stood in disbelief, but it was no use. The horses fled nearly as fast as they had from the marshal's hall and were well on their way to wherever they were going.

"Well that's—just—great!" said Jem furiously, as he watched the fleeting glimpse of his father's horses disappear into the darkness of the sleeping town. "Now we'll have to walk back. Hopefully those idiots are running back to the farm, or it's my hide in the morning."

Lucian said nothing. Instead he sat upon the ground quietly, pressing his thoughts upon whatever was coursing through his mind. Jem guessed it was the key—his friend's newfound dilemma. After a period of getting themselves over what had just happened, and mentally preparing themselves for the walk back into town, they began their trek.

At length they came to the bridge of the miller's creek. Jem stopped, as though it should have been obvious that Lucian would have wanted to dispose of the key after their whole ordeal. Instead Lucian kept walking, aimlessly it seemed.

Throughout the time it took to get to the creek, neither spoke. Jem was still writhing about the steeds running off, and also about Lucian's lackadaisical demeanor.

Before Lucian reached the end of the bridge, apparently heedless to the fact that Jem was not following him, the Fryer boy shouted: "So that's it then?"

Lucian stopped and turned slowly.

"That's it?" Jem repeated incredulously. "You think this thing is yours now, so forget about what it's doing to you and me? Well perhaps *you* can, but I can't. I'm tired of worrying. I can hardly sleep at night knowing this thing is down the street—how can you sleep with it under your pillow?"

Lucian spread his arms, as though at a loss for words. Not even he could answer Jem's questions, and Lucian soon grew angry. "I sleep just fine, Jem. I can't help the part of you that worries."

Jem sighed. "But you can, Lucian. Don't you see? This thing—it's bigger than you and me. It's bigger than this town. You need to be rid of it. It's not right to be hauling it around all day. We just saw our own *marshal* deteriorate before our eyes, all because—"

"*I* will not deteriorate!" Lucian snapped, then recoiled as though coming out of a spell. He realized to his sudden horror that he had grabbed hold of Jem's shirt and was pulling him close. His best friend's eyes were filled with saddened disbelief, as he was not entirely sure who he was talking to on the bridge anymore.

Lucian shook his head as though waking from a daydream. "Jem, I—"

"Save it," said Jem, pushing Lucian away from him. "I'm leaving." And with that Jem stormed past his friend toward the farmhouse, grief-stricken. Lucian watched as his slowly fading shadow disappeared.

Three days had passed since the last exchange of words between the two friends. Lucian sulked around the inn, and had strangely been tending to his studies. Even Mary noted the rarity that was Lucian scuffling about in the morning, gathering his things and heading out the door for school. He and Jem were part of the same gathering of students, and while the two normally sat beside each other, Jem had taken to situating himself in a separate corner of their headmaster's hall. And when school ended, Jem walked out purposefully before giving Lucian the slightest chance to approach him.

Finally, on Thursday evening—four days since their falling out—Mary inquired with Lucian as to his uncommon behavior over dinner. She had closed her services for the evening, and made a fine meal—fit for two—of roasted chicken and vegetables. Lucian, as had been the case the entire week, hardly touched his plate or lifted his eyes from the floor.

"Alright, Lucian Rolfe," said Mary intently, "let's hear

it."

"Hear what, exactly?" played Lucian.

"Don't play your games with me, Lucian. I'm not one of your neighborhood companions—I know you better than you know yourself."

Lucian wanted nothing more than to put the key on the table. More than anything, he wished he could tell Mary all about it and ask her advice about how to relieve himself of his self-induced burden. But for some strange reason, he remained quiet, closing himself off to Mary and everyone else.

"Just under the weather is all," was his only reply.

Mary got up to fix herself another plate, all the while looking at him suspiciously. When she returned she said, "But you've been attending school . . . *regularly.*" She was obviously on to the peculiarity of Lucian putting in nearly a full week of studies.

"Year's almost over," replied Lucian. "I have to show my face at some point."

Mary held her suspicious gaze. "Where's Mr. Fryer been? Haven't seen him around the street in almost a week. Everything alright between—"

"Everything's fine." Lucian's tone was sharp, and he looked at Mary for the first time. There was a fierceness in his eyes, such as she had never seen. Normally she would be quick to discipline Lucian when he spoke in such a manner, but she felt strangely fearful now of her adopted son. Lucian shook his head, coming out of the trance that had become a regularity.

"I'm—I'm going to bed," he said softly.

Mary hadn't any retort. The rest of the night she sat at her table alone with a cup of tea, unable to tell if she feared for—or simply just feared—Lucian Rolfe.

Friday afternoon ended having been Lucian Rolfe's first full week of school the entire year. He was not sure whether to feel accomplished or embarrassed. Jem was yet to talk to him, still fleeing quickly after dismissal as to avoid any contact with him.

That night he headed to MaDungal's for the first time since Jem's birthday. The same lively fiddle was playing, joined by the same beautiful flutist, but Lucian sat alone and weary—not one of his thoughts straying past the friend he feared he had lost for good.

Macintosh rumbled over to him, humming a song to himself and polishing a plate. "Well, well, well," he said cheerfully, "if it isn't Mr. Rolfe!"

"Evening, Mac," said Lucian sulking, fiddling with a nearby fork.

MaDungal was quick to gasp. "Say there, little fellow, yeh sound like y'ain't got a friend in the world."

"That's what it feels like nowadays," replied Lucian lazily.

MaDungal seemed to be trying hard to remember something. "What about that plump chap? The one who had his birthday here last week?"

"Oh, him?" Lucian said as though recalling a distant memory. "I don't know, Mac. I guess I kind of pushed him away."

"How so?" MaDungal had abandoned his polishing to turn his complete, red-cheeked attention to Lucian.

"We had a fight," he answered plainly.

MaDungal sucked his teeth. "Fights are seldom good, lad."

"When are they *ever* good?"

"Well, I s'pose sometimes it's best to let things out, yeh with me? Otherwise yeh'll go through life like one big balloon—just gettin' fat with things yeh wanted to say, or things yeh *should* have said. Then, when it's all said and done, the tiniest little thing can pop yeh open. And that, my friend, is something yeh don't want."

Lucian nodded. For once MaDungal made a bit of sense, much to the credit of his fleeting sobriety. "I suppose you're right, Mac."

The night waned as Lucian and MaDungal conversed over pints of ale. Somehow, MaDungal convinced Lucian that he should go to any length to approach Jem, since it was mostly his fault they had not spoken the entire week.

Thus it was, after finishing one last pint of Eveland Cherry, Lucian left before the midnight hour and headed for old man Fryer's farm.

He immediately regretted approaching the farm so late at night, for he closed the gate harder than he intended to and the noise made the animals stir. *Might as well just knock now,* he told himself.

Old man Fryer's voice sounded from inside, apparently furious.

Lucian heard the old man ranting. "Midnight! Who comes rapping at midnight?" Then his words were inaudible, but still in the same infuriated tone, interrupted by the unpleasant sound of an unsheathed blade. The door flung open, and there stood Lucian Rolfe quivering in the doorway. Samuel Fryer stood before him in the shortest of shorts, the longest of overcoats, and a very threatening blade in his hand. A vain protruded from his bald, rotund head.

"Rolfe!" he exclaimed furiously. "I almost killed you, you know that? This close, I was." He pinched his index finger and thumb close together, just to give Lucian a better idea.

"Is, uh—Jem home, sir?" asked Lucian, holding back the laughter that threatened to break free at the expense of the ridiculous presentation that was Samuel Fryer.

"Jem? My boy? Heard you two lovebirds had a bit of a falling out. Come to kiss and make up, have you?" Samuel Fryer was always amusing himself.

"No kisses tonight, sir," replied Lucian. "Just need to talk to him."

"Not sure he's expecting company this evening."

"He wouldn't be, sir. I just think it's important that I speak with him."

Trying to get anything out of Samuel Fryer was like trying to chew your way through a brick wall. Never a straight answer. Always a roundabout way of getting his point across—points that usually only made sense to him.

"I'm afraid he's asleep, son. Come back tomorrow." He began to shut the door when Lucian gently prevented it from closing with his foot.

"If you wouldn't mind waking him, sir; what I have to say is urgent."

Any other night Samuel Fryer would have retorted enthusiastically, but even he could see the sincerity in Lucian's eyes—the dire need to speak to a troubled friend. After looking hard upon his son's best friend for a moment or so, he nodded subtly and went to fetch his sleeping boy.

"Sorry to have woken you," said Lucian when Jem had come outside the farmhouse and shut the door. Jem shrugged, then the two set out for a walk around the nearby streets.

For a long while, there was a period of awkward silence. Lucian was the first to speak. "Look, I know this is kind of sudden, but you never exactly gave me a chance to approach you in school or anything, so here I am."

Jem rubbed the sleepiness from his eyes. "Here you are indeed," he replied. Jem was quick to notice the lights of the key through Lucian's pocket. "I see you've yet to let go—"

"You know how I feel about the key, Jem. I feel it's right for me to hold on to it for now."

Jem rolled his eyes.

"I'm not here to talk about the key, Jem," Lucian continued. "I wanted to apologize for that night on the bridge—I'm not sure what came over me."

"And because of your stubbornness you won't. But it's the key, Lucian. It changes you—changes the way you think sometimes. I'm worried for you."

The two stopped in the street. "I understand, but I'm asking you to bear with me this one time. I don't have anyone else to turn to."

Jem clearly saw the desperation in his best friend's eyes, thus recoiling was the hardest thing he ever had to do. "I'm sorry, Lucian. I can't be with you on this one. I can't endure anything similar to Sunday night. I can't endure the thoughts, the paranoia. When you sort things out I'll be here—until then . . . I'm afraid you're on your own."

Lucian was taken so aback that he nearly lost his footing. He watched as Jem surreally walked away from him in the street—hands in his pockets, head down.

But he abruptly stopped, just before he was out of Lucian's sight. "Do you smell that?" he asked Lucian, who had not moved since Jem walked away. Lucian sniffed the air and noticed what seemed to be the odor of sulfur

"Smells like something is burning," Lucian replied warily.

Jem examined the air around him, as though detecting the smell for the better. He followed it as though it were toying with him. "It's here now," he said. "Can you still smell it?"

Lucian sniffed around for the smell, but it was gone. After walking around a bit, he detected it again. "I smell it over here."

He had come upon a small opening to a patch of woods. Jem called. "That's odd," he said, "it's over here as well." He moved a couple feet to the right. "But it's not over here."

The two slowly came closer together, now frightened at the floating sulfuric scent on the air. It was easy to distinguish the smell of an oven or campfire, for those were common around town. But this was unlike those smells entirely—this was a deep, pitiful scent that nearly turned their innards to sewage.

Suddenly, the still of the night was breached by the panting of horses, though they were well away from old man Fryer's farm. "Are there horses on these streets?" asked Lucian.

Jem shuttered. "N—not to my knowledge—"

Suddenly the sound of racing hooves penetrated the silent darkness behind them, and Lucian and Jem frantically darted into the mouth of the woods. Though unable to see who or what approached, a threatening feeling caused them to assume a hiding place. The fast-paced hooves seemed to slow to a walk as Lucian and Jem found themselves behind fallen arms of trees and scattered brush. From there they could see the road clearly, and a black horse—saddled but without a rider—stopped before the opening to the wood.

"What the—" began Jem, until Lucian threw a hand

over his mouth.

Where's the rider? was the thought upon each of the boys' minds. Or perhaps it was best they did not know, for the horse was ominous enough. It had reins that seemed to be made of human hides, and was decked with trappings of bone. A white substance oozed from its mouth as it beat its head about restlessly. To their horror, they heard advancing footsteps, though they failed to detect where they were coming from.

The deep, sulfuric scent returned—this time stronger and more grotesque. "What *is* that awful smell?" said Jem, nearly inaudibly.

Lucian held his breath. "I don't—"

And then they saw it. Stooping to the ground, camouflaged by the cover of night, was the most hideous of creatures. Its face and hands were all that were exposed from under its black cloak—red and of claw and fang. Jem gasped ever so slightly, and the creature's pointed ears perked up.

In a sweeping, bat-like maneuver, it advanced on them, never rising from its bent position, and stopped nearly two feet away to take in the scent around it.

It must smell us, Lucian thought, *whatever that thing is. It has to smell us.*

The two friends held each other and closed their eyes. Suddenly, to their incredulous horror, the log behind which they hid was thrown aside and their position was revealed. The creature shrieked the shrillest of cries as sparks of flame flew from around it. The arm of the tree above them rose up in smoke.

For an outstretched instant, they locked eyes with it— yellow and glowing like the belly of a raging fire. Similar cries rose up from the surrounding parts of the wood, as the beast before them reached its clawed hand down to grasp them. The two friends could do nothing but close their eyes, hold each other, and scream for their lives—

Just then, a whistling sound rang through the air, and the creature gave another wail—this time out of pain rather than satisfaction, for a blue-feathered arrow had pierced its chest and it lay panting heavily upon its back on the ground.

"Run!" Lucian cried, grabbing a hold of Jem and racing off to the mouth of the wood despite the presence of the black steed.

Together they sprang away, and when they passed before the riderless beast, it raced onward in rapid pursuit. Lucian could not place a time he ran faster, and neither could Jem. Need drove them headlong into the unpromising night, the hooves of the steed nipping at their heels. It was a fitting beast for the creature it once had borne, for it seemed to snarl and growl rather than whinny and pant like common horses. But, nevertheless, it wouldn't be long before it overtook them.

Suddenly, with the horse's breath misting the two boys' backs, something yanked Lucian's arm from the side, and as he grabbed hold of Jem they were both jerked into a shallow portion of the nearby wood. They turned to see the steed race onward just a bit further before evaporating into thin air, leaving only a black, wispy cloud in the spot where it had been. On the ground where it had raced, no hoof-prints were distinguishable.

Though thankful for their lives, the boys were yet to find their terror alleviated, for as they turned they saw the hooded stranger gazing attentively into the night beyond. Luckily enough, he seemed uninterested in the presence of Lucian Rolfe and Jemstine Fryer—at least for now.

He stood looking out to the road from which he had dragged Lucian and Jem.

Lucian, against his will, spoke to the hooded man. "Who are you?" he asked tensely.

Jem tried earnestly to stop him from talking, but Lucian pushed him aside.

"I've had enough of this, Jem!" he exclaimed. "Who are you?"

But the hooded man ignored Lucian's demands, and turned only to say, "Lucian Rolfe?"

How can it be? But just hearing the voice of the cloaked figure frightened Lucian to the bone, and the spur of anger that had possessed him was gone.

Lucian could only recoil and nod his head reluctantly as the hooded man answered, "There is much you need to know."

12

The Stranger

He requested a private area where they would be able to sit and speak with as much secrecy and as little distraction as possible. The stranger led them hastily along the road, constantly looking in all directions for more of—they boys guessed—the horrid creatures with whom Lucian and Jem experienced a much-too-close encounter. It was a disquieting realization that the stranger was expecting more of them.

"Quickly!" he whispered urgently in the darkness. "There must be some place that will afford us shelter."

Jem, whose heart was on the brink of exploding, turned to Lucian.

"Just do what he says, Lucian!" he implored frantically.

Lucian could hear the wavering of his friend's horrified voice. But, in truth, he hadn't the slightest idea where there was such a place. And what was more, nothing within him possessed any remote desire to speak privately to a stalker, if that indeed was his *only* credential. Nothing about this man suggested that he was the sort to bring to tea.

As they fled along the road, the man consistently implored for a subtle place to hide, and with the pressure to think mounting on him, Lucian could come up with nothing but Mary's inn. That plan, however, would have certainly resulted in waking Mary, which would in turn lay the burden on Lucian to explain not only the hooded man but the dirt on their faces, and whatever those things were now loose around town.

But the stranger was growing impatient. "We haven't all night, Master Rolfe," he said, annoyance present in his voice. "I don't have enough arrows to kill them all."

Thoughts wheeling, it came to Lucian at last that he had access to MaDungal's Pub, for Mac always made sure to tell Lucian where the key was, just in case he became ill and needed a replacement. Thus it was he led them there earnestly.

When they reached the pub, Lucian felt beneath the window where MaDungal kept a bushel of small flowers and breathed a sigh of relief when his fingers came across the small key for the door, and the three eventually fumbled inside.

Lucian and Jem, in particular, thought it strange how a place formerly teeming with life and laughter could ever be this dark and still. The floors of this once lively pub were usually so crowded that it was odd to see the actual wood it was comprised of. Men would raise their glasses high and spill their ale as they clashed mugs together in glee. Thousands upon thousands of songs had been sung here, and the fiddler and flutist would play until they simply lacked the strength to play anymore. But now it was as though the happiness that once filled MaDungal's had fallen to memory, and—watching as the stranger busied about assuring their privacy—Lucian wondered if it would ever know joy again.

Attentively the boys sat, propped up for their still-present fear of the stranger that had loomed about that town for many days.

"Mind the windows and doors, both of you," ordered the hooded man, who had yet to reveal the features of his face.

Thus they took to sitting at a table in the middle of the room while the stranger stalked to each window, and after peering out to make sure they were alone, closed each set of curtains. Then he came to where Lucian and Jem were and lit a tall candle to provide a bit of light.

Now, for the first time, he threw back his hood. The boys gasped, having anticipated something ghastly—something perhaps as inhuman as the creature in the woods. Relief—

and slight embarrassment—fell over them at the realization that he looked no different from a common man; and perhaps, if it was at all possible, lesser. His eyes of brown were mysterious—their piercing gaze stern like that of a great eagle, yet they thought to see a great deal of sadness drooping back behind his expression, as though he were constantly reminiscing on other things more dear to his heart. At his brow and near his neck his disheveled locks of brown drooped, frayed here and there from having worn his hood so long. Upon his face, damp with sweat and seemingly stripped of all innocence, was a grisly beard that may have once been thin and tidy.

Fussing through his pockets, he finally drew a long pipe, and, overturning the candle carefully, lit it and drew in a smoky breath. After a moment, he sent a cloud of smoke into the air and cleared his throat.

"I suppose you two know why I am here by now?" he asked as simply as though he were ordering a drink.

Jem spoke. "Are you intending to exterminate those creatures? If not, then I can't say I know."

Then Lucian said, "You're here because I have something of yours—the key I found in the creek a few streets away. Well, here—" he set the key on the table, the emerald and sapphire lights beamed brilliantly in the darkness of the empty pub. "If I give it to you, will you take it and leave? You're starting to make some of the locals worry."

The strange man looked upon Lucian, his face bathed in the blue-and-green glow, with an incredulous grin, though the hint of a smile played with the corner of his mouth.

"Oh," added Lucian, almost as an afterthought, "and take your friends with you." He was alluding to the horrid creature that had nearly made a meal of he and Jem in the woods.

The man sighed, and brushed a hand through his sweaty locks. "I should have known this would have been more difficult than I expected," he said. "This key is not mine, Lucian—"

"Then whose is it?" Lucian rudely interrupted. Jem grabbed his arm, afraid that the man would surely harm him if he continued being disrespectful—to no avail, of course. "Your father's? Grandfather's? Brother's—"

"I wish," the man said quickly, "that it was only a family heirloom. If that had been so I would be halfway across the sea by now."

It was as though Lucian froze, his mouth never having moved from the last word he said.

But it was the stranger who continued. "This key's owner is one not often spoken of aloud."

"I–I beg your pardon?" Lucian stammered in confusion, trying to find anything to say in retort, but nothing came to him.

The man seemed amused by Lucian's reaction to the sudden news, for a slanted grin came about his face. "You can honestly say you have no knowledge of what this is? Can you not say what it is that fell upon you at the creek?"

Lucian sneered as though sniffing something foul. "Fell upon *me?* It got stuck on my fishing line, and so, naturally, I reeled it in. I had no desire to come across it."

Jem spoke. "He is right though, sir," he said hesitantly, and nearly cowered when the man's attention shifted to him. "We happened upon it by chance. It can't be Lucian's. That would be too much of a coincidence."

"To the naked eye, master Fryer," replied the man, "it would be the strangest of coincidences. But there's more to this matter than is being let on."

Lucian grunted. "And who are you anyway?" he said sharply. "I don't believe we caught your name."

"That's because I didn't give it," answered the stranger resolutely, and Lucian and Jem grew wary. "This land is cluttered with evil ears, and I didn't think it wise to risk my name being heard. But I will give it now: I am Gamaréa of Medric, land of the Moroks, and by the charge of the King Mascorea I am to deliver both this key and its keeper to Medric . . ."

His answer was not even remotely close to what the two boys had expected. Distant lands, kings, Moroks—

"More like 'morons'," Jem bravely muttered under his breath.

142

"I beg your pardon?" inquired the stranger.

The sudden fright on Jem's face was of one who had accidentally soiled himself.

But there was not any hint of falsity in the hooded stranger's voice, and for some odd reason they felt that he was indeed being truthful. Now more than ever they truly did wish he had actually been some stalking peddler from outside the far country.

"Medric?" said Lucian, dubiously. "I've never heard of that place."

Gamaréa expelled another cloud of smoke, this time to the side as to not choke the boys. "Eastern mortals perhaps would not. It's a land far west of here, across the Mid Sea, where war will soon be spreading."

Whether by chance or some other means, the candlelight seemed to dim when Gamaréa spoke of war. It was a word seldom spoken in Amar or any of the humble villages of the east. Ever in their schoolhouse, the prevalent theme of history repeating itself had been nearly branded into their minds, and the legend of their ancestry had been retold almost every year by one headmaster or another—enough at least that each of them understood that it was by war their ancestors lost the west, and in the wake of their escape established small settlements along the eastern seaboard. But it was as though the dancing flame shone a light upon the stranger, and they saw now, in the gaps of his robes, that he bore the armor of a soldier, and when he moved they thought to hear the clinking of mail.

A look of bemusement crossed the faces of the boys. They had been subject to horrid things much too quickly for their liking: the grotesque creatures of fire, disappearing black steeds, a key of pure gold that concealed an evil secret—and now a soldier from Medric?

Jem, who at first was frightened of Gamaréa, became curious. "What is a Morok, exactly?" He was still slightly embarrassed for having been overheard earlier.

Gamaréa sighed. "There is not much time for discussion," he said quickly, as if the subject troubled him somewhat.

"I'm sorry, sir," said Jem, "I just—"

"What is the fastest way out of town?" Gamaréa asked, not heeding Jem and turning his attention to Lucian.

Lucian fumbled for a moment. "Now hold on a minute," he said sternly, though his voice was wavering slightly. "What's going on here?"

But the Morok stood and paced about the windows, peering out from behind the closed curtains.

"You're a fugitive, aren't you?" Lucian accused. "You're a criminal who's made his way to our village, and your trail is being followed."

"That isn't it," the Morok retorted

Then Jem cried out. "Then what is it?" His eyes had been frightened bright with tears.

Then, as if dismayed, the Morok sulked, bowing his head below his drooping shoulders. "You really have no inkling of what this is, do you?" he said softly, as if trying to help himself believe the realization.

"What?" said Lucian. "This thing? This key? I used to think it was just an oddly decorated key—to open what, I don't know. But now, after that display of madness in the marshal's quarters, those things outside, and your presence here, I'm willing to bet that it's something else altogether. Something bad. Tell me I'm wrong, stranger."

"Not entirely," Gamaréa replied calmly, as though trying to restore some order in the room. Lucian had all but grown both frustrated and frantic, as Jem sat beside him with his head in his hands.

"I'm not a fugitive, Lucian Rolfe." And then his eyes grew hard, as though a fire had been lit within them as he peered down intently on the young boy. "You are . . . "

All Lucian could do was sit back in his chair, trying to somehow process the surreal explanation that had been presented to him. A slight smile twitched at the side of his mouth. Then he stood, seemingly annoyed. "I'm done here. Let's go, Jem."

Then the Fryer boy too stood up and headed to the door with his friend.

"Leaving this tavern would be unwise," said Gamaréa just before Lucian's hand could grasp the doorknob.

Lucian turned around angrily. "Why?" he demanded.

"Did I not just tell you that you are a fugitive?"

Lucian snorted. "But I haven't done anything! How could I be a fugitive if I haven't done anything?"

The stranger twisted in his seat, and for the first time they realized how exhausted he truly looked. "In the right sense of the word, you may not be a criminal," he said. "But that key, in fact, does not belong to you."

"Then who does it belong to? Here!" He threw the key at the Morok soldier; the blue-and-green lights spun about the room and for a moment wrapped the pub inside the revolving wheel of its light.

"You deal with it. I'm—"

"It's not mine, either" said Gamaréa quickly. "Those creatures in the woods, they are agents of an ancient force called the Matarhim. They are in the service of Sorcerian, Lord of Nundric, on the cusp of the west, and that being said, they have come very far to find you. Their charge is simple: never to rest until the Key is in their possession, and the Keeper dead."

Lucian shook his head as though trying to repel everything Gamaréa had just told him, as if by doing so could make his words false. Then the Morok spoke again. "Will you sit now, please?" Urgency was more apparent in his voice this time. "Time is pressing. The Matarhim have most likely regrouped by now and will come for us."

The two boys hurriedly moved from the door to sit by the Morok, nervous now of the demon army that had probably resumed their pursuit of them.

"I will tell you everything I can," Gamaréa continued, "but you must make a pact with me here that you will follow me out of Amar."

Lucian started. "But—"

"If you wish to keep your lives you will make that pact with me now."

Gamaréa sternly annunciated every word he spoke, and the two boys simply nodded, utter horror writhing through their veins.

"From here we must venture elsewhere," continued

Gamaréa, "and in distant places perhaps others can tell you more than what I am about to."

He checked his surroundings one last time before beginning.

"This key is an ancient device that was once used in the name of justice. The Lord of the Sages, Ation, created it in the very Forge of Zynys."

Lucian stopped him. "Ation? Sages?"

Gamaréa sighed. Unfortunately, this was going to be more difficult to explain than he originally thought. "The Wizardrim is the most powerful force on earth," he continued. "Or . . . was, at least. Zynys is their dwelling, but it is far from here—the very pinnacle of the world. Ation is their king, and therefore highest of all, from whose very hand the world we now inhabit was formed, and all its people with it."

Suddenly a loud crash was heard from down the way—not close exactly, but close enough to be audible—and the entire attention of the company was caught as Gamaréa continued hurriedly.

"When his creations were complete he forged the Chamber of Fates, in which he housed the fates of the three races: Fairies, Moroks, and Mortals. And this very key—that which sits before us now—he forged to lock it."

Then his face grew sullen. Lucian's and Jem's eyes darted from Gamaréa to the door and back again. "But chaos arose thereafter," he continued, "when Sorcerian, who was of the Wizardrim himself once, rebelled against Ation with a handful of followers. Sorcerian's advance was pushed back, however, and with the entire order of Sages at his side, Ation banished him far away into the bowels of the west.

"It was there the sorcerer was meant to live out his eternal days in darkness. His chasm rests beneath the earth now, at the very base of the world. But he was not done plotting against Zynys, for with his entire host of followers he eventually launched a second assault, rising powerfully from his lowly depths, seeking vengeance on his former kindred.

"This time his ambush was successful. Ation and Sorcerian each rendered each other lifeless with potent spells that have left them dormant to this day, but the Chamber of Fates was claimed for Nundric. With this chamber, Sorcerian's agents were able to molest the fates. Now, instead of living eternally in the realm of Zynys, the souls of the dead are funneled into Sorcerian's realm where he feeds on them. Each new soul brings him closer to rejuvenation. And there is only one way to reverse the spell cast over the Chamber—only one way to restore the former fates and end Sorcerian's scheme for good—and it is lying on this table. Unlocking the Chamber in turn destroys the curse Sorcerian has cast upon it, and thus destroys him."

Lucian's eyes became wide with confusion and terror, but he had become enthralled by the Morok's tale. "But how is it here now?" he asked. "This key, how is it—"

Just then, a shrill cry sounded through the night, a piercing wail that tore through their very souls and nearly made them vomit.

"There was a raid," Gamaréa said swiftly. "The Raid of Nundric, it was called. A battalion of Wizardrim soldiers took on the mission of delving into the pit of Sorcerian's domain to take back what once was theirs. Only one made it down and back up again, and the key was with him. His name was—"

Another cry lifted shrilly through the air as though it were right outside the pub.

"They are nearly upon us now," Gamaréa cried. "We must fly at once!"

Jem sprang from his seat. "Where would we go? They must be swarming the streets out there!"

"Anywhere but here," answered the Morok hurriedly. "Do either of you know back-roads from this pub? We must get Lucian to safety."

Suddenly, just beneath their noses, the key began to vibrate, spinning in a slow rattling circle upon the table. An eerie, pale-blue gleam was beginning to sprout from its shaft, and when they looked, they saw the inscription of a scratchy, foreign dialect.

"What's it doing?" asked Lucian frantically.

"I—I don't know . . . " answered Gamaréa gravely. "I'm not learned in all of this key's powers. We need to get you out of here. Now."

"Why just me?" Lucian asked, exasperated. "What about the townsfolk?" He was nearly in tears, his voice wavering increasingly.

"Because you are the Keeper of Fates. Only by your hand can the Chamber be unlocked now. And, should the fates remain in their molested state, the world will continue to fall—soul by soul—to ruin. Presently, Lucian Rolfe, your blood is the most precious prize on earth; and the Matarhim, the darkest order of evil, are seeking it."

Now a tidal wave of anxiety crashed over Lucian, dragged him beneath its incredible force. The world around him seemed to shrink, as though he were an adult in a child's playroom. All voices became muffled. His senses fled. Thoughts wheeled past him in random sequences: the inn, fishing, Mary, Jem—even school, for he suddenly preferred those long, endless lectures.

He knew at this moment that his life would never be the same.

He heard himself speak softly, as if through a dream. "And where would we go?

And his face became blank and confused, as though not even he could believe he was obliging to flee.

Gamaréa was quick to respond, lunging from the table in apparent anxiety himself. "Away from here. We must find my ship and take to the sea as soon as we can."

Lucian took the key up from the table, finding that it was warm to the touch.

"We must hurry, Lucian," said the Morok as though waking the young boy. "We must leave before—"

But his words were not permitted to conclude, for suddenly a flaming torch was flung through the window of the pub and came crashing into the center of the room. In its wake, the awful wails of the Matarhim rose up.

"Hurry!" exclaimed Gamaréa, reaching for the two boys and seeking an escape route.

Now another torch was flung through an adjacent window, and a fire began to swelter madly on the floor, licking its way onto nearby furniture until MaDungal's became engulfed in mountains of flame. Gamaréa threw his hood atop his head and kicked open the door to the rear exit.

Lucian and Jem, without many choices left, followed.

13

The Razing of Amar

The shrieking masses of the Matarhim pierced the once quiet night, and to the left and right they could see their sweeping black shapes rummaging about the streets with torches, launching them into unsuspecting homes and shops. Waves of flame were now bellowing out of MaDungal's, and they could hear all too plainly the snapping wooden posts and shattering glass before the pub collapsed entirely.

Lucian wondered if any singular mug that splattered to shards had been recently occupied by him, in the many nights he shared with Macintosh MaDungal, who—*if* he awoke—would find his prized possession destroyed. But he was shaken from his thoughts by Gamaréa's arm. Huddling both Lucian and Jem together, Gamaréa drew his sword, its magnificent blade glinting in the light of the rising flames.

Gamaréa was speaking, but Lucian could not hear him. Grief swept through him like a black cloud, and for a brief while he watched as the flames finished off the fallen pub like a pack of wolves upon a deer. The horrific scene seemed to trap him in time. As the place he considered his home away from home sighed and snapped upon the ground, he devoted his attention only to remember . . .

"Mr. MaDungal! Mr. MaDungal!" shouted Mary from all the way down the street. As she dragged a stubborn, seven year-old Lucian Rolfe along with her, the young boy beheld a plump, bearded man with red hair turn to face her. Finally, the old innkeeper reached this Mr. MaDungal—whomever he was—sweating and short of breath.

"Someone I'd like you to meet, Macintosh," said Mary.

The man's eyes turned downward, beholding a fair, innocent boy at the hand of Mary Rolfe. The boy's hair was slicked back, and he was dressed rather formally for a seven year-old. But Macintosh MaDungal was wise enough to know that it must have all been Mary's doing . . . he hoped.

"This," said Mary, yanking Lucian's arm to direct his attention, "is Lucian—Lucian Rolfe."

A sudden cheerfulness erupted in MaDungal's eyes. "Say now!" he exclaimed. "Hello there, little fellow. The name's Macintosh MaDungal, but yeh can call me Mac."

He held out his enormous hand for Lucian to shake. Much to Mary's surprise, the boy did so without hesitation—and what was more, he was wearing a large smile.

"Lucian here," said Mary, "has been staying with me for several years now." Then she mouthed, *Constantly getting into mischief,* so that Lucian would not see. "I thought perhaps you could give him a job of sorts, just to keep him busy?"

MaDungal picked up on the hidden meanings of Mary's proposal. *So the kid is on the wrong track, eh?* he wanted to say, *and yeh wan' me to keep him busy fer the day so he don't go further down it. So let me keep him cooped up in a pub from dawn 'til dusk. He'll know more about ales than he will about anythin' worth knowin'.*

But all he said, in his outstretched, jolly manner was, "O' course, Ms. Rolfe! We'll have a swell time, we will."

He shook the slicked locks upon Lucian's head, and though this was a gesture Lucian had come to loathe, he did not seem to mind when it was MaDungal doing the shaking.

It was then that Lucian stepped into MaDungal's Pub for the first time, and from that day forward the wily bartender proceeded to teach Lucian all he knew about important matters—which was not a long stretch by any means, but at least it was something.

If he was nothing else, MaDungal was a dreamer. "One day I'll build an entirely new pub, see—thrice the size o' this one. Jus' gettin' me feet wet, I am. So enjoy it while yeh can!"

It was something he said perhaps once or twice a year, but for the ten years Lucian knew him, it only remained a dream.

Lucian always found himself being included in MaDungal's chores, which he openly cherished. It was not long before he was eager for the morning to begin so that Mary could walk him to Pub Street.

When he got old enough and could set out for the pub on his own, MaDungal told him where he hid the key to the door, and the owner would often arrive to find that Lucian had already set things in motion for the morning. Macintosh MaDungal became a part of Lucian Rolfe, and the pub his greatest keepsake.

With a final bellow of snapping wood and rising flame, the pub was officially gone.

As though he had been sleeping, Lucian was startled by Gamaréa's cry. "We must head north!" he shouted. The flaming homes and buildings around them had intensified and increased in number, and now people flocked into the streets in utter horror.

"We must head toward the far country!"

But Lucian could not seem to move his feet. The scene was unfathomable. The townsfolk they had known for most of their lives wailed in horror, pain, and sorrow. Some had caught fire themselves. Some cried for trapped loved ones. It was a stagnant, nightmarish maze of broken lives and families, and all the while, the wails of the Matarhim issued from all sides.

Men ran into their homes for family left behind—most only to die themselves. Fathers carried lifeless children to their frantic mothers in the streets. And from the spot where they stood—before the fallen pub—Lucian and Jem watched in helpless torment.

Suddenly Pub Street was overrun by the shrieking Matarhim, racing swiftly atop their hell-spat steeds. One shifted its glowing eyes to the three companions, springing upon them before any of the company could realize what was happening.

They broke quickly apart as the Matarhim warrior came spinning its whizzing mace wildly. Gamaréa was now nowhere in sight. Jem, looking quickly this way and that to find he was alone, darted for his father's farm. Lucian took one final look to the burning mound that had once been the pub, and then raced for Mary and the inn.

Jemstine Fryer did not need to reach the farm to know it too had been attacked. His father's prized horses were scattered about the street, having come loose from the stables along with other animals Samuel Fryer raised there.

He was hesitant to go further, but was spurred forward by the rising flames coming alive around him. Then he saw, coming around the corner, the farmhouse itself overcome by flame.

Jem panicked and started quickly toward the door before the dying house gasped and caved in on itself. He recovered and bolted away to dodge burning debris that had been cast toward him. Then—there in the middle of the empty, burning farm—the Fryer boy fell to his knees and wept in awful realization.

Samuel Fryer could not be saved.

Gamaréa hit the ground hard, completely taken aback by the Matarhim warrior that had forced itself so unexpectedly upon him and his company. He checked for his weaponry, then stood. Lucian and Jem were nowhere in sight, lost somewhere in the sweltering chaos that had befallen the crowd. Houses and workplaces burned steadily in roaring flames. Every street for miles, it seemed, had come alive with flame

From a distance, he could see horsemen riding in from the north—the foremost rider sitting with a proud posture.

Those nearby were exclaiming, "It's the marshal! The

marshal has come with his men!"

But as the horsemen arrived on Pub Street, Gamaréa found it necessary to take shelter. Masses of townsfolk had begun fleeing to scattered areas—many in the direction of the far country. What fate would meet them there, Gamaréa could not be certain.

Nevertheless, it was behind shrubbery he took to hiding, and from there he saw the marshal and his company (four other riders) come to halt. Soon a small band of Matarhim joined them there.

The marshal spoke. "What news?"

One of the Matarhim riders—perhaps their captain—answered, "We've yet to come upon the Key." Its voice was fitting for its appearance, raspy like a growl.

The meeting Gamaréa was witnessing was strange enough, but the fact that the Matarhim were associating with mortals furthered his bewilderment. The flames rose around them now, like a rising red-and-orange wall—flaring, wailing, and cracking. It seemed now that all the residents had either fled or were lost within the pyres, though distant screams remained on the air.

Crowley cursed. "So there have been no signs of the two boys?" he asked sternly. "No sign of Lucian Rolfe or Jemstine Fryer?"

The beast hissed. "We fell upon them in the woods just hours before we set the town aflame, and that was the last we saw of them."

The marshal issued an annoyed chuckle. "And how, Dyseus, did two mortal boys manage to slip out of your sight?"

As though offended, the one referred to as Dyseus growled. "They were not alone," he retorted.

Crowley's gaze inflated with perplexity. Dyseus continued. "A Morok was with them."

Crowley hissed. "Impossible! Moroks would not trouble themselves with business on these shores."

"Then explain this." The beast then felt inside his black shroud and pulled out the arrow that had killed his fellow warrior. "This arrow undid one of our number."

How, Gamaréa thought to himself, *could you have been so careless? Two hundred years of warring and you leave substantial evidence of your presence for the Matarhim to find. We must fly, and with haste.*

Dyseus continued. "It is an arrow only the inhabitants of Medric possess—feathers said to be from Vodaptica, a native bird of Zynys, and blessed by Nepsus, Sage of the Sea; the only arrows crafted outside of the Mountain to which we are susceptible."

Dyseus spoke truth, for the arrows Moroks possessed *were* in fact the only arrows in the world—outside of the blessed arrows of Zynys—that were capable of killing the Matarhim in one fell swoop. The Zynian steel at the point of each arrow extinguished the flames burning within them, and the undying feathers of Vodaptica filled their every flight with purpose. It was but one of few methods, in fact, that actually *could* kill them.

"What orders do you have for us now, mortal?" Dyseus continued.

"Well," began Crowley, "it is apparent it does not seem to matter what orders I have for you, does it? A town one-thousandth the size of your ash-infested homeland and you cannot even find two dimwitted schoolboys."

The beast hissed and drew a long, jagged-edged sword. Off its iron blade, the flames glinted sharply. Dyseus held firmly to its hilt of bone, and pressed it up to Crowley's throat.

"Only the Dark One gives us our true instructions," he snarled. "Only he may direct us. Your pact with him will not prevent your death here, should you continue on this way."

Crowley recoiled his anxious tone, gulping as the edge of Dyseus's blade crept closer to his flesh. "Now—what orders?" repeated the Matarhim soldier.

"Take—take the east roads," the marshal said shuddering, "and burn everything on either side. At sunrise, we will search the debris. The Jewel of the Sorcerer cannot be undone by fire."

Dyseus's company barked and bellowed and spun away

eastward. Gamaréa's need for haste was now intensified. *I must find the mortals,* he thought to himself frantically, *but where could they have gone?*

Springing from hiding, he darted swiftly after the Matarhim. Instead of searching for Lucian and Jem, Gamaréa decided to try to kill as many beasts as possible while their attention was on other matters.

Creeping along, he approached soundlessly. There, but yards before him, the Matarhim had gathered—lighting their torches and casting them away into buildings that were yet scathed. Gamaréa notched an arrow and fired swiftly into the head of the nearest beast. The rider instantly fell from horseback. However, it was not until Gamaréa slew another member of their pack that the Matarhim realized they too were under attack.

As they rounded in his direction, Gamaréa daringly exposed himself upon the road, firing two more arrows before the Matarhim completely acknowledged him. The horses of the two remaining beasts jerked wildly and charged.

Gamaréa took the horses down first, sending the Matarhim warriors flying in a cloud of soot and firelight.

Dyseus was among the two left alive. "Such archery should be commended," the beast said. "But rather, I ask why a Morok has traveled this far east to a peasant village?"

"I might direct the same question your way," the Morok replied, revealing Dawnbringer from its sheath.

The two Matarhim soldiers circled Gamaréa slowly.

Dyseus spoke, low and menacing. "You and I, perhaps, are here for the same reasons."

"And what reason would that be?"

Dyseus hissed. "Do not be coy, Morok. You know well what led us here."

Suddenly, Dyseus's companion charged at Gamaréa from behind, but he parried in enough time to repel its blow. Then with a swift, retaliating swipe, he managed to take it down with little difficulty. The beast's sappy, black blood now oozed off the edge of his sword as he pointed it at Dyseus.

"Will you face me now, Matarhai?" he dared. "Or will you flee to tell your master of the woes you suffered here?"

The two were locked in a slowly spinning circle of hard stares and careful movements—the slain Matarhim warrior lying in a motionless black heap between them. Then, like a flash, Dyseus sprang forward, leaping off his fallen companion into the air toward Gamaréa. The Morok dove out of the way, shielding his face with his sword in time to parry Dyseus's hard swipe. His swing having missed, the Matarhai sent a swift kick to Gamaréa's face, knocking him aside and dislodging Dawnbringer from his grasp.

Kicking Gamaréa's sword away, Dyseus lifted his arms for his killing blow when Gamaréa took an arrow from his quiver and manually delivered it between the beast's eyes. The leader of the Matarhim stood limply for a moment, a dubious look in his glowing, yellow eyes, before joining his fallen team.

Lucian ran off as fast as his legs could carry him, the thought of Mary spurring him faster and faster along the burning streets. She must have been horrified—if not for the terrible occurrences of the evening, for the fact that she hadn't the slightest clue where Lucian was.

Subtle thoughts ran through Lucian's mind as he raced onward—apathetic thoughts that wouldn't normally run through the mind of someone whose village was being destroyed around him. The fact that it must have been nearing dawn was one of them—almost time for Mary to wake and start preparing for the day. But as Lucian came upon his street, he realized no one would be preparing for anything.

Every building on County Street was burning uncontrollably, muffled screams audible within the roaring flames. The inn was entirely engulfed when Lucian arrived. The fire within it had spread all the way upstairs and was reaching out into the night through the windows of his bedroom.

Stepping as close as he dared to the doors he screamed desperately for Mary to no avail. Despairingly he reached for the door, but as he jarred it open, the fire swallowed up the doorway. The inn could not be entered, unless as a suicide attempt. His prized balcony, where he had enjoyed so many mornings, wailed in exhaustion. Suddenly, the white framework that once held firm to the inn snapped and fell swiftly where Lucian paced, lamenting.

Beneath the weight of the withering, white wood, all things fell to darkness. And the last thing Lucian Rolfe saw was the silhouette of a shadowy figure stoop low as if to carry him. It was then, as though he were weightless, he felt himself being taken away. His consciousness faded, along with the sounds of the dying town.

Part 2

"For we cannot tarry here,
We must march, my darlings,
We must bear the brunt of danger.
We the youthful, sinewy races
All the rest on us depend."

~ Walt Whitman

14

The Black Forest

There was a light above Lucian that flickered now and then. A gently swaying breeze passed over him at times, and he could feel his hair rustling in its grasp. Around him there were voices—two, in fact, for what he could distinguish; and they were conversing.

Somewhere beside him, a campfire had been built, for he heard the light crackling of flames and smelt the scent of the burning wood carrying on the air. There were also footsteps that he sometimes heard busying around him. Though he passed in and out of a conscious state, the voices were consistent—soft and muffled with no apparent form of intent. Here and there was the sound of chewing and sipping, accompanied further by the same faceless voices. Now and again passed what Lucian perceived as animal footsteps.

Every now and then, he felt himself hovering, bobbing lightly as though being carried. When another wave of consciousness possessed him, he was able to detect more light, though his eyes remained closed. Again, the voices were present, as was the sound of running water, and a very apparent smell of fish.

When he hesitantly opened his eyes for the first time, Lucian perceived that he was on a soft hillside that delved down to the bank of a moderately swift stream. There at the bottom Gamaréa stood smoking his pipe and fishing, while Jem sat at the tip of the hill, watching him.

The farmer's son turned to see his friend had finally

woken up.

"Lucian!" he exclaimed, hurrying over to his side. "Gamaréa, Lucian's awake!"

The Morok turned and reeled in the last of his line, the bait still squirming off the end, and scampered up the hill.

"It's about time you decided to wake up," said Gamaréa with a jolt of sarcasm. "I was getting tired of carrying you around."

Lucian held his forehead for a moment, as one recovering from a headache, and sat up slowly. At first words escaped him, and he stammered inanely for many moments. "How long was I sleeping?" he said at last.

"I don't know," said Jem, "if you call *that* sleeping."

Lucian looked puzzled.

"You were unconscious," Gamaréa clarified. "Whether it was the smoke in your lungs or the debris that had fallen on you, I can't be sure. But you had a pulse and were breathing almost normally. I had no choice but to get you out of Amar."

At first, Lucian was confused about what the Morok had been speaking of, but then he remembered the horror of his falling town and became filled with grief. He stared aside blankly, remembering.

"Where are we?" Lucian asked at last after a long while.

"Far away," replied Gamaréa simply. "You were lost to us for three days. In that time, we flew across the far country, and made haste through the cliffs at its border only to find every decent wharf within reach has also been destroyed. Some ships are still aflame as we speak, I don't doubt. It was on those bluffs your weight got the best of me, and we stopped longer than I would have preferred. Nevertheless, we had to change direction hurriedly. I had planned to meet up with the ship that brought me east, but there was no sign of it in those ports, and a good thing too. They are probably sailing up the coast now. What they will find there, I cannot say. All we can do is follow these coastal trails in hope of finding them. The Black Forest will be upon us soon. There we may find proper shelter before nightfall—" Gamaréa was peering anxiously into the direction he expected to lead them. "Then in the morning our journey will be long," he finished.

"Where will the forest lead us?" Lucian asked cautiously, looking at Jem who seemed equally concerned.

Gamaréa sighed, a hint of worry in his voice. "If it remains, to the only haven this far east—"

"And why should it not remain?" Lucian asked concernedly.

Gamaréa peered over both of his shoulders; as if to make sure he was not being observed. "I will not speak of that matter here in the open. But it won't be in our best interest to delay further; I came here both to rest and fetch us a worthy supper. As of yet I've accomplished neither."

Talk among them commenced for a short while, then when Lucian decided he could walk on his own they continued on. The place they walked was rigid—as the green folds upon which they had stopped were soon replaced by the jagged, rocky cliffs that Gamaréa had previously spoken of.

Lucian was quick to regret the decision to carry on upon his own strength. Because of his frequent debilitations, they had to stop many times, much to Gamaréa's dismay. The Morok stressed the urgency of making it to the forest before nightfall, though he would not speak of his reasoning. He had taken to acting so strangely that both boys exchanged puzzled looks quite often, constantly spinning around as though he detected someone—or something—behind them. Even the slightest song of the slightest bird seemed to startle him.

Their road became less trying not long after the sun sank deeper into the west. The cliffs were behind them now, having declined steadily away into the soft field below. Ahead of them was the Black Forest, or so Gamaréa mentioned—a vast stretch of woodland that seemed ominous at first glance. Though the last of the sun was facing it, the trees at the mouth of the wood seemed to repel its light, standing luridly dark as though it were night.

Jem spoke. "That's strange," he said. "Look! The sun is right on the trees, yet it's as dark as can be."

"They don't call it the Black Forest for nothing," replied Gamaréa. "Now come! Night approaches."

Like a deer, he sprang away over the final stretch of the field in front of the wood, and in time led the boys into the forest with haste.

The forest was dim even in its brightest sections; elsewhere they had to proceed slowly and with caution, until eventually they were forced to creep an arm's-length away from each other. They tread this way for hours until night had fully fallen. Around them, the air became colder, and the boys shivered as they walked carefully along. Gamaréa, however, walked briskly, seemingly unfazed by the drop in temperature.

Eventually, Jem determined that he had had about enough. "Excuse me," he complained, "don't you think it's time we rest for the night?"

"That depends on your friend," answered Gamaréa. Jem was just satisfied he had not been scolded. "Has he any strength to go further?"

Jem looked at Lucian, who had been clutching his shoulder since they had entered the forest. Lucian slightly shook his head.

"He's got nothing left in him, sir," replied Jem. "We're going to need to rest a bit."

"Then rest we will."

Gamaréa led them a bit further to a convenient glade where the ground was soft and flat.

"This is a sufficient-enough place to rest for the night," said Gamaréa ponderingly.

The boys settled down. Jem helped Lucian to the ground and set up a makeshift sleeping arrangement for him, while Gamaréa lit his pipe and stood at the cusp of the glade smoking.

"It's awfully cold," Jem stated. "We should light a fire."

"No!" Gamaréa spun round wildly, as though Jem had suggested something awful. The Morok collected himself quickly. "We cannot light a fire, master Jemstine. We must not give away our position."

"Position?" Jem asked, confusedly. "To who? You mean

to tell me there are more of those . . . *things* in here?"

Gamaréa took his precautionary stares left and right before answering. "The Matarhim?" he corrected softly. "I'm afraid they are everywhere now. All the Dark One's collected servants have gathered to claim the Key—"

"But are they here—the Matarhim?"

A long, cold silence fell between them before Gamaréa answered, "Yes."

Jem shifted anxiously where he sat. "How do you know?"

"I can smell them," Gamaréa answered plainly.

"But I can't smell anything," retorted Jem, "and I know for sure what they smell like by now."

"My senses are a bit more altered than yours, I'm afraid. They are nearly a day's travel east of us. We can afford a couple hours' rest and no more. We must fly at first light."

When dawn approached—or what could be sensed of it, at least—Gamaréa led them onward. Dew lightly bathed the flora that was about them, and grasshoppers clung to bushes and leaves. It was actually quite humorous how they could go nowhere until it was dryer.

Their journey throughout the morning was relatively simple, for the forest had given way to a portion of scattered trees and natural pathways that stretched for many miles— but before long they were forced to travel close together, and confined to slight, restricted movements.

Lucian had more strength that day than he had the day before, and he walked almost normally while keeping pacc with his companions. He grew tired, however, around noon, and the company decided that it was a proper time to rest again.

"Do you have any food?" Lucian asked Gamaréa.

"I haven't."

Jem held his stomach, which sounded like some kind of carnivorous predator. "I'm starving," he said disappointedly.

"There were fine trout in the stream we saw yesterday," said Gamaréa. "It's a pity we were in such a hurry."

"Are there anymore streams in the wood?" asked Lucian. "Jem and I enjoy fishing."

Gamaréa laughed slightly. "Though you've made a habit

of catching sacred trinkets rather than fish."

The boys could not help but chuckle with him. It was the first time the Key had been but slightly mentioned, and Lucian grazed his hand along his pocket to find that it had not managed to slip away.

Jem spoke. "I haven't even seen any game in this forest," he said softly.

"I made a note of that," replied Gamaréa. "Folk must have hunted this forest bare."

"It's a shame," said Lucian sadly.

But Gamaréa attempted to raise their spirits. "If we make good time," he said, "we should be out of these woods in a day or so. Until then, keep your eyes open for anything with meat on its bones."

They carried on. Behind them, the afternoon dwindled into evening, and the evening further into night. They tread into the gloom—the unearthly darkness—where even their own hands were invisible in front of their faces. No sound was present but those of their persistent footsteps—a twig snapping here, a leaf rustling there. Sometimes they passed quietly enough it was as though they bore no feet at all.

There was a greater angst this night than the one before. Perhaps the cause of this was that they were more awake—their senses heightened to a separate extreme from the last moon. Nevertheless, despite the constant paranoia of things lurking, watching, and waiting, they marched.

"It's a funny thing, the woods," said Jem as they walked on.

"Why is that?" Lucian ventured to ask, just happy to hear the sound of a familiar voice in the blackness.

"Because you know a hundred things can see you, but, for the life of you, you can't see them."

Lucian grew nervous; Gamaréa smiled.

The silence was soon pressing again, and in time they felt cramped, as though the forest seemed no bigger than a bedroom there in the ominous darkness, and it was much warmer now than it had been.

In his mind, Lucian thought of the Matarhim. It was not so much their appearance that frightened him—it was the sounds they made; the blaring wails, the persistent grunts. Their eyes were their most frightening characteristic— glowing, yellow beads within a pit of fire—and when they looked at him, he felt nailed to the spot in which he stood, paralyzed by fear. His mind played tricks to make him believe that he saw their eyes glinting through the distant darkness, like individual, miniature stars in the blackest sky. And when morning came, he was not any more at ease.

That day it rained hard into the afternoon, but the storm subsided at the cusp of evening. The company traveled swiftly despite the conditions before resting again. Gamaréa was displeased with their progress, for he had hoped to reach their destination by that point, but he voiced that they were still some miles away.

They rested against the base of a leaved hill in the darkness. The Morok smoked his pipe and cursed. Jem and Lucian rested quietly, conversing every so often. Lucian would have given anything at this point to have been back in Amar at MaDungal's pub. He deemed, if he had been given the chance, he would have made the finest use of his ales. It troubled him greater than any trouble ever had that it was gone. The pub, the inn, the town—everything. Gone. As though it never were.

He turned on his side, as if to sleep, and wept. This was the first time he thought of Mary. The memory of citizens screaming came back into his mind and he pictured her amongst them, running for her life or wreathed by flames. He remembered what he was doing before he became unconscious. He was going to save her—or attempt to, at least. Then the inn gave way and fell on top of him, and the Morok carried him away. Into his mouth dripped the bitter taste of salt.

On and on Gamaréa cursed, and eventually proceeded to fling his pipe aside and spit in disgust.

"What's he so mad about?" Jem whispered to Lucian.

"I don't know," he replied, "but it's hard enough to sleep in this place as it is, let alone with him cursing the forest dry."

The Morok had been pacing back and forth angrily for a long while. His motions were short. His gaze was stern. But suddenly he stopped and became alert, like a deer who detects the slightest inkling of a predator. Bowing his head, he began listening attentively.

"What's he doing?" asked Jem.

Lucian did not answer, though he had become almost as anxiously aware as Gamaréa.

Quickly, the Morok spun round to the boys. "Run!" he exclaimed.

Almost instantaneously, the boys shot up from their weary states and sped off through the woods behind him. Now the whistling of arrows flying rapidly through the air sounded at their back. Many slammed into the surrounding trees, flying errantly this way and that like pointy raindrops. Gamaréa moved behind the boys with his bow and fired skillfully as Lucian and Jem fled desperately away.

They were not sure how long they had been running, but they soon made it to the edge of the wood where the trees gave way to the rocky shore of a gray, roaring stream, and were dismayed further upon discovering that their way had been blocked by Matarhim cavalry. They must have been thirty strong, and when the others who had closed in on them caught up, they flanked the company. Shoulders touching, the three companions stood together, aware of all the impracticalities of their escape.

A rider came forth from within the grotesque clan, but unlike his company, he was not beastly in physical form. Atop his head, he wore a drooping hood, which he presently removed.

Marshal Crowley's face seemed older somehow, with at least a week's worth of stubble having grown on his once-fair cheeks. They discerned from his weary eyes that he had perhaps not slept in many days, but his demeanor seemed dignified and proud as he propped ruefully atop his black steed and approached.

The horse crept up and loomed over them, drooping its head and snorting in their faces, mucus spraying wildly from its moist snout. Its eyes seemed to mesh in with its silk-like coat, and had it not been for the reflection of the nearby river they perhaps would not have been easily visible at all. The beast's hot breath protruded from its mouth, the crisp cool air soon tarnished by the fumes, which smelled mostly of carrion.

Then Crowley dismounted and drew his horse away, and the companions were pleased—at least for a moment—to be out of the beast's shadow. But now they could see for the better the madness brewing in the marshal's eyes, corrupt now beyond all measure, leading his pack of demons out to feast.

He spoke menacingly. "Your road ends here," he said. Then he spit upon the ground. His eyes fell upon Lucian Rolfe as his horde drew their broad-bladed swords, black like ash.

"You must release the Key into my custody," he said, stretching out his long hand. Lucian could see the scab on his wrist from where he had bitten him.

Gamaréa appeared so quickly in front of the two boys that they barely saw him flinch. "The boy will do no such thing," he said. His voice was stern and final.

Then their eyes locked, Crowley's and Gamaréa's, like an invisible magnetic force protruded from their pupils and bound them in a long, intense gaze. Now for the better they saw the true stature of the Morok, such as they had not taken into account in their time with him. He stood nearly a head taller than the marshal, his shoulders as broad perhaps as Crowley's were drooped and bone-riddled. Neither seemed to waver in the other's presence for a long while, but in time Lucian and Jem thought to see Crowley begin to shudder at the knees. The elder's mouth twitched somewhat, as though contemplating what to say or do— neither of which came quickly.

At last Crowley spoke. "The Dark One sent word to all his faithful garrisons of the possibility of a Morok in pursuit of the Key, seeking to deliver it into the hands of the Wizardrim." Then, for a sudden moment, his eyes seemed to fall dreary and sympathetic. "You have come very far, yet have traveled in vain."

"Yours is the only vain cause, marshal," replied Gamaréa. "He who rides in darkness will never inherit the light, regardless of what you've been led to believe."

The marshal laughed. "Light?" The boys thought to hear authentic amusement in his voice. "And what would you know of light, *half-breed?*" Gamaréa felt his eyes twitch as he reacted ever so subtly to Crowley's insult.

"Yes, I've heard all about you, son of Gladris. Nearly four hundred years old, and a reject of your country for just as long. Do you think your master honestly wishes you well in your trials here?"

Now the marshal saw that his words had begun to seep through the tough skin of the warrior who stood before him, inching ever so slightly toward his heart. And though Lucian and Jem knew nothing of what Crowley spoke, they saw that it was slowly affecting Gamaréa as well.

His purpose fueled, Crowley continued harshly. "It is his one last attempt to be rid of you!" he hissed. "But he needn't worry, for we shall aid him in that regard." He then looked hard upon Lucian. "Give me the Key, boy!"

Lucian recoiled hotly. "No!" he wailed.

Crowley sneered and grabbed hold of Lucian. But just then, from an unseen angle, a green-feathered arrow whistled by and pierced the marshal through the side of his throat. His old eyes glazed, and after fixing on Lucian's for a final moment were expelled of life as he fell to his death.

The Matarhim shrieked and their steeds grew restless. The black horde turned recklessly this way and that in frantic anticipation as a battalion of arrows were launched from the woods beyond the stream. It was as though the wood itself was an archer. Not one dart seemed to fall without a hit. Everywhere the dark soldiers were falling upon the soggy earth with a repetitiveness that was almost rhythmic.

In the hysteria, Gamaréa took to slaying many himself, taking advantage of the distraction to fight craftily with his sword. Then, nearly as abruptly as they had appeared, the waves of arrows ceased and the companions beheld the dead horde around them, hissing, it seemed, as though the moist earth was putting out their flames.

Lucian and Jem's gaze never strayed from the area of the wood where the arrows had been dispatched, too frightened that they might fire again. But Gamaréa seemed poised. Stooping to the ground, he examined one of the dead beasts and surveyed the arrow that had felled it, noting the emerald feathers protruding from its shaft.

Then he stood with some excitement. "These are the arrows of the Fairies," he said with earnest.

He called out beyond the stream, and it was not long before there seemed to be activity there. Then, as though his voice alone had summoned it, a light came shining through the shrubbery, and a horde of fair soldiers stepped lively out of the gleam, their armor glinting miraculously. Golden hair flowed atop them all, and their faces all seemed ageless, but none proved more admirable than their captain, who was last to cross onto the bank.

The soldiers circled around the three travelers, and their captain strode through their golden ring to greet Gamaréa. His piercing blue eyes seemed hard and stern.

"You should be dead," he said bluntly.

Gamaréa returned an equally hard gaze. "You obviously failed to see that I had them right where I wanted them."

"Oh no," Jem muttered to Lucian.

The Fairy captain nodded his head, considering. "Indeed."

Then, simultaneously (and much to Jem's relief) Gamaréa and the Fairy laughed heartily together, and the captain wrapped Gamaréa in a damp embrace.

"It has been too long, brother," he said, a bright smile flashing across his statuesque face.

"That it has, my good Didrebelle," said Gamaréa brimming with delight. "These—"

But Didrebelle's gaze had already shifted to the two boys in Gamaréa's company, and he loomed over them as though scrutinizing their very existence. "One of these is the boy," he commented as though certain. His eyes of blue were somehow more alike to crystal, for they appeared as two jewel-like lamps upon his face. Though he was taller than Gamaréa, he bore a slighter frame, which they presumed gave him swift and agile tendencies. Atop his chest hung an armored vest of silver and gold, with the emblem of an eagle wrought upon its center. From his back drooped an emerald cape, weathered at its base from his many travels.

Before Gamaréa could respond, Lucian stepped forward. "I am," he said. And from his pocket, he took the key and showed the Fairy captain, who at first was expressionless.

But, in truth, Didrebelle had become enthralled. The world closed around him and he was delivered to a harsh place in which nothing surrounded him but blackness. All too clearly a voice was calling, *Dragontamer! Dragontamer! So forlorn the forgotten son.* Then Didrebelle seemed to grow wary again and with a gentle grasp, he guided Lucian's fingers around the Key and clasped them.

"We mustn't expose it here, my friend." His voice was soft and distant, though Lucian did not understand why.

After a short while, he ordered his company away, and the host of Fairies made across the stream again. Watching them wade through effortlessly caused Lucian and Jem to forget that the stream was actually moving swiftly eastward. They crossed, however, without the slightest difficulty.

Didrebelle thought a moment, then told Gamaréa, Lucian, and Jem to follow him along the west side of the stream to where a bridge met them, and they passed over it in a swift line, led hastily by Didrebelle. The bridge emptied them onto the opposite side of the stream, and shortly after Didrebelle's companions joined him. From there, they passed like a gallant pack of wolves, their numbers now swelled to nearly thirty strong, until at last they cleared the forest and reached the top of a high hill, green and sparkling even beneath the gathering dusk.

They were peering out across the expanse of a far valley, but what Lucian and Jem saw there was unfathomable. The stream that had passed beneath the bridge had wound its way downward and passed through the valley, flanked by folding stretches of soft emerald lawns, studded with evergreens. Lucian and Jem thought they had fallen into the most glorious of dreams.

The very ground upon which they stood seemed to be comprised of springs, and they felt weightless. Ahead they saw the path, which led from the hill, winding eastward from there along the ridges of sheer cliffs. Transparent mist hung delicately upon the cusps of the ledges ahead, and the last of the fleeting light of day pierced through and glinted off the water, whose steady current far below had become the only sound.

The Fairy's company had begun traversing along the eastward path. Gamaréa trailed them, but Didrebelle stood with the boys, allowing them a chance to take in all that was before them. "This is Elmwood," he said, "the road to Elderland." His voice was soft and spaced, as though he was in awe himself.

Lucian's eyes did not stray from the valley. "Elderland?" He had said the name mostly to hear it flow off his tongue. Somehow, though he had not seen it prior, he belicved Elderland to be fairer even than Elmwood, which up to this point in his life was the most beautiful sight he had ever looked upon.

"My homeland," replied the Fairy. "We probably won't arrive until nightfall, but even under the moon the land of my people shines. Let us go. My lord is expecting us."

15

Elderland

In time, the company came upon a marvelous city that gleamed even beneath the fallen night. Only in the painter's workshop had Lucian and Jem seen such places, but now they were experiencing first-hand the majesty of superior architecture. There was a lovely farrago of massive towers and shining green lawns that were all tended exceptionally. The single road that had led them into the city diverged into multiple branches. Some sloped downward, others up, and some went straight ahead. It was the headlong road Didrebelle took them by, in the direction of what appeared to be a large palace.

The towers here were not as enormous as those known around the world, however. These were instead like the forest that housed them—gray and of slender length—as though part of the wood themselves. In fact, from a distance, their senses could not perceive a difference between the towers and the roots and tree-limbs that were growing on or around them. They noticed now that the forest, in fact, was present elsewhere as well. Greenery sprouted through the negative space between the wonderfully crafted houses. Multiple stairwells, perhaps formed from the forest stones themselves, rose up in some places and went off to other reaches of this dwelling that Didrebelle had called Elderland.

Somehow, it also seemed to be built in order to harness the river that now poured through, and they saw an ancient walkway that cut across two ledges beneath which the stream was running through aqueducts. Looking up now, they saw another waterway spilling from the great height of a nearby mountain, speeding onward through more aqueducts of similar fashion before channeling into the river under them.

By way of the bridge, the captain of the Fairies led them, eventually taking them up the steepest of the stairwells atop which the entrance to a wonderfully crafted hall rose over them. Evergreen needles sprinkled down gently, caught in the subtle wisps of a slight breeze that was present before they spun to the ground in front of them. Didrebelle and his company seemed eager to enter, and Gamaréa himself had grown fidgety with excitement. It was, as Lucian and Jem thought to recall, the first time they had seen him smile so profoundly.

Now the doors swung open, and the company entered with gusto. Inside they saw the hall was wide and vast, and the echo from the opening doors lingered for a moment. Glistening marble was around them on the floor and ceiling, and save for where the natural light of the moon shone through the open doorway, the rest of the hall seemed illuminated with an iridescent, crystal-like glow, as though the folk of this place had captured miniature fragments of the stars and displayed them like lanterns.

Before either boy could inquire about it, Didrebelle said, "The hall is lit by witchlight, if that is what you are wondering. The entranceway remains exposed to the natural light of the earth, but the further reaches of this dwelling delve into the center of the forest where no light can go. The lord Tartalion makes use of an ancient branch of magic to bring his house alight."

"I *was* wondering how the hall was still so bright," said Lucian wonderingly. "But I figured it was a trick of the light."

Didrebelle smiled. "Nothing but the trickery of sacred spells, my friend. But come! The rest are moving forward."

A winding staircase of significant steepness was further to their right, and they went up to where an open corridor wound in a large, spiraling manner around the entire perimeter of the hall beneath. Didrebelle sifted through the mass of his fellows. Their entire number had come to stop before two great, oaken doors. Didrebelle hesitated a moment, then, with a great effort, parted the doors and led the party into a wide, circular room. Windows that stretched from floor to ceiling wound around its circumference, revealing all of Elderland below, exposed beneath the moonlight, gleaming in pale shades of blue and silver.

Across from the doors, standing sternly upon the step of a well-decorated platform, was another Fairy of strong build. Unlike his kinsmen, his broad structure was more distinguished with muscle, and his eyes pierced them hard, though he most likely knew them well. And in the shadow of this brooding guard sat whom Lucian and Jem believed to be the lord of that country, perched with poise upon his emerald throne.

The guard, as though alarmed at the presence of the company who came with the Fairies, reached for the sword dangling from his waist, his forearms pulsing as his grasp clenched. "Who comes with you?" he asked sternly. His black hair flowed smoothly past his shoulders.

Just then Didrebelle came forward from among the group. "Ease yourself, Darthmonde," he said, equally as sharp.

He drew both of his long swords that had been crossed behind his back and took to holding them at his sides. The ringing of the unsheathing blades echoed.

Darthmonde hissed and finally drew his own. Lucian and Jem cowered and fell back behind the group of Fairies who were now standing alertly, grasping the hilts of their own swords.

"You are in enemy company," bellowed Darthmonde.

"That is apparent," said Didrebelle hotly, "and I would appreciate if the enemy would step aside so I may address my lord properly."

Lucian and Jem felt suddenly unwelcome, but they followed Didrebelle and Gamaréa as close as they could to the lord's throne, walking much too close to Darthmonde than they preferred. The guard's gaze never strayed from them.

Tartalion stood, unfazed and smiling. "You may go, Darthmonde," he said in a kind voice. Getting a better look at his full length, they saw he was perhaps one of the tallest Fairies they had yet seen. His hair was long and gray, but well kept, and his face was fair and seemingly without a hint of age. Through clear eyes of blue, he looked happily upon the guests whom Didrebelle presented.

"You must forgive Darthmonde," he said disappointedly. "He is of loyal heart, yet I fear manners were never on his list of things to learn. And with rumors of the western wars having crept across the sea, he has become ever wary of unordinary things."

His eyes passed quickly over Jem before landing on Gamaréa, upon whom they suddenly came alight with pleasure. "Darkwood," he said happily. "It has been too long."

Gamaréa bent to one knee in acknowledgement. "My lord Tartalion."

Lucian and Jem each exchanged mystified expressions when Tartalion referred to Gamaréa as *Darkwood*.

"That's a strange thing to call someone," Jem whispered. Lucian agreed silently.

Though it was only a name after all, there seemed to be a dreary, almost sad element to it. But Lucian could no longer contemplate the name, as Tartalion's eyes now rested on him, where they stopped and became very pressing, as though pulling his innermost thoughts from his mind.

"You have come very troubled," said Tartalion softly.

Lucian wanted to look away, but the Fairy lord held his gaze. His innards felt twisted inside him—his blood felt hot as though it were boiling. The marble floor felt suddenly like some foul quagmire from which he could not rid himself. Yet, as much as Tartalion troubled him in that moment, Lucian felt secure in his hall. He felt strangely assured that no one could touch him, even if they wanted to. Suddenly, almost as quickly as it came over him, the oppressing feeling dispersed, and Lucian felt the invisible weight lift from him. Now, to his relief, he was able to look elsewhere, as Tartalion began to address the entire group.

"We will arrange sleeping quarters for all of you," he said cheerily. "You'll have to forgive the lack of privacy, I'm afraid, for it is only one room. Nevertheless, there are enough beds. You will sleep comfortably, I deem. As for the morrow, a grand feast is being planned and prepared."

His people knew him as Tartalion Ignómiel, first son of Eróndale, the former chancellor of Dridion, who was of Wizardrim descent. His mother Antónia, however, was of Fairy blood. When Eróndale perished in the Raid of Nundric many years ago, Antónia—who had lived in the house of her husband on the Mountain of Zynys—came down to Dridion with her son, who at the time was but a toddler, to live among her people. Because of her husband, whose righteous reputation was known well in that part of the world, she was held in high regard. And when her son was of age to bear arms he was given the position of one well beyond his years.

This, however, is not to say he was not worthy of his rank. The blood of the Wizardrim ran through him after all, making him strong and fierce, but most importantly focused. Though Fairies themselves were stealth in their ways, Tartalion had somehow mastered the art. He strode softly, using anything in his surroundings to either shield himself or propel himself upon his enemies. After two years of service, the general awarded him the rank of a Specialist—a position assigned to those charged to partake in unique and usually confidential operatives that proved too complex for common soldiers.

After only a decade of service, he was awarded the rank of general—a position he held for over five centuries. When his days of war had reached their end, he sought peace on a large estate on the outskirts of Dridion, in the coastal province of Guinard. There he farmed by day and enjoyed long walks along the countryside in the twilight. It was during one of these nightly strolls that Tartalion thought to see something odd washed up upon the rocky cove. Though at first he disregarded it, a voice became present within him, whispering, *Ignómiel, Ignómiel, look! What can you see?*

And as though the speaker was present, he answered aloud. "Leave me be, specter, or whatever else you are. I see nothing but carrion once adrift."

He walked away then, but was called back. *Should you pass from here, so too shall pass the hope of the world.* The acclaimed Fairy spun round looking left, right, and above for the speaker, when suddenly, from behind him, he felt a gentle touch upon his shoulder, warm as though the sun was glaring on him.

Then he fell back, his eyes of blue blinded by the utmost of lights, as Charon, the Sage of War and Valor, approached. "Tartalion," he said gently, as though speaking to a child. "Why do you weep upon the ground? Stand! You have been chosen."

Dumbfounded, Tartalion crept away on his rear. He had faced countless enemies in war, yet before a Prince of the Mountain, he was stupefied, rid of all ability to formulate a thought. "I don't know of what you speak," he said stammering.

As if in answer, the Sage pointed to the object upon the shore, the tide gently washing over it as it passed in. Tartalion too looked that way, and could see now that it was not a mere object, but a human. Then he turned again, to where the Sage had been, but found, to his dismay, that he had vanished.

Suddenly he leapt up, realizing what the Sage had been asking of him, and sped away toward the shore. When he came upon the man he found that he was motionless, and covered in a thin layer of pale sand—but he was still breathing. Flipping him on to his back, Tartalion could see now that he was a young boy, one whom age was yet to truly touch. Without much thought, the old war veteran threw the boy atop his shoulder and carried him to his homestead where he fixed a large fire in the hearth of his library.

It was not long before the boy began waking, and when he noticed the foreign place for the first time, he became startled. Then he heard the voice behind him, deep and aged, like the voice of time itself. "You are in the estate of Tartalion Ignómiel," it said.

The speaker stepped into the light, the glare of the fire gleaming from the white robes draped over him. Ignómiel stood magnificently, his shoulders wide and powerful. Though his voice seemed ancient, he himself appeared young. Every feature of his was immensely distinguished. His black hair ran polished and smooth behind his head, fashioned in a decorative braid that hung down to the small of his back. He glared upon his guest with eyes of blue so light and clear they seemed more like droplets of rain. His face was smooth, yet there was also something hard about it, as though he were comprised of parchment-colored stone.

And now he too could perceive the boy for the better— the unruly hair dangling into random twists and turns about his face; the eyes that peered from beneath his brow, sunken, perhaps trying to appear firm and unafraid although they seemed to cower; the mannerisms, even as he sat motionless in his chair, that defined someone lost.

Beneath Tartalion's shadow, the boy fumbled for a word, when in a tumult of realization he remembered the events that led him there. *Water,* he thought, *I know there was water. I tried to swim. They were calling for me. Perhaps they fired at me. To the coast—they pursued me to the coast, until I jumped and swam away. Then a storm. Was it a storm? Was it a storm that brought me here?*

"Speak now, child," said the Fairy. "Speak now of your coming."

But the boy would not speak—not for many days. Of Tartalion, however, he was ever wary. From the high window of the room where he resided, he watched Tartalion farming, his body bare beneath the sun, statuesque like his face. He watched as his muscles danced and flexed as he worked, as though they sought to protrude from his skin. In the morning, he found that Ignómiel had provided breakfast, if he wished to help himself to a meal, and at night, he was sure to fix a supper fit for two.

It was a long while, however, before the boy obliged, knowing full well that he had grown deathly famished. His skin was now gray with malnutrition, but even still, he waited for privacy to indulge in the fine delicacies his rescuer provided. Then like a beast he ate, devouring his portions rapidly and without natural manner.

Finally, after a week had passed the boy approached Ignómiel in the fields and said his right name. "Gamaréa," he said softly, as though uttering his name for the first time. The very annunciation of it seemed to surprise the young boy, like he faced a fear he had long been running from, and he said it again more profoundly. "Gamaréa."

For the next decade, Gamaréa worked in the fields with Tartalion and became strong, and his landlord taught him the ways of nature. In the afternoons, they took to a small glade just outside the property and meditated, and in his meditations, Gamaréa became accustomed to the voice of the wind, and in his dream-like states was able to distinguish words upon it, beckoning him.

In the house of Ignómiel, Gamaréa flourished. Tartalion fed him well, and the raggedy, bone-riddled boy he had found washed upon shore a decade prior was but a distant memory. Now the boy had become man. His arms and legs had broadened sufficiently, and his back had grown wide and strong. In truth, as Tartalion often mused, Gamaréa had become a monster in human form, a beast tamed only by his methods.

In his gardens, he taught Gamaréa to fight, providing simple guidelines to become a successful warrior. His master's consistent instructions played continuously in his mind—day by day, moment by moment.

Back straight.

Eyes level.

Arms outstretched—no, no, not that much.

Elbows tucked in.

Both hands on the hilt; keep your grasp firm. Much too firm, my boy, much too firm.

Steady now. Now you've got it.

Chin up. Higher. That's it!

Hands firm now—right over left.
Step lively, boy—left foot, then your right.
Swing with your body, not just with your arms.
Even while working he found himself practicing, using his gardening tools as makeshift swords and remembering. *Back straight. Eyes level. Arms outstretched.* He always knocked his elbows against his ribs for good measure to make sure they were tucked in properly. *Chin up.*

Even at night, Tartalion watched from his balcony as Gamaréa practiced in the moonlight, and he saw his form growing almost to perfection. But as days went by, he noticed something about Gamaréa that he had never seen in the five centuries he trained recruits. His form was perfect. Skills that took Fairy soldiers tireless decades to perfect, Gamaréa had done so in one.

There are many things at work here, he thought to himself. *Many things indeed.*

At dawn one morning, Ignómiel found Gamaréa in the garden, still swinging the broken shaft of an old rake like a sword. It was then, much to Gamaréa's surprise, that he tossed a spare sword at his feet.

"Take it!" urged Tartalion. "I've yet to hear a fascinating tale about a rake-wielder."

Gamaréa inherited a look of confusion. "I don't understand."

"My boy, you know my story. For five hundred years, I trained the finest soldiers this country has ever seen, molding them strictly by the way I had been taught. My practice is war, my skill inherited from the blood of my father. The exercises you so tirelessly perform originated on the high summit of the Mountain itself, as you well know—"

"You speak of this Mountain," answered Gamaréa, "this place that must be of high regard, and say you're from there. If that is so, why are you here in a country not your own?"

Tartalion Ignómiel looked hard then upon his apprentice. "I suppose we all traverse by separate roads at times. My road perhaps is no different from your own. Not many of us reach a crossroads and continue straight—that requires a great deal of courage! So too is courage required to stand so close to kin when you feel so distant from them."

Gamaréa's gaze grew solemn. "I've yet to stand before the mortals."

"*Mortals,* you say?" Then, for a moment, his mind raced upon a thought. "You must come with me."

He led Gamaréa away to a deep part of the neighboring wood and brought him to a tree that seemed to stand alone, thick and broad-trunked. Gamaréa looked upward, and saw now that the canopy was high and wide, and perhaps concealed life within its midst. His master stood against it, peering upward also, as though admiring. Then he said softly, "This tree is of mixed descent. Its lineage can perhaps be traced to an individual origin, but as it stands, it bears the composition of all the famous makes of trees: Spruce, Oak, and Cyprus. It is said that few who live can slew these trees from the ground, but I encourage you to try."

Gamaréa was still gazing at the sheer mass of the great tree. Presently he shook his head. "I don't see how I can cut this tree with even a hundred hacks."

"Surely you must try, my boy. What harm lies in attempting?"

Suspicious, and—though he would not have admitted it—a bit curious, Gamaréa stepped back to prepare for a hack at the behemoth mass of tree that stood before him. He drew his sword and grasped it. *Arms outstretched. Elbows in.* Then his posture straightened. *Back straight. Shoulders up.* His gaze narrowed fiercely. *Eyes level. Chin up.* At last, he flung himself at the tree. *Swing with your body; not just with your arms.*

He hadn't realized, but his eyes fell closed as he swung, and he momentarily thought he had missed, for he did not feel even the slightest of impacts. Then he stepped back, and looked up disappointedly at the tree standing firmly in place. His racing adrenaline tapered down.

Discouraged, he looked at Tartalion, who stood a few meters away, his arms clasped and a smug grin on his face. Gamaréa began to speak. "Master, I—" But suddenly, from behind him, as though the forest itself was crying out, the tree began swaying off of its foundation, and fell slowly like a collapsing statue loud upon the earth. Dust from the wood rose up and circled around for a long while, and creatures that had been hiding scurried frantically away.

Then Tartalion approached him, and as he walked away uttered softly, "It was as I thought," before retiring again to his estate.

Though the dozens round him slept peacefully, lost among their dreams, Lucian found no rest. Instead, he lay awake gazing up at the roof, the soft, velvety covers the lord Tartalion had provided draped over him loosely. There was a small slit within the rafters through which some moonlight seeped, and he thought to himself how different even darkness felt in Elderland. It indeed did not feel dark at all, but a dreamlike wave of luminescence laid over the land—distinguishable as nightfall, yet bearing no quality of it—and Lucian wondered fleetingly if he were in the only place on earth where night felt this peaceful.

For some reason he recalled—more than once—the name Tartalion had referred to Gamaréa by. *Darkwood,* he thought, or perhaps he had said it partly aloud, for the Morok shifted in the neighboring bed. Though he quickly fell back to a motionless state, Lucian still lay thinking and remembering, asking himself why someone of such valor and esteem would refer to Gamaréa so drearily.

The name clung to Lucian like blood from a wound that had scabbed over. *Darkwood.* Then his mind took him far away from the large sleeping-quarters and back to his home in Amar, and he thought of Mary and worried for her, recalling only the burning and the screaming and the crumbling houses as the townsfolk frantically raced on their own ways. He wondered dismally if she in fact had met her end there, imagining the roof of the inn catching fire and falling on top of her, all the while her cries lost amidst the chaos that had possessed the village

He dare not shut his eyes. Foul and unearthly images

plagued his ability to find peace—if so, of course, there was peace to be had. Thus, he crept from the bedroom and went out into the hall. There he came upon a dim corridor, lit in some spots by a hanging torch of Tartalion's witchlight. Quietly he passed along, hoping a slow stroll within the enchanted dwelling would sooth him and put him somewhat at ease. The corridor led to a room without an outlet—a large room that wound in a wide circle. Above, the roof was spherical and comprised of clear glass revealing the starry sky.

I don't think I've ever seen this many stars, he mused, watching them glitter.

He had not taken into account the amount of time that elapsed as he was marveling at the magnificent spectacle above, and when he looked away at last, his neck ached.

But now that Lucian focused his attention elsewhere, he saw for the better the display encircling him. Hanging on the walls, wrung all about the room, were multiple paintings, all of a separate event or occurrence that he thought must have been significant. He approached the very first painting hanging on the wall by the entranceway and immediately found himself immersed in its splendor. *This is . . . wow,* he thought—

"It truly is," said a voice from behind him. Lucian spun round to find Tartalion standing against the other side of the wall, calmly, bathed in the pale blue moonlight glaring through. "That, my boy, is *The Creation.*"

Lucian did not even pass a thought along how Tartalion soundlessly wound up behind him, or cared for that matter. All that traversed along his consciousness was the painting's title. *The Creation.* The title of the work almost instantly justified what the painting seemed to display: a large basin, seemingly made of stone, lost perhaps within a rocky valley of a great mountain. A light was beaming from it, gold and pale silver, depicted so vividly that Lucian found himself squinting as he looked at it. In the midst of the glare, he perceived three hovering, humanoid shapes that appeared to be motionless as if they were dolls. It was not until Lucian's eyes grew accustomed to the brightness that he saw a distinguished-looking figure behind the gleam, his arms outstretched as though professing or proclaiming, bathed in flowing robes of white like his mane of locks and beard.

"What you see here is the Altar of Ation," Tartalion continued. "He too is present, just behind the flaring bulb of his magic." He pointed to where the King of the Sages stood gallantly. "This painting, in fact, is not entirely accurate. Here, Ation is depicted creating the Three Heralds together, in one immense conduction of magic."

"The Three Heralds?" Lucian said, nearly to himself. "The things inside the light?"

Tartalion laughed slightly. "My dear boy! The Three Heralds are much more than mere *things*. They are the founders of each respective culture: The Fairies, Moroks, and Mortals. In the painting we see them together as a sole concoction, but in truth an act requiring this much magic—even of Ation—would have been more than enough to kill him."

Lucian's gaze fell blank and confused. "You mean to say the man in the background created Fairies, Moroks and Mortals?"

"Precisely, though Ation is much more than man. He is a Sage—the Great Sage, at that. Lord of the Wizardrim of Mount Zynys. He chose to create the Fairies first, and thus the first Herald came into being. Ation named him Viridus, and instilled immortal blood within him so that he may spread his ageless bloodline. Because of this, the Fairy race is entirely immortal, safe from withering age and faltering health, vulnerable only to arrow and blade."

Withering age. Faltering health. Tartalion's words cut across Lucian's mind and mustered curiosity. "Ageless," he muttered softly. "Then you must be—"

"Eight hundred and sixty-one." A mixture of sadness and pride fell over Tartalion's voice. At first Lucian did not understand why speaking of his age made the Fairy lord seem so dreary, but then he thought of the talk of war spreading in the west, as Gamaréa had mentioned, and he wondered exactly how much of it Tartalion had been exposed to in his long life.

"When he created the Moroks," Tartalion continued quickly, "Ation found that he had nearly spent the entirety of the immortal blood at his disposal on Viridus. Thus, with only a single drop left to spare, he awarded it to Dimitus, the first Morok, who would pass it on to his kin."

Lucian contemplated. "So Moroks aren't immortal?"

"That one small drop of purified blood is enough to make any living being immortal, my friend, yet only to a degree. The lone drop they bear will sustain their lives and immunity, but over the course of centuries they become subject to all the dooms of mortals—withering and graying like old flowers that once had blossomed so vigorously." His gaze grew sullen. "And once they start to age, my boy, their bodies quickly bear the brunt of all their former days, and the fate that awaits them then is all too human."

Lucian's expression became grave as he thought sadly of Gamaréa, of whom he had grown quite fond. "They die?" he asked, half-whispered.

Tartalion's face too had become somber, his eyes still fixed on the painting. "In time their immunity fades, as I have said, and in many instances becomes as weak as it was strong. When that happens, the slightest chill, even, may undo them."

"But Gamaréa—" Lucian said thoughtfully, "he doesn't seem to be fading."

"Gamaréa is reaching the pinnacle of his age, I am afraid," said Tartalion plainly. "He will soon reach that pivotal juncture in the life of a Morok in which the passing years will begin to take their toll."

"And he will age as you said?"

"Slowly at first, yes—almost unnoticeably; then faster as the years progress. But we needn't worry upon that now, my friend. His better days remain before him. Have you not been witness to his strength? Can you not attest to the brawn your companion bears?"

Lucian looked confused. "I'm not sure I'm following."

"A special trait of the Morok culture—lacking in all else but theirs—is their possession of cunning strength. Even their women are stronger than most grown mortal men, though you would not know it unless you challenge one, which I daresay is unwise."

Lucian pictured a woman such as Mary besting several grown men with only her hands and he could not help but smile. "Even their women . . . " Lucian said to himself wonderingly.

"They look plain enough, mind you," added Tartalion. "Their features are alike to those of mortal women, but I warn you, should you ever encounter one, to pay her the utmost respect."

Lucian took Tartalion's warning into account and peered intently at the painting again, shifting his focus to the rightmost shape hovering within the glaring light. "So this, I'm guessing, is the mortal?" he said, pointing.

"The third Herald, yes," said Tartalion quietly. "The first mortal, Hominis; the foremost of mankind."

When Tartalion had spoken the name of the final Herald it seemed a shadow passed over the moon momentarily, and the room in which they stood fell dim for an instant—a highly noticeable instant, as though time had slowed and supplied the opportunity to encounter all the subtle trappings of a second. Then Lucian looked to the Fairy lord as the light flooded back into the room to find that his face seemed worn and tarnished.

"What happened to them?" Lucian asked, immediately regretting his decision to.

Tartalion sighed. "Perhaps the question at hand is what has *not* happened to them, dear boy. For years, they manned the face of the west, those coasts along the Mid Sea's western reaches. Then in what seemed like an instant, by my standards at least, they declared war amongst themselves. Fires brought down their white cities, which, had they progressed further, would have become more endearing and prosperous even than Dridion, the motherland of my countrymen. Those who survived—a humble lot, to my knowledge—are now scattered along the coasts of these shores, having fled here on their small ships to salvage some form of a life for their children. The rest, along with their monuments and towers and city walls, have fallen to ruin."

A hint of redness was apparent on Lucian's face, as though he were embarrassed of bearing the blood of the race the lord was discussing. This could not have been his lineage. His ancestry could not have been traced back to those corrupt and greed-riddled cities. But indeed, it was his heritage as much as his limbs were part of his body. So too, somewhere within those decaying cities, his ancestors once lived. An ill feeling invaded his innards, and he stood quietly resenting everything about his predecessors, sliding his hand from the painting in disgust.

"What about this one?" he asked, directing Tartalion's attention to the painting to the right.

This was an image of a large golden chest, wrought with diamonds and other colorful jewels. Similar to the moon hanging above them, a golden glare sprouted from it, though it was not as bright as the portrayal of Ation's magic. "This is *The Chamber of Fates,*" Tartalion informed.

"I assume the chamber is referring to this box?" Lucian observed musingly.

Tartalion chuckled lightly. "Of course by now you should know that things are usually more than they appear— in Elderland, at least. But yes, this here is a painting of the Chamber of Fates, the very chest Ation comprised to conceal the fates of the three races he had created, so that when their lives on earth ended they may come to live among the Sages on Zynys."

Lucian grew curious. "What are the fates, exactly? Are they instruments of sorts? Trinkets?"

Tartalion smiled, as though pleased with the question. "They bear no physical qualities. If one were to open the chest and look, they would see nothing. They are instead a life-force, if you will—the energy that binds every living soul on earth to Ation's appointed fate. The very Key you bear was forged to lock it, and is the only device that can do so. Not even the great hammers of the Sages can break the locks."

Lucian fumbled for his pocket and felt the Key still

there—its lights warm even through the cloth of his robe. "But if Ation went through all this trouble to create these races and build this chamber, how could he have let it fall into the wrong hands?"

Tartalion's gaze became perplexed, as though Lucian's question troubled him—and it most likely had to some extent. "Because Sorcerian, the Lord of the Netherworld, did not always reside in those lowly depths. He was of the Wizardrim once, and his name was Sceleris, the brother of Ation—"

"Ation's own brother caused all this trouble?" Lucian exclaimed with incredulity in his voice. Though he did not have a biological brother, he felt that his friendship with Jem qualified as a significant form of brotherhood, and he could not fathom doing something of that magnitude to him. He wondered why it had been such a simple act for Sceleris.

"Sadly, yes," answered Tartalion. "He disagreed with his brother's creations of the Three Heralds. He feared that, as their populations increased, they would seek to expand, in which case they would also seek power, and those seeking power would inevitably cross paths and destroy each other, and forsake the name of their high king. He claimed that, even in their short existence upon the earth, they would litter it with hate, war, and prejudice."

Lucian thought back upon what Tartalion had said of the ancient race of mortals. "He wasn't entirely wrong," he said finally, a hint of sadness in his voice.

"No," said Tartalion distantly. "No he was not. He blamed Ation, claiming that he was neglecting the wellbeing of the Wizardrim by putting his love for others foremost. Sceleris was ashamed of his brother's creations, embarrassed to bear the same blood as their maker—and he was not the only one who shared in that stance."

"You mean to say there were others?"

"Of course there were. The first decade was disastrous. War and death soon encompassed the world. Ation's creations roamed about like savages, forsaking Zynys, caring only for riches and glory. Certainly, the highest members of Ation's council remained faithful, his three children always beside him, but Sceleris is highly persuasive, and he gathered enough of the Wizardrim to protest against his mighty brother. It was a civil dispute at first, until—"

They had now reached the third painting in which was displayed the very essence of chaos. From what he gathered from Tartalion, Lucian distinguished Ation and Sceleris in the foreground—the Wizard king massive and muscular in flowing robes of white, pointing downward with his broad arm, tight and corded with bulging muscle. His companions were behind him, all fair and dressed in glinting armor. Some were expressionless, others with theatrical, satisfied stares as Ation cast Sceleris to the depths of the world. And before the great King of Sages, cowering in the presence of his brother, the other stood, his arms comprised mostly of bone, like a skeleton, his cloak a withering hue of gray, aflame at the bottom as though the flames of earth's core reached up to drag him to the world's southernmost boundary.

"Ation would not be defied, you see," explained Tartalion. "He banished Sceleris from the Mountain, along with his followers. Sceleris then took to calling himself Sorcerian, the Sorcerer of the Deep, using his once Sage-like magic for evil purposes. Those who allied themselves with him now comprise the Matarhim—demonic creatures, a constant fire burning their skin beneath which is only a soulless, black void."

The Matarhim. It was a name to which Lucian had unfortunately become inured to over the past few days. "The Matarhim," he said. "They followed us from Amar and fell upon us at the river, just before Didrebelle and the others arrived."

"And they will follow you still," Tartalion said, as though mentioning an obvious fact. "Only, in your next meeting, they will be impatient and frustrated."

"Why do you say that?"

"No creature outside of the Three Races may enter Elderland. Have you not seen the Citadel?" Lucian innocently shrugged his shoulders. "I cast a spell upon the beacon. It took significant effort and patience, but it is sufficient enough. No being of the Netherworld can enter here, so long as that beacon is alight. You will see it tomorrow, I don't doubt. That is where the feast will be held."

"Feast?"

"Of course, my boy! The nerve I would have calling myself a host without coordinating a feast for this band of heroes!"

It wasn't until Tartalion spoke of the feast that Lucian realized how much he had missed warm meals and laughter, and he was immediately filled with anticipation— both for the next day's festivities and the opportunity to see Elderland in the sunlight. But then he walked on, and his eyes latched on to the next painting to see that it bore a gloomy quality. There was a mass of black shapes descending from a high mountain, though Lucian was unable to tell if it was Zynys. Among them, the only shape distinguishable was the Chamber of Fates.

Before Lucian could even ask, Tartalion said, "This is *The Raid.*"

"This is Zynys, then—this Mountain? But the lights that once were shining are out."

The Lord of Elderland's voice then was bitter and sad. "Sceleris rallied a large mass of the Netherworld and led them to attack Zynys. Ation had underestimated the power of his brother. Perhaps some sort of evolution took place within him, down there in the pit of darkness, on the sweltering, ashen fields they call Parthaleon. But when he rose and led his army heavenward, he struck with force not even Ation could contend with—the first time the world was witness to dark magic. A large sum of the Wizardrim perished. Sorcerian cast Ation under a spell that rendered him dormant, and so he remains to this day—deep in the chasms of Zynys, guarded by the descendants of the old Wizardrim. But they are now a broken people, doomed to passively watch the races their lord created wreak havoc on each other—"

"But why do they stay and do nothing?" Lucian

contended. "If they are the most powerful beings on earth, what trouble would it be for them to come down and fight for what is rightfully theirs?"

Tartalion sighed. "Their spirits are all but broken, their numbers too few even to dream of plotting a war. Tirelessly, they tend upon their dormant king with the hope that one day, perhaps, he may rise again and lead the forces of good in Zynys's name to victory."

"How long has he been idle?"

The lord's voice shrunk to an astonished whisper. "Three thousand years."

"Is there anything that can release him from this spell?" Even Lucian was surprised to hear the disparity in his voice.

"If there is, none have found it, my boy."

Lucian thought for a moment. "But has anyone ever actually looked?"

Tartalion thought hard upon Lucian's query, understanding the boy's point. "I cannot say that they have or haven't," he said at last. "It is likely now that the Wizardrim's hope has all but faded. They tend him now by habit, not by motivation that one day soon he will rise."

A silence overcame both of them. Tartalion thought back upon all that he had said, reliving the origins of life upon the earth through the paintings on the wall, and musing over how, in a whisper of time, things went from bliss to chaos. But then he looked at Lucian, still lost in the artwork and architecture around him, and he knew—knew that it was in simple things that the world must place its hope, when all complex and promising figures faltered. *This boy,* he thought. *He walks in darkness but does not see it. Look how he stares upon the wall at the failures of the world, somehow finding peace. He cannot know the trinket that he bears; he cannot know the burden. Perhaps he never will, until the end of his days—which soon may be upon him.*

"Something vexes you, Lucian?" asked Tartalion, noticing the slight frown that drooped upon Lucian's face.

"There's something I've been wondering lately," he replied hesitantly. "Speaking of the Key and all, there's something about it that I don't understand."

"Go on . . . "

"Before we . . . ran away from Amar"—Lucian seemed openly pained as he said this—"the Key did something strange. It seemed to—I don't know—come alive somehow. Or not come alive, exactly, but, well, there was writing on it, and it was hot, and then it disappeared."

Despite his inarticulate account of the strange writing on the Key, Tartalion appeared to understand what Lucian meant, for he was nodding subtly with his eyes closed. "It is a mockery of Ation's old rally cry. Before Sorcerian's raid, it read, *Shadow will devour nevermore*. But after he vandalized the Mountain, the sorcerer branded new runes upon it, so that *nevermore* has been revised to *evermore*."

"Clever," said Lucian sarcastically. This Sorcerian certainly seemed more and more repugnant by the second.

"What about the jewels?" Lucian ventured to ask. "I was also wondering about them. It's odd to me that two of them are lit up, but I feel as though it's stranger that the ruby isn't lit up at all."

"The jewels represent the division of powers under the Wizardrim," Tartalion said plainly.

Then he took to reciting:

> *Blue for the Moroks, strongest of all*
> *Green for the Fairies of light*
> *Red for the men whose will shall not fall*
> *In the hour of the final fight.*

"The sapphire and emerald are alight, as you have mentioned, because the thrones of Medric and Dridion are currently occupied, their people united under one power. Should you ever venture to the throne rooms of those distant realms, you will find that each throne is crested with a jewel much like the ones upon the Key. And, just like on the Key, those jewels are alight as well. However, I fear the race of mortals is so depleted that the practicality of finding a descendant of the old kings is infinitesimal." Then his gaze grew fixed, as though he was musing. "But fate operates strangely indeed. As of yet the mortal throne is unoccupied, but the search to fill it rages daily, for only when it is claimed will the ruby ignite and the Key be able to open the Chamber."

Lucian sneered, suddenly vexed by the information Tartalion gave him as casually as though he mentioned it every day. "So you mean to tell me that as it stands, this Key doesn't even *work?*" Snatching it out of his pocket, he held the Key up by the teeth. The blue and emerald beams flickered in Tartalion's newly alert stare.

"We were almost killed because of something that doesn't even work?!"

"You were almost killed because of the threat the Key poses in your hands," replied Tartalion almost sleepily. "While out of Sorcerian's keep, the possibility exists that the ruby may yet ignite again and a quest for the Chamber will be launched. And that for him is a discouraging thought indeed."

"And the only way it will ignite again is if someone finds a king?"

"Or, I daresay, if a king finds *you.*"

Lucian's face contorted involuntarily into a look of utter confusion. "Well I guess we'll just sit around and wait until a king comes riding up the road then," he said, without the slightest consideration that he was still speaking to Tartalion Ignómiel. Tartalion, however, seemed more amused than anything.

"Why are we even going through all this trouble to get to Nun . . . Nundrak?—" Lucian asked.

"Nundric," corrected Tartalion.

"Whatever! Why are we even trying to get there now? What's the rush? We'll get to the Chamber and ask Sorcerian if it would be alright to camp out for a little while until we can actually open the door?"

"You are en route to Medric, dear boy, or so I have gathered," said Tartalion waving one of his long hands as if to quiet Lucian. "Not Nundric. To risk a trek to Nundric with the Key yet unusable is a silly plot. It is in Medric you will be safest. Mascorea commands the largest army in the world, larger even than Dridion, and behind the great wall of Adoram you will be well protected. It is there you will wait out the ruby. Until then, it is simply getting there that is your task. It is a difficult enough quest in itself, I fear."

A long silence fell between them. Lucian was at least thankful that Tartalion had clarified aspects of his journey that had been cloudy to him, but his heart was no more at ease. Sorcerian was out for vengeance, and Lucian was the only thing standing in his way. He passed a sweeping glance at the paintings again and nearly fainted to think that he was now part of this battle that had been waging for thousands of years.

Tartalion's voice, though he spoke softly, startled Lucian out of his trance. "Find some rest, dear boy. Tomorrow we will speak again."

Sulkily, Lucian wandered back to bed.

16

The Last Suitor

Gamaréa still saw her in his dreams—the woman named Emmanuelle, daughter of the lord Melinta of Dridion, whom he first beheld when Tartalion brought him to the king many years ago. Presenting Gamaréa before Melinta, Tartalion explained that he was strong and able, yet banished from his people because of their building notion that he was a half-breed. He assured Melinta the contrary—that he was more Morok than perhaps even Medric's generals.

"Stór is a fool," Melinta commented from his high emerald seat. "Look upon this soldier, how tall and proud he stands like a statue." He stood up to examine Gamaréa and thought highly of him, then told Tartalion in secrecy that he must first prove his worth to Dridion before he inducted Gamaréa into his forces.

When Tartalion reported back to Gamaréa in his small, prison-cell of a bedchamber, he spoke of Melinta's proposal. His daughter, Emmanuelle, was in the process of finding a proper suitor. Admirable Fairy soldiers from all reaches of the empire had come to the city to try to sway her to their hand. She had already refused a dozen, but there were more to come.

"The king has requested you as her guard," Tartalion said. "She meets the suitors in Ravelon, the enchanted wood. You must escort her there for her appointments."

"The Darkwood?" he had commented shortly.

"To you it may be known as such, but it is hallowed ground to the folk of Dridion, and your duty now is to the daughter of the king."

Thus Gamaréa did as he was charged, believing her to be the most beautiful creature he had ever seen, and though he had not gazed upon many women in his life, he was not sure there was further need. Her hair fell in sparkling, golden waves past her nimble shoulders. Draped along her body so lean and curved was her white gown, nearly transparent in the sunlight, bearing her every crevice and feature, all of which were stunning.

And from the gazebo in the midst of the enchanted wood, he watched her refuse suitor after suitor, sending them away in utter misery, most of them in inconsolable tears, and thus would lead her away to her father where she told him of her progress. For a year and a day, Gamaréa led her to Ravelon, and for a year and a day his heart secretly longed for her.

Then one day there was no suitor present, and when she brought him to the center of the gazebo where so many more admirable than him had stood, she spoke of her intentions—that she wanted him above all else, for he was the sort who let his heart and eyes speak for him, and those were, she mentioned, instruments incapable of uttering false words. And she wrapped him in her slender arms and peered into his pit-like eyes with a light igniting in her own, and kissed him passionately. It was his first kiss, and her first true one, and he felt that, should the world end that instant, he could have boasted a fuller life than many.

Gamaréa and Emmanuelle met many times in Ravelon after that moment. Twenty more suitors came to pass, and when she officially refused them, Emmanuelle would kiss Gamaréa madly. When she sent away the last of her suitors, she resolved at last to marry him, much to her father's displeasure.

"Emmy," said Melinta, "many sons of Dridion, all of excellent stock, have come this way for your hand, yet you have refused them all."

"I know who it is I want, Father," she contended. "I want the guard you've issued me to bear me toward unworthy husbands."

Melinta grew outraged and began shouting. "He is not of good stock! He is of *no* stock! He is a Morok, and what is worse, he is partly *mortal*. A Morok alone is unworthy of your hand, but a half-breed is not negotiable."

She stood furiously. "You are not the one marrying him, Father. I am. There is no need for you to stress upon my choices. The one I choose to marry is not the one who shall succeed you. That is Didrebelle's right and privilege."

"Your brother will one day be king of Dridion, but we must expand our prosperous family further. Why not Demetrious, my dear? Why not him? His family is wealthy, and his father was an acclaimed soldier once. I fought with him in countless battles."

Emmanuelle now bore an ill look. "Demetrious is a walking serpent, Father. Could you not tell by speaking with him? I could. Everything about him serpentine—"

"You speak harshly of poor Demetrious. He had traveled far to see you, my love—from his home in Idra."

"Then he will have a long journey home. Along with the rest of them. I have made my choice." Then she passed from her father's chamber, utterly displeased with his selfishness.

Just then, a figure emerged from the shadows behind Melinta, and he was tall and thin and indeed serpent-like. His hair was short and black, and his eyes were bright green, nearly yellow; his face was pale and white and fair, but his voice was hoarse and evil.

"Demetrious, my good lad," Melinta greeted him. "You know now what you must do. The Morok has turned in, and Emmanuelle will be in her chamber weeping over our discussion here. Now is the moment. Take it."

He handed him a small vial of poison. "Dispense this in the stone well of wine, there in the midst of the gazebo where she so foolishly refused you. The Morok will be with her there tomorrow, and when they drink they both shall perish, and my mind will be rid of this filth that has so ruthlessly seized it."

Demetrious started. "But, my lord, she is your

daughter—"

"She has disposed of her morals and foundations. No daughter of mine shall dwell in the house of a Morok. She is dead to me, and now you will make it so."

"And what of your other guards, my lord? What will happen should they discover me at the well?"

Melinta contemplated. "They do not patrol the woods at night; the Darkwood is no place to wander beneath the moon. Go now! The heart of night is upon us this very instant. Go now and do my will."

Without further word, Demetrious passed from the king's chamber and pressed on horseback to Ravelon where he found the gazebo pale under blue starlight, and the wine-well in the center. After emptying the contents of the vile, he started for his horse when a voice sounded from behind him.

"What are *you* doing here?"

Demetrious spun round, startled. "My good Didrebelle," he said. "Fancy seeing you here this time of night."

"I might say the same." Didrebelle studied the demeanor of Demetrious. "The word was you had left for Idra at noon . . . when my sister refused you."

The prince's words writhed in Demetrious's stomach, but Didrebelle could not see the impish gaze he bore. "I started off that way," he began, "but I came back hoping her fragrance perhaps still lingered here. My heart, I feel, shall always remain within this wood where I heard her final words. And I too am happy to have come upon you, my prince, though we must part so suddenly." He mounted his steed and was off, quickly through the night like an arrow.

The next morn, Emmanuelle brought Gamaréa to the gazebo where she planned to profess her love for him. Sunlight bathed the wood in marvelous green and gold, and the gazebo was white and glowing as ever. There was a light in her eyes like the apex of the night sky, starry and wistful, as she approached him with two chalices of wine that she had fetched from the well.

"My lady," Gamaréa said softly, "no suitors are scheduled

to meet you here today."

Emmanuelle smiled lustfully. "They are gone, never to come again."

"Then why have we come here?"

She handed Gamaréa one of the cups. He studied it as though it were the first time he had ever seen one, then shifted his incredulous gaze to the woman in front of him. "You mean to say—"

Her voice answered softly. "If you would have my hand, I would have yours and yours alone."

Speechless, he fumbled for a word, but all memory of spoken language was gone, fading into a chasm he did not even know was under him, as he looked on her and realized that she was all he ever needed, and would ever need again. And he thought of all those times he loved her and could not have her, forced to watch her listen to others who sought to take her away. He had nearly cast all thoughts of being with her from his mind. Though they shared several passionate moments in the woods, he thought, somehow, that it was merely her way of training for her *true* love, like how he trained with Tartalion for the day he would be called upon to fight. There was no practical way for him to offer her the many things her suitors had: large estates, great manners, children entirely of Fairy blood. He would never be able to give her any of those things.

Yet now she requested his hand, and, dubiously, he accepted, not realizing the mist of tears welling in his eyes as she clasped her chalice with his and drank. When her chalice was emptied, she approached him.

"You haven't drank," she said disappointedly.

"I do not care for wine, my lady."

Emmanuelle laughed drunkenly. "Then you must care for me tenfold today."

She approached him slowly as he set his chalice down, and nearly fell into his arms. But when Gamaréa gazed upon her soft, ageless face, he saw the light within her eyes was fading, and she could barely speak a word. Her weight brought even him, with all his strength, to his knees as he fumbled to grasp her tightly. Then he held her in his arms and looked down upon her face, dead though still living, every illuminated element about her completely dismembered as she strained for the slightest word. At last, she fell motionless; her eyes still and fixed on the canopy of the wood.

It was the only time in his life that Gamaréa was this horrified. Within moments, a large host of Melinta's guards surrounded the gazebo, armed and eager to locate the disturbance. It was only then that Gamaréa realized he had been screaming from his knees, Emmanuelle's body limp in his arms. Two soldiers stooped, and without a word lifted Emmanuelle from off of him and carried her away.

The others seized Gamaréa, and brought him in earnest to Melinta. In a frenzied uproar, the king accused him for the death of his daughter.

"You poisoned her," he hissed. "You filthy, half-bred rat! YOU POISONED MY DAUGHTER!"

Gamaréa could hardly speak, still baffled by the event that had occurred. In one instant, he felt he could never know sorrow again, yet in another he was bound and tried for causing the death of the one he cherished.

"No, my—" But a heavy strike wailed across his sweat-riddled face.

Just then Tartalion rushed in, filled with worry. "What is the meaning of this?" he exclaimed.

But he was greeted only by the unsheathing of Melinta's sword. "The rat you have brought me has killed my daughter. My *daughter,* Ignómiel!"

Gamaréa saw Tartalion's shoulders shrink in dismay as his eyes so sullenly looked upon him, flanked by two soldiers holding him by the elbows before the king. "Gamaréa?" he said with grief-filled incredulity. "Is this—is this . . . *true?*"

The Morok was silent—hanging between the guards completely and utterly defeated.

"He is silent," said the king. "He knows what he has—"

"It wasn't him, Father," said a voice from the doors. The young prince, Didrebelle, approached. "Just last night I saw Demetrious here, at the gazebo, leaning over the wine-well."

"That is nonsense," Melinta sneered. "He returned to Idra after your sister disposed of him."

"Then who else did I see last night? A specter, perhaps?"

"Do not speak so rashly to me, son. I am your king foremost; your father secondly."

Gamaréa recalled the name that Didrebelle had spoken of. *Demetrious. The last suitor. The one Melinta had said was the most promising.* Didrebelle then became the first thing Gamaréa had taken to paying full attention to.

Tartalion spoke. "Your answer is there, then, king," he said. "I see no further need for explanation than that. A rejected suitor returned vengefully to the place from which his love had cast him—to smite her."

"And I do not think he acted alone," added Didrebelle, passing a suspicious, hard gaze to his father.

Melinta became aggressive. "I will not stand here and be accused of the murder of my own daughter, if that is what you are implying! Is it this—this Morok—this half-breed—that has committed this heinous act! He should be killed."

Now it was Tartalion's blade that rung, and he stepped forward filled with rage. "He has done nothing!"

It was then that every guard present took to brandishing his own weapon, and for a moment ringing steel was the only sound heard.

"Be still!" cried Melinta. "All of you." Then he directed his guards to send Gamaréa away to the dungeon where he would await trial.

When they were gone, the king was left to face Tartalion alone. "You possess a special sort of gall to draw your weapon on me openly, Ignómiel," he said. "Do you not recall our history? You were the highest companion of my father's—"

"—and your father is not here," interjected Tartalion sternly. "He is the lucky one. I wonder what he would think of his son now."

It was as though Tartalion's words had slapped Melinta across his long and sunken face. "What are you saying, general?"

An eternity seemed to pass before Tartalion answered,

"I am not a general anymore."

Their eyes locked then, their swords hanging idly in their hands. "What are you saying?"

"That you are not as your father was," Tartalion answered plainly. "You are aggressive and ridiculous and think with your sword. You know all too well that Gamaréa is innocent, and that Demetrious smote Emmanuelle—you just refuse to accept it. It is easier to condemn a Morok to death than the son of a wealthy family of Dridion, a family with whom you so tirelessly seek to combine."

Melinta clapped mockingly. "The rumors of your intelligence have not wavered. There are bigger things at work here, however—"

"Bigger even than the murder of your own daughter?"

"Do you not see, Ignómiel?" Melinta was growing outraged. "Do you not see what I am trying to accomplish? I am trying to expand my father's empire, trying to stretch it eastward to the coast so that the breadth of Dridion *is* the west. There is a storm coming, you know. All the foes of the Netherworld are gathering as we speak and when they are swollen with dark forces they will come for us all. We must gain as many allies as we can while time remains."

"War and murder is not—"

"Only the strong remain after a war. This is our chance, Ignómiel—our one opportunity to send our forces eastward and gain allies."

"And if they do not concede?"

Melinta glared at his sword's edge, broad and sharp and riddled with the runes of Fairies. "There are many ways to make them concede."

"You underestimate the Moroks, especially the prisoner you have just condemned. They are a proud people, and will not stand for your selfishness. Not to mention your lack of cause to plod there."

Melinta looked at him with a surprised glance. "My apologies, former general, but did one of their own not just murder my little girl? I believe that is a handy cause for war, do you not? The savage murder of a king's only daughter!"

Tartalion stepped back, afraid now of the evil that had encompassed Melinta's eyes. "This is madness!" he exclaimed. "You will bring this land to ruin, and disgrace the name of your house."

With that, Tartalion stormed out, and paraded through the corridors until he came upon the dungeon where Gamaréa was locked and bound and freed him with little difficulty.

They were long into their flight away from Melinta's hall when Tartalion spoke for the first time. "I will lead you to Ravelon," he said, "but no further. From there, it is imperative you return to Medric. You are ready enough now, and prepared to face whatever demons forced you away. There are many provinces outside Adoram where honest folk can make a small living. You might try to explore such an avenue. It is an abrupt ending to our fine tale, but I trust we will reunite in due time."

Then they parted, and for many hundreds of years Ignómiel and his apprentice remained separated. In time, though, the Morok learned of Tartalion's separation from Dridion, and his eventual trek across the west to the coast of the Mid Sea, where with his fleet of a thousand ships he ferried his company eastward where he founded a city of his own. The city, they said, called Elderland.

She walked up through the woods. A light was shining behind her, high and sharp and golden and there was whiteness in its center, like the eye of the sun. Her gown was flowing, white like snow, her hair a bursting, unearthly flare of glaring crimson. And even from a distance, he could see her eyes, splintering and green and full of life. All else under her seemed to spread away, creating the path upon which she walked toward him, smooth and soft for her feet were bare. And he was standing in his lonesome, mounted in the wood as though on a platform, and when he looked he noticed he was on the gazebo, and the wine-well was under him, and it bore the contents of blood.

Gamaréa awoke abruptly, looking left and right, not realizing where he was at first. He saw the sunlight peering through a window across the way, and remembered finally that he was in Elderland. The bedchamber was empty but for one of Tartalion's maids, who had become startled by his outburst. Lucian and Jem's beds were neat and tidy, and he wondered what time it truly was. He dressed and went downstairs where he was pleased to find solitude. Lighting his pipe, he sat in a comfortable chair and closed his eyes in thought, singing an old song to himself in his mind.

Your name I hear
In dreams, in dreams
Alas, you cannot call for me
That precious face
In dreams, in dreams
Lies just beyond my furthest reach
And I so brave, in dreams
Cannot find strength enough to pass along
The solemn streets we once had walked,
The hallowed ground where love was lost.

His mind trudged on. The dream had riled new concerns within him, and he pressed his thoughts on the perils of the roads beyond Elderland, and though there were several routes they could take, there was no way safer than the next. Obstacles would meet them on every path. Of this, he was certain.

The boys, he felt, were unprepared for their necessary venture out of Elderland. Lucian and Jem nearly died of fright when confronted by one soldier of the Matarhim—how would they fair when facing hundreds? Thousands? Not much seemed to bode well in their cases.

It was common knowledge to be wary of mountain passes, as the climes were treacherous and steep, especially in the East, though he knew this to be only rumor. Yet, this information excluded two or three options Gamaréa wished he had. Now the roads would be long and winding, and none could be certain what perils lurked in the valleys and caves and deep, uncharted woodlands. He deemed finally that a road without access to a mountain pass could not be planned with any great accuracy, therefore he did not think much more on the matter.

Just as he was about to get up to leave, he saw Tartalion approaching. "Ignómiel," Gamaréa said startled, and poured the contents of his pipe hurriedly onto his lap. The hot leaves and ash burned his thighs, and a pained expression issued over his face.

"You know my thoughts about smoking indoors," said Tartalion, though his tone did not suggest he was angry.

Gamaréa apologized. "My mind seems to have escaped me."

"I daresay it is best you reclaim it. You're going to need it before long, if you are to lead your company to Medric unscathed."

"There lies my worry," Gamaréa grimaced.

"Lucian?"

"Both of them. The only certainty of our road from here is that it will be perilous."

Tartalion nodded. "As are many roads. It is how we fair upon them that defines who we are."

Gamaréa laughed inwardly. *Glory.* Folk wasted their lives trying to make glory out of a purposeless cause, and he knew this. "I am not here for glory, Ignómiel, you know that."

"Yet if you weather your path, glory will be yours whether you accept it or not. Your name will be written in scriptures for thousands of years to come. The name *Gamaréa* will forever be a fixture in the minds of the many."

"As it will be should I fail them." Then his gaze grew weary, and Tartalion noted how truly exhausted his former pupil seemed. "Against his masses, victory seems folly," he added.

"My son, things are not always as they seem. You know that. A time comes in every man's life—when he is born, when he dies—but a time comes for only few when he lives. You know what you must do—"

Tartalion's voice broke off then and became sullen. "I fear for Elderland, my son," he said. "Sorcerian's forces have already docked and have sought passage through the mountains. I have dispatched troops to meet them there, but I fear their efforts are faltering. The host of Nundric is many, and I fear in time swords and arrows will be of no more use. Before long their lines will break, and passage into Elderland and all the lands beyond granted."

"Then we will risk no road through the mountains," said Gamaréa confirmatively.

"I am afraid," began Tartalion, "that in time those passageways will be teeming with forces of the Netherworld. And one cannot be certain, either, of other paths. I do not follow the happenings of further lands nearly as avidly as I once did, but I would assume fighting has broken out elsewhere."

It was inevitable to somehow dodge fighting, or so it seemed. The more talk spread of warpaths, the more Gamaréa realized all roads would be toilsome, and to endeavor merely half of them would be an accomplishment in itself.

"You have plotted a course along the coast, however," continued Tartalion. "At least that is what I have heard from the gentlemen who came with you."

"When my ship docked," started Gamaréa, "there was no port, no town for many leagues. There were eighty mariners aboard with little food or trappings fit for travel. The Captain told me he would follow the upper reaches of the coast in hope to find a decent enough town or port, though I'm not sure if there are any from the sound of things."

"Then perhaps higher ground would serve you well," mused Tartalion. "At least you may find a vantage point that could reveal the coastline for many leagues. You may yet find your ship, though I am not entirely sure that is the only thing that vexes you." Then Tartalion said the very thing Gamaréa hoped he would dismiss. "You are thinking, too, of Emmanuelle," he said. "I have only known you to take up this ridiculous habit,"—he eyed Gamaréa pipe disdainfully—"when her face enters your thoughts."

He saw from Gamaréa's fleeting stare that he had been.

"I dreamt of her again," he said.

Tartalion reached a hand to Gamaréa's shoulder. "You must let her go, my son. Her death, sorrowful though it was, is centuries passed."

"Referring to me as *Darkwood* does not help matters," said Gamaréa numbly. "I wish it were an easy task to forget her, but she will stay with me always, until my days are done."

"Then you will always be *Darkwood,* I am afraid." Tartalion rose then as if to leave, and extended one hand as if to help Gamaréa to his feet. "Come," he said, genially. "I know just the thing to set your mind at ease a bit. The feast will be upon us soon, and there are quite a few surprises."

17

Surprises and Feasts

Lucian Rolfe had ventured off to Elderland's eastern reaches. There he came upon a fine garden that was sparkling beneath the high afternoon sun. For a time, he walked there casually, then took to laying in the soft grass to watch the clouds slug along.

He forgot about the Key here, though it was still lodged in his pocket. Atop the hill where he rested, he could see for a great distance. Tartalion's palace was still highly visible—its white towers glimmering far away.

After drowsing for nearly half an hour, he then carried on walking. In time, he came upon an orchard that was littered with mouthwatering, plump apples. Excited, he climbed one of the smaller trees and began eating, despite Tartalion's approaching feast. They were perhaps the sweetest and juiciest apples he had ever tasted, and after three fist-sized helpings, he decided he hadn't any room for a fourth.

He stayed there and thought awhile of the things that were to come. It was as plain to him as it would ever be that the most-sought item in the world now sat hidden in his pocket. It was disquieting knowledge indeed, yet even more troubling was the fact that he was consequently the most-sought individual. Tartalion was right: Time does work in odd ways. And in fact, there seemed to be no window between Lucian's normal life and the one he was now trapped in, and he mused how in the blink of an eye one's entire life can change.

Yet somehow, the orchard worked to ameliorate his worries, though he feared they would never subside completely. This distant reach of Elderland soothed him, and it was as though some invisible force crept up through his every orifice and carried out the turmoil writhing within him. Could he be granted one wish, it would be to remain there until the end of days.

Not since his life before the Key had he felt so at peace. He felt that his adolescence had been devoured by the relentless force of adulthood much too soon—forced against his will to become a man when was yet to complete the best years of his youth. In only a week's time, the world was presented to him in such grandeur that the mere thought of its enormity made a queasy feeling boil up inside him. What compounded his weariness, however, was the knowledge that it would grow larger still.

In much too short a time, the dinner bell tolled.

A great company gathered for Tartalion's feast in the courtyard before the Citadel, and Lucian saw the beacon Tartalion had mentioned in the wee hours of the morning, though after he had returned to bed he dismissed it as a dream. The roof of the Citadel, like so many other structures in Elderland, had a spherical roof wrought with clear windows. The beacon sprouted out of the center like a great white beam, pointing high toward the evening sky—a glittering, blue light flaring from its pinnacle like a sapphire sun.

Many who were present were of Tartalion's council or some other branch of high-ranking Elderland officer. Gamaréa was also there, accompanied by Didrebelle and Jem, who had come in from the separate corners of the city having done his own exploring. It took the Fairy Lord a great while to reach the table, across which the lavish meal was displayed upon a long, decorative, heavy-wooded, midnight-blue table, which complemented the gleaming white plates and golden utensils wonderfully.

The courtyard stirred with the welcoming commotion of excited voices. In time, Tartalion gathered everyone's attention, and the entirety of the feasters collected themselves and filed toward the center, as though it were some ritual. Tartalion then stretched out his arms, and the others around his table clasped hands with each other, whether friend or stranger. Then, the lord welcomed all to his feast, and paid special heed to Jemstine Fryer, Gamaréa, and Lucian Rolfe, to whose honorable mission they were to feast to that evening.

Then suddenly he exclaimed, "I cannot forget! There are tidings from the South!" He scampered away, and returned with three guests, hooded, and clothed in the finest garb of Elderland.

When they came further forward, they walked toward the boys.

"They have been delivered by the Sagess Dymitri, herself, guardian of the woodland realms of earth," said Tartalion, cheerfully, as though this were commonplace. "You see, boys—you've more friends than you think."

The guests revealed themselves, and when the boys were finally clear of the wave of shock and breathtaking emotions, they realized they stood before Macintosh MaDungal, Samuel Fryer, and Mary Rolfe, among a small band of other townsfolk who had been rescued from Amar.

It seemed like ages that they stood embracing—tears streaming in rapid currents down each of their faces. It had actually been the first time—or so Lucian could remember—that he had actually seen MaDungal shed any kind of tear. Mary was overwhelmed and held on to Lucian tighter perhaps than his own mother would have, as the Fryers wept too in joyous reunion—Samuel's big, burly arms clasping firmly around Jem, and Jem's face turning slightly purple.

The company at Tartalion's table had been standing and cheering the entire time, and rallied around their reuniting neighbors happily. It took nearly an hour for the feast to begin, as the final guests settled and the night went on—for once without the thought of sorrow and despair.

After great length, their supper was ended, and many sought rest in their respective rooms. Lucian and Jem, however, were awake well into the night conversing with the loved ones with whom they were reunited. To them, it was a phenomenon similar to speaking with the dead. Even Gamaréa expressed his surprise to find Mary, Samuel, and Macintosh alive and virtually well—certain that they had fallen with Amar.

He walked past the reunited families, overhearing many things.

"An enormous white light just came through the room," Mary was saying. "I thought it was the end—the very end! But I felt myself being lifted and carried away, and when I was able to see again I was here."

Samuel Fryer was ranting on near his son. "Damn things nearly scared me to death before they actually tried to kill me. They were right in front of me when the light came. It— it was the strangest thing, boy. It was the brightest light I'd ever seen."

Lucian stayed with Mary until she went to sleep. Together they sat and talked for hours in her bedroom, and she shared stories of his childhood—tales that Lucian remembered vaguely, if at all.

"I remember you had such a fear of going to the bathroom," she laughed. "You were so afraid of going that you would wait until the very last moment. Then you would go right in your pants!"

Lucian was embarrassed, to say the least, but was grateful no one else was in the room. Mary shared similar stories until she retired. Then Lucian went and found Macintosh MaDungal, who—to no one's surprise—was in Tartalion's drinking quarters with a horde of glowing Fairies, Gamaréa, and the Fryers.

"Mr. Rolfe, my boy!" shouted MaDungal somewhat drunkenly. "I was wondering when yeh'd get down here."

"Well," replied Lucian, "I see it hasn't taken you long to find the ale. An uncanny ability . . . "

"Now look here, fella—" MaDungal held up his pint with a wobbly hand, "there's nothin' wrong with enjoying a little home-brewed . . . what's this place called?"—Lucian reminded him—"*Elderland* ale! Better than the Eveland brew, I daresay." He whispered this last part, as though not to offend anyone.

Some nearby Fairies held up their glasses in approval, though none of them were quite as intoxicated as old MaDungal, if they were even able to become intoxicated at all. But this time, Mac had every right to be.

Gamaréa laughed. "You're a bartender, are you?"

"You bet, lad," answered Macintosh. A sullen gaze then crossed his face.

Recognition reached Gamaréa's face. "That's right," he said, remembering. "Yours was the pub in Amar,"—he looked to Lucian—"the one we met in."

Lucian nodded, though his brow furrowed. Thinking of the pub filled him with grief, and he could see that MaDungal's cheeks flushed more so than they had been, for he too was saddened by its mentioning.

"*Was*, I should say," said MaDungal sadly. "A bartender isn't worth much without a bar."

Feeling awkward, Gamaréa excused himself. "Well," he said, embarrassed to have lessened the mood. "I need another pint. Anyone else?"

But Lucian and MaDungal were yet to finish theirs. Beside them, Samuel Fryer nearly choked on his sip of ale, as though something MaDungal said startled or offended him in mid-gulp.

"That's nonsense, all that, by the way!" he shouted in protest. "There are bars everywhere, but bar*tenders*—now that's another story."

MaDungal grumbled a small laugh. "Aye, Sam," he replied, "but the pub was a part of me. Now she's gone." He took another swig. "I suppose it was meant to be; I was gettin' too old for that job, anyway."

Lucian scoffed. "You're talking crazy, Mac. You loved the job and you know it. You can't quit."

"Well there's nothing much anyone can do *now*. The pub is gone. The town is gone. Don't think we'll be seeing the likes of Amar any time soon. It's a damn shame, I'll say—a damn shame. One day yeh're sittin' down enjoying a fine meal, and the next yeh're . . . yeh know—at war, I guess."

Gamaréa returned with a new glass. "The world has been at war for quite some time," he corrected, "though it has spread to the east only recently."

MaDungal wasn't buying it. "Well I don't know what for. It's not like the entire *world* is at fault for all its troubles. Just get rid o' the troublemakers, I say."

MaDungal then carried on into a highly opinionated rant without allowing anyone else's opinion to filter in. Lucian tried numerous times to tell him that the Key he had showed him weeks ago was the central cause for the "troubles" the world was at war over, but MaDungal refused to believe it.

In time, most of the company retired and gradually tapered away until Lucian and MaDungal were the only ones left in the room.

"What do you suppose will become of all this?" Lucian asked him.

MaDungal snorted. *"This?"* he slurred. "Who knows? I suppose you an' I will jest stay in this place with all these fair folk until things settle."

Lucian was silent. No part of him wanted to sink MaDungal's heart any deeper, but he knew he could not lie or disregard the matter.

"I can't stay, Mac," he said heavily.

MaDungal was in mid-sip when he choked. Gathering himself, he turned his reddened face to Lucian with an expression of sheer disbelief. "What do yeh mean yeh can't stay?"

"I mean just that," said Lucian plainly, though he feared he came off a bit sharply, for MaDungal seemed to flinch. Lucian continued in a lighter tone. "Gamaréa says I have to take this Key and go with him."

"That odd fellow?" MaDungal's droopy eyes alluded to the direction in which Gamaréa had left. "A little out to lunch, that one, if yeh ask me."

Lucian laughed lightly. "Regardless, Mac, I have to do what he says."

MaDungal sat back perturbed. "But this world ain't no place fer a boy, Lucian. It's too big and angry for a young lad like you. Yeh'll be killed out there."

"I guess it's my time, Mac—my time to grow and what not." But not even Lucian believed the words that came out of his mouth.

"I can't even be sure," he continued. "I don't even know what I'm saying."

Anxiety grabbed hold of him and he stood pestered by sorrow and despair. "I—I have to go to bed." He began to walk away, even as Macintosh MaDungal called for him to return.

Lucian stood on the balcony of his room, looking out into the night. From there he could see Jem and Samuel seizing the second chance the Sage Dymitri granted them, as they were walking around not far from the palace.

He was upset with himself for the way he ended his talk with MaDungal, but the oddest sensation had crept over him as he sat there: the Key had begun throbbing in his pocket for the first time in Elderland, causing him to abruptly flee. It had subsided to near nothingness now, but just the fact that it had acted up was troubling him.

In time, he stepped away from the window and let Jem and his father be. He readied himself for bed, blew out the light and slid beneath the covers. Taking the Key into bed with him, he held it above his face. The blue and green lights gleamed heavily in the blackened room and lit it as though it were day.

Suddenly Gamaréa bounded through, startling Lucian, who slid the Key under his pillow.

"What is it?" Lucian asked, half annoyed.

"News," replied Gamaréa shortly. He ventured to the balcony doors, opened them and stepped outside, lighting his pipe.

Lucian could not believe his eyes. "I guess courtesy isn't popular in Medric?" He could not believe the amount of inconsideration Gamaréa was displaying.

But, unfazed, Gamaréa blew a puff of smoke into the night. "What's the matter with *you*?"

Lucian recoiled, and held his tongue, which had grown

aggressive. "Nothing," he said. "I—I'm sorry."

Gamaréa blew out another wisp of smoke. "I'm sorry to lay this upon you in such fashion, but we are to depart at noon tomorrow."

"Noon?" exclaimed Lucian, who had come on to the balcony to meet him. "Why do we have to leave so early? We've only just arrived! What about Mary and MaDung—"

"They will remain here, Lucian." Gamaréa's tone was sharp. "Tartalion has sensed that the warpath will branch out further toward Elderland in a matter of days. If we are here, Lucian, they will find us. Elderland is not capable of parrying organized attacks. The city no longer bears the weaponry or manpower. We must not bring war to a defenseless kingdom."

Lucian stammered. "We are not bring—but the beacon! The beacon will hold them off."

"The beacon once kept forces of the Netherworld at bay, Lucian, but the foes in the mountains are of different stock. They will not shudder under its beam. Any place that bears the Key and its keeper is subject to battle. We must flee. Noon is a sufficient time to set out, though I fear even then may be too late for my liking."

Lucian's tone shifted to near desperation. "And what should I say to MaDungal? What should I say to Mary?"

Gamaréa's answer was plain. "Tell them the truth. Tell them what your true cause is."

"*I* don't even know what my true cause is—how can I explain it to others?"

Lucian had inadvertently gotten in the face of the Morok, as if to match him fist for fist, but when he realized his aberration he quickly recoiled.

Gamaréa blew a cloud of smoke into Lucian's face. "Firstly, take a step back." Lucian stepped aside coughing.

"You know your cause better than anyone—" Gamaréa continued, "whether you can put it into words or not is your own business. But regardless of whether or not you tell your loved ones, they will find out eventually. News has a way of traveling on the wind."

Lucian stood contemplating, and then a hint of sudden

realization fell upon his fair yet dreary face. "Will they be safe here in Elderland?"

"As long as they are under Tartalion's protection they will be fine," Gamaréa insisted. "Once the Key is gone, attacks will not be plotted on this realm. You must rest. I will send for you a couple hours after sunrise. Sleep well. It will be the best sleep you receive for a while."

18

The Departure

There was fire. Fire and darkness. Black masses creeping through the nearby wood, their shapes perceivable as they approached the lights of the beacon. Lucian watched them from his balcony. In Amar or Elderland? He could not see. He could not see behind or around him. His gaze was forced headlong, where there were the shapes approaching the hill before the great beam of the Citadel, advancing with no intention to stop. Did they know they could not pass there? Did they not see their way was blocked? So unknowingly, they crept onward. They mounted the hill. Now they swarmed over it. Now they saw him on the balcony, and the light of the beacon flickered and went out. Then they were upon him and wrestled the Key away.

Lucian woke in Gamaréa's arms, screaming. His eyes darted in every direction, as though he did not realize where he was. Near the bed, the balcony doors were closed. Sunlight peered through the glass.

"You were dreaming," said Gamaréa. "An awful one, I suspect."

Lucian rose wearily and clasped his head in his hands. "You've no idea." Then he remembered what the Morok had told him the night before. *This will do,* "Is it so close to noon?" he asked.

"Closer than I wished to fetch you," he said, almost sadly. "Are you readied?"

"I guess I'm as ready as I'll ever be."

Lucian then became contemplative. "But I have to see

Mary before I go," he said frankly, "and—and Jem as well."

The Morok looked at him, surprised. "Jem?"

He could hear the sadness in Lucian's voice. "I don't think he should follow us from here. I—it's too dangerous for him. Besides, there really isn't any need for him to put himself in danger."

"Then it is up to you to tell him—" It was then Gamaréa saw the tears building in Lucian's eyes. "Why have you come to this decision so suddenly?" he ventured to ask.

But Lucian, in fact, could not answer Gamaréa. Not even he knew why he felt this way. The very heart of him longed for Jemstine Fryer to be alongside him through every peril he would face from there, but he knew that his concentration would not entirely be devoted to the mission. He knew he would constantly be bending his thoughts on Jem—his wellbeing, strength, and health.

"I just think it's best he stays here," Lucian said softly.

Didrebelle was in the armory at sunrise, and it was there he stayed for a great while; long after his companions had risen and dispersed to separate areas to distribute their farewells. There he inspected several bows of various lengths. There were two that were much too short for his long arms, and another still too long. It was long before he found one that suited him well enough, as he was somewhat of a connoisseur of good bows and understood just what to look for in a proper one.

The bow he selected was just taller than waist-height, and the wood it was made of was smooth and tan, and twinkled with a light glaze. *This will do,* he thought to himself. He lifted it as though he were about to fire and bent the string, determining that it was to his liking even more. *This will do indeed,* he thought smugly.

A voice sung from behind him. "That was *my* bow," said Tartalion, "when I was a young soldier."

Didrebelle's gaze was now full of wonder. "It must have served you well for you to have displayed it this way." He noted the golden wall-mount Tartalion had hung it by.

"Indeed," answered Tartalion. "I remember the first

battle in which it served me, but that was a countless age ago."

Didrebelle slipped the bow back on to its mount and stepped back, his eyes still fixed on it. "I was hoping it was a spare," he said. "I would have selected it for myself."

Tartalion looked confused. "Has someone said you cannot?"

Didrebelle grew excited, and a childish wonder filled his eyes. "You mean—"

"What use do I have for a bow of any kind, Dragontamer? Those days are well behind me; it must serve its destined purpose now. Take it, and use it well. I trust that it will bring you great victories."

Didrebelle took it up and fastened it across his back in a leather sling.

"Now, then," said Tartalion, clapping his hands together. "Do you have your blades?" asked Tartalion.

"I have."

Didrebelle drew slender scimitars that had been in their crossing sheaths on his back.

"Ah, the Dridion scimitar, I see," replied Tartalion. "And of excellent craft as well. Who is to say you are unprepared?"

The young Fairy's look then grew sullen. "I suppose there is not a true way to prepare for something such as this—this war to end all wars."

"That is why there is such a thing as courage, my boy. Such a thing as intrepidity. Without the understanding of fear, no man may call himself fearless."

Didrebelle returned his blades to their sheaths. "I suppose, Ignómiel. It troubles me so, that I will almost certainly cross paths with my father again—he who has grown so corrupt and hateful. I trust he will not receive my return there welcomingly—not since I fled to the East with your company."

Tartalion laid a gentle grasp upon his shoulder. "My dear child," he said, "you bore enough years to make your own choice. It was your only chance to make your stand. You know he framed Gamaréa in Ravelon. You know he tried to make it seem as though he killed Emmanuelle. And he did so to gain a motive for waging war with Medric. He sacrificed his own flesh and blood for his own cause—so that he may expand his empire; an empire built on lies. I would have been much more curious if you had *not* fled."

"Indeed my heart has filled with hate for him." Didrebelle's tone was grave, and Tartalion noticed that his fists were clenched with fury. "I am not sure my eyes can bear his sight."

"Stay your course, Dragontamer," replied Tartalion coolly, placing a hand on Didrebelle's shoulder. "Make decisions when they need to be made and no sooner." He smiled. It was a smile behind which hid sadness and strife.

"I must go for now; I must see to your companions."

"And that is why I must go," finished Lucian Rolfe, taking the Key from the table in front of him and returning it to his pocket. It took nearly an hour for him to finish telling Mary the story behind the Key, and how he found it, and what he was now charged to do, and she sat beside him in disbelief, the color completely flushed from her wrinkled skin. They were conversing in a brightly lit foyer toward the rear of Tartalion's palace, and from the hanging window at their left the Citadel loomed, tall and wondrous, the beacon alight and shining with the day.

"You will be traveling with that Morok you've been speaking of?" she asked. "The fellow who rescued you from the town?"

"Yes." He sensed the worry in her voice. "He's very knowledgeable of the world and its evils—knows the bad roads and what not. He won't take us down those paths."

Mary sighed. "From what I've been hearing, my dear, there are more than you think."

Lucian nodded. "And that number will increase if we wait any longer."

Mary seemed downtrodden and weary, as if every word that Lucian spoke hurt her physically. "So many roads," she whispered. "So many evils. I hadn't thought this world was in such a bind."

Lucian at first said nothing. Instead, he sat and thought

of the world as he had known it for the last seventeen years—peaceful without the slightest hint that it bore other qualities. His town, which seemed so big and broad, was but a microscopic fragment amidst the true mass of earth.

"It's my task to complete," he said at last. "And I have to take it to Medric by whatever road Gamaréa leads us down."

Mary looked at him in a way she hadn't before. It was not a sad glare, or of one who is deeply upset—instead there seemed to be pride in the way her eyes were studying him, and he felt no longer like the child he had been at the inn.

"Alright, Lucian," she replied softly, as though giving him permission to spend the night at Jem's house. "If it's what you must do, then I suppose you should do it." Her face then winced as if to cry. Covering it with a hand, she began sobbing.

Lucian knelt before her. "Don't cry, Mary," he said sadly. "I'll be with Gamaréa; he'll protect me. When it's all over—" Then he refrained, uncertain as to whether or not to complete his statement. He did anyway. "When it's all over I'll come back."

She nodded her head, her face with all the trappings of someone who knew what to say but did not know how to pile it into words. She could only hold him, as she did when he was a child, and their embrace was warm and sincere and long. When they came undone she reached into her pocket and pulled out a necklace—a string of leather to which the medallion of a small, silver lion was tied, prancing with its head back to roar. She tied it around his neck.

"This was Mr. Rolfe's," she said. "He always wanted to give this to his son. I want you to have it. *He* would have wanted you to have it."

Though he didn't speak, Lucian was entirely grateful for the gift, and he looked at Mary with sadness, and felt similar to the way he had felt before his very first day of school. He did not want to go. He was afraid that, if he went, he would never see Mary again. Fear flooded through him, a horror such as he had never known. Lucian wanted to implore Mary to make him stay, as though he were still a child—to refuse to let him go.

But it was Mary who made to speak first. "Lucian, I . . . when you came to me, there was a letter . . . concealed within your cloths. I believe it was from your mother . . . "

Lucian studied Mary's morose face. Her eyes stared blankly.

"I've kept it all these years," she continued, as though ashamed. "I never thought it a proper time to tell you . . . "

"From my mother?" Lucian repeated incredulously.

"It was destroyed in the fire, but I remember it word for word. It said—"

But from the Citadel now a great horn blasted, summoning the group that was to depart at noon.

"Another time, then," said Mary, sadly, shedding a final tear before Lucian sped reluctantly away.

It rang up occasionally as Lucian made for the Citadel. On his way, he looked for Jem but could not find him anywhere, wandering through every wing and every corridor of the palace in search. Gamaréa caught up with him when Lucian entered the eastern wing. "Come," he said. "I must take you to the armory."

Lucian inquired, nearly disbelievingly, "Armory? You never said we'd actually par*take* in fighting. Are weapons necessary?"

The Morok looked at him baffled, as though the answer should have been obvious.

"You're right," he answered. "I suppose our politeness and striking features *are* rather difficult to resist; our enemies will be sure to allow us passage."

"But I've never held a sword," said Lucian worriedly, completely ignoring the Morok's sarcasm.

"No need to worry. It wasn't long after I first held a sword that I was engaged in battle." They had now come upon the armory—a spacious room of glossy stone and glittering steel. The walls ran high until they arched to a spherical roof, upon which an enormous, curving window displayed the morning sky. It had become a lovely day indeed. Hanging upon every wall were an abundance of weapons and armor. They were more like artwork than crafts of war, Lucian realized—something about the way the sun peered in through the window and glinted off the iron and steel gave each individual piece of weaponry a profound glamour. It was unfortunate, thought Lucian, that their purpose was antonymous to their beauty.

Gamaréa was busying himself with sorting through swords when he suddenly lifted one up to show Lucian. The blade was of sizable length, and the hilt was a marvelously glistening gold, wrought with Fairy runes running horizontally along the hilt.

"Take it," said Gamaréa, as though distributing a gift.

Lucian hesitantly reached out his hand and took up the sword. Initially, he was surprised at its extreme lightness, for upon first glance the sword appeared very broad and heavy.

"It's incredibly light!" he exclaimed.

"The steel of the Fairies is the lightest element the world has ever seen. It would take a man of great strength to wield this blade effectively had it been forged in the fires of mortals or Moroks."

"Why is their steel so light?"

Suddenly Didrebelle entered, leaping up like a feline onto a high ridge of the armory where he began examining bows, though one was already fastened to his back. "Our steel was once forged by the fires of Zynys itself," he said. "The High Lord Ation has enchanted it so that the blades would be both lethal *and* light—as you can see."

Gamaréa looked up at him. "Have you been here this whole time?" he asked.

"Nearly since sunrise—"

"This is amazing!" Lucian exclaimed happily, waving the sword around as though in combat with the air.

"Will you be *careful*?" Gamaréa scolded. "We've already discussed how lethal Zynian steel is."

"I'm sorry," Lucian laughed, "it's just the first time I've ever held a sword."

"Well there will be plenty of time for that once we take to

our way—and you won't be swinging it at air, I assure you."

Didrebelle leapt down to meet them. "Must you be so hard on the boy?" he said. "Still your tongue and we will only just *assume* you are old."

Gamaréa missed the humor, and looked as though he was about to respond when Tartalion entered.

"There you are," he said, nearly relieved. "I've been in endless search for you three. Have you made your selections?"

"Nearly, my lord," said Gamaréa. "Lucian here has chosen his blade."

Tartalion walked over to Lucian and held up the blade he bore. He sighed in awe of his own craft.

"Excebellus," he said admiringly. "How incredibly curious."

Tartalion's reaction puzzled Gamaréa—and Didrebelle too, apparently—for they each wore perplexed expressions.

"Curious, Ignómiel?" inquired Didrebelle.

"Curious indeed, Dragontamer—this being only a recent addition to the armory. It was . . . given to me by . . . well, let us just say, for all intents and purposes, a friend." Tartalion's gaze grew distant, and it seemed as though he were attempting to piece a puzzle together in his mind. His voice startled them when he spoke again, genially. "May it serve you well, Lucian Rolfe, may she serve you well indeed. And what about you, Gamaréa? What weapon have you chosen?"

His abrupt change of subject only added to their confusion.

"I have already come equipped, my lord," answered Gamaréa. Tartalion stared admiringly for a moment at Dawnbringer resting at Gamaréa's waist.

Tartalion shifted his attention to Didrebelle. "You, my son, are here now for a second time. Are you displeased with your choice of bow?"

"Not in the least, Ignómiel," said Didrebelle. "I too was in search of my companions and only fell upon them moments ago. But I cannot stray from examining the crafts within this room. Each one is grander than the next."

"Indeed, indeed! And what of armor, my friends? Have you made your choices?"

"Not yet," said Gamaréa. "We were about to."

"Good. When you have readied yourself, I ask that you make your way into the courtyard; the crowd to see you off is massing."

Gamaréa instructed Lucian as to the proper coat of mail to acquire, and the three then fastened themselves with what they saw fitting. Tartalion issued his expertise as they were fitting themselves with jerkins and wrist-plates, and when they were entirely readied, the group made as if to leave the armory together, when Tartalion pulled Gamaréa aside and waited until the others were out of earshot.

"You must listen closely, Gamaréa," said Tartalion earnestly. "It was not by chance that Lucian came upon that sword."

"You mean to say the one your 'friend' gave you?" Gamaréa's tone suggested there was more to the story than Tartalion had let on.

"Perhaps a week ago I was visited by Charon himself, who appeared to me in his true likeness and nearly frightened me blind. He told me of the passage Lucian would take from Amar, and the role you would play in leading him. Why Lucian is so dear to Zynys he would not say, though I have my suspicions. Excebellus was with him. He brandished it as if to smite me where I sat, but merely ordered me to assure that it passed into Lucian's keep."

"Running some last minute errands before abandoning us for good, I see," said Gamaréa bitterly.

Tartalion bore a confused expression.

"They appeared to me as well," he continued. "In my cabin on the galley on which I crossed the sea."

"They?"

"There were three," said Gamaréa, recalling. "Nephromera, Nepsus, and Charon. They stressed their affection for Lucian as well . . . "

The horn blew loudly from outside.

"That is odd indeed," mused Tartalion. "There may be many fascinating things that are brought to light before the end, my son. Until then, keep Lucian close, and guard him with your life. He is precious cargo to the Sages, apparently."

Again the horn blew.

"We should get out there," Gamaréa suggested. "It must be nearly noon."

Tartalion agreed, and together they passed through the great length of his palace, their footsteps echoing through the empty halls. The main doors were open to the courtyard, upon which the sun beamed off every element that was there. Before the doors they saw Lucian and Didrebelle conversing. Didrebelle was moving his hands around animatedly, and Lucian was issuing a frightened-looking smile.

"About time," said Didrebelle when he saw the two coming. "We thought one of you fell in . . . "

Just as they were about to advance through the doors, however, a familiar voice shouted from the high ridge of the nearby stairwell.

"Lucian!" called Jem Fryer, exasperatedly.

Jem's mere exclamation of Lucian's name nearly shattered every bone that was in his body. He had hoped, once his tireless search for Jem came up empty, that he would not be burdened with speaking to him before his departure. Pitiful though it was, Lucian would have welcomed being spared the agony that conversation would involve.

But Jem, who must have been sleeping, for his clothes were wrinkled and his hair unkempt, seemed well aware of the situation. He raced down the many stairs faster than any time he had run before, and when he reached Lucian he was panting, sweat running down his cheeks—or perhaps tears.

"Lu—wh—where are you going?" he bent as if to catch his breath, just now seeing Lucian's sword and armor and the intent in his green eyes.

Lucian fought hard to speak despite his accumulating sorrow. "I have to leave now, Jem," he said heavily.

"*Leave?*" He was still short of breath when he suddenly

realized that this was it—the moment that Lucian's journey would be set in motion. A wave of fury and despair fell over him at once, crashing down in one cataclysmic wave of emotion. He wanted to scream at him, yet weep at the same time. The very organs within him felt like they were twisting and coming loose and would at any moment spill from him. A thousand separate words flushed through his mind, and he wanted to exclaim them all, but managed only to mutter: "Without . . . *me?*"

Lucian bit his tongue. "I can't take you with me, Jem—it's too dangerous."

"Dangerous? We've never cared about anything like *that* before." He laughed slightly, as though doing so would lighten Lucian's mood. But Lucian was stoic as he had ever been, and Jem suddenly realized his words were like water upon rock. "You really *are* leaving without me, aren't you?"

"It's for your own good, Jem," said Lucian after a moment of hesitation. "There's more out there than you or I can comprehend. The world is a place you should avoid, if you can. Stay here with your father. You've been given a second chance with him—would you really make him suffer the way you were suffering?"

But Jem's eyes only became more teary. "You're talking like you won't return. You *are* fixing to come back, aren't you?"

"Well of course I'm fixing to come back, Jem—anyone would be fixing to come back. It's just . . . unlikely."

"So this is it, then? This is goodbye?"

Lucian gave a blank, answerless stare. He did not see the courtyard behind him or the Citadel's gray stone beaming amidst the evergreen trees of the forest that surrounded them. He did not see the crowd, or the beacon shining. He did not hear Gamaréa calling his name, or Jem beginning to weep openly. All he saw were two young boys over the progression of seventeen years, running, laughing, playing, and sometimes even bickering. He recalled the embraces, the splendid, simple times, and the fleeting whispers of a little conversation they shared as children on the bridge of the miller's creek—the very spot that had initiated their separate courses.

Will you always be my friend, Lucian?

I'll always be your friend, Jem.

Then his surroundings began to grow clear again, and he heard Jem speaking. "All those years between us," he said. "It's all . . . gone. Just like that."

Lucian, though shattering within, held his ground. "Gone to memory, Jem. And memories are something no one can take from you, or burn. Don't look back on me and think of today, but the days we spent in Amar—before all this. It's the only solace I can offer you. You'll always be like a brother to me. But now I have to go."

The horn blew one final time, loudly and monotonously. Lucian and Jem exchanged one final gaze, then Lucian passed sorrowfully on and met Gamaréa and Didrebelle in the courtyard. The crowd had gathered to an immense number, throwing white flower pedals into the air where they fluttered on the wind before landing at the companions' feet. Lucian would not have guessed that so many folk resided in Elderland.

Out of the crowd came Mary and MaDungal, both in tears.

"You take care of yourself out there," Mary warned. "Do you hear me?"

Lucian smiled, though the salt of his own tears started leaking into his mouth.

"I will," he replied.

"And you—" Mary yanked the unsuspecting Gamaréa in front of her by his shoulder. "You take care of this one, you hear me? I don't want anything happening to him."

"I will do my best, my lady," he answered cautiously. Lucian was definitely smiling now.

"Don't *my lady* me. You will, or so help me—"

"Alright, Ms. Rolfe, alright," interjected the raspy voice of MaDungal. "Poor lad's got enough on 'is place without you threatenin' him an' all."

Mary released Gamaréa, who looked at Didrebelle awkwardly. The Fairy, however, seemed highly amused.

"Yeh really should keep an extra eye out though,"

MaDungal said to Lucian as Mary looked on. "Nasty boggers out in the wild, I hear. When yeh come back, drinks're on me."

"I'll be sure to take you up on that," said Lucian with a bittersweet smile.

Then a deep, wizened old voice came from over Lucian's shoulder.

"Lucian," said Tartalion. "It is time."

Lucian turned to see Gamaréa and Didrebelle standing purposefully as though awaiting him, and as the sea of onlookers parted, their path became clear. Solemn and quiet, the trio took their first steps away, but only Lucian looked back, seeing the masses watching after them, and seeing, very faintly, the distant figure of Jem slouching in the doorway of Tartalion's palace, and tried to convince himself that dismissing him was the right thing to have done.

19

The Path of Provinus

For many days, they traveled in the open. The breadth of Elderland had given way to the wide, open land that Didrebelle said the Fairies referred to as Viritérra. The mid-summer day had become hot, yet became more bearable as it passed on. Gamaréa was ever wary of the skies, and Didrebelle would constantly run off and scout ahead, his Fairy-sight able to see long and far across the plain.

To this point, much to the surprise and gratitude of the trio, the land they walked was quiet. Gamaréa still debated upon which road to take, for there would come a time when they would reach a crossroads, and have to choose between the passage into the mountains of Provinus or the Adixus Valley.

"If the weather stays agreeable," suggested Didrebelle, "we should stay on the Adixus path, for that would be less riddled with war, I think. Should the weather prove stark, however, Provinus may ironically become the safest road."

Gamaréa took a moment to consider. "I suppose the mountain path would have sufficiently better shelter than Adixus, though I fear we may seek shelter from many things should we attempt to venture through."

Treading much and speaking little, the companions pressed onward. After several days, they reached a large river that ran northwestward, and in the calmest portions of the current took to refreshing themselves.

Lucian wondered if there were fish in the river, but Gamaréa told him that it was highly unlikely, and even if it was teeming, they would be impossible to catch with the current racing as it was. Nonetheless, Lucian was deathly hungry, having eaten only a handful of berries he managed to pick about two days prior. The Morok began to complain about the lack of game Viritérra offered, saying that a fine buck would prove to be a worthy supper. Didrebelle, however, was content with the lack of food supply, for like his countrymen he could go long durations without food or drink.

And so in his hunger Lucian laid back and peered up at the mid-afternoon sky, his stomach rumbling, remembering fondly what Mary had told him before departing.

You are like a son to me, Lucian. I can't even say like the son I never had because you are my son. I don't care if you've got syrup in your veins, you're my son through and through and I love you and I want you to take care of yourself out there. Do you hear me? Do you hear me, Lucian Rolfe? Take care and come back.

The words were like ice pouring over him, despite the growing heat. A fear lingered within him that he would perhaps break another promise to a loved one.

A week after their departure from Elderland, June was upon them. In time, though he traveled well off the headlong path to do so, Gamaréa managed to kill a buck of fair size and cook it for his companions. He instructed Lucian and Didrebelle to eat hardily, for the skies were growing gloomy, and he determined that storms were approaching. So it was he reached the decision to brave the mountain pass of Provinus, where, Gamaréa explained, the many caverns and caves would provide ample shelter, and the many high ridges might afford them a far look along the coast.

But it was not only the path itself that worried Gamaréa. It was something Tartalion had mentioned before they set out, while Lucian had been talking to Jem near the courtyard. Something he remembered perhaps more vividly as the days progressed and fleeted away. *I am aware that Provinus may be a probable route for your company, but I strongly advise that you try your best to stay away. There are giants in the canyons, and Sageless tribes of men, it is rumored.*

I am aware, Gamaréa recalled saying. *I know of the giants and the tribes.*

There is one thing else, Darkwood. One thing above, perhaps, all else. Word has reached my ear of the resurgence of the Queen's Council, she who calls her home the Mountain of Dreams. Though there are several magic mountains that we know of, the Queen's is different. Many elemental evils linger there that have awoken in its darkest reaches. I cannot say I know it to be true, but the threat is present. Be wary! And remember to keep your back straight and arms outstretched, and keep in mind those elbows—

I know, Ignómiel.

Here comes Lucian.

And it was indeed Lucian's slight voice that woke him from his daydream. "Who's fighting out there anyway?" the boy ventured to ask as the company rested after supper.

Didrebelle had prepared a wonderful fire that still roared and sprung up wildly, even after a couple hours of life.

"Mountain tribes," Didrebelle said. "Primitive cultures of men. But there are other things as well . . . "

Lucian grew keen to the uncertain tone of the Fairy. "What do you mean 'other things'?" he asked.

"Provinus," Gamaréa interjected, "is one of many mountain ranges that bears various sorts of inhabitants."

"Why are they there?" asked Lucian, who had taken to snapping twigs. "Why have they taken to the mountains?"

"Most of them have gone there seeking refuge, as Didrebelle said," replied Gamaréa, taking a bite of smoking deer-flesh. "Ever since Dridion allied itself with Nundric the power of Sorcerian's realm has increased mightily—"

"And now that fighting has reached these shores," added Didrebelle, "their need for shelter is more urgent than it once was."

"And they are mostly men?"

"Mortals," answered Gamaréa, as though correcting him. "Ever since the fall of their last king the mortal race has divided into a scattered lot of peasant villages and nomadic clans. They came a long way to escape, both from warring and each other." Lucian recalled Tartalion speaking to him of this matter. Gamaréa's gaze grew weary. "Their worldwide locations are almost entirely decimated—including your village."

Lucian turned away in sadness, wondering why he had been so detached from the outer reaches of the world. To his ignorant mind, it seemed like a misshapen place upon which he hadn't any purpose.

"I regret ever coming across this Key," he said suddenly. "I regret that day I found it in Amar."

Gamaréa looked hard upon him. "The Key was yours to find, Lucian," he said, as though it should have been obvious to him. "It would have come into your keep if it had to fall out of the sky and land atop your head. This is the way of fate."

The rest of what they presumed to be their last night in Viritérra waned quietly, but Lucian could not sleep. The fire was dying, but still released enough light so that they were able to see relatively clearly. Didrebelle had wandered off several meters where the land crept up into a soft incline and looked upon the night sky in wonder. The stars, he remarked, were quite wondrous there in the open range of the Fairylands. Though none of the company spoke of them aloud, they had all observed the beauty of the Viritérran nights. It was as though a barrel of diamonds had been strewn wildly across a velvet carpet, shining atop them like millions of miniature suns. But over the mountains of Provinus beyond, they noted, loomed an ominous sort of gloom.

Gamaréa had made his way toward the fire. He brought the antlers from the buck he had slew and began breaking them into small, sharp fragments, then with his dagger began crafting small, decorous trinkets and dozens of arrowheads while singing soft songs to himself.

After a time Lucian came to sit beside him. "What's that song you're singing?"

The hint of a smile crept along the edges of Gamaréa's

lips. "It is an old hymn I learned when I was a young soldier. Prayers for peace have long been sung."

Lucian bowed his head and fiddled with one of the objects Gamaréa had crafted.

"You look troubled," said Gamaréa, who was putting the finishing touches on what looked like a small bear. The fire crackled before them.

Lucian sighed. "I don't feel that I'm ready," he said heavily.

"Ready for what?"

"This journey, fighting—all of it. I just don't feel that I'm prepared in the least."

Gamaréa set down his dagger for a moment and focused intently on his companion. "And you feel like you should have had some preparation before we set off? Some training of sorts?"

Lucian nodded hesitantly. "I guess," he said with some reluctance.

"Hear me, my friend: I've fought in many battles. Many have died by my hand, and in my arms. There is no armor strong enough to repel the stroke of life—no secret to better prepare you for its ambush. If this world desires to claim you, it will." He blew the small shavings away from the finished pieced and tossed it aside with the others. Then he looked hard at Lucian, and the light of the fire ignited his stare. "But my name has not been called yet," he continued, "and neither has yours."

Lucian sighed, and Gamaréa saw the sadness in his eyes, like a basin within which a week's worth of water was collecting and would dispense at any moment. "Maybe it's readying its voice," he said softly.

"Try not to trouble yourself with such things," assured Gamaréa. "In time I will work with you, and try to hone whatever skills you have. Until then leave the fighting to me, and do well to hide."

Just then, a faraway clap of thunder rolled over the distant peaks of Provinus, and the rains began falling lightly upon the edge of Viritérra where they camped.

"That does it then," said Gamaréa plainly. "Didrebelle's

guess was accurate. It seems that Provinus will prove the better road after all."

The sun rose behind clouds, and the earth was now drenched with the steadily falling rain. The final stretch of Viritérra was soggy soil upon which Gamaréa's and Lucian's feet became caught on numerous occasions. Didrebelle, on the other hand, had no such trouble, for he scampered weightlessly upon the wet ground as though it were dry.

What was left of the green field finally subdued to the rocky soil at the base of Provinus leading into the mountain range. The first great stretch was a rocky passageway that wound frequently and bent around rows of jagged rock protruding from the earth. For hours, it continued on in a similar fashion, until the relatively level path descended further into a steep slope, down which they had to proceed with extreme caution.

They presumed it was noon when they took rest for the first time. Lucian sat on the flattest stone he could find, and Gamaréa lit his pipe. Didrebelle, in the meantime, had run ahead to scout the path, and returned after a short while with no news of a hindrance ahead.

"Alright," said Gamaréa excitedly, "I suppose we've got a bit of time on our hands."

He set his pipe down. Didrebelle and Lucian had both given him an odd stare after his random exclamation.

The Morok walked toward Lucian. "Get up."

Lucian seemed bewildered, and slightly afraid of Gamaréa's demanding tone. "Wh—what?" The Morok seemed all the more brooding standing over him now.

"Come on. Get up!" Gamaréa practically took to throwing Lucian clear off the rock on which he sat. Staggering somewhat, Lucian finally managed to reclaim his posture.

"Draw your sword," Gamaréa demanded.

Lucian did so, still a bit confused.

"No, no, no," lectured the Morok. "Always steady your sheath with your other hand when you draw; it decreases the risk of your blade getting stuck."

Lucian now unsheathed Excebellus the proper way.

Taking a moment to perceive it for the better, he noticed the golden guard was fashioned in the likeness of an eagle with its wings outstretched. The hilt was long enough for both his hands, and the pommel was designed in the likeness of an eagle's tail-feathers. Wrought there, glittering sharply even in the light of day, were the same three gems as upon the Key. They were aligned in the same order and presentation—the glowing emerald and sapphire flanking the dim ruby.

"That's better," said Gamaréa when Excebellus was fully drawn. "Now, I want you to charge me."

Lucian sneered. "What?"

"*Charge* me." Gamaréa was so enthusiastic it seemed to Lucian as though he were asking for desert.

Didrebelle took a seat like an anxious spectator. "Behold!" he exclaimed. "The blind lead the blind in Provinus!"

Lucian shrugged confusedly. "I'm not sure what you mean by *charge.*"

The Fairy stood up, and stood beside Lucian. "Step aside," he said, "and pay attention."

Didrebelle slowly drew his two swords from behind his back, and he and Gamaréa began circling each other. Though they seemed like brothers the entire time Lucian had been with them, there was something ferocious in each of their eyes that suggested otherwise now.

Didrebelle bluffed toward Gamaréa, and then recoiled. After another slow rotation, Gamaréa bluffed toward the Fairy. In this manner they behaved for quite some time, until at length Gamaréa charged the Fairy with great speed, only to find that Didrebelle had leapt up with incredible agility and flipped over the charging Morok, landing firmly behind him.

Now they crossed blades, and ringing steel echoed through the pass. Didrebelle proved much more cunning and agile than Gamaréa—constantly leaping, flipping, rolling, and swinging his long, thin swords with excellent speed and craft—but Gamaréa's profound strength repelled all of Didrebelle's attacks.

They battled for what seemed like an eternity, and Lucian

sat watching in mesmerized horror, fearfully anticipating the fatal blow to come from either combatant. Suddenly, however, they abruptly ceased and began laughing, throwing their arms around each other's shoulders and walking back toward him.

"*That,*" said Gamaréa, "is what I meant by *charge.*"

Didrebelle laughed excessively.

"You want me to do *that?*" Lucian exclaimed.

"No, my friend—I want to teach you how," laughed Gamaréa, waving a hand to assure Lucian otherwise. "Now step toward me. You already know how to draw your sword, so we have started admirably. Next, hold your sword in front of you. That's it. You must be aware of your grip at all times—you mustn't hold it too loosely or too firmly. Now I want you to swing your sword as though you are going to try to slay something."

Lucian swung his sword as fatally as he could, which apparently wasn't impressive at all, for Gamaréa stood scratching his head as though pondering ways to greatly improve it.

"You're swinging horizontally. Try coming down vertically." Lucian did so. "Better. Not good, but better. Now I'm going to stand in front of you, and I want you to repeat what you just did."

"Absolutely not," protested Lucian. "I'm not going to raise my sword to you!"

"You need to practice, Lucian. You are an apprentice on his first day; I have crossed blades with warlords. I think I will be alright."

Against his will, Lucian raised his sword and swung— vertically, as Gamaréa had suggested—and whether by some friendly act in order to boost Lucian's esteem, or simply because his stroke was mighty, Gamaréa bent beneath the weight of the hit and fell to his knees.

"I'm sorry!" Lucian exclaimed. "Are you alright? Do you need water? Did I hit you?"

Gamaréa seemed utterly confused. "I'm fine," he said after a moment. "I'm—I'm alright."

Didrebelle had come over to his side and helped him

to his feet, dusting him off as he regained his footing. In a short while, Gamaréa became more aware. "It seems you've selected a worthy blade," he said. His voice still seemed shaken. "She will prove a fine companion, Lucian."

Rain began falling once more.

"We should continue," suggested Didrebelle.

The company carried on.

Night came over Provinus. The companions had carried on a great while and became tired, resting near the mouth of a looming cave that was to their right. Hours prior, they reached a portion of the path that elevated and scampered upward a long way until it became level again, but the air now was colder, and with the night came steadier precipitation.

There were no stars above like there had been in Viritérra. The storm clouds had become very dense and blocked out whatever light was trying to pass through, and a heavy mist hovered above them. Not even the moon was visible.

Lucian suggested constructing another fire, but was quickly reprimanded; Gamaréa was uncertain of the whereabouts of the indigenous tribes, who reacted harshly upon any unfamiliar passerby.

"But they are just men," said Lucian, "aren't they?"

"Men with troubled pasts," replied Gamaréa. "They are now bereft of any trust they may have once possessed. A fire would draw them to us." The storm worsened as the night progressed, and the company took shelter in the opening of a nearby cave.

As they rested and thought about the quietness of the mountain pass, a distant sound, like a war-horn, carried through the air, blowing long and emphatically through the night, disrupting the eerie stillness surrounding them. Yet, though it seemed warlike at first, it seemed also to harbor a sadness—a stretched out wailing of sorts, deep and longing, as a mother lamenting a fallen child.

Haunting as it was, Gamaréa and Didrebelle did not appear fazed. Lucian, contrastingly, became horrified.

"There is stirring in the Maior," said Gamaréa calmly and softly, as though an afterthought.

"The what?" said Lucian.

"The great canyons several miles ahead."

"You mean to say that sound is *miles* away?"

Didrebelle, who was lying quite comfortably with his hands behind his head, laughed slightly. "Giants have a way of making their voices heard," he said.

Lucian rolled his eyes and shivered from the cold emitting from the rain. "Giants?"

"Yes," replied the Fairy. "They account for some of the 'other things' I mentioned earlier."

Gamaréa must have seen the worried expression upon Lucian's face, for he was quick to intervene. "Hardly do they venture from the canyons, however," he said. "You needn't worry."

The rain continued through the following morning, but the companions pressed on nonetheless. They came upon a portion of the mountain pass that was laden with tall pines sprouting up and tapering to a point nearly twenty feet high, and Gamaréa said that Arlaurus was this valley's true name.

Various other flora were scattered about as well—small shrubs and bushes littered the way with their gloomy shades of green, for nothing about the plant-life seemed splendid beneath the falling rain. Through Arlaurus they passed for some time, keeping their steps steady, for the path became unpredictable in some parts—frequently dropping or rising without warning.

Suddenly, for one reason or another, Didrebelle became extremely aware, running on ahead of the company a few steps as though to hear or see something for the better. Gamaréa stopped Lucian in his tracks before he continued further.

Didrebelle returned. "A tribe approaches," he said, "nearly a furlong ahead."

"How armed?" said Gamaréa.

"Spear-armed, and some archers also."

Gamaréa's eyes grew wide. "Hunters," he muttered.

"Look there!" said Lucian. "They're coming! Should we hide?"

"It is too late," said Didrebelle, "their chieftain has spotted us."

Without a moment's notice, thundering hooves charged toward them, throwing up thousands of miniature rocks in their pursuit and leaving thick clouds of mountain dust in their wake.

The horde surrounded the company, who stood with their backs to each other, hands raised at spear-point. The tribe was barebacked, with nothing of clothing save weathered, cloth bottoms that reached down around mid-thigh. Their physicality was astounding, for they were muscular men who sat broodingly upon horseback. All were of bearded face; each man's blacker and thicker than the next.

Not one of their clan, however, was more masculine or brooding than their chieftain, who came forth through the crowd of horses, and before Gamaréa, Lucian, and Didrebelle, slammed his spear through the rocky soil so that it stood upright like a post.

He walked first to Gamaréa, who stood as though the tribe did not frighten him in the least. The man's straggly hair dangled to his shoulders, thick and dark and dirty, and his dark eyes pierced all them menacingly. His shoulders stretched outward nearly a yard, the muscles in his body bulging and twisting like cords.

"Such a small tribe, yet so diverse," he said. His voice seemed to bellow, deep like a horn, but was negotiable in nature. "Never in all my years have I seen mortals and Fairies together in the same clan, yet this miniature horde passes so openly through Arlaurus. Speak! Who has sent you?"

"First I should correct you, chief," answered Gamaréa, "for but one of us is mortal. I am Gamaréa, son of Gladris, of Medric. We come from Elderland on a mission of great importance."

"A Morok?" exclaimed the chief. "You do not seem like a Morok to me. For in the west I saw them—in the west long ago—and no feature of yours is alike to theirs. But I will leave that alone for now. You say you've come from Elderland. And if indeed you are of Medric, old Tartalion would never have allowed the likes of your kind in his hall."

Didrebelle spoke. "The High Lord Tartalion has separated himself from Dridion," he said sternly. "He has broken from Melinta and has set laws of his own. He welcomed us openly."

Didrebelle's response did not seem to satisfy the chief. "Is that so?" he said. The spears around them condensed, and they could smell the iron spewing from their points.

"We are friends," said Gamaréa. "We mean no harm to you or Arlaurus. We were just passing through."

The chief decided then to take Gamaréa aside, and ordered his men to maintain their guard of Didrebelle and Lucian.

When they gained privacy, the chief said, "Days are upon us now when trust is difficult to distribute. You must tell me your true purpose here, Morok, or I will be forced to treat you and your company as trespassers."

"I have told you, chief. We come with business from Elderland that carries us west. I will not say more."

"You will need to say more if you wish to go west with your life."

Gamaréa held what words he wished to say, and instead confessed Lucian's burden to the chief.

"The boy?" asked the chief.

"The boy."

"It is true then, the word that has come across the plains of Enorméteren far west where men used to dwell— by whose way Darkness has long passed. There from the shadows of all the Demon has claimed whisper fading voices. *Osti umbra*, they say. "Shadow's Key is found.""

"And we are taking it back."

"Back?" exclaimed the chief. "To Nundric? With but a threesome?"

"If we have to. Medric is our immediate course, however. The land of my people."

"Your mission is folly. Even should you manage to reach

that dreadful door the key will not work unless a rightful king of men is found and sitting in his throne. And if you didn't know, the line of kings ended when Amarog was destroyed."

"That aspect we will leave to hope. Our journey is long, and will take much time, and we hope that the mortal race may rekindle and at least appoint a king. But we haven't time to tarry on it ourselves. I humbly request your understanding, chief. Our mission affects all."

The chief mused for a moment. "Alright," he said finally. "I will allow you passage, though I am not as easily persuaded as you have seen." He bid his men release Didrebelle and Lucian, and the companions met again before the mighty lord of the mountain tribe. For a moment, their gazes locked—his old, weathered eyes that had seen many days and hardships, and Lucian's young and innocent, whose hardships they had yet perceived— as if to say, *Good luck to you.* The company from there carried on through what remained of Arlaurus, followed by the guard of the mountain tribe until they would follow them no more.

From Arlaurus their road became more troublesome, for the rain had become consistently hard and cold and the company sought shelter more times than they wished. For another three days, they passed on—traveling little and resting often in the storm-riddled mountain pass—until the weather was fair enough to continue.

In a day's trip, they came upon an area where the peaks of Provinus had broken off and wound around, and the flat land before them delved steeply downward for many hundreds of feet. Didrebelle said that they had come upon the Maior—the stretch of canyons he had spoken of earlier.

Though the ridges of the canyons were not narrow by any means, they were sure to maintain caution as they passed along. They followed them until nightfall, when Gamaréa offered them rest before the final stretch of the pass.

Lucian for one was much obliged with the idea of rest—

that is until the wailing and horrible, elongated bellows of the giants sounded up from the unseen depths below. He had nearly forgotten them. Now, from directly below them, their cries were bone shattering, earsplitting, like the sounds alone had the power to slay them. Lucian covered his ears and rolled around frantically, as though the wailing was wrenching every organ within him. Didrebelle and Gamaréa, though cringing, seemed relatively content.

Then came a sound unlike the other bellows; a deep, ringing cry like a low-toned war-horn, and when it stopped the canyons shook with vengeance, as some earthquake had suddenly befallen earth and looked to shake it from its foundation. As if for reassurance, Lucian looked to Gamaréa, who looking aside said only, "Tantus."

There was anticipation in his voice, as if speaking of something dangerous or of someone powerful. When the land became still again it remained quiet for some time. Eventually the wailing they originally heard sounded up again and droned on, but it was not long until it was interrupted by what Gamaréa had referred to as *Tantus* and the canyons shook again.

The Morok urged them onward, and the companions stole through the night upon the shaking earth. There were times when it ceased and they were left to a level road upon which treading was simple, but then the quakes sprung up again, conducted by the sorrowful bellowing. When it stopped, seemingly for the last time, the company was far too winded to continue with any great haste, and so they sat and panted, both in weariness and fear.

Gamaréa, who did not sit, peered out into the darkness where the canyons fled behind them. The sky was blotched with varying hues of black, and only the vast silhouette of the peaks of Provinus were visible as the median between the deep velvet sky of night and sheer darkness; and at the bottom of that darkness roared the one called Tantus.

"Tantus is restless," said Gamaréa. Didrebelle and Lucian paid heed to where he was looking.

Just then, the wailing commenced, without the rumbling earth, yet at this point it seemed to be in shorter, quicker spurts, and seemed to suggest anger rather than sadness or despair. Then there were sounds like thunder or great war-drums, separated by a matter of seconds, in a haunting repetition that seemed to last for an eternity. And as the sounds grew louder, the earth began to shake with them, until suddenly a massive form, of this world or another, emerged from the depths of the canyons and crashed upon the ground before them. It was a shape, when its silhouette was slightly distinguishable, that could only be described as an enormous hand.

Suddenly the Morok bid his companions flee, and looking back, they could see a grotesque, astronomic figure lifting itself upon the straining ridge of the canyons. When it came to its feet and rose to full posture, it was nearly thirty feet tall, and bellowed toward the flying company who were running faster than their legs could carry them. Then he charged, Tantus, Lord of the Maior, King of the Giants, with great speed toward them, and they found difficulty in gaining consistent footing as they pressed on.

For a far length, they ran out of need and fear, despite their weariness. Bounding into the unpromising darkness, they fled on. Relentlessly the giant chased them, but it was not long until they could see the canyon's end before them. Beyond it, another stretch of the mountain pass rose up, rocky and cluttered with obstacles they would never be able to pass over swiftly enough with Tantus on their heels. The only solution Gamaréa could muster in the short time he had to think was to take for the cave ahead of them, its opening looming like a shadow nearly beckoning them toward it. "Come!" he cried, and his companions followed as Tantus came flying to the front of the cave wailing and screaming. Then the giant peered through and called one last time with his lowly and pathetic earsplitting howl, watching the shadows of the company fade into the darkness he could not breach.

20

The Mountain of Dreams

The trio raced into the darkness of the tunnel even after the cries of Tantus died away. Lucian wondered if perhaps this was the darkest place he had ever been in his life. The surroundings made even the Black Forest seem like a brightly lit corridor. Though not even an arm's length separated the companions, neither could see the other's back. It was the kind of darkness that seemed to not only affect sight, but sound as well. Though Lucian could not speak for his companions, he was having difficulty breathing.

They slowed their pursuit after a while, and took to filing cautiously along the path. Before long, Gamaréa and Lucian felt Didrebelle shift from the rear of the line and up past them, and they heard his light footsteps continue beyond them for a moment or so before he stopped and whispered back to them.

"I cannot see a thing," he said, surprise evident in his voice. Then Lucian remembered that, being of Fairy descent, his eyesight was perhaps the keenest in the world.

They thought to hear him shift forward some more and come to a halt again. What he began to do then the others could not see. He had pressed his ear gently upon the cold, stone wall of the tunnel and was listening closely, as though the more attentively he listened the more likely it would have been for the rock to begin speaking. But, in fact, he was measuring the thickness of the stone, thinking that he could render a clue as to how deep the tunnel ran into the mountains, and also if anything was on either side of the walls. Yet there seemed to be something about this place—a distinct element that made it nearly impossible for the skilled Fairy to reach any sort of calculation or conclusion, and they passed on aimlessly hoping for the light.

They may have wandered well into the night; they could not have been certain. Everything was night here. From all directions, the arms of darkness seized them, but they were too far now to turn back. And even if they could have, they knew the giant would be there, living suitably at the mouth of the tunnel waiting for them to turn their course back toward him. For he knew none ventured into this place and came out the other side; he knew no one weathered the Mountain of Dreams.

The darkness smelled of horrible things. There was the stale smell of dust and things that had come to rot. They may have been people—tribesmen that had gone there to stay warm in the winter with their fires—or perhaps small animals that had ventured by that way. Who or whatever had come to pass there had not fared as well as they perhaps hoped they would; or maybe, each member of the trio silently mused, they had in fact gone there to die.

They would have taken rest had it not been for the uncertain road stretching through. The ground became uneven much too often, and they found themselves stepping over mounds of hard and soft objects. Though their minds tried to conjure a multitude of explanations, they knew they trudged atop the deceased. But they pressed on over flesh and bone as best they could, never bending or straying or taking to the ground. The smell eventually became unbearable.

Perhaps an hour into their trek, the road began declining awkwardly. Feeling the momentum of the descent pushing them forward, they held on to the sides of the walls to maintain balance.

Not a moment passed without regret for Gamaréa. Though he knew it was impossible, he felt that Tartalion Ignómiel was sitting in his hall in Elderland completely and utterly ashamed of his decision. *But Tantus had driven us there,* he would have said. *Tantus of the Canyons—the rogue. He wanted to make a meal of us.* But Tartalion would have found a separate way, if he had not turned and tried to smite the giant first.

He is not here, he chided himself. *I did what I thought was best.*

Gamaréa knew the giant was too fast for the group. He knew Tantus would have overtaken them had they not fled into the tunnel of the Mountain of Dreams. But he still did not forgive himself—did not rid himself of guilt for leading his companions to a premature doom.

At long length the first words were spoken, as Didrebelle stopped for the first time since examining the walls. "Unless my eyes deceive me, it seems to be getting darker," he muttered.

Gamaréa snorted from a meter or so behind him. "If that is at all possible," he said.

Then Lucian thought of the Key and the lights that shone from it and began taking it out of his pocket. Suddenly the emerald and sapphire glare emitted wildly, the blaze so pronounced in the stifling darkness that it was nearly blinding.

Before Lucian removed the key entirely Gamaréa threw his hands upon him and covered the lights. "No!" he exclaimed. "You mustn't expose the Key here. This is an untrustworthy realm; we do not know who may be watching, who may be lingering in the shadows."

The exhale of Lucian's breath was enough to make Gamaréa realize that he was frightening him. "It is just a precaution," he continued softly. "We must go on."

"Normally," started Didrebelle, "I would be able to summon the light of Zynys through my eyes. It is a gift I received from the Mountain itself when I was cleansed."

"I thought the only capability of that gift is to tame dragons and other beasts?" said Gamaréa.

"Dragons, mostly; I wouldn't know about other creatures."

Lucian listened and remembered the name Tartalion

would refer to Didrebelle by. *Dragontamer,* he thought. *I see now.*

"Perhaps," continued the Fairy, "I can try to summon it here, though I doubt it will be successful."

"No harm in trying," said Lucian, his voice with all the trappings of a plea. It was odd to hear his own voice spoken for the first time in a long while.

The Fairy stopped again and they could hear him chanting to himself, lowering his voice and speaking in a foreign language that Lucian could not understand. It was a language ancient enough to also pass beyond the extremities of Gamaréa's knowledge. It was the language of the Wizardrim.

Lucian and Gamaréa were standing close behind Didrebelle as he conducted his ritual. Lucian was frightened and curious; Gamaréa was simply hoping for any kind of light to guide them. Suddenly Didrebelle curled up and wailed as though in pain. Lucian instinctively sprang forward to aid him, but Gamaréa held him back.

"Wait!" he whispered fiercely. "He is acquiring the light."

Didrebelle's cries soon rang throughout the tunnel, echoing along the way by which they came and that which they had yet traveled. Then his wails ceased abruptly, and, forcefully, his golden head jerked back, and from his eyes protruded white beams of light comparable only to exploding stars.

"I cannot look at you," he said as though in pain, sensing that Gamaréa and Lucian were fumbling forward to see if he was alright.

"I will blind you," he warned. "But follow me now—now that we can see."

It took a moment or so for their eyes to settle in the new light blazing from Didrebelle's eyes. In an instant, they had managed to ascend from one extreme to the other. Whereas they once walked in utter blackness, they were now guided by a source of inconceivable light. Yet, though the light made their passage easier, it also cursed their eyes, and it was not long before they wished for Didrebelle to extinguish it. For revealed to them now were the multitude of bodies scattered at their feet.

They were strewn about almost as if they belonged there, as though part of the tunnel itself. Contorted and disheveled, they lay grotesquely, each corpse in a separate stage of decay. The remains of their garments had nearly been torn away completely. Pieces of dirty rags were strewn about the scene, some having grown filthy, bloodstained, and hard. Only bones remained of some bodies; others seemed to be fresh cadavers. Then there were some in the stages between—of shriveled flesh that had grown pale and shrunken upon the bones. Many of their eyes were missing, probably having been eaten by small, tunnel-dwelling rodents that had feasted on their misfortunes. Some were missing limbs or other features—a finger here, a nose or ear there. Some were sitting up against the walls, their heads tilted over as though sleeping.

"You see," said Didrebelle softly from behind them, his voice teeming with despair, "some gifts can also be curses."

Gamaréa, nearly in awe, bent to examine one of the fresher bodies. It had been a man, as he distinguished by the exposed chest. His mouth was dangling open loosely. Perhaps he had been screaming when he died. Had it been for the presence of eyes Gamaréa might have been able to determine the state he had been in when he perished. But now he saw only an open mouth on the expressionless ghost of a face—the eye-sockets deep and hollow and fringed like little black tunnels. The cheeks had deflated and sunk against the cheekbones—perhaps his skull would be surfacing soon. The cartilage from his nose was missing also, now bearing a blood-dried, triangular hole over his shriveled mouth. Gamaréa could tell through the gap between the rows of remaining brown teeth that his tongue was missing also.

When the light came and Lucian was able to see the scene for the better, he fell back in horror, and Didrebelle nearly had to catch him. Spinning immediately from his grasp, he turned away to vomit.

"I am turned toward you now, Gamaréa," Didrebelle warned. "Tell me when you are turning."

"I cannot turn any more than I am turning inside," he said solemnly. "What do you suppose befell them here? What fate could have undone so many?"

Lucian cringed against the wall, his voice weak and his throat hoarse from vomiting. "It probably all started with just a handful," he mused, wiping his mouth with his sleeve and looking revolted. "Then when the others saw them they probably died of fright."

Didrebelle looked around for the better. "There seem to be whole tribes in here," he said. "Many of them lie cluttered together and bear the same fragments of garb. But—"

"There are no weapons," Gamaréa noted suddenly, surveying the floor for any form of weaponry.

Didrebelle was baffled. "They did not think to meet their ends here," he remarked.

Lucian came back and met them, his eyes partly closed, his face a pale-green hue. "I'm sure the giant had a thing or two to do with them coming here," he said, grabbing hold of his stomach again.

"Watch the boots!" exclaimed Didrebelle, spinning Lucian away from them and back toward the wall to vomit once more. He stood behind Gamaréa and spoke softly despite the distracting sounds of Lucian's predicament. "The boy hasn't the stomach for what he is about to encounter," he whispered.

Gamaréa, his eyes transfixed on the bodies, was wide-eyed and possessed by disgust and sadness. "Do you, Didrebelle?" he whispered. "Do I?"

Soon Lucian returned, and Gamaréa spoke to him without lifting his gaze from the bodies. "Are you alright?"

"Fine," he said shortly. "Can we move on now? This place is beginning to make me uneasy."

Didrebelle laughed quietly. *"Beginning?"*

"I'm sorry," started Lucian, "I've just never seen a dead bod—" his words were cut short, for just then a black, sticky substance dropped from the ceiling and plopped atop his foot. Soon after, a second drop fell upon Gamaréa's hand.

Simultaneously, Lucian, Gamaréa, and Didrebelle looked upward and saw that the roof was cluttered with dozens of boulder-sized spiders; and for each beast were twelve beady eyes that leered back. Lucian screamed and fell back as Gamaréa leapt up from the ground, nearly tripping over one of the bodies. When Didrebelle looked up at them, however, they seemed to cower in the light and disperse to other reaches of the tunnel. But now they came down from the circling sides, and some hovered down by their strings of thread.

They sprang after the companions quickly after touching down, but the trio did not wait for them to get settled. Speeding on behind Didrebelle and his light, they were dismayed to find that the path ahead proved more hindering than it had been behind them. Here the corpses were more plentiful, and for a while, they made as best they could, the inane chattering and heavy tapping of the spiders' long legs sounding directly behind them. Suddenly Lucian lost his footing on the outstretched arms of one of the corpses and fell hard upon his face. To his utter horror, he felt the Key fly out of its pocket and clang upon the ground just out of his reach.

"NO!" he cried.

Gamaréa spun quickly and saw him there on the ground, the eight-legged legion all but on top of him now. He called to Didrebelle for aid, and the Fairy joined him with his bow, the light from his eyes hindering the spiders momentarily as the two of them fixed arrows and fired. With their darts, they slew many, but two more seemed to replace each one that fell. By the hundreds, it seemed, the spiders funneled in from all reaches. Some now were approaching from ahead of them, and they found themselves flanked.

Gamaréa pulled Lucian from the ground and stood before him, drawing his sword. Then Didrebelle too resorted to his blades, and when the creatures advanced the Morok and Fairy slew them wildly, and their cause was spurred on to see that Lucian was doing the same. Now the three companions battled fiercely, splattering the thick, black blood of the beasts all over the tunnel—chopping off legs and burying their blades between their many sets of eyes—until the host retired and scurried away to whatever nest belonged to them.

Gamaréa approached Lucian. "I see Excebellus has not misled you," he said, a hint of a smile upon his face.

But Lucian's face was pale with worry. "I didn't draw it soon enough," he said, almost in tears. He saw Gamaréa's expression fade, his eyes becoming hard and fastened almost upon Lucian's very soul.

"The Key came loose in the fight," admitted Lucian heavily, saying the words as if he himself did not believe them.

"It is not here!" said Didrebelle worriedly, scouring the ground wildly. "The creatures must have taken it."

Gamaréa remained collected. "I saw some disperse that way." He acknowledged the road yet traveled. "They must be delivering it to the Queen."

"They must be her agents," said Didrebelle, anger apparent in his voice.

"What are we going to do?" said Lucian frantically.

Gamaréa rested his hand upon the wall of the cave, tired and worn and disgusted. "We have no choice now but to follow them."

The ensuing path was steep and cluttered still with the dead. They managed with as little regard as they could, although in time—as wrong as it seemed to them—they became used to the company of the fallen, rotting bodies. In the distance ahead Didrebelle heard the spiders fleeing, though his companions could not, and in their direction, the Fairy led them onward with need and great haste.

Lucian Rolfe could not imagine what foul distinctions this place had—this Mountain of Dreams. The name itself seemed serene, as though they pressed toward a place of tranquility, like Elderland had been. But Gamaréa spoke ever shortly of it, as though he wished to say nothing more than he had to, and even in his stride Lucian saw that he was hesitant.

And in fact he was. He knew what fate awaited them there. He knew the Sorceress was longing for them. Now her henchmen bore along a useful trinket, and would lay it at her very feet. *As though escaping this place was not difficult enough,* he thought with frustration.

Maybe after another several hundred yards they could all hear something ahead of them, but it did not seem like it could have been a band of rogue spiders. It instead sounded like flowing water. And indeed it was. At length they saw an intersection of streams flowing in from either side of the tunnel, channeling into a large pool where the tunnel ended at long last.

Now they came upon a large open cavern within which a shallow pool was glowing under the dim light of torches. Towers of rock protruded from there and supported the roof of the cave, tall and slender and burnt orange. Beyond, where it led away to other reaches, they could see nothing. Didrebelle concealed the light of his eyes and he was able to look at his companions again. He saw that they were worn and dirty and bruised, splattered with the black blood of the Queen's miscreant agents.

Lucian was enthralled by the place they had just entered. It was not the grandest of locations, but half a day's march through the tunnel that led them there was a worthy foil for any place. He took a step forward, but Gamaréa pulled him back. "You mustn't step in the pool," he said.

"Why not?" Lucian demanded.

Gamaréa could see the angst within the boy's eyes. "It is not meant for us to wade through, I don't think."

Lucian looked hard upon the crystalline pool, glittering even through the dim. "But I can see the bottom," he retorted. "There's nothing there."

"That is hardly the bottom. It appears as though it is, but everything within this Mountain is an illusion."

"But this is the Mountain of *Dreams,*" whispered Lucian confused, and slightly disappointed.

"Yes," answered Gamaréa, "but who said anything of good dreams?"

Then they saw a woman emerge slowly from the water, her naked body nearly as tan as the rocks she blossomed beside. She rose quietly enough that they at first did not realize she was present, but when they saw the figure standing there, seemingly atop the water itself, they fell back and looked on in wonder. Her fair skin was glistening, not from moisture (she was oddly dry), but perhaps from something else. Her auburn hair draped down over her breasts, which they could tell were round and supple. At her sides, her thin arms hung idly, swaying subtly back and forth near the curve of her waist.

It took only a moment for Lucian to realize that she was the most beautiful woman he ever fixed his eyes upon, and she held his gaze for what seemed like an eternity— her eyes of green and yellow mixing with his and keeping him there, unable to move. He did not see his companions cowering. He did not hear them pleading with him to look away. He heard only her soft voice speak to him, though she had not once opened her mouth to talk.

Lucian. Lucian, my love. You must come. You must come at once.

And so he listened to her, wading after the woman through the pool with a blank and trance-like expression on his face.

From behind him, Gamaréa and Didrebelle were calling, but Lucian could not hear them.

"He has fallen under her spell," said the Fairy anxiously. "The Enchantress will claim him now for sure."

Gamaréa was sitting now at the mouth of the tunnel, his head bowed into his hands. "She knew he was the youngest of us," he said. "She knew she could use his inexperience and innocence against him."

"She knows too, perhaps, that he is susceptible to the weaknesses of men," added Didrebelle. Then a thought occurred in his mind—a sudden, frightening thought. "Do you think she knows he is the Keeper of Fates?"

Gamaréa contemplated for a moment before speaking. "I cannot be certain, but I doubt it."

He had heard of this Enchantress only through tales Tartalion had told him, and he fought to recall them. "The Enchantress does not trouble herself with outside affairs," he continued. "She simply waits to feed on the souls of men who venture to her lair. She does not care what their intentions are, or who they may be, or where they may be going."

Didrebelle stepped a few paces ahead, looking out to where she and Lucian vanished. "You would think this Queen—whoever she may be—would try and be rid of her."

"I'm sure she would have it no other way. But the Enchantress cannot be killed by magic, which the Queen would seek to use to her advantage. Nor can a common blade smite her. She will meet no end until her lover's blade pierces her heart, it is said."

A light flickered in Didrebelle's eyes. "Then we must get to Lucian at once! We must tell him to smite her and be done with it."

Gamaréa grew even more sullen. "It is no use," he said slowly. "Lucian cannot hear or see us now."

The fair face of Didrebelle contorted with despair. "I do not understand. What are you saying?"

"Did you not see how his gaze fixed upon her? He would accept no other sight; hear no other sound. The Enchantress devours all that is around her victims. They see only her as all else becomes a black void of nothingness. Even if we stood beside the Enchantress, she would not see us. Nor will he hear us if we advise him to kill her."

"There has to be a way to him. We cannot abandon this mission so easily."

"We are not abandoning the mission, Dragontamer. The Key is still at hand; the spiders carry it to the Queen as we speak."

"But the Key is nothing without Lucian."

"Even in Lucian's possession the Key will remain useless until the ruby is alight. In the meantime it is our charge to keep it safe—"

Suddenly the cavern began to rumble somewhat, and the rumble escalated to a near quake, lifting the companions from their feet to fall upon the ground. From all directions, rock came crashing down, barreling into the pool, and threatening to block the passage ahead.

"Come!" shouted Gamaréa over the chaos. "We must find the Queen!"

They barely made it to the path ahead with their lives. Rocks in large fragments had been thrusting toward them from all reaches, hindering their pursuit onward. But by cunning agility—even among the obstacles that thwarted them—they managed to reach the road they hoped would lead them toward the Queen.

Tartalion had not spoken much of her, and the little information he had once provided was all Gamaréa knew. She would seem beautiful and evil all at once, he had explained, and her voice would be sweet and wooing, like the coo of a dove. And she has means of showing those who venture there the truth, if they ask it of her. But she is not a Sage, nor is she capable of Wizardrim-like magic; for hers is sorcery, and used only in her dwelling.

They pressed on. Didrebelle in time had to light the way again, but on this occasion the summoning of the Light was easier. There were no bodies upon this road, to their relief, and the only smell was dirt and dust, and an odd, stale scent they thought originated from the horde of creatures that had passed there.

In time Didrebelle inquired with Gamaréa as to his thoughts on the length of the path they walked, but looking ahead, the Morok could not see any discrepancies in the road that suggested its end. But he walked on, looking this way and that for any clues or signs, and after a moment or so his ears perked up and he became attentive. "Did you hear that?" he asked quietly. Didrebelle looked as if he didn't understand him. "That sound—that voice?"

"I heard nothing but the crunch of stone beneath us," assured Didrebelle.

Gamaréa walked forward only to stop abruptly. "There it is again," he whispered. "It spoke my name this time."

Again, Didrebelle claimed to hear nothing.

Gamaréa could hear voices all around him now, or it may have been one solitary voice that was circling him. But it referred to him by both *Gamaréa* and *Darkwood* multiple times.

"Phantasms," Gamaréa said at last. "There are spirits here that beckon."

"Spirits in the mountains? Spirits of whom, I wonder."

"I do not wish to understand or learn of them," said Gamaréa at long last, fright apparent in his whispering voice. "Come. We must press on."

In another hour or so, they were able to reach the end of the path and were pleased. The road had brought them to a well-lit hall whose walls were glistening and floors were tiled, and lovely, glass chandeliers dangled from the ceiling like hovering diamonds. Looking behind them now they saw the path was sealed and appeared as though it never was—its only remnants being the sprinkled dirt from the companions' boots, the continuance of the walls around them where the entrance to the path had been. Didrebelle extinguished the Light.

They passed on slowly, wary of all that was around them. Gamaréa noticed upon the floor the black substance some of the spiders had emitted, droplets of which had fallen along the tiles. "The spiders came this way," he said softly. "We are on the path to the Queen."

They sped quickly onward. After they passed the last of the chandeliers there was darkness, and they came upon a corridor—the length of which they could not calculate. The walls were of stone, and tapered up to a high point. Upon the thin, cold air, the wisps of their breath rose.

Gamaréa peered as best he could down the way. "Can you see anything?"

Didrebelle too had trouble seeing. "I see nothing," he said disappointedly. "Nothing but the darkness, which has never before hindered me like this."

"Perhaps—" but Gamaréa's voice was cut short, for an arm's length before them a small light flickered. It was a candle, and holding it was a young, innocent-looking girl. Her initial presence frightened them and they sprung back. But when they saw her, they noticed her eyes were filled with joy, and she smiled widely there in the darkness.

She stepped forward with her candle, the dull flame lighting only her face, and they saw her brow was distinguished and her eyes sunken beneath it, heavy shades of brown with little discrepancy between the pupil and the iris.

"Welcome," she said softly, like a child. "Welcome to the Mountain of Dreams."

The companions fumbled for a word, their nerves still tingling from the abrupt presence of the young girl, standing so confidently before them in the darkened corridor in the midst of a lost realm.

"Young girl," Gamaréa started, "I am—"

"Gamaréa Windswept," she said kindly, almost happily—as if she were speaking to a long-lost friend.

Windswept? Gamaréa exclaimed inwardly. *The very name of my childhood.* Didrebelle too was surprised when the name was spoken.

"We have been expecting you, Gamaréa," said the girl, "as well as you, Didrebelle Dragontamer."

Didrebelle stepped forward. "Young girl," he said sternly, "how have you come to know of us?"

She said nothing, but the look she passed to Didrebelle nearly made him cringe with fear. It was an innocent-enough gaze, but beneath it Gamaréa and Didrebelle could sense evil urging to seep through, as though she was a distortion of something foul.

"Come," she said softly, as though nearing sleep. "I will show you the way."

There seemed to be no concept of time as Lucian was following her. It no longer seemed as though he was still in the cavern with his companions. In fact, he could not recollect much of the world around him at all. He knew only that she was there—this woman who miraculously emerged from the pool and led him away with her. He gazed amiably at her flowing hair, reaching elegantly to the small of her back—gold and brown with hints of red—and her legs were dazzling, long and slender, the toned muscles inflating and deflating as she strode away without a sound.

He did not even feel his heartbeat within him, and was not conscious of any desires except that he must have her and make her his. It seemed like years that he was following her, slowly and hesitantly, afraid that should he approach quicker she would flee. He watched her movements like dancing, there in front of him yet seeming so far, and he wished to reach out and touch her, or at least derive some form of speech, but he was stilled and silenced. Perhaps somewhere in the chasms of his mind that still functioned he knew he could not distinguish anything in his peripherals. But he did not bend one thought upon that.

When at last she turned and faced him, all else he may have vaguely perceived dispersed entirely, and it was only her.

In the corridor, they each heard voices now—fleeting whispers that echoed as they passed away. *Welcome!* They were saying. *Honorable guests of the Queen, the Mountain welcomes you.* They could not distinguish a specific direction as to where the voices came from; they seemed to be everywhere. Gamaréa and Didrebelle remained a comfortable distance from the girl—having not taken to trusting her completely—and not once did she look back at them. She simply strolled along, holding her candle out in front of her, the dull light casting a pale-orange glow around them.

Soon a distinct smell was in the air, sweet and wonderful—much too delightful for the dank corridor through which they passed. Neither companion spoke of it, or acknowledged it save for a glance each other's way, and when they looked again the girl was gone and an abrupt wave of light flooded over them like a rising tide. They saw now that they strode about in a well-lit, boundless room where folk were well dressed and dancing, and looking at each other they saw that they too bore different garb, sparkling and wonderful as though dressing for a ballroom. No walls seemed to exist—instead the room itself seemed to fade away into darkness, as though the hall was hovering somehow in the midst of the night sky. Through the dancing crowd, they saw a high stairwell, gold and twinkling beneath another massive chandelier that hovered above the floor without a chain.

"Didrebelle," started Gamaréa, "that stairway must

lead to the Queen—wherever she may—" Suddenly he was yanked away from his companion and brought to a separate corner of the dance floor by a young woman who sought a dance from him. He noticed looking at her that she bore many colorful flowers in her hair—pink, white, and red— and her eyes were bright and yellow like two miniature stars. She smiled playfully, but Gamaréa only feigned enthusiasm, as he was much too wary of Didrebelle's whereabouts. It seemed she had taken him exceptionally far from his companion. Looking out, the room was filled to its endless capacity, and Didrebelle was nowhere to be found.

The Fairy also had been looking for Gamaréa, as he found himself abducted as well by another dancer shortly after his companion. But when the music stopped the dancers settled for a moment, and Gamaréa was able to break free and steal through the crowd. Finally, he reunited with Didrebelle, crossing gazes with him from a distance and meeting him.

"We must move," Gamaréa said hurriedly. "We must stay together."

They climbed the stairwell, and looking back now they saw the ballroom had disappeared beneath black and gray clouds and it had become utterly cold. They were surprised to see that they were wearing their original garb again, with their weapons fastened just as they were before entering the dance hall.

Nothing flanked them now on the stairwell—not a protective railing or wall that they could use to maintain balance, thus they stayed huddled in the center and pressed upward to where there seemed to be a large door in the sky itself—gray and black through which beamed lightning. As they climbed higher, it seemed the door crept steadily out of reach, and it seemed, to their building frustration, that they stayed in place for a great while. It became such a tedious venture that Gamaréa eventually sought rest— sitting and looking down the thousand steps they already traversed and seeing only blackness and flashing lights. But Didrebelle had taken to carrying on, and eventually yelled for him over the roaring wind, "Look! The door! The door!"

And looking now Gamaréa saw that the door was a meter away.

"What is this place?" Didrebelle said worriedly. "I have never witnessed such strange occurrences as these!"

"It is a realm built upon dreams, my friend. Everything we just witnessed were but figments of our own minds."

Suddenly the door began to open slowly, and they heard it creaking upon the howling wind. At length Gamaréa stood and led cautiously on. They now entered a room in which large shards of glass hung randomly about. A thousand images of themselves peered back at them.

Didrebelle walked ahead a step or two. "This place seems endless," he said. "What is this madness?"

"The path to the Queen would be limitless," answered Gamaréa. "Perhaps none are meant to find her."

Didrebelle continued onward slowly. "I cannot determine which way to pass."

Then he looked around, and was dismayed to find only himself in the reflections. He called for Gamaréa, but the Morok did not answer.

Didrebelle had, in fact, unknowingly closed himself off from the Morok. By walking a separate way, he fell into the trap of the Queen's mirror-maze, and was forced now to follow it along the only path available. He could not hear Gamaréa calling for him on the other side—calling to all the mirrored images of his companion as the true form of Didrebelle stole away.

It troubled the Morok greatly to think that in such a short span of time he may have lost both of the companions he set out with from Elderland—one of whom being the Keeper of Fates himself. At hand remained only the pursuit of the key—which, he felt, could still be salvaged. And so he pressed on, down the spiraling path winding on through the mirrors until it was no longer available to him.

Then there was nothing but a black void, and though he hadn't virtually any depth perception, he felt that he was elevated well above flat ground. Now from under him the world began to shake, and he maintained what balance he could until he could stand no more and fell from the ledge into the void.

To his surprise, he landed rather gingerly upon a silver floor, sparkling here and there as though comprised entirely of jewels. But when he looked up, he saw that more chandeliers were hanging and glinting off the floor, affording the room exhilarating décor. Suddenly he felt himself lifted from the ground, and noticed that he was being carried forward by six of the Queen's spidery agents to the middle of a large, circular room that burst with invigorating color, and in the center he saw her—the Queen sitting tall and proud upon her high throne.

Her face was ghostly pale, but there certainly was a beautiful quality about her. It might have been her eyes, which were dark and piercing, their gaze intensified by her pallid skin. The dress she wore was gold and bulbous and plated with fine jewels. She advanced in a fluttery, girlish manner, as though she were merely waltzing about in her lonesome.

The spiders delivered Gamaréa at her feet, and he rolled off just as the Queen was all but on top of him.

Gamaréa bent on one knee. "My lady," he said softly.

With a gentle touch, she lifted his bowed head. "Gamaréa," she said, genially. Her voice was more delicate than he had anticipated, and he stared into the shadows of her eyes. "You have done well to reach my steps; for there have been none who can boast that they have done so."

"I am not here for my own benefit, or for any right into songs or tales," assured Gamaréa frankly. "The plot of my original course was ruined, and it was the giant Tantus that forced us this way."

The white-faced Queen sucked her teeth. "Then I am truly sorry for the inconvenience the rogue has caused you, my child. But—if so I may inquire—what is a Morok doing within the Provinus in the first place? You being so far from home, of course."

Gamaréa looked up to where her throne was perched,

golden and wrought with various diamonds and flowers. On a small stool beside it, he saw the Key shimmering. "I think you know that answer, my lady," he said.

She answered without looking back. "The *Key?* Is that why you are here?" It was plain to Gamaréa that she was feigning her ignorance.

Gamaréa nodded.

"And what importance does it have to you?" she asked, studying him with her black eyes. "Surely it must unlock something that conceals great worth?"

"In many ways."

"I am very sorry to hear that," she said. She was staring hard at him now, and he understood what Tartalion meant when he said she bore evil qualities as well; for though her tone was gentle, her eyes suggested madness lingered within her.

"Unfortunately I cannot simply *give* it to you," she continued, and Gamaréa became dismayed. "It is not often I am delivered treasures from outside. You must give something to me in exchange."

This confused Gamaréa, and looking about him, he noticed only his sword and bow. "I bear only weapons," he said hesitantly, "and you have no use for those."

"Right you are, my child. I do not engage in warfare, and if I had I would use my sorc—my *magic* as my weapon," she brought one of her small hands to her lips and giggled playfully. "Do you distrust my magic, Darkwood? Do you not think I am a worthy witch?"

"I have said no such thing, my lady."

She laughed slightly. "Your eyes suggest it."

"I assure you otherwise."

She sucked her teeth multiple times. "You challenge me," she said, almost playfully. "Look!" She suddenly stepped aside, and Gamaréa fell back at the sight he now beheld. Now, walking slowly and elegantly down the steps from the Queen's throne strode Emmanuelle, dressed in the gown he remembered her wearing the very last time he saw her.

He bent away. "No, my Queen!" he exclaimed, his voice

wavering intensely as he covered his face. "Do not show me this image! Your magic will not—" but then he felt her touch, the warmth of her hand that could come from no other, as it drew his arm down gently and brought his face up to hers. And Gamaréa saw her plainly now. Their eyes met for the first time in two centuries. Suddenly he remembered her every element and feature as though those years had simply been moments.

"Emm—my—" he stammered, searching for whatever word he could muster. But what could he say? What *should* he say? She bent and guided him upward by his hands, and his eyes met hers now as they had so long ago. And he knew of nothing else to do but kiss her, and he closed his eyes and leaned toward her, and felt only air where she once had been.

The Queen was standing before him when his eyes slowly opened. "What do you think of my magic now, my child?"

Gamaréa was outraged—and though he had not been conscious of them, tears were coursing down the sides of his face. He drew his sword and raised it to her, wailing in fury, but she raised a hand and stilled him. His sword fell to the ground behind him, ringing through the vastness of the hall. She lowered him slowly, and the smile returned to her face. "Now," she said, as though nothing had happened, "as for the Key!"

"What could you want from me that I possess? You do not want my weapons, and I bear nothing else."

"Oh, you naughty fibber," she said, shaking her finger at him. "That is not true! Why must you lie to me? Have I yet been untruthful?"

The Morok thought hard for a moment. He truly had nothing else to offer. *My clothes?* He thought. *What could she possibly want with those?*

The Queen spoke again, and she seemed disappointed. "Perhaps this would be easier if I showed you, darling." She rose her hand up again, and Gamaréa felt something lift from the collar of his shirt and up in front of his face. It was a necklace. A necklace Emmanuelle had given him. A gift he had long forgotten—too saddened to ever look upon it—having fallen to memory atop his heart since her death.

"There now!" gasped the Queen happily. "I ask but this from you, my child. Your necklace for the Key! I barter honestly. I deem this trade fair. You seem to disagree."

For a long while Gamaréa could not speak. "But—I—"

"Come now, child," said the Queen, "if you fail to accept my offer I will have to ask you to leave; my time is precious."

He was in his sleeping quarters—the quarters issued to him by her father, Melinta, the new lord of Dridion. In the darkest hour of the night, she woke him without a word. Her presence sitting at the foot of his bed drew him from sleep. When he saw her sitting there, he was startled, for beneath the sheets, his naked body lay, and he was embarrassed.

When she saw that he appeared so, she smiled. "You needn't worry," she said. "I will not stay long. I've only come to tell you that the line of suitors my father has issued is ended."

"I knew this, my lady," he answered. "I knew when Demetrious was sent away."

"I must give you something." He saw that she held in her clasped hand a golden chain from which was fastened two silver threads that twisted together into an individual point.

"My lady?"

"It is a symbol of my people that represents love—two souls coming together as one. I want you to have it."

There was stirring in the corridor outside.

"I think my father has woken," said Emmanuelle. "I must go. In the morrow I ask that you take me to Ravelon one last time."

"But no suitor will—"

"Please. Just one last time. It is of great importance to me."

Before he could answer, she had risen to leave.

"This chain is of great worth to me," Gamaréa said at length. "I cannot part with it. You may have whatever else you desire."

The Queen sighed. "I will ask for nothing else but this, my dear," she said, seemingly saddened, as though she was bound to seek this chain. She must have noted the despair on Gamaréa's face, for she approached him and spoke gently. "Come. There is another thing I must show you."

She led him to a large stone basin in the midst of a larger chasm, accessible through a tunnel not far from her hall. A light was emitting from it—the only light in the room—and all else was illuminated stone. "Look," she said, "in the basin."

At first Gamaréa refrained. "I will not."

The Queen seemed disappointed. "Must you make everything so difficult, my dear?" Then her gaze fixed hard upon him, and he felt as though she was grabbing his head and forcing him to look within the water. "What can you see, child?"

There were many images of various lands—places he had seen and some he had not yet encountered. He noticed his homeland of Medric, and an image of Mascorea. Then images of Dridion and Mount Zynys and Nundric passed, and then an image of somewhere he could not place—a city that may once have been inhabited but now lay in ruin. Now there were flames and legions of the Netherworld seizing the realms of the Three Heralds and razing them—their people fleeing and eventually mutilated. And then he saw the souls—all those lost to the void of the plains of Parthaleon where Sorcerian fed on them.

Then suddenly he heard the Queen. "The choice is yours, Darkwood," she said softly.

He rose from the basin, his eyes swelling with stubborn tears—whether for the sight he just endured or the choice he was about to make. But he clasped the chain about his neck and yanked it away, and without looking handed it over to the Queen.

"Now," she said, "that wasn't so difficult."

When Gamaréa looked to her, he noticed her magic had returned them to her hall, and they stood beside her throne. She handed him the Key.

"I trust your treasure is of profound importance, Darkwood" she said, "for you to part with something so dear in exchange."

His eyes bore down to the floor. "Allow me now to take my leave," he implored heavily. "And call me Darkwood no more."

It seemed as though Didrebelle had passed on for hours, but when the maze of mirrors had reached its end, he noticed he had arrived inside a cavern of sorts, where stone pedestals seemed to be holding up the roof and an opening revealed the early morning sky outside. What light shone in was glaring down on two objects in the center—Lucian and the Enchantress. Even from where he stood, he could see Lucian's gaze and how captivated he was. Didrebelle, in fact, thought it to be much too eccentric for his liking, but he considered the circumstances.

He crept along the ridge of the cavern—a shadow inching along—and remembered the words of his companion. *She will meet no end until her lover's blade pierces her heart.* Even from where Didrebelle stood, he could see the glare from Excebellus glinting out of its scabbard upon Lucian's waist. *He may not have a mind to smite her,* Didrebelle thought to himself, *but I most certainly do.* He inched along, devising a scheme to somehow manage to spring up behind Lucian and pierce the heart of the Enchantress with Excebellus, but it would not be an easy task.

He cleared his mind, and in no time at all darted rapidly from his position with speed that surprised even himself. With a cry, he claimed Excebellus for his own and pushed over its mindless bearer. Closing his eyes, he thrust it forward and into the heart of the Enchantress, and her piercing scream filled the air of the cavern. Suddenly the area began to quake and rock came loose from all directions, raining down upon them all. Then he saw the most horrid of sights; for now the Enchantress seemed to be deteriorating, and as her body caved in on itself she became grotesque and serpent-like, her skin and eyes green like muck before she evaporated into a cloud of reeking smoke that filtered out of the orifice above.

Then Lucian, now flung from his trance, awoke to the crumbling room of the cavern and was delighted to find Didrebelle standing before him. Together they broke for the opening, and after much toil stole away into the coming morning. From the plateau upon which they surfaced, they heard the cavern below falling to ruin. But their spirits were abruptly lifted when they saw Gamaréa, too, who was racing off ahead of them.

Didrebelle called to him, and at long last, their trio was whole again. They looked out over Provinus and saw the sun rising just over the peaks in the east, a gray mist circling beneath the pink-and-red-blotched sky.

Didrebelle inhaled deeply, and a look of pleasure came to his face. "Do you smell that?" he said happily. Neither companion answered. "Salt!" the Fairy exclaimed. "The sea lies just beyond those peaks."

Gamaréa laughed. "For a moment I—" he looked upon his companions hard, realizing now that everything he needed—and could ever need—was standing intact before him. But he could not finish what he was about to say, for an all too familiar cry lifted over the hills at their back, and Tantus, with renewed vigor, came barreling after them.

21

Beelciber

From behind them, the giant came barreling, thrusting himself clumsily down the final stretch of Provinus at the fleeing threesome. They could distinguish his features clearly now in the light of the coming sun. There was nothing remarkable about Tantus except for his size. Everything about the wild, flailing beast was absolutely revolting. His face seemed confused and misshapen, with a large nose and a protruding forehead that shadowed his deep, dull eyes brimming with madness. His limbs emerged awkwardly from his body, heavily muscled, jointed by disgruntled elbows and knees. A beard—or what could only be interpreted as a beard—sprouted from the lower part of his face, circling his wide, lipless mouth in which rotten, dagger-like teeth were housed.

Though his strides were long and carried him quickly, the company maintained a fair distance from him, and when they reached the end of Provinus, Didrebelle was the first to proclaim, "Look there! A ship! A ship is moored further out!"

Now all of them saw it—a war galley, it seemed—moored perhaps a hundred feet from the shore. Though he believed he never would again, Gamaréa drew a wide smile when he saw *The Sojourn* resting at the pier, just on the cusp of the shoreline.

Fate does work in wily ways, he thought merrily for once.

It was not long before Gamaréa, Didrebelle, and Lucian

were forced to plunge into the water, otherwise Tantus would have surely enjoyed a sizeable breakfast. Running out into the murky waters, they dove in, swimming for their lives. All the while Gamaréa was shouting for anyone on the ship, racking the water with his arms as he swam quickly and with great cunning. It was Gawaire's face they saw first, as he poked his head over the prow with his pipe in his mouth and a stern look on his face.

"I'll be!" he shouted jovially. "Lars! Fetch the throw-ladder! We've got ourselves some company!"

A rope ladder was flung over the starboard side of the galley, which the dripping companions climbed eagerly.

Just then, the terrible figure of Tantus cascaded over the small hill leading down to the shore, his monstrous cries piercing the calm morning.

"What on earth did you do?" said Gawaire, helping Gamaréa onto *The Sojourn*. "That thing can't swim can it?"

"Not for its life," replied Gamaréa cheerfully.

Lucian boarded after Gamaréa, and once Didrebelle was helped aboard Larstus lifted the ladder and Irie the anchor, and from there they passed swiftly against the gentle emergence of the morning tide. Off their stern, they heard the crying Tantus shouting through the mist; crying, for he would return prizeless to his canyons, knowing years would wither before others dared to venture there.

Gamaréa gazed headlong off the prow of *The Sojourn*. Didrebelle had made his way to the tip of a high mast and perched there for a time, for the vision of Fairies is extensive, and he thought he could serve the company well as they crawled along the sea. Lucian, however, sat troubled, then rose troubled, and then sat again; for it seemed that before he merely blinked an eye he had been attacked by a demonic horde, watched his village burn, was thwarted by mountain tribesmen, and chased relentlessly through a quarter of Provinus by a thirty-foot giant—and on account of a Key. *A Key!* he thought. *Something as commonly used as bread and butter.*

It was a curse, and he was not entirely sure he deserved

to be cursed. Perhaps someone somewhere in the long range of his ancestry did wrong to someone who could have made this hex possible. Maybe, even now, they were watching through some magnifying device laughing—laughing as Tantus chased them to the sea, and laughing even as they traveled further, leaping from net to net, to be caught and then escape only to be caught again. But in time, thought Lucian, a net would claim them too cunning from which to wiggle.

The day had fully broken, and for what they could fathom, it would be similar to the last. They passed beneath a gray sky, which was flanked by lighter grayness blotched with thick storm clouds. The ship, however, hastily trudged along the waters, guided by the extroverted wind within which Didrebelle's garb flailed wildly from atop the mast. He constantly shouted down to Gamaréa about the time they would be making if indeed they were pressing toward a specific destination, for the beach had long disappeared beyond the impenetrable mist behind them.

Sometime in the afternoon, Lucian—who had drifted in and out of a nap—made his way to Gamaréa, who since they came aboard the ship gazed from the tip of the prow like the figures of mermaids often do, speaking frequently with Gawaire and Gellun about a proper course. The three were standing confident and steadfast, as though the seaward breeze soothed them like a lover's touch, and extracted a power hidden deep within their souls.

"Where will this route lead us?" Lucian asked candidly.

It was Gawaire who spoke. "This is the one, then?" he asked.

Gamaréa nodded before responding. "To the coasts of the west," he replied, "if the Mountain favors our journey." Though he knew the Sages' attention was elsewhere, it was a phrase he had grown accustomed to saying.

"And how far into the west do we have to go to get to Medric?"

"Unless I'm mistaken," said Gellun, rubbing specs of dirt from his compass, "Stormbeard Bay is still a few days' sail."

"If our journey favors us," added Gamaréa, "our course is set to deliver us to the port of Dwén Alíl. From there it is not even half a day's ride to Adoram."

"And from there," said Lucian hesitantly, as though about to ask a question he hadn't any desire to ask or have answered. "How far to Nundric?"

A distinct shadow seemed to loom over *The Sojourn* now, such as Gellun shuddered, and Gamaréa and Gawaire looked warily around them. Even Lucian felt a heaviness overcome him, and for a moment felt the uncomfortable pangs of seasickness.

Yet the shadow passed in a moment's time, and it seemed as though the sun were out even in the little light the gloomy day provided.

"Another time, Lucian," was all Gamaréa said.

But for some reason, a dire need overcame Lucian's mind, and he felt it was imperative that he understood where Nundric was and how to get there. It was beginning to settle in that he had reached the point of no return. The east was fleeting behind *The Sojourn*, and the remnants of his old life with it. He was deathly afraid of the changes the west would force him to adjust to, and the responsibilities that he would need to accept once he stepped off of Gawaire's vessel.

The rowers' chanting songs beat on behind him. He stood there, denied, as Gamaréa took up a conversation with Gawaire again, racking his mind for a way to retort. This was his mission and his burden to bear, and he was furious to be denied information regarding it. Yet even he was surprised by his own persistence, as he reached for Gamaréa's arm and tugged at it, interrupting his talk with the captain.

Gamaréa sighed, as though he knew Lucian's intentions all too well. "Yes, Lucian?" he asked lazily.

"A word, please?" answered Lucian shortly.

Gamaréa was less than pleased to be dragged below deck by a seventeen-year-old mortal. A small cabin afforded them at least some privacy, though the chanting of the rowers and the smacking of their oars were very distracting.

"What is it now?" asked Gamaréa sharply.

"I want to talk about Nundric," answered Lucian.

Gamaréa grunted, apparently frustrated that Lucian dared broach the subject again.

"I thought I told you," scolded the Morok. "Another time."

Realizing the main topic of Lucian's meeting, Gamaréa made as if to shift his way out of the cabin when Lucian grabbed on to his mailed shoulder and stopped him. It is difficult to say which one seemed more surprised, but all movement ceased and their eyes locked for a brief moment—Lucian's filled with desperation; Gamaréa's with incredulity.

"I–I want to know now," said Lucian sheepishly, releasing Gamaréa's shoulder as though it had started to burn.

Gamaréa wanted to ask him why the thought of Nundric was at the front of his mind when they still had a long journey ahead of them once they docked, but he refrained. After a small moment, having realized the worry in his companion's eyes, he felt as though he owed it to Lucian to answer whatever questions vexed him.

"What is it you want to know?" asked Gamaréa at last.

Lucian's lips fumbled wordlessly for a moment. He had so many questions regarding Nundric, yet now that it was time to voice them, he fought to recall just one of them.

"I–well, I guess I don't understand what it looks like . . . Tartalion said something about Nundric, but then about another place—I forgot the name . . . "

"Parthaleon, surely," answered Gamaréa. "It is the underworld realm that lies beneath the ashen fields of Nundric. That is where the souls of the damned are massing. It is in Parthaleon that he has secured the Chamber of Fates."

"But what about Nundric itself?" asked Lucian confusedly. "What's there?"

"Nundric is the first tier of Sorcerian's realm, the tier in which his living hordes are assembling. Over the centuries, they have been sworn to his service, and have taken to building fortresses and watchtowers of thick stone in preparation for the day that someone dares to enter Parthaleon and seek out the Chamber.

"But they cannot enter Parthaleon themselves, mind you, just as no living soul can do so without perishing. Thus, they litter the Darklands by the thousands, and their sum increases by the day. In the end, with the forces of Nundric, Parthaleon and Dridion combined, we will certainly have a fight on our hands."

Lucian's heart was beating rapidly, and a very distinct heaviness fell over him, such as though he felt welded to the spot in which he stood. The more of his questions Gamaréa answered, the less he wished he had asked them. But he could not stop himself from asking more.

"How far underground is Part-Parth . . . ?"

"Parthaleon. There are none who have released a true measure of its depth. Perhaps there are some who have tried, but I cannot say. I can only speculate that it delves many leagues beneath the earth, for he was cast there with such vengeance from the highest summit of Zynys with all the powers of Ation cast against him—"

Lucian became contemplative, as though trying to recall something distantly. "I have heard stories about Darklands and such," he replied at last. "Mary used to tell them to me when I was little. Nundric reminds me of some of the places she spoke of—"

"No, Lucian," Gamaréa said softly, yet there was a very stern tone to his voice that seemed to close Lucian off even to the sound of the rowers beyond the door. "Nundric is unlike anything you have ever seen or heard of on earth. It is a place not meant to be visited; a realm littered with death, woe, darkness, and turmoil—the air more stifling than all the world's deserts combined a hundred times over. As children we are taught never to speak of it, never to even imagine being in any kind of vicinity to it, yet there we press. Prepare yourself, Lucian, as best you can. It shall be the most evil you encounter in all your years of life."

There was not much more to be said. Lucian, for one, although he felt as though he had more questions remaining on the subject, did not dare ask anymore.

They finished speaking then. Gamaréa went back above to converse with some members of the crew, but Lucian remained behind for a long while. Didrebelle remained atop his mast, peering out into the far distance. As evening approached the mists began growing lighter, and the sky smoothed over with a layer of velvet that looked as though it was silk draped neatly across the breadth of the heavens. Stars began emerging faintly where the storm blotches had been throughout the earlier parts of the day, and Didrebelle was proud to announce that their nightly voyage would progress without many obstacles.

Larstus was specifically thankful for the Fairy's expertise. "Someone ought to thank that agile fellow over there for me," he remarked sarcastically as he manned the helm.

Lucian wished now that his mind would carry on as steadily as their vessel, but instead he lay upon a bench at the ship's stern and gazed up to the night that had completely fallen, watching it slowly drag away as *The Sojourn* passed on. He felt the Key firmly in his pocket, heavy as though it were some large stone he had claimed possession of—that he could not be rid of. Upon the wooden deck of the galley, he saw the ghosts of the gem's blue and green lights casting their iridescent shadows.

Two more days of *The Sojourn's* voyage passed, eating salted jerk and stale bread and drinking from some casks of Gawaire's mulled wine. Lucian had grown accustomed to taxing his jaw trying to chew the rough, hard meat so that it was swallowable, but the wine was a poor substitute for the many drinks he enjoyed at MaDungal's, whose hardy rum would have served him well now in the chill of the nightly sea.

They were eating one night upon makeshift plates when Didrebelle inquired of Gamaréa as to the remaining stretch of their journey at sea. The Morok responded by telling him that by Gawaire's calculations they would reach Stormbeard Bay in a day or so. He paused for a moment, then elucidated that, should in fact *The Sojourn* manage to keep its *current* pace, it would be thus.

Though Didrebelle made no apparent remark and bore relatively no expression, Lucian could tell he was displeased with the Morok's news. Didrebelle pressed him further, as though by doing so his report would change and the remaining duration of their trip would lessen. Gamaréa relayed the same information. Didrebelle was silent throughout the remainder of their dinner, and did not speak again for what Lucian heard.

As the sky churned shades of plum and indigo to ebony, it proved to be another night of restlessness for Lucian, who fiddled with the Key, tossed and turned, then fiddled with the Key again. In time, he abandoned his attempt to sleep and listened to his companions, who he could hear speaking quietly, as if in secret, at the prow.

Lucian crept beside the captain's wheel, at which Larstus was now working, and listened as best he could. Didrebelle and Gamaréa were weaving in and out of the common and foreign tongues, but for what Lucian heard, Gamaréa said, "We knew this journey would bring us here, my friend. Any route we chose would have led us to the sea."

And Didrebelle replied, "But I had hoped our time across would have been swifter; the sea is perilous to those who tarry."

"Our vessel cannot tread faster than it is. The rowing crews already toil endlessly below and have nearly divided our trek west to half of what it took to go east. We must continue at our present speed and cling to hope."

Hope? Lucian thought. *Hope for what?*

Then Didrebelle spoke as though revealing information he meant to keep hidden. "Beelcibur has been tracking us for a day, now," he said softly, as though the very name he had just uttered would shake them from their foundations.

The Morok straightened. "I have sensed him also," he replied.

Gamaréa peered over his shoulder, and Lucian crept further into the secrecy of the darkness near the wheel and masts.

"We are passing over his territory as we speak," observed Didrebelle. "It will not be long before he lets us know that."

Beelcibur? thought Lucian to himself. Just the word rattled his bones, as though it described the very name of evil—a name profound enough to make two warlords whisper it. But now Gamaréa and Didrebelle had broken apart, and headed for the stern. Lucian quickly retired from his hiding place, went back to the bench where he originally tried to sleep and pretended to do so.

There Gamaréa and Didrebelle peered over him.

"Look at him," said Gamaréa softly. "He is sleeping peacefully."

"He hasn't a clue," added Didrebelle. "Not a clue of what awaits us—in these waters or elsewhere."

Soon after they retired, Lucian rose again and paced about the ship. The night air was soothing, and the salty breeze passed over him calmly. No sounds were audible, save the gentle chopping of the waves upon the ship, and the occasional exhale of a whale who would surface now and then.

High above the moon peered from the velvet sky, wreathed by scattered stars that gleamed off the unusually placid sea ahead. Lucian walked to the prow and thought. He wondered now how Jem was fairing, and was impaired by further regret that he had left him so abruptly. But it was for Jem's own sake, Lucian would justify. Had Jem partaken in this venture alongside him, Lucian's attention would certainly have been divided between the Key and his friend's wellbeing, and that was something he could not allow. In Elderland, he determined, Jem was safe.

And as the ship etched further into nothingness he thought of all else he had left behind. Perhaps it was the coiling stillness that was around him that made him ponder such things so deeply, and soon his mind was stifled by guilt and sorrow and fear that he would never return to see any of them again. What little hope and confidence he had in himself burned to the ground with Amar, even before Gamaréa led him through the Black Forest. Those roaring flames were still all too present in his mind, and in his heart he wept for all that was lost, and cursed himself for having introduced a peaceful village to such grief. And as he thought of the Key he felt it pulsating in his pocket like a heavy, demonic, negative energy that was ever present in times of hardship; something he could not shake or hide from, something he feared would follow him even if he cast it to the bottom of the ocean beneath him.

It pulsed on, intensifying so that it was nearly audible, throbbing against his thigh like a burning flame. And so he took it out, almost involuntarily, and gazed into the gleaming lights of blue and green, and heard its voice whisper his name, hauntingly, without intent, like a child. It pulsed within his hand now, tickling his palm, vibrating his enclosed fist, rattling his finger-bones to the point of pain, and on and on the voices continued, continued on into the night.

Then suddenly the sea was not still, and the pulsating Key became lifeless again. Upon the ship, the waves crashed harder, and *The Sojourn* bobbed left and right—sometimes violently—despite the lack of wind. Lucian grasped firm to the starboard rails as a sound sprung from below like an impish shriek promptly followed by an enormous strike upon the ship's rightward side, nearly capsizing the vessel. With a sound like a falling tree, one of the masts toppled, blanketed by the flags it had flown.

Again, the same shrill cry rose up, this time further up the starboard side, and the ship was struck again. Upon the open sea, it quaked as it was attacked and thrown about, like some invisible fleet had sprung upon it in the night and lay siege to it with missiles. Lucian was thrown from his feet and slammed against the wall of the deck. Trepidation engulfed him while he watched as the Key he once held onto firmly flew from his hand and hovered above the sea for an instant before it fell to the malevolent depths beneath.

"NOOO!" he cried, but it was no use. He could only lay there in horror, gazing down at his hands in disbelief, as though it was their fault to have let go of something so precious, even in such freak conditions. Though the wailing and slamming continued on, it seemed to be drowned out by the realization that the sole purpose of his journey was lost in an instant, and in moments, as all the wrath of the sea conspired against them, he felt he would share the same fate.

Just then Gamaréa and Didrebelle leapt swiftly to the deck, and Gawaire and his fellows came with them, soon to be joined by the alternate crew of forty rowers all bearing spears or bows. Didrebelle leapt cunningly atop one of the masts that still stood and peered into the darkness of the brutally active sea.

"Beelcibur!" he cried above the cacophony. "Beelcibur is upon us!"

Gamaréa ordered Lucian to run and hide below deck, but a certain shock had come over him since the Key had fallen overboard, and he was unable to retain anything the Morok said for a moment. Gamaréa found that he needed to repeat himself numerous times before Lucian paid him complete attention, and even then the young boy was resistant.

"I have to stay here," he insisted. "I can fight with all of you."

Gamaréa looked upon him doubtingly. "I will not have you raise your sword against Beelcibur," he said. "He has claimed many skilled soldiers' lives. You have to retreat below deck at once!"

Before Lucian could rebut, an enormous, scaled tentacle, drenched in seawater and slime, fell heavily upon the deck, and the black-and-green life form wrapped around Didrebelle's mast, tugged twice and yanked it from its hinges. The Fairy, however, did not budge until the last second, and used the momentum of the falling mast to leap upon the tentacle where he immediately began chopping swiftly with his swords until he managed to hew a sizable portion of it away, causing Beelcibur to shriek again as its separated limb spewed oil-like blood erratically upon the deck.

For a short while, it was dormant, but in time rose up again with fury, and set about wrapping the ship with two of its snake-like limbs. One of these nearly fell upon Lucian.

Gamaréa swung his sword wildly, raising it high above his head and dropping it down so rapidly that blinking would have resulted in missing it having happened. Didrebelle had returned his swords to their sheaths upon his back and resorted to firing arrows at the tentacles. Now he leapt upon the edge of the ship, keeping excellent balance and posture despite its swaying, and fired arrows into the sea below, hoping some would befall the sea-beast.

"Show yourself, coward!" Didrebelle cried with rage. But Beelcibur had yet surfaced entirely. Lucian also ran clumsily alongside them, carrying Excebellus tentatively, but causing much damage when he struck.

In time, though their trial was exhausting and repetitive, the companions managed to rid themselves of Beelcibur's relentless attack, and its tentacles—or what was left of them—retired back into the sea and it fizzled for a long while before becoming still again.

The companions gathered round at the starboard side of the ship, facing the sea, expecting Beelciber to rise up at any moment and strike again.

"It is still here," said Didrebelle quietly. "I can smell it."

Gawaire grew restless. "Whatever Sage you talk to, friend, now would be a good time to summon him."

They prepared themselves. Gamaréa and Lucian held firm to their swords and Didrebelle had an arrow fixed to the string of his long bow. The spear-armed rowers looked warily about, their pikes at the ready. Then suddenly, with a shriek livelier and more bone shattering than any other it had released, Beelcibur unleashed itself from the sea and showed itself fully above the water. A barrage of seawater spewed this way and that, spilling onto the deck of *The Sojourn* in salty waves. Now they gazed up into its glowing eyes, yellow, like rebellious flames that had ascended from the depths to smite them.

They could see that it was more serpentine than anything. Its body was long and slender, stretching high above them, looming over the prow, drooling hungrily from its fang-riddled mouth. In one fell swoop, it bore down on them, using its body like a makeshift sword to split the ship in half and drag the companions down to the depths with it. Shards of wood splattered everywhere, and everyone flew off in different directions, left to nothing but the beast, the sea, and the night.

Beelcibur submerged once again, and came up swiftly in moments beside Gamaréa, who tried to grab onto it but slipped off its slimy body. Didrebelle bobbed calmly in the water, even as it swirled frantically around him, but he had set aside his bow and released his swords again. When Beelcibur was in reach, *he* attempted to mount him and was successful. Running up the slime-covered slope of its body, he took to wrestling the beast when he reached its head. When Beelcibur was aware of the courageous Fairy, it cried out in fury and flailed its head around to try to throw him off. Didrebelle's focus and determination, however, were too intense even for the horrid creature, and having grown weak and weary, he managed to slit its throat with two fatal strokes of his swords.

Yet as Beelcibur—bobbing now in the sea, confused and dying, with long streams of black blood oozing down its slender neck—ebbed into eternal slumber, they bore witness to a defiantly strange occurrence, for from the water around the companions came flying what appeared to be arrow-like projectiles. Beelcibur, pierced by their majority, submerged for the final time, sinking swiftly to the bed of the ocean from which he would rise no more.

Then, from beneath them, the companions felt what appeared to be gentle hands grab hold of their dangling legs and drag them earnestly below the sea. When they looked, though it was dark under the disrupted water, they saw that strange beings had taken hold of them, and they delved beside the shards of their ship and the sinking corpses of Beelcibur and *The Sojourn's* brave crew, until all around them went dark.

22

The Woods of Ravelon

Lucian could tell that it was morning. Though his eyes were closed, he could sense a light shining on him, and it was humid. Sporadically he heard the calls of gulls, and the soft rumble of the tide as it rose up and around his ankles. Now for the first time he opened his eyes, and saw for the better all that was around him. Gamaréa lay sprawled to his right as though dead, and to his left was Didrebelle drenched and covered in white sand. For the moment, neither was moving, but in time, he heard Gamaréa groan, as one waking from a drunken slumber, and Didrebelle was quick to stir after.

It took much effort for Lucian to rise, and when he did so, he removed his worn boots and planted his feet in the cold, soggy sand over which the tide trickled. He relished in it as it passed, closing his eyes and enjoying for once a fresh breath. Things were beginning to come back to him now as he stared across the sea. *The Sojourn's last voyage,* he thought sadly, thinking of Gawaire and his unsuspecting crew. There would come a day when his company would be entitled to bear ill tidings to many wives, but that day was far off, and it was not yet proven whether their deaths were in vain.

A cold breeze flew in from the east and fleeted by. Sliding a hand upon his pant pocket, Lucian was startled when he remembered that the Key was irretrievably lost somewhere within the wilderness of the waves.

But a strange thing happened then, as he stared

far beyond the blue horizon before him. At his feet, he felt something odd, like the touch of metal, and looking down he beheld, inconceivably, that which he feared was lost forever. Stooping, he picked up the Key, which was seemingly unscathed, and placed it in his pocket once more.

Behind him Gamaréa said, "Lucian?" with an air of confusion in his voice.

Lucian turned, half-startled. "Yes?"

The Morok had taken to scratching his sand-covered head. "Are you alright?"

"I am. And you?"

Gamaréa's was disheveled, and he was squinting heavily from having just woken. Looking over to Didrebelle, who was awake yet slow to rise, he said, "I'll be just fine."

Didrebelle's weak voice sounded then. "It would seem as though Nepsus is not dormant after all," he said.

"I don't think it was the Sage that aided us," replied Gamaréa. "He was adamant about the temporary cease of the Mountain's intervention. We were helped, I think, by other means. There is good *and* evil in the seas, my friends, just as there is good and evil on land. It was by an evil stroke *The Sojourn* was undone, but by a righteous deed we have been spared."

"The Aquilum, you mean?" said Didrebelle incredulously.

"I think it may be so."

"The Aquilum?" asked Lucian, intrigued.

"Yes," replied Gamaréa. "It must have been, though I have only heard of them through tale. They are a tribe that inhabits the depths, and are said to follow in the wake of troubled vessels lost at sea. Though *The Sojourn* was not lost exactly, they must have sensed our hardships and aided us anyway. Rendering us unconscious was the only way they could transport us to this shore, and thus they have delivered us our lives, but little else. Fate led us to *The Sojourn,* or perhaps *The Sojourn* to us, but just as quickly has steered us off course. Yet we have to press on while we still have strength, and be thankful for such gifts. We have met a better fate than those intrepid souls who gave their lives for our cause, and we must never forget the part Gawaire and his crew played. *The Sojourn's* last voyage will be etched forever in the histories of the world when better days are upon us."

Then Gamaréa stood wearily, and peered out to sea beside Lucian, a look of longing upon his battered face. "It might also be that they recovered the Key for you as well," he said, as if an afterthought.

Lucian's face flushed, embarrassed to learn that Gamaréa knew he had momentarily lost the Key. But to his relief Gamaréa left that topic alone.

"We can tarry here," said Gamaréa, contemplatively, "but only for a short while. When we regain our strength we have to press on, and find out where on the face of the west we've landed."

The beach gave way to small cliffs through which a pathway stretched, and by that route, Gamaréa led them well into the morning, not seeing much of anything but stone and dust. In time, however, the cliffs delved steeply downward into a soft, green landscape that was flat in many spots, through which a galumph river passed, bending westward out of sight.

"We will follow the river," Gamaréa stated confidently. "It is our only hope to maintain accurate knowledge of our whereabouts."

Gamaréa stated later that it seemed the river would eventually pass through Dridion, and that there was a forested area that was popular among the ancient Moroks called Ravelon, which Didrebelle too seemed familiar with. In the time when there was peace between Medric and Dridion, Gamaréa said his kindred would often take to the forest to hunt large game, but that presently, however, he feared it was one of Melinta's most guarded stations; thus, should they be discovered there, their journey would meet an abrupt end. Nevertheless, with a lack of options presented as to a proper route, Ravelon afforded the most shelter, and thus became the trio's chosen path.

So it was they went on, slipping softly abreast of the

erratic current of the river for hours now, and to their dismay saw that it still led on for a great distance. Looking ahead, they saw the sky held blotches of darkness that loomed ominously over the far stretch of fields they had yet traveled, and determined a storm was approaching.

After the better part of four hours, the grass became tall, and the river grew calmer and narrower, running down into a calm pool at the foot of a small hill atop which was the entrance to the forest Gamaréa had mentioned earlier. Here the limbs of the trees sprouted long and slender from the ground, their shapes swaying like fair threads of a gorgeous tapestry, frolicking carelessly upon the calm breeze. And whether by the natural position of which they grew or an enchantment of sorts, they formed what looked to be a doorway, standing tall and arching, clasping on to one another like swords beneath which honorable soldiers stride, and in this way they carried on, they guessed, until the forest's end.

Gamaréa carried on up the hill to the doorway in the woods, and Didrebelle joined him. There they stood, blanketed by the light of the sun shining in at the path laid before them. It was silent but for the twittering of the forest birds, and as of now things seemed to be working in their favor.

When Lucian carried up the hill, they slipped away, silently as though moving passed sleeping serpents. The forest roof was high above them, woven delicately, as though by hand, with the thin, elegant branches of the wood.

Lucian gasped. "I've never seen anything like this!" he exclaimed. "Who could have made this place?"

"No architect had any say in the forging of this forest," answered Didrebelle. "Ravelon sprouted from the first seeds of the earth, and has grown since. We have just passed the door of Everdell, and we now walk in his hall."

"Everdell?" replied Lucian. "Was he a king? A Wizard? A sorcerer, maybe?"

"He was a legend of my people," answered Didrebelle plainly, "who believe that all that is green and glowing was created by him from his high seat in the clouds. And Ravelon was his first creation; and so it is said he blessed this place with his spirit, and the trees began to separate, forming a doorway open to a leafless path in case he ever descended to come walk in his palace without hinder."

"It figures there is a story," Lucian said sadly. "I doubt anything so beautiful would simply *sprout* from this earth."

For what they could tell, the day had waned nearly to dusk. The path shone golden before them in the sunset, the trees of Ravelon sparkling. Every so often the remaining remnants of the sun would glare through the woven branches—and now, gazing upward at the intricate canopy, it seemed surreal to them; and even the Fairy, who knew every word of the story of that place, looked on in childish wonder.

As the crest of the fading sun shone through the intertwined limbs for the last time, it made them appear carefully built; yet when night fell and all grew dim they looked as pale, ghostly tendrils, like visible gusts of a rapid wind frozen in time. The trees along the path stood high and thin, like tall pedestals along the path of kings; but a little further on, they came upon a large stone mounted by a small, leafless tree, and Gamaréa stopped the march.

"I should like to rest now in this sanctuary," he said, sitting to rest upon a stone. Lucian and Didrebelle agreed and did the same. A good rest, they felt, would be sufficient.

The company settled. Gamaréa slept for a short period of time, only to rise again and stand beside Didrebelle, who had rested long enough and now kept close watch a few yards ahead, standing like a fair statue with his great bow in hand. Together they stood peering down the path yet taken, the Fairy's blue eyes wandering ceaselessly.

"It is a quiet night," said Gamaréa. "I had forgotten the feeling of peace."

"Cling to it then, brother," replied Didrebelle, "for it will be short-lived. The night wanes; day approaches. My mind feels threatened."

He noted the graveness in the Fairy's tone. "How long have you felt this way?"

"Since the river's end." The Fairy was whispering, as though things lurked around him that may have been listening. "I do not think the Matarhim are ahead of us, but I can feel a distant shadow closing in from behind."

"But of yet we've seen or heard no sign of them, or the soldiers of Dridion for that matter. You and I can detect a Matarhim beast from a good distance, and *you* are also very capable of detecting your own countrymen."

Didrebelle's gaze seemed further troubled then. "And that is why I am most bothered; for a smell of familiarity is in the air; not dark, but sweet and soft . . . It does not comfort me."

"At dawn we will make haste, then. As for the remaining night, my trust is strong in this enchanted wood; that it may shelter us long enough to hold our tread 'til morning."

"And woe to us if we are discovered before then. We do not have the strength to fight. How should we prosper if attacked?"

"By our pride and will; war is more than strength in arms."

Didrebelle looked unsatisfied. "You speak from nearly three hundred years of experience. You were not so quick with words when the Crossing was taken long ago and Dridion marched over Medric. You were young then, and I have refreshed your mind somewhat, but you have become a great warrior in the time since then, and your name perhaps is worthy to be spoken among the legends. Yet we walk now with a child. You know Lucian cannot fight yet, though he is mighty at heart."

"In dark times," replied Gamaréa impatiently, "perhaps a stout heart can lead you better than a steadfast sword."

The Fairy sighed. "Perhaps you are right," he said softly. "I was wrong to doubt our companion. It seems I am overcome with anxiety. So much has happened since we left Elderland that our road becomes a mere blur of grief to me. Perhaps some rest *is* in order. Dawn will be here soon. Then we will fly."

And so dawn came. The forest was rank with an enchanting red gleam. It was silent but the soft chatter of birds far up in the boughs, and the company rose well rested, though having slept little.

They went on, Gamaréa and Didrebelle flanking Lucian in a single-file line. The path ahead seemed endless, and in time, the red glow of dawn faded and the wood was bright with a new day.

Suddenly, Didrebelle lashed from behind them, running past the front of the line hurriedly and nearly frightening Lucian out of his wits. Gamaréa signaled to stop. There alone in the middle of the bright path the Fairy stood, his bow in hand and an arrow fixed to the string. Didrebelle's gaze pierced every branch as he bent his bow and concentrated, his eyes locking on a target in the trees twenty yards or so up the path, but when he intended to fire, he realized he had been pursuing a mere forest bird.

He lowered his weapon for a moment, but suddenly another sound sprung up—small and almost inaudible to the rest of the trio—from the boughs above him to his right, and without hesitation he fired into the trees with hands quick as lightning, and a short while later they heard a heavy crash upon the ground. Didrebelle ran to where the thing had fallen, Gamaréa and Lucian advancing quickly in his wake.

"A scout!" he called in fury, and the company beheld a soldier of the Matarhim lying dead upon the ground, dismantled from his fall—an arrow through his throat.

Didrebelle quickly fastened another arrow to the string, but soon they heard the low, grim chanting of many deep voices, the tip-taps of iron-shod feet, and the unsheathing of many swords. Looking desperately in every direction, they saw in horror the Matarhim coiling around them like one giant, fire-riddled asp.

Many things ran through Gamaréa's mind, foremost of which his past shortcomings on the battlefield. He was skilled in war and he knew this, but he failed to recall a time when his skill aided an entire cause. The Moroks historically had fallen short in disputes, yet he always managed to live on, to fight another war, to watch his countrymen fall as he went on to wield his sword for the sole purpose of bloodshed. But this day, he deemed, would be different. This day, though he now anticipated it as his last, his efforts would stand to provide a shimmer of hope for the world beyond.

He leaned in toward Lucian and whispered softly, the marching soldiers of Nundric closing in around them like a great storm upon a small, defenseless village. "Take the Key," he said, "and go by the path I make for you. Fly to the end of the forest, and do not look back to see what will happen here. Perhaps, one day, we will meet again, when the doom of this world is decided; but I must leave you now—for a long while, maybe."

Didrebelle had listened in, and without a second guess, knew the plan of his strong-willed companion, and he took a long, slow breath, preparing his mind for the coming storm. Before Lucian could respond to Gamaréa, the Morok went charging like an arrow from the bow with Didrebelle alongside him. With sheer strength, the two warriors plowed through the front rings of the Matarhim and made their way, slowly but surely, through the thick circle that enclosed them, drawing all attention to themselves. And Lucian, though his heart had been dismantled, obeyed his leader's final order, finding fleeing as his companions fought behind him the hardest thing he had to endure the entire journey. But as the swordsmen cleared a bloody path through the amassed horde, Lucian stole frantically away. *Come on!* Lucian thought to himself. *Don't stop now. Move! Move on!* And he bounded off further, the ringing sounds of clashing iron behind him.

Meanwhile the battle raged on. Gamaréa and Didrebelle fought fiercely to keep the Matarhim at bay, and for a while, not one went far passed their barrier. Gamaréa rapidly lashed his sword through the air, seemingly invincible. He slew many almost effortlessly, and in time, it seemed as though his foes merely stood and watched in amazement before they were smote themselves. Didrebelle had gone twice through a quiver, putting his swords to use afterward, but when the number of Matarhim dwindled, he retrieved more arrows and continued his lethal bow-work.

Gamaréa hewed one of the largest beasts among them, and in its dying fall, it dragged the Morok to the ground. When he stood again, a green-feathered arrow whistled by, nearly striking him, and it bobbed in the bark of a nearby tree.

"Will you watch where you're firing?!" he shouted at Didrebelle. But to his horror, his companion was behind him, and could not have possibly fired the arrow that nearly missed his head. Then, in a white-and-gold wave, a horde of Dridion soldiers advanced through the scattered trees, prancing like mighty bucks, and in the ruckus and distraction of the newly approaching foes, the remaining host of Matarhim broke through and tread in the direction of the fleeing boy.

Didrebelle watched hopelessly as the beasts stole away, but his gaze was suddenly drawn left of him, as Gamaréa called, "My friend! It is over! Fly! Fly to Lucian before they claim him!" Didrebelle turned to behold Gamaréa thrown upon the ground and bound at the hands, then carried away by a group of Melinta's men.

Didrebelle, left alone, stood in sad, helpless thought, as though the occurrence before him froze him where he stood. His eyes never strayed from his friend, who was being borne elsewhere, sinking into the distance. And now, as the forest once rank with calamity fell silent, he felt as though a swarm of ghosts hovered around him.

He thought of Lucian and the Matarhim battalion that had passed their hold and wondered if the boy would be able to escape them. Walking wearily to a tree, he leaned against it and bowed his head as if resting. He remained standing this way for a long while, beyond perplexed.

Suddenly he heard a sound behind him, and he spun round wildly with his bow drawn, to find that it was pointing at the empty wood beyond.

Now you are losing you mind, he thought, frustrated.

Sorrow filled his heart then, as the realization that he truly was alone fell over him like a shadow. He turned back to the tree, as if to support himself, when suddenly he fell to the ground in fright as he found himself standing face-to-face with the towering figure of a man decked in splendid, shimmering armor.

A blinding light was shining, and it seemed to be emitting from the hulking man himself, as he offered his hand to Didrebelle as if to help him to his feet. Didrebelle felt himself yanked off the ground as if he had been weightless, and he peered into the crystalline eyes of the hard-faced stranger in fear.

"There is not much time," he said earnestly, in a gruff and raspy voice. "I must return promptly—my sister cannot know that I have been here. But do you know what you must do?"

Didrebelle could not believe his eyes, as he fumbled dumbly for a word. "Wha–I–and you are . . . ?"

The man looked annoyed. "I am Charon," he answered plainly, "and you, Didrebelle Dragontamer, son of Melinta, know what you must do."

"On the contrary," said Didrebelle, dumbfounded, "I cannot say I do."

"You must not fret over Lucian," he said composedly. "There is a different path laid out for you. Follow the road of your countrymen. Gamaréa of Medric will not be able to outlast them on his own. He will need you to come to his aid before the end."

"But Lucian—" said Didrebelle, nearly in tears. "He is not ready—"

"Lucian will be well taken care of," assured Charon, and Didrebelle thought to see the edge of a smile flicker across his face. "You must trust me."

In his heart, Didrebelle did not object to aiding Gamaréa's cause, for he knew that his capture would inevitably lead to his death. Yet there was something holding him back.

"I do not wish to see my father again," said Didrebelle sheepishly, cowering before the massive figure of the Sage.

Charon's expression became firm. "And yet you must confront him eventually. These are the times when we must rally all our courage to do the things we fear to do."

"But—"

"I leave you now, Dragontamer. I feel my sister's presence

is close. I will surely never hear the end of this."

And it seemed as though Charon vanished before he even finished speaking. Didrebelle, left alone for a second time, stood with his heart racing.

You know what you must do, he told himself. *Though you may not want to do it.* He racked his mind to try to understand what Charon had meant by *Lucian will be well taken care of,* but he hadn't the slightest clue. The Sage spoke as though he were breaking some sort of rule coming to speak with him in the first place—would he be so daring as to aid Lucian next?

I must trust him, he told himself reluctantly. *He is more knowledgeable than I will ever be. And if he says that Lucian stands a chance, I must believe him. Gamaréa, however . . .* There was certainly no denying that Gamaréa's road would only lead to death. Melinta hated the race of Moroks, and seized every opportunity to persecute, and eventually execute, any who trespassed on his territory.

Determination rising within him, Didrebelle summoned his courage, and, scouring the bodies of dead Matarhim scattered around him, he filled his quiver once more and stole away through the trees, the uncertainty of his decision lessening as he ventured down the road ahead.

Dridion, he thought, would play host to many surprises in the days to come.

It was not long before Lucian heard thundering feet behind him—foul cries shattering his ears—and he turned to see a large group of Matarhim standing and waiting, and they were joined, it seemed, by Fairies, who were similar to Didrebelle in appearance.

Never before had Lucian been this afraid, but in spite of his horror, he stood helplessly in the middle of the path. Was this truly the way it was to end? So quickly, so alone? He stood firmly like an uprooted tree shaking in the wind. Now came the Matarhim, weaponless, and Lucian bore Excellebus and killed the first of them swiftly, wielding the great sword with skill that surprised even himself. He raced on, driven by the overwhelming fear that gripped him like a vice.

But in spite of his efforts, he was soon taken down, and lifted effortlessly upon the shoulders of the beasts and carried away. Their scent was putrid, and even through their thick black cloaks he could feel their burning skin. Lucian cried out in vain, as though Gamaréa or Didrebelle would hear him—as though Mary could rush to him and scold the beasts like she did whenever he was picked on as a child—but no one answered his call. All that was heard were the grunting beasts as they rushed off with their cargo, as they pressed swiftly onward, bearing him away.

23

The End of Exile

The Fairies did not leave a path by which Didrebelle could follow in his pursuit of Gamaréa. The way ahead felt weighted, as though an invisible force was hindering him, keeping him from gaining speed against the pressure it applied, and as he struggled along, he questioned the decision he made back on the main road, despite the Sage's instructions.

No, he contemplated sadly. *There is yet hope for the boy. For Gamaréa, however—for my friend—hope is certainly fleeting.*

Wherever they were, Didrebelle guessed, they must have been well ahead of him. He stopped numerous times to scan the path ahead for the better. Though he was fleet of foot, it seemed the swiftness of those he hunted had doubled since they stole away. But he ran because hope yet lived. Though he knew Gamaréa was more than capable of defending himself for the time being, he went with all haste, knowing well that days had grown dark between Dridion and Medric. *And they will show him no mercy.*

The Fairy sprung onward through the slim, enchanting trees of Ravelon, the wood lit by golden threads of sunlight, peering sharply through the canopy like magical spears. Morning broke into noon, and yet it seemed like days since the trio had parted. He went on for at least another mile when suddenly he stopped before the forest's end, as though facing a door he wished not to open.

For a moment he was silent, his eyes bolted to the light

outside the trees. *I have arrived,* he said to himself. Past the trees ahead lay Dridion, his former home, yet in this moment, he felt he would have preferred an unfamiliar place. He bent his golden head solemnly. He had lived for so long, yet it seemed as though his entire world was swept from under him in an instant. He felt ashamed that his emerald vest bore the sigil of his former land, for it now represented selfishness, greed, and betrayal, when once it stood, above all else, for honor.

Didrebelle was keen enough to his father's ways to know that he would do whatever it required to gain the utmost power. He took a slight sniff of the air. For the first time that he could remember, Dridion reeked. It was not hard to distinguish the unmistakable scent of the Matarhim. He was now in deep thought, playing riddles through his mind, silently peering out as far as he could manage, and he realized the scent of Sorcerian's army came not from the wood but from Dridion itself. And he reached the ledge of the forest and looked out, beholding Matarhim soldiers by the thousands polluting the fields that once were green, bearing his country's sigil of white talons.

It disgusted Didrebelle to the lowest depths of his soul that his father was tangled in the thick, unforgiving web of Sorcerian. But then, it was only typical of him. Melinta had always sought power, and by any means necessary.

In any regard, it was the king's own path to tread. But now he had Gamaréa captive, and Didrebelle could no longer keep himself idle; he could no longer avoid the monster his father had become. He stood on the cliff overlooking the glistening white city. Everything his eyes perceived was of superior beauty. But there was evil in the air—an evil so foul it nearly made him, an immortal, sick.

Nevertheless, he cloaked himself and progressed downward and into the city. From a great distance, he could see his father's tower rising like an acclaimed monument above all the cluttered buildings. He needed to retrieve his companion above all else, and he knew only one way to do so.

For the first time in nearly half a century, Didrebelle

stepped into his homeland and carried on to the king's hall, and there he stood, hooded, before his father's great, white tower, at the base of its many steps. The sun was hiding behind the tall peaks of the mountains stretching westward when Didrebelle arrived in the courtyard of his father. The parchment-colored road of clay he had been perusing along gave way to a steep incline of white marble staircases. Looking left and right, Didrebelle noticed that there were three such staircases, each separated by about fifty yards or so.

It led up into the courtyard, which was dramatically different from what he remembered. His sister's plants once decorated the courtyard magnificently. Her colorful flowers once grew along some of the walls. Evergreen trees once sprouted up here and there and complemented the white marble perfectly. They made the courtyard—and consequently the king above—seem tranquil and at peace.

But plants and flowers no longer bloomed here. Emmanuelle's garden had perhaps died with her. Now it was barren, save the erroneous, glistening white marble that was almost too much for the eye. Contractors walked about conversing, carrying long scrolls containing blueprints of future projects. Looking up he saw his father's tower, stretching so high over him that he strained his neck to see only its midsection. To the right, outside of the courtyard, he could see the giant shaping of a marble bust cloaked in wooden scaffolding. The king's slaves worked vigorously upon it, chiseling and hammering, carrying large stones along the base to be transported up to where they were needed. It was completed to about the shoulders, but Didrebelle did not need to see the completion of the face to realize who it was.

Disgusting, he thought. His grandfather would have been severely displeased at the very least. Didrebelle bowed his head and continued toward the causeway leading to the entrance of the tower. When he reached the large, heavy doors of stone, he was approached by two legionnaires. They were armored in the customary guard of Fairy soldiers: vests of silver and gold, under which jingled their well-polished sleeves of mail. The bottom of their brown tunics sprouted from beneath their iron plates upon their chests, reaching to about the middle of their thighs, and at their shoulders were draped dark emerald capes.

"You there!" said the soldier who approached in front of his companion. "You will go no further unless you seek an ill fate."

"Yet an ill fate awaits whether sought by you or me," replied Didrebelle.

The legionnaires drew their swords, displeased with Didrebelle's tone. It was then that Didrebelle unveiled himself, throwing off his robes to reveal his natural garb, and the guards saw then that he was undoubtedly of Dridion himself. His golden locks were more evident now that his dirty rags were thrown aside to disclose his emerald vest.

Didrebelle stepped forward. "What would your king say," he began, "if he heard that his guards drew their swords upon his son—upon their very prince?"

The guards each fumbled for any sort of words, embarrassed and afraid. They could do nothing but kneel at Didrebelle's feet, humbly pleading for forgiveness. He actually thought it was quite comical the way he made them act as mischievous children do after they are caught in an improper deed. Didrebelle smiled as their heads were bowed, but he straightened out his face so that he wore a makeshift, stern expression.

"Rise, guards," he said finally. "Take me to the king."

Epilogue

The Dormant King

Nephromera sat melancholy beside her ailing father. Though it had been three millennia since Ation had been undone, the Lord of the Sages did not seem to have aged a day. His white mane of hair flowed silkily behind and atop his broad shoulders, and his distinguished, snowy beard remained thick but tidy. The King of Mount Zynys bore all the characteristics of one locked in a very pleasant dream; his eyes closed, but not clenched beneath his bushy brows, and a very placid look upon his hearty face.

The Sagess—his only daughter, and the eldest of his children—sat in a chair beside his hovering bed, her white-gold head bowed morosely, stroking his soft, limp hand. The many nights that she spent in her father's golden chamber often remained wordless. Whatever words she meant to say always seemed too inadequate for her liking, though she knew for certain that her father would not be able to hear her. Sometimes her brothers would wander in. It was Nepsus mostly; their father's predicament weighed too heavily on Charon, who actively avoided spending more time than needed in his father's sullen room.

There were other Sages who passed through regularly also. Evandrus, the Sage of Light, applied new light fixtures with his lightning bolt-shaped staff the first day of every other week so that the glowing room never lost its radiance; Annoria, Sagess of Music and Harmony, whiled away hours playing soothing melodies on her golden harp; Baron, Sage of Bards, often sat beside Ation and told him the stories he always treasured in the days when he was strong.

Every Sage (and there were hundreds) paid their respects frequently in their own unique and special way, always inquiring as to any progress the King may have made, but it was Ela, his wife, who was a mainstay in the chamber. With a wave of her wand, the Sagess of Fertility applied new sheets to her husband's levitating bed, and changed the decorations and color of the room nearly every month. The constant changes, she always said, helped her forget how long her husband had been gone. There seemed to never be a moment when Ela was sitting as calm and still as Nephromera was sitting now. Her mother was always gliding about the room in her sparkling, velvety robes, mending, replacing, or cleaning something. Nephromera did not need to ask her mother why she never remained still, for whenever she was not busying about, her sorrow took hold and she would weep beyond the point of consolation. This was also something Charon could not bear. His siblings always quipped that he was a "mother's Sage" at heart, but there was certainly truth in the claim.

Bending her head to kiss her father's hand, Nephromera whispered that she loved him before she set it atop the other, resting on his barely-moving chest. But as she turned, she saw her mother in the doorway, leaning sullenly and wearily against the frame of the large oaken door. Ela's eyes, which had once been more piercing even than her daughter's, seemed to have been drained of most of their splendor. Though her appearance was that of a young woman, age was certainly discernable on her face.

The Queen of the Sages was standing in her silken, white nightgown, her arms crossed as though defending against a chill. Her red hair, like freshly kindled flame, stood out brighter than ever when complemented by the pale hue of her skin. Lack of sleep and millenniums of sorrow had certainly taken their toll on her appearance. Ela's face was as gaunt as ever, and her sunken cheeks applied to her features a very emaciated look. But for the first time in a long while, Nephromera saw the hint of a smile at the edge of her mother's dry lips.

"Neffy," she whispered. It was startling to hear her voice despite its very low volume. "I called you that when you were no older than a mortal girl. Do you remember?"

Nephromera, though flustered, smiled. "I remember it plainly, mother."

But Ela's gaze moved past the shoulders of her daughter to where her husband lay dormant in his floating bed, and her dull-blue eyes began brimming with tears. Lips quivering, she reached in her gown for her wand, but Nephromera took hold of her hand.

"Let me go!" cried Ela sheepishly, her voice wavering.

"No, mother," answered Nephromera sternly. "You must let *this* go." Ela's eyes widened dubiously. "You have reformed this room twice already this week. It is time you leave it alone. Redecorating will not bring him back."

Ela's lips moved sporadically, mouthing silent words that she was unable to formulate into audible speech. It was not long before she sunk to her knees, and though frail her weight dragged Nephromera with her to the floor where she wept inconsolably into her daughter's silken robes.

"I know, Neffy, I know—I have always known," sobbed Ela. "I miss your father more than words."

These were the only words Ela was able to utter for a long while. When her anguish finally subsided, she spoke again. "It is more difficult, I think, that he is still with us," she said, straining her gaze upon the bed where her husband unconsciously rested. "If your uncle—"

"Do not call him that," hissed Nephromera. "Do not *ever* call him that. He is no relative of mine—"

"If . . . he . . . had ended him for good, perhaps I would have coped with it by now. But this . . . "—she used the sleeve of her gown to dry her eyes— " . . . to have him so close, and yet so far from me—it is too much to bear. Far too much to bear."

"He never had the power to destroy father," said Nephromera matter-of-factly. "And he never will. Those at his service think that he may rise again, and finish what he started . . . "

"They may be right—"

"NO!" and Nephromera's voice rattled the walls of Ation's chamber so that even her mother's eyes filled with fear. "Forgive me, mother," she said softly, subduing her gathering rage for the moment. "He has not yet fed on enough souls to reclaim his former body. Yet even if that day comes he can be defeated simply by opening the Chamber—"

Ela laughed, but not with glee. *"Simply?"* she sneered. "It is no simple assignment to unlock that Chamber. It is in the bowels of Parthaleon, as you well know, where no living soul can enter, and none can be certain what kinds of charms your—*he*—has cast upon it."

"But we must try, mother," answered Nephromera sternly. She, for one, was growing utterly disheartened by her mother's air of doubt, she who had always been an optimistic rock on which to lean.

But Ela seemed too distant to be listening. Her nearly-extinguished eyes had passed again to Ation and filled once more with tears. It was at that moment that Nephromera muttered something that drew Ela's utmost attention. *"Lucian* must try . . . "

Now the eyes of both Sagesses locked, Nephromera's gaze demanding, Ela's pleading.

"My poor child," whispered Ela, as if to herself. "He is just a baby—"

"His eighteenth year is nearly upon him. Soon he will be able to set his task to purpose."

A long, downtrodden silence fell between them. Neither Sagess knew what to say. Nephromera was wondering what thoughts were now passing through her mother's mind; Ela was contemplating the possibility of losing both her husband and youngest son to the malice of her brother-in-law.

In time, it was Ela's defeated voice that shattered the silence. "Where is Lucian now?" she asked desperately.

It took a moment for Nephromera to answer. The last time she had tuned in to Lucian's journey, things had taken a turn for the worst. She could only imagine what kind of trouble he was in now.

"The last time I checked," answered Nephromera, prepared to lie, "he and his company had just entered the woods of Ravelon . . . "

An incredulous look came over Ela's face. "Ravelon?" she asked with a tone of fright in her voice. "So close to the Fairy lands? I believed their course to be toward Medric?"

"It was, mother. However, there seemed to be a skirmish at sea, and their vessel was lost. Beelcibur, or so they call the sea serpent, sunk their ship and altered their course. Had it not been for the heroics of the Aquilum, all may have been lost. It is a blessing that they managed to come ashore unscathed."

"My poor child," said Ela under her breath. "He must be so frightened." A moment passed before Ela added, "You know, Neffy, I barely got to hold him. When he was born I looked into his eyes, and I thought I saw him smile. Then the midwife took him—to cleanse him, I thought—but that was the last time I ever saw my dear Lucian. Of course, I have looked through that blasted contraption you and your brothers are always playing with, but it does not do it justice. A mother needs to hold her children, nurture them, be present for them—not view them from a distance, raised under the guidance of another woman—"

"It is what needed to be done, mother," assured Nephromera.

Ela smiled plainly, and for the first time. "You sound like your father," she said nostalgically. "Always have. It is a blessing that you have managed to remain steadfast through all this. It weighs heavily on your brothers—Charon, mostly. He hardly speaks of it; but you know how much he loved your father."

"We all love him, mother. And we are all working to restore him. The day that he returns will be glorious. Nundric, I daresay, will be in for a rude awakening."

Ela shifted her gaze from her daughter to her husband, and then from her husband to the floor. "And if that day never comes, Neffy?" she whispered sadly.

The determination in Nephromera's smile could have frozen a molten stream. "Ah," she said, "but what if it does?"

Nepsus peered into the Luminos, frowning. Since he heard of his brother's departure from Elderland, he had spent many hours glaring into the all-seeing basin, watching in horror as he and his company braved the Provinus pass and escaped Tantus. Though he never admitted it, he was ready to give up on Lucian when he was subdued in the Mountain of Dreams by the Enchantress, thinking for certain that he was going to succumb to the very mortal vice of lust. Those obstacles weathered, however, Nepsus did not think the Luminos could possibly reveal to him anything worse. That was when Beelcibur attacked and feasted on the wooden planks of *The Sojourn*. But, the Aquilum having managed to save Lucian's skin, he was beginning to believe that there was not any circumstance that his youngest brother could not manage to wriggle out of—until Ravelon.

Now he watched as Lucian was being carried away by a host of Matarhim soldiers, and his heart became filled with grief. *He should never have been chosen,* Nepsus thought angrily. *There is no way he could have prepared for a quest of this magnitude. Father was mistaken . . .* In a tumult of fury and sadness, Nepsus detached himself from the Luminos only to run into Charon, who was cursing.

" . . . blasted! . . . never gets easier . . . "

"Do not tell me you have done it again?" said Nepsus incredulously, his heart racing from having been startled.

A look of surprise fell over the chiseled, bearded face of his elder brother. "Done what?" he managed to answer feebly in his gruff voice.

"Come off it," replied Nepsus angrily. "You know well what I mean."

Charon shouldered Nepsus away. "Check your tone, brother."

Walking to the Luminos, Charon leaned up against its stone wall, his features becoming lit by the pale radiance emitting from within.

"We are under strict orders," Nepsus reminded him.

Charon chortled. *"You* may be under strict orders,

brother, but I have grown fond of making my own rules." He gestured to the Luminos with a bob of his head. "I am sure you have seen the predicament our brother is currently in?"

"I have."

"And you would remain in these climes and do nothing?"

Nepsus stepped up to his brother hotly. "I did not say that—"

"That is quite enough," said the voice of Nephromera, who had emerged from beyond the shadows of the basin. "What is the meaning of this?"

"Nephromera—" said Nepsus, clearly caught off guard. "I was . . . "

But Nephromera's gaze pierced the eldest of the two brothers. "You have done it again, haven't you, Charon?"

"For the last time," answered Charon, "I haven't a clue what either of you are talking about—"

"The leaves clinging to your cape betray you," answered Nephromera casually.

Charon was silenced. Nepsus suppressed a laugh.

"You were in the forest," said Nephromera, clearly frustrated. "In Ravelon."

Charon could not see any point in stretching the lie. "So what if I was?" he said defensively. "Someone has to see to Lucian's protection!"

Nepsus started. "The Fairy meant to go after him—"

"I sent the Fairy away," said Charon plainly. "I instructed him to go after the Morok. We cannot have him perishing. He's yet a part to play."

Neither Charon nor Nepsus recalled a time when their sister was more furious. "You directed the Fairy *away* from Lucian's cause?"

Nepsus cowered, but Charon remained steadfast. "I did," he said matter-of-factly. He may have been referring to leaving a window open and letting in a draft. "The Morok must have aid; otherwise he will surely perish at the hands of the Fairy King. Didrebelle is the only one who stands a chance of rescuing him."

"And what about Lucian?" asked Nephromera behind

gritted teeth, her fists clenched so tightly that they claimed a ghostly shade of white.

"Have you forgotten, sister?" said Charon, almost gleefully. "Have you forgotten whom father has dispatched to that side of the world?"

Both Nephromera and Nepsus straightened their postures. A subtle smile crossed Nephromera's face as she stood recalling, though vaguely, an ancient pact her father made ages ago, just before his fall. Her rage began to subside.

"The Protectors," she muttered, as though tasting the name.

"Indeed," said Charon. "Ever the forgetful sort, Neffy. Lucian will be well taken care of, I suspect." Charon noted the look of consideration that his sister's face now hosted. "Ah, now my plan bears fruit!" he exclaimed smugly. "My rebellious nature paves the way to a brighter day! You, my dear sister, are *more* than welcome . . . "

"Come off it, oaf," said Nephromera, shoving her daunting brother aside. "Forgive me if I have forgotten a pact made millenniums past, but, if you haven't noticed, I have been attending to important matters myself. Our dormant father, for one—you remember him, do you not?"

Her mighty brother's brow furrowed. "And what is *that* supposed to mean?" he said icily.

"Interpret it as you will—"

"I think there is only one interpretation . . . "

"Alright, alright," the voice of Nepsus interjected, as he came walking forward as if to separate the bickering siblings; but Nephromera shoved him aside.

"You cannot face our father's dilemma," said Nephromera, clearly agitated, and whatever glee she may have owned a moment prior flooded from her demeanor. "It is only your body that has been awarded strength. It seems your heart and mind have been neglected such gifts."

Charon's bellowing voice filled the chamber. "How dare you suggest such a thing?"

"*Suggest?*" exclaimed Nephromera. "Brother, it is concrete a fact as they come, yet even now you deny it.

When was the last time you even stepped foot in the wing of his chamber? Dare I even ask when last you ventured to the very landing on which he rests?"

Charon's gruff voice began to break. "I have been tending to my own matters—"

"Matters in which our meddling is forbidden!" replied his sister relentlessly.

"You have done it as well—"

"Only when the need was dire and necessary. For you it is now just a silly habit . . . "

A deafening silence encompassed them, as was broken sporadically by the faint bubbling of the Luminos. Nephromera anticipated a response from her brother, but he did not issue one. Nepsus, who had been taken aback by the confrontation between his siblings, backed into the shadows.

The next voice to speak was not issued from either of the three present. Ela, who had been listening to the tail end of Nephromera's and Charon's confrontation, emerged from the shadows, her eyes red and her once-elegant face troubled. "Is it true, Charon?" she asked meekly, nearly whispering.

Charon's eyes widened, and with his hands behind his back, he bowed his head and slouched backward a step or two. "Mother . . . I . . . it was only this one time, I promise—"

"Not that, Charon," said Ela, in a tone that suggested she almost did not want to hear the true answer to her question. "About your father? Your presence has indeed been scarce, I must say . . . "

Nephromera slumped and swept quietly away beside Nepsus, who looked on in worry. Charon, as though with the mannerisms of a small child being scolded, cast his eyes to the floor and began to idly tap the tip of his boot with the other. "Mother, I . . . "

Nephromera, who was standing closest to Charon, thought to see a small tear trickle down the side of his statuesque cheek. If he indeed was shedding a tear, it was the first time she had every seen him cry.

"I cannot abandon Lucian," he said at length, his voice,

once strong, beginning to waver. "I cannot watch another member of our house fall. I—refuse to . . . "

Charon's look of desperation was reflected in his sister's eyes as his gaze fell on her. Beneath his well-groomed beard, his lips began to quiver. He said nothing further. Instead, he turned on them all, his cape flapping behind him like drapes in a windstorm.

Nepsus made as if to follow him, but Nephromera held him back. "Let him go," she said, not surprised to hear herself whispering, for despair began to fill her too. "He needs to be alone right now."

"He cannot keep running from this," said Nepsus calmly. "There must be a way for him to cope with what has happened. We have all managed to do so . . . " But gazing now at his depleted mother, her small, skeletal figure bathed in the pale light of the Luminos, and the weary look on Nephromera's face, he wondered if his statement bore as much truth as he thought. " . . . haven't we?"

Neither Sagess spoke for a long while, until Ela said dismally, "Charon must grieve in his own manner. Certainly your father needs him . . . " It was then that Ela dipped her crimson mane of hair into the Luminos and saw the predicament of her youngest son being carried out in front of her with the vividness of a fever dream. When she removed herself and looked again on Nephromera and Nepsus, they could see plainly the look of fear wrought across her face. " . . . But I think Lucian, at this moment, may have indeed needed him a bit more . . . "

ABOUT THE AUTHOR

Nicholas T. Daniele was born on June 9, 1988 in Norwalk, Connecticut and discovered his passion for writing in the second grade. Roughly two decades later, he has authored his debut novel The Jewel of the Sorcerer, being the first installment of The Keeper of Fates trilogy. He earned a Bachelors degree in English and Secondary Education from Framingham State University, and hopes to produce future classics while teaching those from the past. A dedicated writer, avid reader, and die-hard Yankees fan, Nicholas currently resides in the New England area near his close friends and family.

28856636R00189

Made in the USA
Lexington, KY
06 January 2014